Praise for *Hunter's Choice*

John Hager knows the outdoors, he knows the human heart, and best of all he knows how to tell a hell of a story!
Steve Hamilton
author of the Alex McKnight novels

John knows what he's writing about, creating an inspired, adventurous read I highly recommend. I can't wait for his next book.
Joseph A. Greenleaf
author, editor, adventurer

An action-packed read with dead-on descriptions of the quarry area's stark beauty during the winter. I expect to see a cabin in the repair shed and Matt Hunter there to greet me when our field season opens..
Aubrey Golden
President, Michigan Karst Conservancy

Hunter's Choice

Hunter's Choice

A Matt Hunter Adventure

J. C. Hager

Greenstone Publishing
Rapid River, Michigan

Hunter's Choice
by J. C. Hager

Copyright © 2008 by John C. Hager
Cover Art by Kerrie Shiel

First Edition
Manufactured in the United States

ISBN: 978-0-9797546-5-4 $15.95

Library of Congress Control Number: 2007931758

Information: www.GreenstonePublishing.com
                    1-906-280-8585

GREENSTONE PUBLISHING LLC

          Publisher's Cataloging-in-Publication Data
Hager, J.C.

Hunter's choice / J.C. Hager.

p. cm.

ISBN 978-0-9797546-5-4

1. Adventure stories. 2. Organized crime—Fiction.
3. Michigan—Fiction.

PS3608.A44 H86 2007
813`.6—dc21   2007931758

Dedicated to the memory of

George F. Hager (1910–1976)
*A wonderful father, never given enough
credit, so good and smart he didn't care.*

Rachel Bottrell McGillviray (1893–1987)
*She needs a book of her own: logging camps,
Fiborn Quarry, and oh! those cinnamon rolls.*

1

Cessna

THE CESSNA WOULDN'T CLIMB. The pilot could see the beads of rime ice on the wings and nose cowl. The resulting drag on the controls and the increased rate of fuel use had plagued him for the past hour. Although certified for flight into icing conditions, his classic Cessna 310 couldn't handle this much ice, despite its rubber boots on the wing leading edges. Deicing fluid kept the windscreen clear, but every minute more and more ice was building up on the twin-engine plane. The weight was only part of the problem; the icy bumps stole aerodynamic lift from the normally smooth flight surfaces. The plane's performance slowly had deteriorated until it refused to climb; more ice and it would refuse to fly.

The pilot counted the ice buildup as strike two. Strike one had occurred a half hour ago when the Gore Bay Airport ILS localizer beam became intermittent. The Gore Bay tower calmly reported they were under Instrument Flight Rules due to reduced visibility by blowing snow. Crosswinds greater than thirty knots slammed their single 6,000-foot, north-south runway.

The pilot thought it was too risky to land his ice-heavy plane under such conditions. Experienced with crosswind landing techniques, he calculated that the risks exceeded his comfort level. With his newly installed GPS, reflecting the pilot's practice of keeping the plane in state-of-the-art equipment and perfectly maintained, he could have tried a GPS-only approach in lieu of using the intermittent ILS localizer, but he didn't. He had elected to keep pressing on, and now there was no turning back.

With 20/20 hindsight, the pilot would have given all he owned to be back at Gore Bay on Manitoulin Island with an opportunity for a challenging landing. He had planned an easy flight from Montreal, leaving before dawn to avoid the storm forecast for later in the day. These charter customers paid big money to be flown where they wanted to go without any questions about passengers or cargo. The business from these mysterious, sometimes dangerous, clients had kept him flying and in money for more than a decade.

He looked at the large man next to him who seemed to recognize their problem but said nothing. The beautiful woman in back was cold and bundled in her fashionable down vest that she probably wished was a jacket. Four large, military-type duffel bags filled the space between the front seats and the single back seat. Since they weighed several hundred pounds, he thought they could be jettisoned to give them a few more minutes of flying time—if it came to that.

A veteran pilot, he had experienced icing many times. He replayed this latest sequence of events in his mind: a strong tailwind had helped compensate for the initial ice drag, leaving most flight parameters acceptable. Well, except for the high gas use and sluggish controls. Heavy icing started when they were between Ottawa and Sudbury. He rejected Gore Bay to go for Sault Ste. Marie. The Sault had several runways and the crosswind conditions were less of a factor. The Sault's Automated Surface Observing System broadcast reported light snow with two-mile visibility.

During his radio contact with Gore Bay regarding their plans for the Sault, they had reported the transmission was static garbled.

At an altitude of 6,000 feet along the north edge of Drummond Island, they hit turbulence. The two engines strained to bring the heavy plane up to 8,000 feet as the pilot searched for better air with less water and, therefore, less ice in it. The pilot's pride and the nature of his cargo and passengers stopped him from declaring an emergency after passing Gore Bay. Now he fought against the hard bumps from the unstable air that hammered the lightplane.

After a particularly violent bump, both the pilot and the passenger caught the acrid odor of burning insulation and saw the puff of smoke rising from the panel. The pilot immediately shut off the master electrical switch and began bringing equipment up one system at a time. When he hit the avionics, the smoke returned. The avionics were again switched off, eliminating both GPS and radio. Strike three.

The storm from the southwest hit them with wind, snow, and more icy hail. Intermittent patches of forest flashed by below them through holes in the clouds. He grabbed his maps and tried to read the bouncing and spinning magnetic compass. He tried to keep heading west into the storm but was unable to maintain altitude. Where were those two major highways or the huge former Strategic Air Command base south of the Sault?

The pilot fought the controls as the storm slammed the plane up, down, and side to side. Eyes widening with fear, all three on board desperately sought some kind of landing spot. The pilot asked about dumping the duffel bags. The big man growled for him to shut up and just get them down.

After another half hour, the twin fuel indicators were bouncing on their lower stops and the plane's altimeter read 1,000 feet. The pilot battled the wind-driven turbulence with sluggish, ice-laden controls—a battle he was losing.

Through a break in the white curtain of blowing snow, he spotted a patch of white amid the dark forest. A small lake. The port engine coughed. Only two choices now—land on the lake under some kind of control or later dive into the solid carpet of forest they had been over for many minutes. The densely packed canopy looked smooth and soft but was in reality a fanged monster that would shred the aluminum plane, leaving parts and people impaled on branches or crushed on the forest floor.

The pilot tightened his seat straps; so did his passenger. He instructed the female passenger in the back to get on the floor and brace herself against the large bags. There was no time to throw the bags out, and their soft bulk would protect the woman better than a single lap belt.

The pilot thought about putting the wheels down and trying to limit damage to his treasure of a plane, using flaps and props to shorten the landing. The option went away when the port engine stopped. He mashed the right rudder pedal to counter the sudden left yaw and wrestled the sluggish ailerons with all his strength and skill to level the wings. He knew he must descend quickly onto the lake to have as much landing surface as possible. Treetops cracked against the nose and wings. Pine branches scraped the windshield. One jagged crack shot across it. He fought the urge to duck as the sweet, but incongruous, smell of pine hit him. His mind and fingers raced over procedures and switches he had rehearsed hundreds of times in practice and in nightmares. He killed the right engine, feathering both props to reduce drag and engine damage. He set his jaw, concentrated on glide angle, clicked switches off, fought to keep wings level, reached for the flap lever with his right hand, all the while wincing at the deafening sounds of his first crash. Then a sudden silence produced a surreal moment as forest changed to lake.

No one said a word as the white expanse of the frozen lake filled the windshield.

The Hunt

THE BUCK STOPPED EATING ACORNS scraped from the forest litter, sniffed the freezing morning air, and looked around the hardwoods. Snow crystals started pelting the dry oak leaves and the forest floor. The storm approached with a noise like a distant waterfall that was magically moving closer. The deer was alert to the weather change, wanting to eat as much as possible before the snow made ground food unavailable. He sensed the storm would be a severe one. Thirsty after eating his fill of bitter acorns, and wanting the water and the shelter of the cedars, he moved upwind toward the lake and swamp. He disappeared among the large white spruce trees that formed a picket line between the hardwoods and the thick cedar swamp and lake.

Forty yards south of the buck, Matt Hunter crouched in an old deer blind he and his grandfather had built nearly thirty years ago. The woods shared a lot of history with Matt and his grandfather Manfred. The pair had built the blind like a bunker, on the "military ridge" or just off the top of the hill. Manfred was an expert with a rifle and hunting tactics; Matt remembered the whispered shooting instructions as he looked through the blind's slit opening. "Don't breathe on the scope…keep your head back or that scope will bite ya."

Matt touched the cedar logs and thought, *Like a sponge, these logs are going back to the soil they have grown from.*

Sphagnum moss covered the entire roof, which was supported by logs, corrugated steel, and dirt. At one time the blind commanded several hundred yards of cedar swamp edge and fifty acres of clear-cut white pine and hardwood stumps. Now he looked down a narrow logging trail going north through the hardwoods then west toward the swamp. Matt could see through and under the large cedars. The browse line along the cedars to the left was perfectly cut five and a half feet from the ground. The hardwoods to the right still had a lot of oak leaves and only gave intermittent views into the forest.

The blind was too high for the present growth. But Matt never passed it without going in for a period of time to relive all the exciting and rewarding hours he had spent listening to the whispered lessons of Grandfather and his cronies. He could almost smell them—the aroma of damp cedar, wet leaves, and moss conjured up the smell of wool, leather, wood smoke, and tobacco smell from so many past hunts. All gone now. The old deer blind would soon cave in from a heavy snow, or some animal efforts, or just from the relentless force of gravity and the chemistry of nature.

An hour earlier Matt heard the buck pawing the leaves before he saw him. He picked him up in his rifle scope a little after first good light and just watched him. Matt cranked the Leupold 3.5 to 10-power scope to maximum magnification and looked carefully at the fine animal. The area's limited gene pool seemed to produce strong deer with distinctive markings. Bucks tended to get very dark on the back and rump. However, old bucks could be so tough that when they finally reached the hunter's table you couldn't stick a fork in their gravy. His mother and grandmother would send hunters out to get table meat with the admonition, "Remember, you can't eat the horns." Matt thought of all the hunting camp sayings while he watched the buck move into the swamp area.

For the first time in over twenty years, Matt could hunt during the second week of the gun season. For twenty-three years he had been a high school teacher and a coach. The classroom, football, and wrestling had taken most of his time from August through early June. Now he had taken early retirement. Though he had loved teaching—and preached that there was nothing more important than helping students learn and mature into mentally and physically strong individuals—he had lived through many cycles of dissatisfaction with the teaching system. But each fall and each sport season started with total optimism; last year, the optimism didn't come. He wanted to gain control of his time and pursue several not-yet-defined ambitions. At forty-eight he said, "Today,

I'll hang up the old Acme Thunderer whistle and return my pound and a half of keys to the office."

If teaching in high school had a sabbatical he would have taken it but, facing burnout, he had no alternative except to take the early retirement. Matt forced professional frustration and guilt out of his thoughts. He vowed to enjoy the moment and the woods. Though still honed in on the buck, he didn't want to shoot it. He had dropped a nice eight point on opening day, and he was now hunting on his second deer tag for a hunter's choice that could be filled with either a buck or antlerless deer. He just wanted to hunt—to listen, see, smell, and learn from the woods.

Matt felt good about himself. He was fit and healthy with a well-muscled six-foot frame. His coaching activities had kept his weight below two hundred pounds and his heartbeat below sixty at rest. Still wrestling tough, his body did what he asked it. His brown hair was thick enough to keep his head warm, and his hazel eyes didn't need glasses yet. He was on land he owned. His name was in the plat book for over nine forties, 360 acres of very remote Upper Peninsula land in Mackinaw County. The land included a quarry last active in the 1930s, a lake, multiple ponds, over one hundred acres of hardwoods, ridges of pine, and a hundred acres of cedar swamp and grassy fields. He owned part of the largest cave system in Michigan; several branches of the Hendrie River flowed through the lowlands, and he was nearly surrounded by the eastern part of the Hiawatha National Forest. The land, inherited mostly from his grandfather Manfred, was part of the least populated county in the Upper Peninsula.

All his cousins, relatives, and friends had hunted hard and most successfully during the first week and were now back at jobs or homes scattered across many states. Matt had chosen to be alone in this magnificent country with no agenda except to appreciate the trails, trees, swamps, and associated critters of his property. The land never failed to provide what he needed when he felt down or had to plan a strategy.

Matt felt and saw the wind change. He could feel the warmer, more humid air. He knew a major storm was forecast and he had come into the woods to observe the heightened activity of the animals preceding a storm. He thought, *The best hunting and fishing is just before a storm.* His second deer tag made an excuse to stalk the woods. Understanding the reason for taking does to maintain a healthy herd balance and save more of the scarce winter forage for growing bucks, he was enjoying the hunt much more than the prospect of shooting a doe.

His cabin was nearly a mile away. He had prowled through the predawn dark along a sphagnum-covered path up to the hill, and then eased up the hill with its frozen leaves and its skiff of snow. There was little snow on the south side, but more on the north as he looked out of the blind.

It became very quiet after the buck disappeared into the cedar swamp. Matt could hear the snow pelting the dry oak leaves on the trees and ice pellets hitting the leaves around the blind. He left the blind to watch the storm come in. Thinking, "I should level this blind before it caves in on someone."

The storm hit hard. The wind whipped the tree limbs back and forth. The snowy mixture of large flakes and small crystals simultaneously wet and stung his face. He pulled his old black Kromer cap down on his head and brought up the hood of his hunting jacket, then started down the hill for the mile walk against the southwest wind and storm. The snow and wind were so strong he couldn't look up. He just followed his familiar path generally south. A hundred yards later, he was halfway down the slope, the snow was already two or three inches deep. He couldn't see fifty feet ahead. The wet snow stuck to his clothes. He anticipated the warmth of the cabin, some brandy-laced, reheated coffee, and the W.E.B. Griffin paperback he had been enjoying.

Then Matt heard the plane.

3

The Crash

M ATT HEARD A WHISTLING ABOVE the howling of the wind. His brain had no catalog for that sound. Then he felt and heard a plane pass over the top of the trees, bucking the wind toward the swamp and lake. The Doppler effect gave the sound a living quality as the pitch of the engine first rose, then fell, competing with the roar of the storm. The plane cracked, snapped, and splintered the tops of the pine trees. Matt realized he was holding his breath and that there had been no engine sounds for five heartbeats. Then crunching metal, the low, bell sound of a large object slapping hard on the frozen lake, and the pop of ice cracking, followed by several concussive thuds. Finally, only the sounds of the storm.

Matt froze for several seconds, calculating his next actions. Having once worked as a lifeguard instructor at a Boy Scout camp, he knew and had taught that the first instincts in an emergency are usually wrong and can be fatal. Matt reminded himself that half of the people who jump into the water to rescue a drowning victim die in the attempt. Running directly to the wreck scene wouldn't be the best action. The lake was nearly a mile away to the west and south through thick cedars. His cabin was generally south, also nearly a mile, but the best trail to the lake went from the cabin.

With his decision made, Matt jogged toward the cabin. There, he could get material to help a rescue and a snowmobile to get him to the crash faster.

Originally the prefabricated office of an oil pipeline company, the cabin was moved into the huge, old, quarry machine shop, a barn-like structure with concrete walls and floor, steel beams, and a metal roof. The large vertical windows of the old machine shop were open slits. At one time, railroad cars and engines entered its Gothic-scale main door for repair and servicing. Matt and his relatives and friends had reinforced the cabin, added plumbing, and put on a second-floor bunk room.

Matt reached the quarry and jogged across its flat, boulder-strewn floor to the machine shop building. Several snowmobiles and assorted boy's toys scattered across the floor—from canoes to old three- and four-wheeled all-terrain vehicles. He put his deer rifle in the cabin to dry. Matt checked the fuel in one of the Polaris XLT Indy snowmobiles. Nearly full. It had a towing hitch, but its towing sleigh was gone, probably used to bring out a deer and not returned to the shop. He needed something to haul materials and maybe victims and didn't have the time to look for the sleigh. He took the seventeen-foot Grumman canoe off the wall rack, dumping out paddles, life vests, and assorted coolers and buckets that had come to roost inside what had become an impromptu shelf. Into the canoe he threw various ropes, two plastic tarps, a short shovel, and a coil of plastic anchor line. He ran into the cabin and retrieved the camp's large first aid kit, a fire extinguisher, and a gallon of water. He placed the items on the canoe bottom and secured them with the tarps and the shovel wedged under the thwarts.

He tied the canoe to the Polaris with less than two feet of leader between them. The powerful Indy machine started with one short pull. It was a 1993 XLT with three carburetors, nearly 600 cubic centimeters of engine, and more speed than any sane or sober rider should attempt. The wear rods on the skis bit into the concrete floor, the carbide studs spun and caught, the machine and canoe shot out of the wide main door. Matt had no helmet or goggles. The snow and wind lashed his face. He further impaired his vision by running the machine at over fifty mph, noting the 6,000 rpm on the tachometer dial. If he hit an old limestone block, his rescue mission would be over and they might not find him until spring. He slowed to twenty mph and negotiated his way up and out of the quarry floor. The road to the lake, once large and paved with crushed rock, now had forty-foot trees encroaching from both sides, leaving only a ten-foot-wide path, a path that appeared to have had other traffic on it in previous weeks. The 4x4 tracks and snowmobile tracks led to the lake and several scattered deer blinds. The road came down a slope to the swampy lake edge. Matt drove out onto the frozen surface. Away from the edge, the lake had more than eight inches of ice for safe travel. However, both the swampy east and west edges had springs and even small, flowing streams. The water wasn't deep, but several feet of decayed vegetation and black muck covered the lake bottom.

Matt could not see any plane or tracks. He headed west down the middle of the lake. Nearly half way down the lake, he saw clear marks from a plane's belly slide, scouring through the snow into the dark ice. He ran the Indy as fast as he could while still being able to stop if the track ended in a hole in the ice. The plane's track turned into slush and water with visible wing or engine marks. Matt went wide of the marks. He knew the west shore would appear soon, but with the blinding snow and wind and his focus on the skid mark, he had no frame of reference to pinpoint his position. He slowed without braking; the canoe gave him a light bump to assure him it was still behind him. He smelled gasoline. Raw, not burning. He saw the broken ice slush and tortured path where the left engine had dug into the ice. The swamp area—delineated by cattails, hummocks of grasses, and old dead tree stumps—loomed ahead. The plane's path continued across this lake border. Matt couldn't see the woods' edge yet through the fierce storm. Thirty to forty mph winds howled, with the ice and snow as hard on his face now as when the speed of the snowmobile had artificially increased its fury. He stopped the machine and turned off the motor.

Only the sounds of the wind and the whack of the snow and ice against his windshield. The smell of gasoline mixed with other chemical odors. He restarted the snowmobile, realizing that the 600-pound snowmobile could get stuck in the swamp. He had no reverse. If the skis fell down between snow-covered hummocks into the icy slush between them, he was done as a rescue unit. He eased ahead another fifty feet then turned sideways to the wind. He retrieved the 100-foot nylon anchor rope and tied it to the rear bar of the Polaris. With the line, if he broke through the ice, he could pull himself out of the swamp and also find his way back to the machine.

Matt carefully moved parallel to the skid marks. With visibility less than twenty feet across the wind and less into it, he could not see trees where he knew they must be. The cedar swamp was extensive on the lake's west side. Its trees were thirty to forty feet tall with some fifty- to sixty-foot tamaracks and pines, but he could see only snow, a dark water streak, and the closest grass hummocks. He moved from grass clump to grass clump, as close to the plane marks as he could. Between the clumps were stands of water caused by the skidding plane breaking the ice. He knew the swamp area generally formed a fifty-foot border between the lake and the cedar woods. He paid out his nearly frozen plastic line that refused to uncoil easily.

He concentrated on the line, the hummocks, the smells, and the open water, cautiously working into the wind and storm. He was sweating under hunting clothes chosen for stalking and hiding rather than jumping across grass clumps. If he opened his jacket, the snow and freezing rain would immediately soak him. He slipped off a clump, plunging one leg up to his knee in water and muck. He rolled onto his hands and knees across several hummocks and began working himself to his feet. He wondered whether his boots would keep his feet dry. As he got to his feet, his head hit the plane with a painful thud.

The white horizontal stabilizer was invisible in the storm. The jar hurt his jaw and neck and nearly knocked him between two large hummocks. He grabbed the horizontal stabilizer and simultaneously saw the vertical part of the tail, also white but with a red tip and stripe. Ducking under the tail, he could make out most of the plane. A twin, mostly white but with a red stripe. He saw several windows. One propeller blade stabbed upward. The plane's nose had slid into the cedar trees. A large, uprooted cedar tree root had snagged the right wing and turned the plane sideways. The plane's wings were level, the body burrowed into the muck and grass.

It looked like a medium-size Cessna with the entry door on the right side. The plane had spun enough to swing the tail and fuselage clear of the broken ice of the skid path, but the left wing remained out of sight in the cedars, grass, and snow. When he had hit his head, he had dropped the line. Finding it at his feet, he saw only a few remaining coils, maybe ten feet. Matt edged along the starboard side of the plane. He found a storage hatch just before the wing and tied the last of the rope around the pop-out handle. Climbing onto the wing, he brushed snow away from the side window, though it was too dark to see anything inside. Five to six inches of snow covered the windows and kept the cabin dark. No sound except the slap of wet snow and the gusting wind. The wind muted the pings and crinkling sounds of the cooling engines. Although fainter, the gas smell forced him not to use his hunting lighter for light. Matt pried the door open several inches but still could not see much in the cabin.

Matt wiped the snow from the windshield to allow light to enter the cabin. He lay across the cracked windshield with his face near the plastic. Despite the dimly lit interior, he could make out a form draped over the left controls. He rapped the windshield with his gloved fist. No responding movement or sound. His breath clouded the windshield, and the snow covered any cleared area within seconds. He needed to enter the plane.

Matt crawled back from the front window onto the wing. He could now see cedar trees looming over the plane. The trees broke the wind, reducing the snow and sound. He pulled on the passenger door, and it reluctantly opened; then he pushed it nearly parallel with the wing. Two people sat jammed against the Cessna's dual control yokes. Soft-sided travel bags and large military duffel bags wedged the seat forward against the passenger, a large, older man. Matt took off his gloves and touched the man's neck. Warm flesh, slow pulse, blood on his forehead. His shoulder and arm were jammed forward, his right leg bent at an unnatural angle. Matt pulled a duffel bag out of the plane, then several luggage bags. He moved into the space he had produced, finally reaching the pilot whose skin was cooler and without a pulse. As Matt felt for a pulse, he also felt the head's loose connection to the body. Broken neck.

Matt toughened his mind against the tragedy of death before him and returned his attention to the passenger. He worked to find a seat belt release embedded in the passenger's belly and clothes. He had no choice but to move the person. It would take hours to get emergency help to the location. His cell phone didn't work at camp, there was no landline phone, and the nearest home with a phone was more than eleven miles away on the road to Trout Lake . The man had to be moved and brought to the warmth and comforts of the cabin. Matt moved the passenger seat back. It clicked on its adjustable track safety catches, which had not held during the crash. The man moaned and mumbled unintelligibly. He opened his unfocused eyes, turned his head, and tried to see where he was.

Matt said, "Your plane has crashed, I need to get you out…can you hear me?"

The man said, "Help me, I hurt. Ribs. Legs."

Matt found the seat belt release and pressed it. The man gave a groan and tried to move his inside arm. He moaned again, then fell silent.

Matt needed more room inside the plane. He removed the remaining bags and luggage jammed against the front seats. The plane seemed filled with bags, heavy but soft. He pulled out more bags and pushed them out the only door. With the door open and with his eyes now adjusted to the inside light level, he could view the cluttered cabin. He pushed bags backward when he could no longer push them outside. More light streamed in with the door now held open by bags.

The pilot's seat was pushed foreword. Matt checked the passenger again. His pulse was strong and regular. He had stopped bleeding from his ear and was breathing regularly. Matt looked around the cabin. It seated five, but the space for the middle seats was used for duffel and luggage bags. He needed to clear a path to remove the passenger from the cabin.

The unrelenting snow had piled over eight inches on the wing and his footprints were almost undetectable. Visibility was nearly zero as the strong, gusty wind drove the snow into swirls. Matt knew it was getting colder; the previously wet flakes were now sleet, ice crystals, and dry flakes.

In the plane's cabin, Matt again checked the passenger's pulse, respiration, and temperature. No change. Matt wanted to keep him warm for the trek back. Although small, the dead pilot's leather sheepskin jacket could help keep the passenger warm. As Matt unzipped the flying jacket, he was shocked to find a shoulder holster and a pistol under the left arm. For no reason other than curiosity, Matt thumbed the holster release and pulled out the pistol. Even in the dim light, he recognized the SIG Sauer, a fine pistol. Long interested in guns, rifles, and pistols, he couldn't leave it out in a wrecked plane on a dead man. After checking the chamber and finding a shell, he thumbed the decocker, which safely dropped the hammer. Matt slipped it into his hunting jacket pocket. He then worked at unfastening the passenger's seat belt, moved him back in his seat, and covered him with the pilot's leather jacket. Then he left the plane.

Matt grabbed the plastic anchor rope and followed it through the wind and snow to the ice and finally found his Indy. He retied the knot of the anchor line on the snowmobile, wrapped the line around the towing bar twice, and finished with a half hitch. He then put a simple overhand knot in the remaining line to keep the slippery plastic from working its way back through the hitch. He pulled in the line and repeated the knots on the canoe's bow painter attachment. He now had the canoe attached to the Indy by a long rope. He went to the stern of the canoe and pulled it back to the plane. Nearly a foot of snow covered the grass mounds and filled the areas between them. The lower temperature was freezing the water between the hummocks. He stepped on the ice to test the freezing strength. It held him despite some spongy give under the snow. He struggled back to the plane in a minute. He was sucking wind, not in as good shape as he made his athletes achieve. If he were one of his football players or wrestlers, he would have yelled, "Suck it up, Hunter...you hoser..."

He took a long breath and dragged the seventy-pound canoe up to the plane fuselage behind the right wing, opened the folded plastic tarps, and made a bed in the canoe, leaving plenty of plastic to cover the passenger.

Inside the cabin, the passenger had moved a little, sideways over the controls now with his head touching the pilot. His vitals didn't seem to be any different than when Matt had left him. Matt brought his face close and yelled, "Can you hear me?"

Instantly, he felt dumb for saying such a thing. The man opened his eyes and tried to focus on Matt. He mumbled something, totally lost in the wind sounds.

"I'm going to pull you out of the plane. Help if you can," Matt yelled.

The man gave a quick shake of his head and closed his eyes against the blowing snow curling in.

Matt removed the pilot's leather jacket and put it aside. He grabbed the passenger's jacket by the shoulders and slowly pulled him out of the cabin. The man groaned but looked up, wordlessly saying keep going.

Matt slid him out of the plane and down the wing. At the canoe he stopped. How to do this? He turned the canoe on its side, dragged the man into it below the mid thwart, and pulled him under it to the middle of the canoe. Then he righted the canoe and adjusted the man on the bottom of the canoe. He was very careful with the right leg, which felt broken. The passenger had plastic under him; Matt put the pilot's jacket and more plastic tarp above him to cocoon the man from the weather and stabilize him for the mile trip across the lake and quarry.

Matt went back to the bags he had pushed out of the plane cabin and shoved them back in so he could close the door. The wind blew the snow, now well over a foot deep, into major drifts wherever it could. He moved into the cabin and moved the bags to the rear so he could close the door. As he turned to work his way through the litter and baggage to leave, he heard a cough and a moan.

He held his breath, thinking the wind and storm noises had fooled him. He shouted, "Hello, where are you?" though he was embarrassed for yelling in a cabin about the size of a club cab pickup truck. He then heard a movement under the avalanche of bundles.

The light was poor, the windows covered by a foot of heavy, drifting snow. The cleared door window offered some weak light. He started to move bundles to the front of the plane. He felt like being in a life-sized Rubik's Cube. On the floor of the cabin he found an ankle covered by a dark stocking. A very nice ankle. He went one way and found a very nice foot in a moccasin. Drawing on his vast anatomical knowledge, he worked his way up the ankle and, predictively, found a knee, then a thigh. After the thigh he found a skirt bunched around a very impressive group of warm feminine goodies.

A SIG and this on the same day?

Matt moved bundles until he could see the rest of the person attached to the ankle, knee, thigh, and goodies that his first exploration had discovered. Her dark hair blended into a dark turtle neck sweater, and both framed an oval face with a small nose and well-formed lips that could belong to a female of twelve to thirty-five. Out of her seat, she lay in a fetal coil on the plane's floor. She must have been in the small seat at the rear of the cabin. Matt lost a few seconds, struck by her beauty and vulnerability.

The complexity of this find called for thought. Matt had a very severely injured person outside, possibly dying and surely freezing in an aluminum canoe on an ice covered lake—and now he had another very much alive, warm, and good-smelling survivor.

Triage…the word popped into his mind. How do I save these two people?

The man was in poor condition. The girl, although unconscious, seemed in better shape, literally and figuratively. With an outside temperature in the low twenties or even the teens, he couldn't leave her. He had one trip to reach the warmth and comfort of the cabin. He had to move them both at one time.

Matt touched the girl's face. He continued to the neck, the pulse strong and regular. He felt her neck. Normal. He worked down each shoulder to the arms and hands; he found no abnormal lumps or conformations. He couldn't straighten her out without knowing the state of her backbone, neck, or head injuries. She didn't have any leaks he could see or feel in the limited light. He would move her to the canoe, hoping he did her no further injury. He lifted her to a sitting position. Everything seemed to move normally. He found a down vest on one arm. He put it on her and zipped it up, pulling its collar up. He moved her toward the left side behind the pilot, stepped over her, and left the cabin. The weather couldn't have been any nastier. Wind and snow came in antagonistic gusts.

Matt's grandfather had always told him, "There is no such thing as bad weather, just bad clothes." Matt knew how to dress and move with various weather. However, the two comatose victims were not dressed for this storm. Matt needed to move quickly; he had over a mile to transport both people down the lake and through the woods in subfreezing temperatures with a wind chill below zero.

Matt went to the canoe and opened the plastic tarps slightly; the man was still warm and had a strong, steady pulse. He seemed to be breathing better stretched out. Matt quickly returned to the plane, pulled and carried the girl from the cabin to the canoe. He thought he heard sounds from her, but the wind was too strong to be sure. She felt solid and strong as he carried her to the canoe. He pushed her feet first under the mid thwart from the stern. Her legs came to the man's waist. Matt packed her into the canoe and wedged the plastic tarp back around the man and her legs and waist. Matt put his wool hat on the girl and it pulled down well over her ears and forehead. Just as he closed the tarp around her and tucked it under her and the stern seat, he felt a movement. He leaned close to her head and yelled, "We are going back to a warm cabin. Just hold still. Don't move. Don't move. I'll take care of you."

He found the plastic line and then found his Polaris. It took two pulls to start it. After all three carburetors had finally agreed to put the right amount of gasoline into the cylinders, the engine ran smoothly. Matt slowly took up the slack on the nearly one hundred feet of anchor line. As soon as he felt the canoe move, he went off at an angle that wouldn't allow the canoe to hit the tail. He was worried about falling into the plane's icebreaker skid path. After about thirty feet of slow travel, he stopped the machine. He went back to the taut line. It extended out of sight into the howling snowstorm. He pulled on it, and it came with the expected amount of effort. He pulled hard, the thin line cutting into his wool army glove liners. The wind and snow made it impossible to see even a few feet. He felt the canoe getting close, the angle of pull changing as the canoe's bow slid to within a few feet of the snowmobile. He retied the line around the snowmobile and threw the remainder of the line into the canoe, tucking it in under the bow seat. He checked the two passengers in the canoe. They seemed well covered, with their weight balanced. He didn't open the plastic to check any vital signs. He couldn't do anything for them anyway and doing so would only cause them to lose a lot of heat.

Matt jumped on the Indy. The powerful machine didn't like to go slow, but it did. It pulled the two victims and Matt across the lake, onto the shore, through the woods, then down into the quarry. By going directly downwind on the lake, he found the shore edge about where he had come onto the lake. Blowing snow totally obscured the path to the cabin, leaving old landmarks snow covered. The low speed further disoriented him. Matt finally made out the old base of the crusher building, like a huge double garage. He went on; without a hat and its protective bill, the snow swirled constantly around his face. He had his jacket's hood pulled tightly around his head. The wind came from his back and made vision a little better. He drove, kneeling on the machine to see better. The machine's light did nothing to help. Midmorning with such poor light that Matt could see blowing snow sparkling in the headlights. He was on the right road and soon came to the cave-like maw of the door to the huge building that covered his cabin. He pulled into the cover of the building and across the relatively snow-free floor to the cabin door. He hit the orange kill button on the right handle bar and ran to the cabin door, opened the screen, and held it open with the device on the pneumatic spring. Then he opened the inner door and blocked it with the large rock that, over the years, had been trained for that purpose.

With some effort, he unpacked the two victims from under the several inches of icy snow covering the plastic. The girl was easiest to remove— lighter and not packed under the thwart that would impede Matt's lift. She moaned, and he felt some muscle tension as he lifted her. He carried her into the cabin and put her on one of the two couches. She breathed regularly and had good color in her face, lips, and fingertips. He covered her with a quilt that lived on the couch. Moving the man was a lot harder—bigger, heavier, and lodged under the center thwart. Matt could not lift him with his hands under the man's back and legs but only drag him by holding him under the arms.

Easily two hundred fifty pounds, the man would have wrestled as a heavyweight, Matt thought as he tried to move him out of the canoe. He pulled and slid the man out of the canoe, laying him on the cement outside the cabin. Matt went into the cabin and returned with a six-foot rag rug that normally lay in front of the kitchen sink. He worked the man onto the rug and grabbed the rug by its edges, curling it around the man, then dragged him into the cabin. It was as smooth a way as he could think of for getting the man into the cabin. He dragged him to the other couch, facing a coffee table that separated the two couches. He grabbed the man's coat and lifted him partially onto the couch. After his hips reached the couch, Matt lifted his legs onto the couch. He got a blanket from a bedroom on the second floor and covered the man, then turned the propane heater's thermostat up to seventy-five and listened as it obediently kicked in.

Matt searched the refrigerator for the gallon jug, remembered it was in the canoe, went out and got it, and took a long, cool drink. On his second drink, he looked at the injured people on his couches and contemplated his next steps.

Victims

ALMOST NO WIND NOISE REACHED THE CABIN. The two-story building had beds upstairs and cooking, eating, and lounging areas on the first floor. A small bathroom and shower also occupied the far corner of the first floor. There was electricity with a backup generator system and hot and cold running water. The propane tank held five hundred gallons and had been filled just before Opening Day, the sacrosanct 15th of November. Matt had some staple foods in two large cupboards, and the refrigerator held more beer than anything else because it was too cold to store it outside. But the cabin was not a hospital.

The girl's moan brought Matt back to the immediate problem—two injured people who needed medical help. His Yukon with the back seats down would make a bed. Even with the vicious storm, he could still get to the highway if he left soon. If he waited very long, even the Yukon couldn't negotiate the three miles of rutted dirt road and the eight miles of county gravel road to the paved highway. Given the storm and another hour, the highway could be impassable with wind-blown snowdrifts. The nearest hospital was in St. Ignace, over forty-five miles away, and Highway 123 could be tricky with any drifting snow. With two feet or more of drifting snow, the drive would be challenging. Newberry had a good hospital and better roads leading to it, but it was ten more miles. He would have to make the go or no-go decision within the next hour or the point would be moot. They would be snowed-in for several days.

While thinking about hospital trips, he checked his patients for cuts, breaks, and bruises. The man had not changed—still breathing slowly with a good heartbeat. A cut lip and blood in his mouth, but his teeth were not broken and his tongue was normal. He had skin off both hands and a scalp cut just at the front hairline. Matt removed the man's jacket, opened his shirt, and raised his undershirt, revealing a distended stomach either from injury or practiced obesity. His broken right leg showed no bones threatening to break the skin. Several inches below the knee, the break seemed to be the tibia. The girl had a large bruise on her left temple and a discolored and swollen left wrist. Broken or sprained? Her face and mouth seemed unhurt. He continued the examination down her chest, abdomen, and hip areas, trying to think as clinically as possible. She also had a large bruise on her left knee.

Matt went to the refrigerator for ice but found no cubes, only a package of frozen meatballs and spaghetti sauce in a Cool Whip carton. He dumped it into a large ziplock bag, wrapped it with a dishtowel, and put it on the girl's head bruise. Next, he retrieved the first aid kit from the canoe and found a variety of Ace bandages to wrap the girl's wrist, which he then iced with a snow-packed ziplock. The cabin had a good supply of bags used to carry the hunters' lunches. While filling several with snow blowing into the windowless, doorless building, he checked the progress of the storm. More than two feet of snow covered the ground, with drifts of four to five feet. The snow blew almost horizontally, dropping visibility to less than fifty feet. A hospital drive looked like a bad idea.

Matt covered as many of his patients' bruises as he could with the cold packs. He treated any bleeding scrap or cut with hydrogen peroxide followed by an antibacterial cream. The lesser scrapes got a shot of aerosol Lanacane. He elevated the girl's wrist on a pillow.

The broken leg was his final first aid project. He used two small, old canoe paddles for splints, after sawing the handles off and splitting about a third of each blade with an ax and hammer. Old sheets provided padding for the splints and bandages to secure them. He pulled on the foot very carefully. There was no real reason to reduce the break, but it seemed like a good idea. The splints were across joints above and below the break. He would read the first aid manual later to see if he was missing something about circulation, but he felt the immobilization looked well done. While ripping and tying the sheets, he heard a very feminine voice ask, "Where are we? Who are you?"

The woman's short brown hair, hazel-green eyes, small nose, and strong chin completed her oval face. She was looking at her wrist and its bandage, slowly testing her fingers. Her fingers were more functional than delicate, nails well-kept but not painted. She started to sit up but changed her mind; using her abdominal muscles caused her to wince.

"May I have some water?" was her third question.

Matt found a glass, filled it with water from the plastic gallon jug, and brought it to her. She had brought her legs off the couch and had her wrist on the pillow on her lap. She looked at the meatballs and, understanding what the package was for, laid the bag on her wrist with the bag of snow under it. She drank about half the water in the glass.

Matt thought, *So much for stomach injuries.*

Her color seemed good—well-tanned or maybe just her heritage. Very attractive eyes. Matt wondered how they went with a smile.

Matt said, "Your plane crashed, the pilot died. This man is badly hurt. We need to get to a hospital but there is a mother of all storms out there right now."

She asked, "Is it night?"

"No, this cabin is inside another large building." Matt gestured at the windows. "Those look out into a dark building. But it's midmorning, and you're in the woods of the Upper Peninsula of Michigan. This is a hunting camp. We're miles from even a good gravel road. I'm Matt, Ms...?"

"Tanya Vega. What happened to the plane? Did it burn?"

Matt caught a little Spanish accent when she said her name. "The plane is about a mile away; it tried to bulldoze its way into a cedar swamp after skidding down an icy lake. There was no fire, but it'll be a big mound of snow by now. I left the pilot inside and all the luggage you were carrying." Matt paused. "We need to try for a hospital immediately. Your friend is way beyond my first aid ability."

"I work for him," she said with a slight shake of her head. "Ivan Lesky."

So, she's not his girlfriend.

"Where were you going?" he asked. "Didn't you know there was a major storm forecast?"

Tanya hesitated before answering, "We overflew the airport where we were planning to land. We left Montreal this morning planning to land at Gore Bay on Manitoulin Island...in Canada."

Matt nodded.

"The pilot didn't think it was safe to land there. Our instruments stopped working while we tried to find the Sault Ste. Marie Airport, and we got lost in the storm. The plane was icing up. We were looking for a landmark or a highway. That's all I remember until I looked up at your wall of deer horns."

Matt finished splinting Ivan's leg and checked his neck pulse. Strong and steady. Matt pushed back an eyelid, then the other lid; both were equally dilated and got smaller as light hit them. He felt pressure against his fingers as a hand grasped his wrist.

"Where are we?" Ivan's voice was low and accented.

"My hunting cabin. We need to get you to a hospital," said Matt.

"No hospital, no doctors, I know people you can call." Ivan fixed his ice-blue eyes on Matt.

Matt said, "We have no phones, my cell phone has no service here, and we have snow outside that is ass high on a tall Indian."

Tanya slowly moved off her couch and knelt beside Ivan. "I told him we were flying from Montreal and we overflew our airport. I told him how we iced up."

Matt became suspicious with the way she seemed determined to keep their stories straight.

"Tony is dead, and the plane is about a mile away," Tanya continued. "It didn't burn and is in one piece,"

"Where are we, exactly?" asked Ivan, lifting his head and trying to look around.

Matt went to a large wall map, made of four U.S. Geological Survey topographic maps, stuck on thin plywood and covered by clear plastic. There was a grease pencil hanging from a string down the center of the framed maps. They used the map to plan their hunts, establish their blinds, note deer movements, and generally let others know where they planned to be. Matt pointed at a junction of several dotted road lines and a set of crossed picks followed by the label QUARRY.

"We are here..." He drew a small circle. "Your plane is here."

Matt made a small X at the west end of the lake. "This is the closest paved road" drawing a black line along an unnamed road between the towns of Rexton and Trout Lake. "It is about 11 miles through roads I'm not sure we could drive out on right now."

Ivan couldn't see details but appeared to accept Matt's explanation. He lay back, pushed the couch side cushion under his head...and winced. Holding his stomach, he looked at his leg without comment.

"We have things in the plane we need. I have a satellite phone that is good anywhere on the planet. All my identification is there and my papers, too. It is all in a black metal briefcase. Could you get it?"

Tanya added, "My purse is there, in the back. Black leather."

Matt replied, "I can get your stuff after the storm lets up. Now, I couldn't even see to find the plane, and the tracks were all covered ten minutes after we made them. In the meantime, could you take some warm soup and whatever food I can scare up?"

Tanya got up and walked to the kitchen area. She opened one cupboard and considered its cans of beans, soups, cereal boxes, flour, sugar, many types of coffees and teas, and nearly every cracker brand known to man. She went to the stove, lifted a teakettle, and went to the sink to fill it.

"No, use the water in the gallon jug." Matt told her. "You'll find more under the sink. Our water is a little rusty and smelly here. It's just surface water we bring in from a sand point. Okay for washing, toilets, and showers, but we don't cook with it."

Matt wondered if she could lift the gallon jug with her injured wrist, but she managed with some effort but no request for help. She began heating water for soup, arranged crackers on a plate, and sliced some brick cheese and sausage from the refrigerator.

Matt checked Ivan's splint and the color and warmth of his toes. Everything seemed satisfactory, but he worried about Ivan's back and stomach. Ivan said nothing while Matt fussed over him.

Matt finished. "How do you feel?"

Ivan tried to prop himself on the arm of the coach and sucked in breath from his various pains. "The leg is busted, but I can live with that. I think I'm busted up inside; my ribs hurt when I breathe and I feel sick to my stomach. I can't seem to get a deep breath. I can feel my legs, but my back is out of whack. My head hurts."

"You have a scalp cut. I've cleaned it and pushed it closed and put a cold pack on it. It's not bleeding, and a scab has already formed. You're a good clotter," offered Matt. "I'd give you aspirin but it will thin your blood which wouldn't help any internal bleeding problems. Your eyes are tracking evenly, but you really took a shot from the seat belt and controls of the plane. I can Ace bandage your ribs, give you a little sipping whiskey for the pain, and keep you still. I don't know what more we can do here. "

"Get me that briefcase from the plane and we can communicate with people who can help us," said Ivan between pained breaths.

Matt noted Ivan's gray color as he eased farther up against the arm of the couch.

"Let's get the radio on and see if we can get any weather reports. You listen and I'll go out and eyeball the storm," Matt said. Then he turned on a paint-spattered boom box, already tuned to a local oldies station, probably from the Sault or St. Ignace. The announcer predicted school closings and severe weather. Matt appreciated that weather emergencies gave local radio engineers an excuse to steal a bit of airtime instead of just playing ten oldies and two canned commercials for local businesses like Menard's and the Native American casinos.

Matt went out of the cabin and snatched the coat he had hung by the door. He pulled it on, noting the extra weight of the SIG in the right glove pocket. The snow still came down hard, but the wind had gone down. Nearly three feet of snow covered the ground with drifts that only a photographer could appreciate. The snow pushed almost fifty feet into the building in a delta that tapered from several feet deep at the entrance to almost nothing. The road to the lake could stop a snowmobile with drifts this deep.

Matt had a great deal of experience "drift busting" with friends: one machine would go until the snow stopped it; then another would race up the packed track, pull around the slowed machine and, with its greater speed, smash through the drift and keep going; the first machine then steered onto the new trail and followed the new leader. The operative word was "machines"—plural. One machine could easily get stuck in new, drifting snow. Matt knew a person on a snowmobile could go in ten minutes where a walker would require several hours through waist-deep snow. Even snowshoes helped little in new, deep snow. Animals solved the problem of blizzard conditions by curling up under shelter for several days.

Matt shrugged, reentered the cabin, and hung up his coat. He looked at his two guests. "I'd suggest we stay put for at least twenty-four hours."

"I don't know if I have twenty-four hours," breathed Ivan. "I'm feeling dizzy, and it's getting harder to take a breath. I need to have my phone. You have to make another trip to the plane!"

Tanya stepped close to Matt, offering a cup of hot cream of chicken soup. She made eye contact and said, "It is very important that we can make contact with people who can help us."

Matt's fingers touched hers as he took the warm cup. They felt warmer than the soup and sent heat rushing through his body. He considered her for several seconds. Using more testosterone than brains, he said simply, "I'll give it a try."

Matt changed his turtleneck polypropylene undershirt for a dry duplicate, put on a heavy wool sweater, wrapped a scarf around his neck, pulled on his hunting jacket and Kromer, and pulled up his jacket hood and tightened the tie straps. "The fastest I can do this will be about twenty minutes. If I get stuck, it could be over an hour. If I fall into the lake…the keys are in the Yukon. You just push the 4D button for four-wheel drive. Study the map, make a drawing, take it with you, and you might get to the highway.

Driving through drifts with a bad wrist over narrow roads won't be easy. No one will come here to check on me for many days."

With that last dash of information, Matt left. He didn't know if he sounded like a Jack London character or something from Robert Service's *The Cremation of Sam McGee*. He had given them important information about their survival, but maybe more than he wanted them to know about his isolation. But like Service said, "A promise made is a debt unpaid."

Second Trip

MATT UNTIED THE CANOE FROM the Polaris. He took a pair of long snowshoes that framed the cabin door—decorative, but also totally functional. They were made in Shingleton in the U.P. of super-tough neoprene webbing—much more serviceable than gut, and animals won't eat it. He bundled them together, put them on the snowmobile's seat, secured them with a bungee cord, started the machine, and headed into the storm. He could have put them on the side of the seat but if things got rough, he wanted them easily accessible. Better to have them uncomfortably under him than unfindable if he got stuck or started sinking in icy slush.

The storm proved a real challenge. Despite the powerful, heavy Polaris—made for this type of adventure—vision was a problem. He could only see by turning his head from side to side so that alternately one eye at a time saw clearly for a few seconds. He had rejected the helmet legally required by the regulatory overzealous DNR. He needed unimpeded sight and hearing, and goggles or a helmet visor quickly would become useless in the clinging snow. Familiar landmarks were few as he sped across the quarry floor and down the wooded road. The trees cut the wind, allowing him quick progress to the edge of the lake. He took his Silva compass from his jacket breast pocket and put its tie string around his neck. He sighted along the compass for the westerly bearing he wanted. The southwest wind would keep the snow against the left side of his face.

Out on the lake, the wind and snow dropped visibility to less than twenty feet. Matt worried about hitting the open water made by the plane's crash, by now likely thin ice covered by snow and nearly invisible. He spotted the two-foot-wide canoe groove left by his earlier passage, covered but not quite hidden by the snow. He followed the trail. It disappeared several times but gave a true bearing to the plane. He slowed the last hundred yards, showing respect for the trail on one side and the icy water on the other. He found the plane, only a few yards south of the trail. The snow had filled in between most of the hummocks, but Matt could feel his passage over them. He stopped with plenty of room to turn before he reached the wing.

The snow had drifted over the plane, hiding the door. Matt dug snow from the top of the door down and pushed it lower on the wing. He felt for the handle and pulled the door open, just enough to squeeze in. His small Maglite flashlight brought very bright light into the basically white cabin interior. He looked at the pilot again.

Sorry, Tony, but I want to see what else you are carrying.

He found another SIG magazine under his right arm. He removed his wet wool gloves and popped out a shell, .357 SIG hollow point. He put the shell in his pants pocket, pocketed the magazine, and removed Tony's shoulder holster, shoving it into his large coat pocket. Leaving an empty holster would raise too many questions.

He found the black metal briefcase wedged between the passenger seat and the instrument panel and lifted it free. Heavy with a combination lock. Matt tried one number each way on each of the four dials to see if it would open easily. It did not.

Ivan isn't lazy or stupid.

Matt located Tanya's handbag on the floor. Her wallet contained a Florida driver's license with an Islamorada address in the Keys. Also, phone and credit cards, school pictures of grade-school-age children, a PADI scuba diving card, and some group pictures of college-age revelers on a sunny beach. The rest of the bag held makeup items, mints, gum, a small Kleenex package, and a black plastic film container. Inside the tightly closed film container Matt found a handful of .22-caliber hollow-point long rifle shells wrapped in a Kleenex. He dumped everything out of the bag onto the carpeted cabin floor. The bag was still heavy. A large bag made by Coach, it smelled of fine leather and faintly of perfume. He could not feel a gun from the outside but an outside flap covered the stiff, thick side. He had opened all sections and zippered areas. Then he felt along the edge of the bag and noted how the one side was stiffer and thicker on one end. He pulled on the thicker side and heard Velcro opening along the seam. A small .22-caliber semiautomatic occupied the exposed cavity—MOD. 21A-22 LR on the slide and P. Beretta on the plastic grip. His hands were too cold to bother checking the action, so he put the pistol in his left pants' pocket. He replaced the rest of the bag's contents.

Now, he wanted to see the cargo, hoping for an explanation for all the firearms. Plastic ties secured the duffel bags. He cut one with his Swiss army knife. The contents were multiply wrapped bundles of powder.

I bet this isn't flour for Girl Scout cookies .

He had never used any type of dope. He didn't know how to identify cocaine. All the movies and TV had the people rubbing the powder on their teeth or gums.

Why not?

With his old Victorinox Swiss blade poised to punch into a package and retrieve a small amount of the crystal powder, he wondered, *What if it was poison or anthrax?*

Not very smart. So, was he now sharing his cabin with dope dealers and his lake with a plane full of cocaine?

He had no idea of the value of the cargo in the large duffel bags. A small, soft-sided gym bag caught his attention, locked with a small Master lock. Matt separated the double handles on the bag and eased the zipper apart, finding bundles of $100 bills. They looked well circulated, without consecutive serial numbers. The yellowish wrapper read $10,000. "Shit…" Matt said aloud. "I'm a dead man."

Matt carried the money bag out to the Polaris and, with difficulty, stuffed it into the rear Velcro-closed storage compartment. He also took a bag of the white powder, just a couple of pounds.

Maybe a kilo, he thought.

He unzipped the turtleneck of his undershirt, stuffed the bag inside, and wiggled it down until the belt of his pants stopped it. He bundled back up.

He scanned the many dials, levers, and switches on the plane's instrument panel but could not make sense of it. He traced Tony's headset to the radio area. He couldn't see any way to turn anything on. He left the plane, careful to shut the door firmly.

He mounted the Polaris and stored the briefcase between his right leg and the seat, jamming it into the ice and snow that covered the foot space. The handbag he stuffed between the instruments and the inside of the windshield. The engine started with a short pull. He made a tight turn and headed back along his rapidly disappearing track. He went slowly, trying to think. He could make a run to Rexton or Trout Lake and find a phone. What about Tanya? What about Ivan? There was no vacillation on his position on dope. He had seen its effect on school kids and knew of the human disasters and social disruption it caused.

How much money am I dealing with? Way out of my league in every way.

He decided to confront his cabin guests, protect himself, and see to their needs, planning his next actions once he knew more about the total picture.

With the decision to return to the cabin, he concentrated on driving through the storm and finding the way off the lake without running into a cedar swamp or a boulder of limestone. The tracks were still plain as he roared up the drifts onto the trail to the cabin. He could see better with the wind behind him. No bad drifts on the generally north-northeast trail, despite more than three feet of fairly solid snow. Ramming a hidden block or log worried him more than sinking and getting stuck. He also needed to keep up his speed to give him momentum when he did come to a drift. He soon came to the large opening of the huge building that protected his cabin. He drove to the front door. At nearly noon, the light had an evening quality.

Matt hung the snowshoes back up to show no suspicious movement if his guests watched from the cabin's dark windows. He stepped around the side of the cabin and checked the SIG in his coat pocket. Familiar with the SIG Sauer, he cocked the hammer, slid the slide aft, closed the breech, and popped the magazine out. Checking the hollow point looking up at him and the weight of many shells, he snapped the magazine in solidly and pushed the decocking lever, which safely brought the hammer down. No safety on the double-action pistol. The first pull cocked and released the mechanism. He didn't know exactly how many shells filled the magazine, but probably more than the two or three he could see. He unzipped his coat and jammed the gun under his belt on his left side. With his gloves off, he walked into the cabin carrying the briefcase and handbag.

6

Bad Guys

TANYA KNELT BESIDE IVAN, holding a damp cloth on his forehead. His bulk stretched out on the couch. She looked up when Matt entered, but Ivan did not.

"I'm glad to see you back. Ivan's worse; dizzy and can't focus. I don't know what we can do," she said.

With his eyes closed, Ivan whispered, "Do you have the briefcase?"

"It's right here." Matt placed it on the coffee table that separated the two couches.

"Combination 0000, never changed it." Ivan tried to chuckle.

Matt set the chrome dials to 0000 and pushed the single catch release. The case popped open. The locking mechanism ran all along the edges of both the top and bottom—a formidable obstacle to breaking into the briefcase.

The briefcase contained no gun but, rather, several manila folders, flight information, some loose papers, several maps in pockets, a laptop computer, and a brick-sized phone, along with various plug-in chargers.

With one eye open, Ivan pushed himself onto one elbow. "Hand me the phone."

Ivan took the phone from Matt, opened the cover that turned into a mouthpiece, extended the short antenna, and pushed the "on" key. Both Tanya and Matt could see LEDs activate.

"Marginal. Only a level 2 connection," said Ivan, handing the phone to Tanya. "Find Webb in the directory and dial him. Then give it back to me."

When the beeps indicated dialing, Tanya gave the phone back to Ivan.

Ivan held it to his ear. After a few seconds, he spoke, "*Dobroye utro Gyorgy...net...net...Da, kazhetsya, ne ochen' harosho...*," followed by rapid-fire Russian.

Matt heard Montreal but could not recognize any other words.

Ivan handed the phone to Matt. "I told him we've crashed and I am not well. Tell him where we are."

Matt took the phone, impressed that it worked under two roofs and through a snowstorm. "Hello, can you hear me?"

"Yes, what is your location?" A distant voice with no particular accent.

"Well," Matt said, "we're in a cabin in the Upper Peninsula of Michigan, west of Interstate 75 and south of Michigan Highway 28. The closest town you might know is Sault Ste. Marie, where the locks link Lake Superior and Lake Huron. Our closest good road is Highway 123. That's the best I can do without showing you a map. You couldn't get a vehicle in here through the snowstorm on our poor roads. Ivan needs medical attention. I can now call a doctor, but how would we move him?"

Matt thought *over* and handed the phone to Ivan. Matt knew the description would narrow their location to somewhere in the eastern part of the Hiawatha National Forest but, outside of a few old farts from Rexton and his relatives, no one could find this place in five summer days. You had to stand on the edge of the quarry to see into it. Even from the air, the quarry had enough growth and trees to make it hard to pick out. The pipelines and the big building would be coordinates he would give to a rescue helicopter if he got a chance.

Just before closing the phone, Ivan said in English, "Yes, I don't think so, okay, sure, *do svidaniya*." Then, he lay back with a deep sigh.

"What's the plan?" asked Matt.

"They'll call us back, so we wait."

Matt moved to the kitchen table, keeping Tanya and Ivan across the room. As he passed the door, he removed and hung up his coat, hat, and scarf. He rearranged his sweater, which had been tucked into his pants, and smoothed it over the pistol. He then pulled up his undershirt, took out the bag of powder, and tossed it on the coffee table, next to the briefcase.

"I suppose if you were from Iraq you would call this baby formula," said Matt.

Tanya and Ivan looked at the package like it was a rat on a dinner table, then looked at each other. Ivan lay back.

"We need to talk," said Tanya.

"This is a great time and place for it," replied Matt.

Tanya stood up from her perch on the arm of Ivan's couch. She moved past Ivan toward her bag, also on the coffee table. "May I get something from my bag first?"

Matt shrugged.

She picked up the bag and without revealing her disappointment at its lightness, looked at Matt.

"I hope nothing important fell out on the trip back here," said Matt.

She opened the bag and took out the small pack of Kleenex. Taking one, she blew her nose perfunctorily and put the used Kleenex and the pack back into the bag. Moving around the room to get closer to Matt, she said, "You are involved in something way out of your league."

With Tanya at the end of the table and Ivan across the room and more than 90 degrees separating the two, Matt thought, *Enough of this cute shit.*

He pulled out the SIG, cocked it for a deliberate audible effect, and aimed it at Tanya.

"Put your purse down," he said, hoping he sounded like a blend of Clint Eastwood and John Wayne. "Move back to the couch with Ivan. If either of you move anything fast, you'll be shot, wired to some B Blocks, and sunk in about six feet of loon shit before this storm is over."

Tanya paled. Ivan mumbled something that probably translated, "Oh shit, what more could go wrong?" although his look said he knew Matt's bravado was so much bullshit.

Tanya stepped closer. Matt leveled the gun at her chest and wondered what four pounds of pressure felt like when running on about 110 percent adrenaline rush.

Matt said nothing, but Tanya sensed another step might kill her. She moved back to the couch. Matt pulled out a chair at the table and sat facing his two guests.

Matt started, "No more warnings, if I need to shoot, I'll shoot you both. Now, what is this, how much is in the plane, and how much money is in the luggage? And are there any more interesting surprises in the plane?" He paused and considered the silence.

"Okay, do I need to print these questions on the board?" Again he waited.

They watched him silently.

"No need to raise your hands." They missed the joke. Matt felt like Barney Fife in a New York precinct.

Ivan and Tanya remained silent. Matt squeezed the trigger.

Boom!

The bullet sped over their heads and tore through the far wall.

Tanya started, eyes widening. Ivan jerked reflexively.

Matt figured some silicone sealant inside and outside would fix the damage. The bullet should have passed through the big door opening on the south end of the building.

The shell casing bounced across the cement floor and rolled to the front of the room. No other sound for several seconds. Matt's ears rang. With the muzzle facing them, Ivan and Tanya could probably barely hear.

"Talk to him," said Ivan, color draining from his face.

Tanya started to stand, but Matt waved her down. She eased back down and began, "There are 200 kilos of top-grade cocaine—440 pounds. Coke wholesales for maybe $20,000 per kilo, street value as much as $90,000. So, the plane's got maybe four to eighteen million U.S. dollars of coke plus another quarter-mil of laundered money. Coke's a commodity, its value fluctuates. The money…is money.

"How much do you make a year?"

Tanya's eyes considered him as though she waited for the first kiss of the evening.

The question, preceded by facts he couldn't quickly assimilate, caught Matt off guard. "About two and a half bags worth of your white shit, but I taught, not poisoned my students," Matt did not break eye contact with her, realizing he was arguing with his brain but falling in love—lust?—with his heart. Or some other parts.

Tanya went on, "We don't sell to kids either. We sell to people who sell to stockbrokers, lawyers, and politicians. Do you have anything against that?"

Her first smile unnerved him. With difficulty, he broke eye contact and checked his watch. Not even 1:00 p.m. and he had a SIG, millions of dollars of a controlled substance, and a woman whose smile made him want to wag his tail, run over to her, and lick her all over.

Matt felt some pressure against his leg at the thought of playing puppy and his next sensation was the little automatic pressing against the other side of his left leg. Both sensations told him to tread carefully with this beautiful, but dangerous, woman.

Realizing her smile had worked, Tanya started to capitalize on her accomplishment. "We could make it very worth your while to help us get to civilization."

"You're dead if you don't help us," Ivan croaked, eyes still closed. "You're dealing with powerful people and a big organization. They don't let people get away with their money or goods. You told them where you are. They'll call back and expect cooperation."

"We need to get the money and goods to some people in Chicago. Will you help us?" asked Tanya, giving Matt a helpless look.

"I can use your phone and have the police here in a few hours. Your plane's emergency locator may be transmitting right now," Matt replied. "I need to think about this. How can I trust you?"

Matt reclaimed the satellite phone with its blinking standby light. Having never seen a phone like it, he just punched a cousin's number he remembered. He wanted to tell someone he was okay and have him call others, including his neighbors, so they would not send out a rescue party. He had friends who would brave a storm just to get to Matt's beer and brandy. He punched the send button, the phone rang and was answered but only with static and a fax-like squeal. He broke the connection and tried it again with the same results.

"It's scrambled, and I can't remember how to take it off scramble," said Ivan, eyes still closed. "As for the plane's emergency locator, we kept the battery just charged enough to keep the idiot light off on the dash. You'd need to be within about a mile to pick it up. I'm not even sure our crash was hard enough to set it off." Matt pursed his lips in thought.

"Look," Ivan pressed, "I'm not in good shape. I feel dizzy if I sit up, and I can't breathe if I lay flat. My leg hurts like hell and so do my ribs. You got any pain pills or some booze?"

"Liquor's in the cupboard over the refrigerator and a few Vicoden tablets are in the bathroom medicine chest."

"Tanya, get me something to drink and check on the pills. I can't think straight hurting like this."

Tanya looked at Matt and got an approving head shake. She went into the bathroom, and Matt heard the medicine cabinet open. In a minute, she came out with a plastic vial, went to the refrigerator, and opened the cupboard. She looked at the score of bottles but couldn't easily reach them.

"How about the vodka?" she asked. "Could you get it?"

Matt moved to the refrigerator after enjoying the sight of Tanya trying to stretch over the top of it. He remembered how, back in the plane, her legs had gone all the way up. But he hadn't really appreciated the total package when she was all curled. Matt reached up and retrieved an almost full bottle of Smirnoff. Tanya took it and picked a glass off the dryer rack. She poured two fingers into the small glass, shook out a Vicoden, and gave them both to Ivan. He took the pill and washed it down with the vodka in two swallows. He seemed to appreciate the attention.

He gave a small cough, winced in pain, and frowned. "American vodka. In Russia, we start fires with stuff that's better than this."

Propped up on the couch, he laid his head back against the cushion. He looked gray.

Matt motioned Tanya back to the other end of Ivan's couch. His now-stiff fingers had clutched the pistol for too long. He thumbed the hammer down and tucked the gun into his belt. Without turning his back on Ivan or Tanya, he filled, charged, and turned on the large Mr. Coffee on the counter. Hungry, he eyed the cheese and sausage plate, still on the table. Matt buttered several crackers and layered them with cheese and sausage. He ate two in as many bites, not graceful but neat. No crumbs fell. He opened the refrigerator and pulled out a Coors light. Not much taste, but wet and cold. He wanted a Heineken or four, but needed his head clear.

Matt piled three inches of crackers on the cheese-and-sausage plate and took it to the coffee table in front of Tanya. "Want something to drink?

"Some wine?" she replied, looking up at him. "Anything that's not sweet."

Matt got a gallon jug of Carlo Rossi burgundy from under the sink. He poured some into a real, long-stemmed large wineglass, fashionably above half full, and presented it to Tanya. Another smile. More puppy thoughts.

He took the briefcase and phone to the table and sat facing his guests, safely separated by the table and other couch. He started to rummage through the papers in the briefcase.

Lists of private flying clubs and small airports. Copies of news clippings about flying clubs. A report by a business consultant about the effects of 9/11 on the lightplane industry and private flying, as well as a half-inch-thick, glossy advertising magazine by Cessna Aircraft Company, two *U.S. Pilot* magazines, and several other magazines all cut up and underlined. He saw Experimental Aircraft Association clippings and aeronautical charts of Michigan, Ohio, Wisconsin, and Illinois, and a map of Ontario and Quebec Provinces .

Matt looked from Ivan to Tanya. "Why the interest in small planes?"

"You don't want to know," she said.

Ivan blinked at them both with one eye, looking like a poor imitation of a lighthouse.

Matt was hot. The room was in the seventies, and he still wore wool pants and sweater and polypropylene underwear. He needed to chill out, figuratively and literally, but mostly he needed to slow his life down from its recent frenetic pace. A tidal wave of events had crashed onto his small shore and now threatened to suck him and everything around him out to sea. He needed more than to keep his head above water, he needed some direction and a sense of control over the course of events.

Is this all my own karma, fate, joss, luck, or whatever? I damn well better find the pony…because I'm drowning in horse shit.

He took off his sweater, unzipped the neck of his underwear, and swigged the cool Coors. Tanya. More than cute, less than a classic beauty. But perfectly proportioned and very sexy. Wonderful eyes and a totally captivating smile. She moved gracefully, always in balance. Matt could usually tell the sport of an athlete. Tanya? Probably a swimmer, judging from the scuba diving card and address in the Keys. Her muscles were long, like a swimmer's. He could also imagine her playing tennis, although he hadn't noticed a difference between her left and right wrists or forearms and hadn't checked her thumb for a callus. He wanted to spend time with her, but needed her to have enough fear, or respect, that he wouldn't have to tie her up or, worse, shoot her. He had heard of women who could smile at you while dropping the hammer on their pistol.

Matt considered Ivan. Head and internal trauma, either of which could be fatal—with or without medical help. Still, the body is a tough mechanism, and Ivan seemed a tough person. So, they had a waiting game, and Matt could only try to adhere to the first part of the Hippocratic Oath, "First, do no harm."

With oldies music wafting softly from the radio, Tanya reapplied wet cloths to Ivan's neck and forehead. Jarring musical notes burst from the satellite phone. Classical, but nothing Matt could name.

Matt picked it up, pulled out the antenna, and snapped it open. "Yes?"

"Who's this?" demanded the same voice he had spoken to earlier.

"I'm the guy with the hunting cabin in the woods. Who are you?"

"None of your damned business," the voice snarled. "Let me speak to Ivan."

Matt handed the phone to Ivan. "Speak in English. Anything else, and I stop the call."

Matt motioned Tanya away from Ivan and stood by Ivan's head, in easy reach of the phone. He moved the SIG to his left hand.

"Yes?" Pause. "How the hell should I know? That was Tony's department. We left before dawn, it was clear. We couldn't land at Gore Bay, and then we missed the Sault. It was a hell of a storm. Either ice or gas or both. Shit, we're lucky to be alive and not wrapped around some tree burned to a crisp…" Pause. "Ya, the money bag and goods are in one piece. Tanya's fine, she just banged her wrist a little." Pause. "I haven't a damned clue." Pause. "He's got a gun on me now, that's why. Here, he wants to talk to you."

Ivan held the phone out to Matt, who put it to his ear.

"Listen, *dolboy'eb*, give that gun back to Ivan and do what he tells you or you'll get yourself and everyone you love killed."

Matt responded, forcing the butterflies in his gut to settle down, "I can tell you're from Chicago. All you flatlanders have the same trouble getting along. I'd like to see a bounty put on every one of you. I'd like to see us stop every Illinois car every ten miles and collect thirty-five cents—exact change…"

"All right, I get your point. What we got to do to get along here?"

"We could use some medical advice in the short term, and I want to be sure I stay alive in the long term."

"I'll have a doctor here in thirty minutes. What's your name, and where is your place?

Matt thought a second. "I don't want you knowing my name or location at this time. But what should I call you?"

"Mr…Webb is good enough for now," said the Chicago voice. "And what about our money and other goods?"

"All in the plane under two or three feet of snow."

"I'll call you when the doctor gets here." Webb broke the connection.

Matt put the phone on the table and went to the large wall map. With his Swiss army knife, he cut out the part with the quarry and surrounding roads. He got his Bic lighter from his hunting coat, lit the map pieces, and dropped them in the sink to burn.

"Now, unless you have photographic memories and 20/10 vision," Matt said, "you have no clue where you are. And even if you know where you are, you don't know how to get to civilization. And if you knew where you are and where the closest city with street lights might be, you could never get there in this storm."

Matt checked his watch; it was after 2:00, early afternoon. He felt like he had been up for days, and the warm cabin made him sleepy. Ivan was sleeping, or at least immobile, on the coach. Tanya ate some cheese and meat and had drunk most of her wine. She, too, looked sleepy. With the light filtering through the front window, he could see his Yukon and the large empty windows of the machine shop across the 40 feet of open area in front of the cabin. The snow still fell, but more slowly.

Matt went to Tanya, who was sitting on the arm of Ivan's coach. "May I look at your wrist?"

Tanya lay down on the other couch with her left wrist on the outside. With a serious expression, she presented her wrist. Matt carefully unwound the Ace bandage, rolling it up as he went, and knelt beside her.

Although his back was to Ivan, he would hear the couch springs creak if Ivan moved. He held Tanya's hand and softly touched her wrist—discolored and puffy. Tanya moved her fingers, but winced when she tried to bend the wrist.

"Looks like a sprain," said Matt. "It can take longer to heal than a break. I think the best we can do is use the RICE rule; Rest, Ice, Compression, and Elevation." His first aid advice came from one part of his brain but touching Tanya excited the rest of his brain and body. He fought for objectivity.

He rewrapped the Ace bandage, put a pillow under her wrist, and recharged the ziplock bags with packed snow from outside. After two aspirins washed down with water, Tanya seemed quite content to lie on the couch. He also put ice packs wrapped in a damp dishcloth on Ivan's head. Ivan looked gray and didn't open his eyes while Matt worked on him.

Matt turned down the cabin thermostat. The excessive warmth made him logy and tired. His visitors could just cover up if they got cold. He cracked the door open to get a few breaths of cold air. Matt's brain had overloaded.

I can't trust dope-dealing gangsters. I'm friggin' out of my league.

Facing classrooms of students, adversarial teams and coaches—even the lawyer for his ex-wife—hadn't prepared him for this chess game played with millions of dollars of illegal substances, mob money, special phones, a dying man, and a woman he'd like to have met at an after-church coffee hour.

The satellite phone's classical tones sounded. Tanya picked it up on the second group of notes, moving very quickly from her couch. It made Matt think that she hadn't been resting or sleeping after all.

She answered, "Yes, yes, not much change. No, no, I'm not sure..."

Matt took the phone from her and moved around the table. He wanted space between them. "Hello, who is this?"

"This is a doctor, can you tell me about Ivan's condition?"

"Well, he got whacked hard on the right top of his forehead, leaving a gash and a lump larger than a golf ball. We treated it with an antibiotic salve and cold compresses. He has a broken right leg—at least the tibia. He didn't need reduction and it's splinted. His toes are not cold or discolored. What else?" Matt thought a moment. "He's complaining about his ribs. Shortness of breath when he lays flat and dizzy when he sits up. His eyes seem to dilate equally. We gave him some Vicoden and a little vodka about two hours ago when he was in a lot of pain."

"Is he awake?" The doctor added, "You seem to have had medical training."

"He's not awake." Matt's immodesty almost got the better of him with bragging about coaching and hours of first aid classes and his science background. Then he remembered his difficult situation. He lied, "I watch a lot of *ER* on television."

"What about his pulse and temperature?" Matt checked Ivan's neck for a pulse. Was there one? He tried to still his own pulse and tried Ivan's wrist pulse. Just barely detectable, so he timed it with his watch.

To the doctor, he said, "Forty but very weak. Warm and clammy to the touch."

"Do his pupils dilate when you lift his eyelids?"

Matt checked both eyes one at a time, then together. Was anyone home in there?

"Yeah, but slowly, and his breathing's slowing down. Not good…"

"Let me speak to Tanya, please," said the doctor.

Covering the mouthpiece, he warned, "Stay within an arm's length of me, and don't say my name or anything about our location."

"Yes?" Tanya said into the phone. "Just like he told you. Ivan's not moved or talked for over an hour. Is there anything we can do for him?"

Tanya listened attentively. "No, we can't. We're in the middle of a serious snowstorm that's shut down the roads. It'd be over an hour to any hospital, anyway." She paused again. "This guy dragged us from the plane in a canoe pulled behind a snowmobile." Another pause.

She looked at Matt. "Try to wake him up and elevate his chest some more."

Matt lifted Ivan's shoulders and slid a cushion and pillow under his back and neck. Ivan remained limp and quiet. His breathing deepened, and Matt heard gurgling.

"Hear that gurgling?" Matt asked.

Tanya, with the phone, started to relay the information, but the doctor had heard Matt and continued speaking. Tanya turned the phone so Matt could hear. "There isn't much more you can do without medical assistance. He needs IVs, a surgeon, and an ICU. He may have abdominal and or head injuries with internal bleeding. We have no way to get a blood pressure reading. His lungs may be filling or…" Ivan made the issue a moot point by gasping, stiffening, and finally gurgling his last exhale.

"I think he's all done dancing," said Matt. He thought about CPR but instead just checked Ivan's vital signs and watched a person become an object.

"Ivan just died," Tanya whispered into the phone.

After nearly a minute, Webb returned to the phone and said, "Put the hunter on the line."

For a heartbeat, Matt wondered how Webb knew his name before realizing it was just a convenient label.

"What now?" Matt asked Webb, keeping the phone so Tanya could listen.

"Here's what you're gonna do. Go through his clothes; leave only his identification, it was on the flight plan anyway. Put him back into the plane."

"You expect me to cover up for you?"

"Shut up and listen. Stash the money and goods from the plane someplace safe. Be sure to clean out the storage compartments behind the engines. Don't let the bags break open, they are special, without any chemical residue."

"Like hell I will, you—"

"You don't, and people you care about'll die. Are we clear?"

" Go ahead." Matt fumed mentally but decided to keep it to himself. He saw a pleading look in Tanya's eyes, she touched his hand that held the phone. *Maybe I shouldn't anger this asshole.*

"If the authorities find the plane, there'll be federal and local law up the ass. You clean out the plane and deliver the goods and money, we'll pay you and you can walk away with no more trouble. Just tell me where we can meet—someplace on a good road—and we'll pick up Tanya and our property and be out of your life. Deal?"

"I suppose, but once they find the plane, they'll find me, too. Which means so can you. Then you can take back anything I get for this—"

Tanya placed a hand on his lips and shook her head, holding her hand out for the phone.

Matt looked into her eyes, exhaled slowly, and gave her the phone. *Maybe she had a better idea.*

"Let me discuss this with…our host," Tanya told Webb. "I'm sure we can work out a good deal for everyone. I'll call you back tomorrow when we've had time to think and make plans."

She listened a few seconds and turned off the phone.

7

Third Trip

C'MON," TANYA ORDERED. "We've got to get him in a chair, so it'll look like he died sitting up with his blood pooled in his lower body."

Businesslike, in control, and apparently not sad that Ivan was dead, Matt watched her rifle Ivan's coat, shirt, and pants pockets, checking for a money belt or inside carrying device. She even checked his watch and shoes. She dragged an old leather overstuffed chair across the room and to the couch. To Matt, she said, "Help me."

They removed Ivan's splint and wiped the salve from his head wound. The two of them wrestled the dead body into the chair, where he looked every bit like everyone Matt had ever seen in that chair after a day of hunting, some warm stew, and several Hartley brandies. Peaceful and relaxed, resting from a long day in the woods.

Tanya's efficiency and purpose impressed Matt. The plane would be found for sure in the spring when a few relatives arrived to fish the lake. Hell, the emergency locator might summon inquiring minds before that. Tired, he just wanted to sit down beside Ivan and say, "Some day, hey?"

Tanya looked at him, "We need to get him to the plane as soon as we can. And bring the other stuff back here. Is there another machine I can use?"

"You know how to drive one?"

" I've done it before—once in Canada and once in Yellowstone."

"And your wrist?"

"It's good enough."

What the hell am I doing? Aloud, Matt said, "It'll be dark in less than an hour, and the storm's still howling. We can do the canoe thing again, I suppose, and you could be some help in digging the plane out and another sled could haul cargo." He looked her over. "You're going to need more clothes and better boots. Skirt, knee socks, and moccasins will only get you frostbite."

Do I trust her? Matt wondered. *She's assuming I'm going to do what Webb had ordered.*

Not exactly what he had expected.

What the hell, old Ivan has to be somewhere. Why not the plane?

Getting the cocaine and money into his safe keeping seemed a good idea too. Maybe he could gain some control. Anyway, the storm and lack of local communications would keep them isolated from the authorities for some time.

Looking into her eyes, using all his control to keep mind and body from caving in to her beauty, he asked, "And why should I trust you or help you?"

"We've got to do something with Ivan anyway, and we need to get the money and packages out of the plane. We can talk later about what we do after that," she said logically.

" Okay. Let's see what we can find for you," Matt said, heading up the stairs to the bunk area. The room was undivided except by two roof supports; bunk beds were in the middle area, and two queen-sized beds were at opposite ends of the room. Clotheslines drooped across one end of the room above a floor register directly over the space heater below. Two tin closets lined one wall. Here, Matt found a pair of size seven Sorel boots—his son's from many years ago, too good to throw or give away. He also found a medium-size snowmobile bib and a pair of sweat pants.

"Get into these the best you can. Your sweater's good, and there are snowmobile jackets and gloves downstairs that will work."

Tanya dropped her wool skirt right in front of Matt. Her tights show-cased her fine figure before she slipped into the sweat pants that came up to her armpits. She pulled on the bib, sat on a bed, and pushed her feet into the Sorels.

"Too big," Tanya remarked. "Do you have any extra socks?"

Matt found some almost new Wigwams in a small size and helped her into them and back into the boots. He snapped, adjusted, and zipped her bib. Matt, having enjoyed the intimacy, helped her down the stairs.

He looked at her and laughed at her new roundness. "You look twelve years old, and I expect you to tell me you need to go to the bathroom."

"Actually I do," said Tanya with a smile that made her look ten.

Matt unsnapped and unzipped her, and she left for the bathroom.

Matt found an old black Skidoo jacket with a hood. He also found a wool navy watch cap, unused by the men because it was so small that it would slowly work its way to the top of your head and fall off.

Tanya came out of the bathroom, got resnapped and zipped. Matt put the watch cap on her. It fit Tanya very nicely, covering her ears. She rummaged through the glove box, finding a good pair of leather gloves lined with Gortex and filled with Thinsulate, men's large, big enough to fit over her bandaged hand.

Matt and Tanya dragged Ivan out to the canoe, where they wedged him between the front seat and the middle thwart, more or less in a sitting position.

Matt returned to the cabin, put on his sweater, jacket, and dry gloves.

He tucked the plastic tarps tightly around Ivan, put in a second shovel, a five-cell flashlight, and an old railroad broom. Used for cleaning switches on the old Soo Line, the broom had an ice scraper on one end and a broom on the other—good for moving snow, chipping ice, and most importantly, sweeping out their tracks. Even snow-covered tracks would reveal themselves as the snow melted. Their paths to and from the plane would still show after the March thaw. How long depended on temperatures, rain, and sunshine.

Tanya looked around inside the large building, filled with all its hunting vehicles and paraphernalia, ladders, ropes, axes, tree trimming saws, and a general store's supply of outdoor equipment.

"Why did you build the cabin in this big building?" Tanya asked.

"It seemed a good idea at the time. We got a free building from a pipeline company just for moving it. This building has a good cement floor. We were just going to store it here, but then we put it together for one deer season, hooked up gas, water, and electricity; a couple years later we put a bunk room on it. Now we can't get it out the door if we wanted to. We don't have to worry about snow load and can store all the toys in here, too."

The sun, low in the southern sky, was just a bright spot on the horizon at 4:00 p.m., only an hour and a few minutes of light remained. The storm still blew, but without as much snow as before. They could make it to the plane in daylight, but the return trip would be in the dark.

Matt started another Polaris. It had enough gas for their needs. He started his machine and tied the canoe on as before, with only a few feet of leader. He tucked the excess rope into the canoe and confirmed he had the plastic anchor rope. He double-checked the load.

He asked Tanya, "Can you steer that machine?"

She thumbed the gas lever and showed she could move the handlebars side to side, though with some difficulty.

"The trail is fairly straight. Just follow me closely. We won't go very fast and I'll pump my brake lights when I plan to slow down. It will be hard to see out on the lake. If you get in trouble, use this high and low beam switch to let me know. Otherwise, leave it alone. Ready?"

Tanya gave a thumbs-up.

Matt got on his machine and drove out of the building. He looked back several times and saw Tanya was doing fine, even smiling, as she followed him.

They reached the lake without incident. Though the snow and wind made vision difficult, this return trip proved easier. Matt could still see tracks through the drifts and blowing snow. A few minutes later, Matt stopped thirty feet from the plane and untied the canoe. Tanya parked beside his machine and followed the trail broken by Matt pulling the canoe. Matt pulled the canoe right up to the right wing, or at least to the snow mound where the wing should be. Over three feet of snow drift covered the wing and almost as much covered the fuselage. He got the shovel and started to dig down to the door.

Tanya helped with the broom and the other shovel. She favored her wrist but still got snow moved. After five minutes, they got the door open. They removed the bags and hauled Ivan from the canoe and to the plane. Matt edged into the cockpit and with great effort pulled and pushed Ivan back into his seat. He rebuckled the seatbelt. Matt put the leg back in the same position he had originally found it. Ivan wasn't really stiff yet.

Meanwhile, Tanya moved the four duffel bags and the soft-sided luggage bags from the plane. They could only get three duffel bags into the bottom of the seventeen-foot canoe. They tied one bag on top of the others with the plastic anchor rope, leaving the load a little top heavy. Matt would have to go slowly on grades and turns.

"There's more!" Tanya yelled. "We haven't emptied the wing storage areas on the engine cowlings."

They had to shovel a lot of snow to get to the right wing compartment. It held a smaller heavy canvas bag about half the weight of the large bags, maybe forty pounds. They closed the right wing storage area and shoveled the snow back.

Tanya pointed to two bags she had set aside, "This is Ivan's and that's the pilot's. We should leave them in the plane."

Matt noticed she didn't open them and thought, *I don't want another weapon showing up.*

Tanya looked in the plane, "Where's the little gym bag with the money?"

"I've got it in my sled," yelled Matt above the wind, as he entered the cabin.

While Tanya held the flashlight, Matt found the emergency locator box in the aft cabin. Using his trusty Swiss army knife, he unscrewed the mounting screws and pried off the rubber-gasket-sealed cover and carefully loosened the positive connection, leaving the wire dangling several inches from its terminal. He resealed the box.

"Good," Tanya said, her breath rising in frosty clouds.

They left the quiet, dark cockpit, closed the door, and shoveled snow back into the cave-like opening they had created. Matt swept it smooth with the broom. The wind and snow would finish the sealing job.

With a great deal of effort, they climbed and pushed and tumbled over the plane and to the other wing. Matt dug hard to get to the wing, trying not to dent it with the shovel. Below the wing, Tanya pushed the snow away as Matt dug. Matt opened the compartment using the broom's scraper as a lever.

"Help!" Tanya screamed above the roar of the wind.

She was slipping out of sight between some grass hummocks into the watery slush below the wing. Matt grabbed the hood of her jacket and stopped her sinking. He pulled her up and out from under the wing, wet to her armpits.

Tanya flashed him a weak, shaky smile, her eyes wide and face pale, still showing fear from slipping into snow, ice, black water, and muck where you don't touch bottom.

"We have to get you back, NOW," yelled Matt. The baggy snow pants would stop the wind and hold some heat, but she would freeze in the wet sweat pants if they delayed at all. He quickly emptied the left wing compartment and kicked snow down into the hole they had dug. He grabbed the shovels and broom and pushed Tanya ahead of him back across the plane. No time to cover their tracks. He'd have to trust that the snow would soon fill the exposed area.

Matt pulled two of the large duffel bags off the canoe, replacing them with the smaller bags and roping them down, making the canoe now nicely bottom heavy. He secured the two remaining duffel bags by their D-shaped top locks with ten feet of doubled line to Tanya's machine.

He started Tanya's machine; she got on.

"Follow me, same rules. Don't let your mind wander. You need to get to the cabin and get warm," Matt yelled above the wind.

Tanya's dragging cargo would help to cover the snowmobile tracks. The plane would have to cover itself. Matt kept a steady speed, glancing back every few seconds. Tanya's headlight never wavered or flashed for help during the fifteen-minute trip back. Now dark inside the huge quarry building, parked side by side. Matt noted the two bags trailing obediently behind her sled and the canoe's load still secure. He put thoughts of dope or money aside to concentrate on getting Tanya safely inside and warm.

She just sat on the machine without moving. Matt hit its kill button, and the silence engulfed them. She just stared at him.

Matt knew hypothermia was sneaky, sometimes grabbing a person in mid sentence. The body just shuts down, throwing all its levers to keep what little warmth it has left. He needed to warm her up in a hurry.

He helped her into the cabin and started the hot water running in the shower. She didn't say a thing while he undressed her. He had her down to panties and bra and into the already-steamy bathroom, when she whispered lazily, "Enjoying yourself?"

"You bet," Matt said. "You're a hunter's dream. But I prefer my women warm."

"C-cold," Tanya said through slightly blue lips. She started to shiver as the room filled with steam. Matt switched on the exhaust fan and felt the temperature of the spray. The sulfur smell was a little strong.

"Need any help getting into the shower?"

"I can handle this by myself, thank you."

Matt brought his gaze from her body to her eyes. She seemed in control.

"I'll make you a hot drink. I'll bring it in to you. I want to see you in that shower."

Then he left while that pleasant double entendre danced through his mind.

In the kitchen, he poured about two cups of wine into a saucepan, turned on the burner, and brought the wine to steaming temperature. He added four teaspoons of sugar to the wine, stirred it, poured the mixture into a large mug, and went back to the shower.

Under the steaming water, Tanya's body launched fantasies in Matt's mind. She turned to him without covering herself. He handed her the cup while trying to just look into her eyes.

"It's a sure cure for being cold. It works wonders. Just warm red wine and sugar. Drink what you can. Stay under the shower until you feel warm all the way through. There's an old terry cloth robe behind the door. I'll bring you some heavy socks and your moccasins."

Matt left the bathroom door open and did what he promised. He put the socks and shoes inside the bathroom. He caught a tantalizing view of Tanya with soapy water running down her body. She had her eyes closed, and Matt took full advantage of his opportunity.

Matt hung up her wet clothing to dry and put her travel bag upstairs. He put the SIG in the liquor cabinet, too high for Tanya to reach without standing on something. He looked at the Beretta—thumbed the lever to pop the tiny barrel open and made sure there was a shell in the breech and a full magazine in the handle. Matt closed the little semiautomatic, thumbed the lever by the hammer into the safety position, and put the gun in his right pocket.

Hungry, he set to work on supper, which would consist of breakfast fare. He dropped toast in the toaster, started eggs frying in bacon fat, put some potatoes and ham to reheat in the microwave, and got coffee dripping through the Mr. Coffee.

A hair dryer hummed in the bathroom.

8

The Invisible Business

TANYA CAME OUT LOOKING GOOD and smelling fragrant. The robe went nearly to her ankles.

"I never knew men had so many shaving lotions. I now smell like Members Only." She walked over to inspect the eggs. "I'm famished. Nearly freezing puts a real edge on the appetite."

They sat at the table, wolfing down the eggs, potatoes, ham, and toast, washing it all down with hot coffee.

"So," Matt said between bites, "Tell me about yourself. How did you get involved with drugs and gangsters?"

Tanya chewed thoughtfully for a few seconds and took a sip of coffee before answering. "It's a long story. You've saved my life twice, I suppose I can trust you."

Matt nodded.

"My father was career Air Force, his last assignment was to help shut down Homestead Air Force Base, down near Miami, then he retired. Before that, he was stationed in other Florida bases, so I've lived my whole life in Florida."

Tanya massaged her wrist and pulled the robe more discreetly closed so Matt could concentrate on her story. "I spent four years in the Air Force after high school, then got my degree in Marine Biology from the University of Florida. I went to work for the State of Florida at John Pennekamp State Park. My folks run a dive and charter fishing shop on Islamorada but never made much money. One day, a party asked Dad to help them find a boat that had gone down, said they wanted to get the fishing tackle and stuff. The fishing tackle turned out to be plastic bags—dope. Dad took the money they paid and kept his mouth shut."

Matt shrugged. "Easy money can be hard to turn down."

"Uh-huh." She sipped the wine she'd carried from the shower. "That was just the first time. Far from the last. Sometimes, they had Dad make the runs alone to pick up who-knows-what. He couldn't get off the tiger he was riding."

"How did you get involved?" Matt asked, wiping up the last of his egg with the last of his toast.

"He told me how he was making his extra money. I said he should go to the law. But…they made it very clear to us that any trouble could lead to all kinds of accidents and legal problems. We had so many worries Mom developed an ulcer. Dad wanted to sell out and move, but no one would buy the place and he was told to relax and enjoy the money."

"Hooked him on money the same way they hook people on drugs, I guess," Matt said.

She nodded. "Now, he's got several boats regularly chartered by people you just don't ask any questions of. Sometimes they book long charters, pay big deposits, and don't show up. Dad came to rely on that money coming in."

Turning pensive, Tanya toyed with the remaining food on her plate, pushing it around before finally piling some on the fork. She chewed thoughtfully, gazing out the window beyond the confines of the cabin.

"That's your dad." Matt said, "What about you?"

"I got pulled into the picture when a routine inspection turned up some planted crack cocaine in my locker at work. The State fired me almost immediately, no hearing, no nothing. Later, the charges were dropped by the DA's office. So, I went to work for Dad, leading diving groups and working in the store."

"That had to be a tough time." Matt said.

She chuckled. "Right. I'm telling you all this so you know you're in a serious situation with very determined, dangerous people." She finished the last of the eggs and toast and pushed the plate back. "They can be very seductive, getting you to do seemingly harmless things until you're in so deep you can't see the light anymore."

Matt gathered the two plates and utensils. "Don't suppose they'd just let you walk away."

"Not these guys. I'm to the point now that I need to do anything they ask. I'm in the middle of drug trafficking and smuggling, and they have my Dad deep in their control."

"So, what's the deal with you and Ivan?" asked Matt.

"I am going to tell you things I shouldn't. I'm doing it because I need your help and I want you to trust me.

"Ivan went to Canada on a mission from Webb. I was along as interpreter, because he was meeting with some Colombians, and I suppose as window dressing. Also, Webb likes checks on everyone—even his old buddy Ivan. The drugs were to be left in Canada for some people on the island. The cash was clean money, for expenses I guess. I missed the reason for the meet because the Colombian spoke better English than I do. He was a banker—they were talking off shore accounts and major payoffs, but when the negotiations got good, I was asked to leave the room."

"How big a deal are you in?" asked Matt, pouring more coffee for himself. Tanya covered her cup with her hand and nodded at the gallon jug of wine on the counter. Matt got a clean glass and poured it full.

Tanya took a long sip and then another. "Webb's operation is mind boggling: many nationalities, billions of dollars, smuggling people and packages in and out of the United States. Webb has built the UPS of international crime. It's an invisible business. With the southern boarders getting lots of attention, Canada is the easiest entry right now. We were flying to an executive lodge on a Canadian island. The lodge is one of many that can be a stopping point for people and products getting into the United States. The next step would be another small plane, a car—or in the summer, a boat. The northern part of the U.S. is a sieve. The risk-to-reward ratio is very good for people smuggling, better than drugs…"

The background radio suddenly changed to a series of beeps, silencing Tanya. They next heard about a plane missing. Matt jumped to the radio and turned it up, getting the last of the message that asked for information from anyone hearing or seeing or knowing anything about a Canadian twin-engine commuter plane that was lost south of the Sault area.

Matt turned the radio back down and sat at the table. Tanya reached across the table and touched Matt's hand, "If you don't help me get the computer and cocaine to Webb's people, they'll destroy you, me, and my parents."

Matt looked at her beautiful face tight in a worried frown, "It may be out of our control, a downed plane isn't easy to find, we had one crash near here many years ago and it wasn't found for 13 years—they had some ground information but found nothing until bear hunters came across it. We can't get out for a few days, no one is getting in here. But if it is found, I won't risk jail and my land being seized because of Webb's threats."

Tanya looked at Matt, pleading with her eyes and touch, finally she broke both contacts.

She left the table, pulling the robe tightly around her neck, at the steps to the upper floor she turned to Matt, "I need to get more clothes on and rest awhile."

As Tanya quickly climbed the stairs, Matt knew he had just experienced a classic female rejection ploy: quickly leaving the room, morphing from a loose bathrobe over a naked, perfumed, totally perfect woman, to a distanced stranger, covered in multiple layers of protective clothing.

Matt yelled up the steps, "I'll put away the duffel bags before some critter gets into them and has a party."

No answer came back down the steps, a tin closet door shut harder than needed.

Matt bundled up and went out to the snow machines. He knew he started the slippery slope when he unloaded the plane. Now, hiding the bags just increased both the slope and the slippery.

Well, if some weather-fearless friends show up, I might be able to explain Tanya, but not these damned bags.

9

The Cave

WHILE TANYA FUMED UPSTAIRS in the cabin, Matt suited up for another excursion outside. He wanted to hide the cocaine and money and knew the perfect place.

The expansion of the quarry over the years had cut into large limestone deposits that also had caves. All but one of the caves had been destroyed in the limestone production—the one in the southeast corner that drained into the South Branch of the Hendrie River. Back in the 1920s and '30s, many of the townspeople used it as a walk-in refrigerator and meat locker. It had a double door system that Matt and his relatives had kept functional, repairing and rebuilding as needed. It was on the lowest end of the quarry walls; large boulders partially hid the path to it. Trees now grew on the banks, and anyone backing up a pickup truck to the entrance would have to worry about breaking a rearview mirror.

With the two bags they'd towed behind Tanya's sled carefully loaded and balanced on the canoe behind Matt's, he eased out into the dark, snowy evening, monitoring the load for shifting. As he negotiated around a snowdrift, the snowmobile wrenched sideways. Matt fought for control and stopped. He twisted around on the seat. The damn load had shifted and tipped the canoe onto its side.

"Damn it all," he muttered. *Maybe it's an omen.*

He tried to force the canoe upright but only succeeded in losing his balance as his feet slipped out from under him. Raging at the storm, he unloaded the canoe, righted it, and carefully reloaded it. He rocked it side to side, readjusted the load a bit, and decided it was as steady as he could get it. More carefully now, he motored down the trail to the cave entrance. Snow and wind had formed a five-foot drift that almost covered the entrance.

Cursing again, Matt dug a shovel out of the canoe and cleared the opening until the shovel clanged on something—the sleigh supposed to be stored back in the shop building. Someone must have used it to move a deer to the cave and just left it there. Another damn delay.

Okay, calm down.

Matt walked into a small storage area and dead-air space common to root cellars. He selected a battery powered Coleman lantern from the several on a shelf and approached the metal second door—a watertight door and hull from a ship fitted into the limestone with great effort and skill. Put on in the late 1950s, it had been repainted or touched up with anti-rust paint every few years. Graphite and lithium grease kept all the moving parts in perfect shape.

After heaving the heavy door open, he entered the cave's foyer—a room about ten feet square and over seven feet tall. This landing opened onto steps that descended into a larger, pit-like area that could have taken a small house. Its size absorbed all the light, and Matt couldn't see the far wall. The well-built steps and handrails led down into the darkness, where he found the deer carcass doubtless brought in on the sleigh. A large cutting table with drawers held knives, sharpening tools, and various wrapping papers and plastic bags. An old swing set served as a hanging rack. Various hooks in the ceiling could suspend lanterns while butchering deer. Matt dragged the duffel bags two at a time down the stairs and loaded them on the shelves built under the stairs—thick cedar more than strong enough for the four duffel bags and two smaller canvas bags.

So this is what 440 pounds of cocaine looks like.

Matt left the money bag in the Polaris, wanting to distance himself from the dope but unable to resist keeping the money close.

He snatched a sharp butcher knife from a magnetic rack holding half a dozen and boned the round steak off one deer leg. He double-wrapped the meat—one layer of plastic wrap and a final wrapping of butcher paper. Out of habit, he picked up a grease pencil and wrote "round steak" on the outer wrapping. He cleaned the knife and replaced it.

Matt closed the metal door, taking the lantern with him as he shut the outer door. He worked for some time freeing the sleigh from the major-league drift that had buried it and the cave door. He put the sleigh where it belonged behind the snow machine and tied the canoe on behind the sleigh. He had everything aiming out by the time he finally started the machine. With the Polaris lights on, he returned the Coleman to the cave anteroom.

Outside, the snow still fell and the wind still blew. He drove quickly back to the cabin, glad to have rid himself of the unwieldy load. Almost an hour had passed. He shut down and returned the sleigh to its normal spot, hung the canoe back up, piled up the normal stuff that got thrown into the canoe, and put the money bag in the Yukon, fascinated at having so many neat $10,000 bundles and amazed at how little room twenty-five bundles took up.

Inside the quiet, warm cabin, Matt turned off most of the lights, poured himself some brandy, and sipped it as he prepared the couch for sleeping. Then, he padded upstairs to check on Tanya, who slept soundly—breathing deeply with a little snore at the end of each breath.

Downstairs again, he left the bathroom light on so Tanya could easily find the stairs and tucked the SIG under his pillow.

What a day.

10

Meetings

MATT WOKE UP TO THE SMELL OF BACON; so much for light sleeping. Tanya—in heavy gray-and-red wool hunting socks and a long, dark green-and-gold Packer Super Bowl T-shirt—looked very domestic as she quietly worked on breakfast. As she pushed the bread down in the toaster, Matt heard the coffee maker burble its last to announce mission accomplished. She knew how to time a meal to have everything come out together.

"Time for breakfast," she announced. "I hope you like eggs over easy, toast, bacon, and coffee."

Matt put on his Levis, stretched his tight back muscles, and walked to the table, picking up the briefcase to examine as they ate.

Tanya served the food on plates, brought cups of steaming coffee and sat on the same side of the table as Matt. Matt thought she looked great without any makeup, smelling of soap and bacon, and wanted to hug her. With one leg curled under her, the Packer shirt exposed a nicely tanned and well-formed leg.

She very pleasantly surprised him by giving him a hug and a kiss on his cheek. "That's for saving my life."

"My pleasure." Emotionally off-balance, Matt forced his attention back to breakfast. He didn't want his morning testosterone to make his decisions. He ran a finger around the rim of his cup. "I put the cocaine in a very safe place and the money in my car. We…might get visitors if the storm lets up.

If I don't get to a phone, people might come to check on me. The worse the weather, the greater the need for Yoopers to go out in it and check on other people. If someone does come, how should I introduce you?"

Smiling, she said, "Say I'm your girlfriend that just flew in."

"Okay. What do we do with Webb and his people?"

"Make a deal with them. They'll want the cocaine, money, and—most of all—Ivan's computer. I'll get a ride home, and you'll get some money for your trouble."

"And I go to the gray-bar hotel for aiding and abetting—no thanks."

Tanya pursed her lips briefly, then reseated herself and squared her shoulders, showing more leg and a wonderfully stretched T-shirt and capturing all of Matt's attention. "If you ever believed anyone, believe me now. Webb and his people have raised extortion and coercion to an art form. If they can't control a situation—people die. Webb will send folks to kill you and get the goods if he can. The weather and location are our allies. I've been thinking…if we can get him to come here personally, he might not take a chance of being involved in a killing. He knows my father would go crazy if anything happened to me. I've known Webb for many years. He uses our marina and spends a lot of time with my father. I even captained his boat several times. He's promised to look after me. As weird as it sounds, his word is good. I suppose you could say he's a complex man."

With her sitting so close, her lips beckoned, her eyes drew him in, and he had to work at listening…and breathing.

Tanya continued, "No one's ever testified against him. He'll threaten your family or get you so dirty no prosecutor would touch you. That's just you—he already owns me and mine. Help me get us through this."

They ate in silence for several minutes. Matt pondered her use of "our" and "we" and "us."

I've got to protect my son, Tanya, myself and be able to look in the mirror when this is over…

He turned to her and said, "Tell me more about Webb."

Tanya thought for a few seconds. "He's deadly but has advanced degrees in economics. I think his real name was something like Vankov. He came here before 9/11 and, between Soviet-doctored records and our State Department bureaucracy, he got U.S. visas. A natural leader, he'd worked his way up in the former Soviet Transportation Ministry, then got in trouble. After a few years in prison, he'd developed some powerful ties in both criminal and government channels. He and Ivan go way back—when Ivan got drunk, he bragged about Webb. Before I knew what he really was and what he did to my father, I actually liked him. He always gets what he wants."

"Damn." Matt considered his food, but no longer felt hungry. "Look, maybe we can set something up, someplace away from here. When the authorities find the plane, which they eventually will, Webb'll know where this place is…and who I am. That lake is too shallow and too clear to hide anything plane size, and the black bottom would make it easy to see from the air. Pipeline patrols fly over all the time and the air searches will start as soon as the storm lets up."

She held his gaze steadily. "Look, I'll do what I can to protect you. I won't tell Webb any more than I have to. If we're careful and get Webb involved personally, we might pull it off clean. If he just sends his people, we could have trouble…a lot of trouble."

"Look," Matt said, easing up out of his chair, "I have no experience dealing with people like this."

"I know," she said, putting a hand on his arm. "But I do, so let's work this out together."

Her warmth seemed to spread up his arm. Hoping to keep his head clear, he started to pace across the kitchen. *This is really life-or-death, Matt ol' buddy.*

"There's another thing about Webb that might help us. As a Russian, and maybe a throwback to their communist background, he needs to show he isn't afraid or too good to get his hands dirty. But he's a chess master— always thinking several moves ahead—but likes to flirt with danger."

Matt turned slowly at the bottom of the stairs, shaking his head. "I'm not sure how much danger I'm ready to flirt with."

"I think we can minimize that," she said. "Any ideas on where we could set up a meeting?"

He paced slower, staring at the floor. "Depends on the storm and what's open. What about a public place? Or a very private place that we could control? Some highway rest areas stay open all year. Maybe plow out a single lane to force them into a tight spot where they'd have trouble pulling anything tough?"

"Webb would prefer someplace private, someplace not too hard to get to."

"He'd probably also prefer me dead." Matt headed for the door, stopping to take the SIG from under his pillow. As he pulled on his jacket, he said, "Look, I'm going to get my road map from the car, see what the storm's done to us, and…think a bit. I'll be back in a few minutes."

She began collecting the dishes. "Good idea. I'll clean up while you're… thinking." After retrieving his new road map from the Yukon, he checked on the snow conditions outside several of the building's windows and its main door—three feet deep with five and six foot drifts. The Yukon would need help getting out, but snowmobiles could move easily.

He stretched the map out on the Yukon's hood and studied it. He wanted a cleared secondary road and a place he could have plowed out off that road, someplace a stranger could find easily.

Garnet Lake?

Only a few miles north of Highway 2 and marked on maps, it had good road signs that should be above the snow banks. A lot of locals used H40 road, so it was kept open almost as seriously as US 2. He could get the road going into Garnet Lake plowed as far as the camping area, tree covered and partly concealed from the road. Matt would bring Tanya by snowmobile.

What about Thanksgiving? Lots of people at home and on those snow trails.

He refolded the map and tossed it back in the Yukon. He sucked the cold air deep into his lungs. It felt good. Raw but good.

The Monday after Thanksgiving might be good. Most people would be back at work. I could get in and out of there fast on a snowmobile.

He knew all the trails and most of the roads that could be used. He could finish the rest of the planning in the warmth of the cabin.

Walking in, he noted how nicely Tanya had cleaned and tidied the kitchen. She was just hanging up the dish towel.

He waved a hand at the kitchen. "Neater than it's been in years."

"Idle hands..." She smiled that resistance-melting smile.

"Yeah," he said. "Before we call Webb, I need to know if you could stand being here for a few days. Or do you want to get to civilization as fast as you can?"

"With all the pressure I've been under for so long now, I could use a little simple cabin life in the piney woods. But first, I'd like to check with my folks so they know I'm alive and well."

He quickly outlined the plan he'd just cooked up. "Unless they bring a snowmobile, they couldn't follow us, and we'd have decent control of the situation. We would spot tracks coming in if they tried to set up any surprises for us. We ought to be able to see them before turning over the goods. They're going to need a big SUV or extended-cab four-by-four truck. No big black limos in these conditions."

"Okay, but watch out. Webb may have other ideas. He likes to control everything."

Matt took the satellite phone from the briefcase. Fully charged. He turned it on, worked the menu to WEBB, and pressed SEND. The complex phone did its magical thing, and in a few seconds Webb said, "*Privet?* Hello?"

"This is the hunter," said Matt. "I've got an idea for a meeting place where you can get your goods and Tanya. Interested?"

"Maybe. What do you want out of this?" growled Webb.

"How about I keep the money for my trouble and silence?"

"How 'bout we take it all and let you live?"

Matt swallowed hard, decided to ignore the threat, and forced calm into his voice. "Look. That money would be real good for me right now, and its chump change to you. If you don't want the deal, you can kiss everything goodbye, including the phone and computer. I'll give Tanya to the cops and lead them to the stuff. Oh, one more thing. I want you at the meeting. What do you say, Mr. Webb?"

Matt's suggestion met only silence. He could almost feel Webb's phone being subjected to plastic-crushing pressure.

After several seconds, Webb replied, with controlled, carefully spaced words, "Where and when?"

Matt answered, "About seven miles north of US 2 and 40 miles from the Mackinac Bridge. I'll tell you exactly where once you pass the Cut River Bridge. This phone is really a wonderful thing, but I don't trust it. You'll need a large SUV or better yet a four-door, four-wheel-drive pickup truck with a covered bed. No limos or multiple vehicles. I'll be able to see anyone following you, but you'll never see us."

"When?" Webb asked.

"Next Monday. Most of the Thanksgiving tourists will be gone by then."

"I can't be in any vehicle carrying anything it shouldn't, so we'll need two vehicles. I'll pick up Tanya, the phone, and computer. My men in the second vehicle will get the rest. I'll want to see the money. You'll get half."

"All of it sounds more reasonable to me. You want my silence when they find the plane. You want your cocaine back and all of Ivan's information, including his computer with all his contacts."

"Listen, you shit..." started Webb. Then he paused and took several breaths. "Okay, we'll be on Highway 2 on Monday. I'll be coming up from Detroit. I want Michigan people and plates. What time?"

"Let's make it 2:00 p.m., Eastern Time. I'll call you at Cut River Bridge and give you the rest of the directions. Should take you about thirty minutes to get to the meeting place from there. Oh, you should remember, this is the U.P. People from Detroit stand out like ticks on a blonde girl. Wear hunting, or at least casual outdoors, clothes."

"You're a damn pushy bastard." He paused. "We'll go with your plan. Call at 2:00 next Monday."

Matt's hands shook slightly. *I don't think I'm cut out for this crap.*

He exhaled slowly to still his nerves. "If you're not on the phone when I call, the deal is off. I'll ask questions about what you see along the road to make sure you're really there. Two vehicles is okay."

Matt disconnected and put the phone down.

"That seemed to go well," said Tanya. "How far to your meeting place?"

"A little more than ten miles from here. I'll have somebody plow the road. We've got a few days now to figure out whether we take one machine or two."

She stepped close enough to him that he could smell her hair. "Whatever you decide is fine by me."

Several possible interpretations of her comment filled his thoughts. "We can make a snow-machine run later today to where I can use my cell phone. It's going to be really beautiful on the trails with all this new snow." Tanya looked up into his eyes and smiled. "A little fun sounds...pleasant."

She smiled, turned away, and moved up the stairs. Matt watched, and enjoyed her every step, barely able to breathe. The Super Bowl XXXI T-shirt never looked better. He wondered if this was a signal to follow her.

Down, boy. Don't ruin the weekend right at the start. Get yourself cleaned up and shaved, then let the days and the nights play themselves out.

11

Thanksgiving

ATT AND TANYA ROARED through the great door portal on the two snowmobiles, into the beauty of fresh snow under a brightening overcast sky. Matt led them up the trail heading south out of the quarry, then north on Quarry Lane, winding around on trails and logging roads to the easily followed Quarry Road where he again turned south. The overcast day and the need to watch the machine ahead would make it nearly impossible for Tanya to know her position or direction. She could backtrack, but Matt doubted she would find the quarry any other way.

The fresh snow was packing, the temperature had gone up to nearly freezing, and the wind had gone to almost zero. Matt stopped several times to let Tanya enjoy the breathtaking vistas so unlike her Florida home. Every time she took off her helmet, she smiled at Matt. Her wrist did not appear to interfere with driving. On the old railroad track that was now the main road into the quarry, Matt accelerated to 60. A quick glance backwards confirmed that Tanya held her position well. About four miles down the road, Matt came to a stop and turned off the machine. Tanya pulled up beside him. She stopped with the brake, controlling the machine very well. Matt removed his helmet and reached into his inside jacket pocket for the cellular phone.

"I've got a good signal here," he said, checking the signal strength. "I can make all the calls I need."

Matt got his neighbor's answering machine and explained he was fine, snowed in at camp, and enjoying the day. He said he wanted the time alone and would return to town by the end of next week. He added two names and phone numbers and asked his neighbor to pass the message along. He then called a cousin in Garnet. Leon Johnson ran heavy equipment during the construction season. Leon had a large Ford four-wheel-drive truck with a new Boss plow—a technical wonder that automatically adjusted to multiple positions. An expert like Leon could handle almost any snow-moving job with it. Leon answered on the fourth ring.

"Leon, this is Matt, I really need your help for some snow plowing."

"Sure, no problem," Leon said. "I need to get out of the house and breathe some clean air to work off all the food I'm going to eat today. My grandkids will love it. You at the quarry?"

"Ya, but what I need plowed right now is the east road into Garnet Lake. Just into the edge of the camping area by the water pump. Put in a turnaround area big enough for a truck pulling a snowmobile trailer. I've got some people coming up Monday, and they'll need a good bank to make it easy to get the machines off and on. I'll meet them on my machine for a few hours on the trails. I'd really appreciate this. Maybe you can do me later Monday afternoon and have some beers, but I need the lake road done Monday before noon."

"No problem, glad to do it. I'll get the lake road done today and clean it up if we get more snow later. Why don't you come by for turkey leftovers or pie? They got football all weekend."

"Thanks a lot, but I've got some plans for the whole weekend that will keep me busy and happy," said Matt. He glanced at Tanya, and she had that smile going again. "Oh, and another thing, my cell phone battery is getting low, would you call the gang at Lamoreaux's and tell them I'm fine and don't need plowing out or rescuing and I'm eating on the venison they left hanging when they didn't put the sleigh back where it belonged."

"They'll be here later today for the kids to play together, but I'll call them. You getting lucky or something?"

"Maybe, or something," said Matt. "I appreciate your help and I hope you have a great holiday and you don't lose too much money on the Lions. Hi to everyone. I'll drop by before I go back to town."

Matt turned off the little cellphone and put it back into his inside jacket pocket. Tanya sat on her machine, looking inviting and looking at him.

"Are you getting cold?" Matt asked.

"Maybe a little, but not when we're going and I have the helmet on. This is really wonderful. Where does this road go?"

"This will get you to a paved road if you go far enough. We should head back, and I'll show you some of the hardwoods and some beautiful trails along the river."

"Could I make a call to my parents in Florida?"

"Sure, but don't mention my name or anything about your location other than being in a nice warm cabin in the U.P. You could be back in Florida next week."

Matt brought out the cellphone and punched power. Good signal, and the battery showed two of three bars.

"Battery's getting lower, but you can talk several minutes."

Tanya punched in the numbers and waited for the call to go through.

"*Ola,* " she said after several seconds, then went into rapid and emotional Spanish.

Matt picked up a few words he knew—*nieve, frio, bosque* and a very few others—but wished she'd speak English. She seemed so happy to talk to her parents he couldn't take the phone away from her. He didn't hear any words that sounded like local towns or roads.

She talked for several minutes then handed the phone to Matt.

"It's my father, he wants to talk to you."

"Yes?" Matt tried not to sound suspicious.

"Hello, I'm George Vega, Tanya's father. She said she owes you her life. Her mother and I can't thank you enough. She's all we have. Please know how grateful we are to you. Take care of her on those machines and in the snow. You are very welcome to come to our island and enjoy the sun and sea. We are the only Vegas on Islamorada. Here we have the little Key Deer but there is no hunting them. However, we can go hunting fish above and below the water. We even have fish that hunt you. You know, you got to be careful with the sharks. *Via con Dios.*"

He's talking more than vacation talk...

"I'm glad I could help. I'll take good care of her." The phone's beep warned Matt the battery was almost done. The cold had further reduced its power. "My phone's almost out of power. Don't worry about Tanya in the Upper Peninsula. Goodbye."

Matt turned off the phone and put it away. Tears welled up in Tanya's eyes, but she quickly changed her mood and brought back the wonderful smile.

"Let's go—and thank you again for everything."

They mounted their machines. Matt led them down trails and roads through the woods and river areas. He finally brought them back to the quarry by a northern trail, hoping to keep Tanya disoriented enough that she couldn't find her way out or in again.

Matt wanted to trust her, but felt safer if she couldn't give a clear location to anyone. After they parked, he checked the fuel tanks—plenty left for further rides, including the run to Garnet Lake.

They stood by the machines, now silent except for some cooling pings. Matt took Tanya's helmet as she looked through the large window opening of the huge shop building. Tanya leaned against Matt. The window framed a view of the twin arches of the crumbling crusher building. "Like an old master's painting of a Roman ruin….it's wonderful, and so are you." said Tanya as she kissed Matt's cheek.

Inside the cabin, they stripped out of their snow gear and into casual light clothing to offset the relative warmth of the cabin after the cold ride.

"Hungry?" Matt asked.

"Famished. What do you have to offer?"

"How about venison, shrimp, vegetables, and wild rice?"

"Sounds great."

"Let's turn it into a stir-fry on rice, with a fairly fresh lettuce salad and biscuits. I'll start the rice and chop up the meat, green peppers, and onion. Can you make the biscuits?"

Tanya nodded. "No sweat. I saw Bisquick."

They enjoyed Carlo Rossi burgundy as they cooked and set the table.

They ate hungrily and talked about their high school days, their university days, their various love lives and love failures, their dreams and some of the realities that had altered their dreams and ambitions. They ended their dinner with coffee, brandy, and a shared Hershey's Special Dark Chocolate bar and an old Twinkie whose shelf life was measured in decades.

They stacked the dishes and the few cooking pots. Matt put the small batch of leftovers into the refrigerator. They got closer and closer as they worked around the refrigerator and sink. After several passes when they almost touched, Matt finally took her waist and turned her to him. He looked into her eyes. They closed as she offered him her lips.

The kiss was a winner. It was just like what teenage boys dream about: warm, solid, enthusiastic, and time stopping. Matt felt her lean into him. She moved her whole length against him with a definite pressure that moved an inch or two from side to side. Matt brought his hands from her waist to her side. She brought her arms up between them and put one hand on his neck and one on his face, pulling him to her. The movement made space for Matt's hands to go to her breasts. Her hips pushed into him. Without moving, Matt was happily pushing back. She moaned and moved her hips in a small circle. Her nipples became hard, one after the other. Matt reminded himself to breathe.

"Your place or mine," mumbled Matt.

"Mine," said Tanya and led him up the stairs.

What a Thanksgiving. Matt didn't care who won the football game.

Matt and Tanya spent the next three days enjoying each other. Tanya said she felt comfortable and safe for the first time in years, Matt felt he was in a dream. They were perfect together. Matt never felt an age difference. They never mentioned the problems that awaited them. They made a game of foraging in the cupboards and freezer for food. They used snowshoes and cross-country skis, new activities for Tanya. Matt experienced some new adventures he had not tried before also. Showers became fun and interesting. The maple syrup made from a sugar bush only a few miles away took on new uses. Matt had never felt so happy. Whether love or lust, he didn't really care.

Tanya talked about growing up as an only child on air force bases. She told of the problems of military moving and never really building the life-long friendships that town kids establish. She talked about her many-year relationship with an air force pilot that continued into her college years. She put all her trust and love into it and had her heart crushed when the man went to his class reunion by himself and fell back in love with his old high school sweetheart.

Matt told her he was an only child too. But he had a large, loving extended family. His father's parents raised him. He gave her a tour of the cabin's many pictures on the walls. They showed his *Opa*, grandfather, at many ages—with his brothers and sons—including Matt's father. Matt skipped his family history, where so many men in the pictures died in wars. He brought down one smaller black-and-white framed photo of a man with his arm around a teenager—both standing by a hanging buck. "This was the fall after my mom died of polio, *Opa* was tough on me but he was always there. I went to the same school with the same kids all my life, it must have been tough always changing schools." Tanya nodded and held the picture, looking back and forth several times to see Matt in the child and grandfather. Matt continued talking about the land and the seasonal activities that defined his life as a teacher.

They feasted on each other's histories, making no judgments, seeing their previous lives as pieces of a mosaic that made the artwork they had become.

They talked about their favorite pastimes. They both loved to dive, travel, fish, go to the end of the road, usual stuff—but they also found they shared a superstition about always picking up lucky pennies, they were ardent window peepers as they jogged or drove in the evening and they carried dog yummies when they went camping or hiking for all the four-legged friends they met. They loved boats. Tanya had captain's papers to run dive and fishing charters. Matt went through the series of boats he owned and how he sold his twenty-four-foot Star Craft Islander two years ago. He talked about his ambition to run a charter fishing boat on Little Bay de Noc, one of the best walleye fishing areas in the United States. They both liked to be alone or at least away from others at times. They saw a lot of similarities between being on the water and being in deep woods. They talked about places they had dived, discovering many common favorites.

They talked for hours about adventures they had on the water and under it, enjoying each other's tales. They slept together well. They packed as much as they could into each day and each night.

Monday morning came too soon.

12

Garnet Lake

MONDAY MORNING STARTED EARLY. Tanya was up before Matt, making biscuits, using the last of the milk. They were also out of bread, eggs, juice, and bacon. Tired of pancakes, they were out of maple syrup anyway. She checked the empty syrup jar and gave a sad sigh before calling up the stairs to the bedroom, "Biscuits, jam, and coffee will be ready in ten minutes." After a quick shave and shower, Matt sat down at the table just as she poured the coffee.

"I've got to load up the sleigh this morning," he said, stirring his coffee to help cool it. "It'll take us less than thirty minutes to get to the campground. I'd like to get there early and set up in the woods about 100 yards from where the cars will be. If you don't want to go, you can stay here," said Matt.

"I've got to go." Tanya paused and stared at the plates on the counter. "I've got to go back with them, right? Besides, I can identify Webb. You can't. If he doesn't show, he might send his top muscle man. Volcheff. I think it means wolf in some language. He's a big guy with a cue-ball head, you really don't want to meet him."

"What does Webb look like?" asked Matt.

She turned around, leaned back against the counter, and took a deep breath, letting it out slowly. "He's built like the weightlifter he used to be. Keeps his hair cut short. From offices in Chicago and Detroit he controls most of the Midwest smuggling operations. His goal is to be able to move people and material anywhere in the world—the UPS of the invisible business. He owns several legal businesses that employ nearly a thousand people."

"How do you know so much about him?"

"Webb's known me from the first days he worked with my father." She seemed not to want to look directly at Matt. "I…I think I remind him of his daughter. I captained for him several times He seems to talk about himself a lot, but he's really wheedling information out of others. He makes you want to share your life stories with him. He's tough, even cruel, but he also can be very charming and likable."

After absentmindedly putting the empty plastic half-gallon milk container back in the refrigerator, Tanya wiped the counter for the third time. "Look," she said, contemplating the rag in her hand, "Webb's only going to come here to get me and probably the computer and phone back. He'll get miles away from the drugs as fast as he can. They're going to ask me lots of questions before they send me back to Florida. I'll do everything I can to protect you, but they have ways of figuring things out."

"Don't worry about it," Matt said with more confidence than he felt.

"Uh-huh." She pulled the tray with the biscuits from the oven. "You might want to think about disappearing for awhile."

She sat across from Matt and smiled thinly. "Maybe, when this has all blown over, you could take a nice drive to the Keys. I could show you some great diving places."

Tanya's smile made Matt's ears ring from a rush of blood.

He just looked at her for several seconds before daring to break the spell of the moment. "I've been thinking that maybe we should ride double to the meeting. The sleigh leaves distinctive tracks, but one machine is harder to follow than two. I'll siphon gas from other machines to get a full tank."

"Whatever you think is best."

"Better kiss me now before I taste like gasoline." Matt stood.

Tanya rose with him and came to him. They kissed and clung to each other for a minute, knowing that soon they'd be back in their own, separate worlds of self-preservation.

Matt slipped into hunting clothes and considered the weather—overcast with little wind. He gassed up the XLT Polaris Indy with its ten-gallon tank, topped off the oil, and confirmed the antifreeze level. Matt had replaced the original windshield with a lower, racing model after someone had cracked the original by opening the cowling into a pickup truck tailgate. The lower profile would better suit Matt's purposes today.

He hitched up the sleigh, then threw all sorts of potentially useful material into it—a couple of old life preservers, a moldy pop-up tent, a pair of padded hunting seats that fastened to the hunter's belt, and three plastic tarps from shelves near the canoe rack. He grabbed anything with some bulk but not weight, including ten goose decoys with detachable heads.

Satisfied, he roared out of the building heading to the cave. The snow had settled to about two and a half feet on the flat, perfect for snowmobiling. Being overcast made it easier to see the snow contours.

At the cave, he repacked the drug bags with the bulky odds and ends he'd brought. Not totally sure of his next steps, he knew he didn't want Tanya associated with the drugs. He would give them anything they wanted, after he knew she was safe. He knew his ploy could backfire—dangerously backfire—but his gut said he had to try. He tied down the bundles with complex knots he planned to pour water on back at the cabin, just out of orneriness.

Matt dragged the cutting table to the middle of the room so the overhead lights would hide the bundles in shadows behind the stairs, in case someone came for their deer. He expected visitors anytime but hoped the word had gotten out that he was "entertaining," so friends would leave him alone. Back at the cabin, he left the Indy and sleigh pointing out the large, open door.

He took the money to the old quarry shop with its stone forge, four feet high and about the same square. Rocks, dust, and debris filled its air hole that, at one time, led to the fire pit. Matt took a crowbar and removed most of the rocks from the base hole. Then he reached in and pulled out most of the loose material, making the hole large enough to hide the money. He drove the Yukon near the forge, so Tanya could not see it from the cabin, and transferred the money. A tight fit, he packed it like a cannon barrel, using the crowbar like a ram. He got it all in. Then, he covered the hole with loose rocks and sprinkled the area with material in the forge. He kicked snow around and even used a snow scraper from the car to remove his tracks. Matt finally hung the battered gym bag on the canoe rack.

Next, Matt got his rifle from the Yukon. He loaded it and put it in his padded gun case. A loaded rifle on a snow machine was a "no-no," but he would only be crossing two roads and had little chance of being stopped by the ever-vigilant DNR. He had three shells in the rifle and three more in his pocket. He also had the SIG in his zipped jacket pocket.

He found the cabin clean and neat with Tanya just finishing laying out her clothes, including her original ones from the plane in a small bundle by her travel bag.

Matt had put two Cobra citizen band radios on the double charger the evening before. They worked well up to two miles with light headsets that muted the main speaker when plugged in. He attached the headset cord to his radio. Tanya would carry the other one with no headset. He liked the idea of talking to Webb via radio while looking at him from over a hundred yards through his scope. In case they also had rifles, he added a winter camouflage tarp to the sleigh's load. He would wait on the edge of the woods with trees above him and drifts around him, very hard to see. He knew the Garnet Lake area well from many years of road hunting for partridge. Matt was well prepared for the meeting, even if he didn't know how it would work out.

They tied the briefcase and Tanya's bag on the sleigh. He put the fully charged satellite phone inside his coat and his cell phone in his inside pocket. Matt poured water on all the knots holding the bags on the sleigh. He checked the towing connection. It was solid with the pin in and locked.

Matt handed Tanya one of two blaze-orange hunting vests. "It's hunting season, and we don't want to be moving along a drift and look like a deer. There might be trolls around."

"Trolls?" Tanya looked puzzled.

"Ya, people that live under the Mackinac Bridge…lower Michigan people. Some people shoot at anything that moves. Not many hunt in this area, but we need to be careful."

At 1:30 p.m., Matt, with Tanya sitting behind him, drove the Polaris to where they had made their phone calls, then headed south until he hit the main road, now plowed. He carefully came off the plowed bank onto the snow-covered road and ran south for several miles, passing one truck going toward Trout Lake. Matt didn't recognize the occupants. He picked up the regular snowmobile trail just south of Caffey Corners. The trail paralleled the road east for several miles then turned southeast through woods and by several lakes. Passing Seven Lakes, they followed old logging trails well-marked for snowmobiles, angling northeast to the field just south of Garnet Lake.

Matt scanned the field and saw the nicely plowed lane curling into the campground area, ending in a cleared turnaround area just as he'd requested. He cut behind the trees that surrounded the opening, off the trail now but easy going in the packed snow. At the west end of the lake, he turned onto the unplowed road that came to the lake from the west, around the south side, and brought them to the plowed turnaround area. He stayed up on the bank. Tanya got off, and he unhooked the sleigh. Anyone driving up the plowed road could easily spot the sleigh. A few trees and brush between it and the lake concealed the meeting area several feet below the drifting snow. Beyond the turnaround, Matt could see across the lake to a short stretch of the main road.

"It's almost 2:00. Let's call Webb. Then I'll disappear. I'll be in the woods right over there." He pointed to the south across 100 yards of field and a few scattered bushes.

She nodded.

"Look," he said, "I don't want to leave you now…or maybe ever…"

It sounded a little corny but, once it came out, he realized he meant it.

Looking sad, she seized his arm and stretched to kiss his cheek. She looked small dressed in the oversized clothes. She whispered, "I know we will be together again. Just keep the dream, no matter what happens."

"I'll try." Matt brought out the satellite phone and turned it on. Glad to see the strong signal and fully charged battery indications, he put the call through to Webb. He planned to keep the phone as, he hoped, another form of leverage.

"Yes?" came Webb's voice.

Tanya leaned closer to hear him, easy in the cool, quiet air.

"What do you see on both sides of the bridge? Be specific," said Matt.

Webb described the parks and turnoffs, businesslike without wasting time with threats.

"Good," Matt said. "Drive west on Highway 2 until you come to Borgstrom Road, about ten miles. Watch for the sign. If you get to the Black River, you missed the road. Turn north on Borgstrom Road, go 4.8 miles to the Hiawatha Trail Road. It's the first crossroad you come to. Turn east, right, for 2.2 miles and you will see Garnet Lake on the right. There should be a sign for the campground, but if it's snow covered, turn right on the first plowed lane you come to. The lane goes in about a half mile. There's a turnaround area. Tanya and the goods will be there. Got it?"

"*Da* , we understand. Where are you going to be?"

"I'll be here too." Matt slowly closed the phone and smiled at Tanya. "They can be here in fifteen or twenty minutes. Now, the fun starts."

They hugged and held each other's gazes for a few seconds.

Matt took his rifle and camo tarp from the sleigh, hopped on the Polaris, and headed down the plowed road. He glanced back and saw Tanya leaning on the sleigh.

Matt took the plowed lane down to the highway. He ran east about a mile and turned right into a field and ran south until he cut his original trail. Back at the field, he could pick out Tanya's blaze orange vest as he maneuvered into some pines and brush and stopped the machine parallel to the field. He broke two long balsam pine boughs on the side of the tree away from the field and laid them like a bridge from the handlebars to the rear seat of the Indy, then spread the tarp over the boughs. He dug snow out on the side opposite the field and scattered it on the tarp and skis. The arrangement left a perfect shooting slit under the tarp. The bushes and trees behind and on both sides of him formed a dark background. They wouldn't see him if they looked right at him, while he had a fine view of the sleigh, Tanya, the lake, some of the highway, and part of the plowed lane.

Matt uncased his Remington 700, 7 mm Magnum with a 3.5x10 Leupold scope. Very accurate, it weighed nine pounds and kicked. Matt used 150-grain noisler partitioned bullets that left the barrel at over 3100 feet per second and only dropped a few inches at several hundred yards. He had it zeroed at 150 yards. At the range to the sleigh area, with no wind, he could hit a stationary poker chip consistently from a steady rest, like the snowmobile seat provided. He took off his helmet, put on his Kromer, and removed the orange vest and sat on it. He maneuvered himself into a good shooting position with the seat supporting his gloved hand under the rifle. He propped the rifle on his left palm and right shoulder.

Through the scope, he could see Tanya looking for him and for Webb approaching down the road. He set the scope's front lens fine-sighting adjustment for one hundred yards and the magnification to seven, allowing him to count buttons on a coat with wide enough field of view to see part of the turnaround. In hunting mode now, he took several deep breaths, relaxed, and let his heartbeat slow down. He was ready. He took out his Cobra radio and put the earpiece in his left ear. His right ear rested on the cheek rest of the wooden stock. He pushed the button on the cord mike and watched Tanya jump as the radio he'd left on the sleigh sang its loud trill.

She grabbed it and fumbled until she found the talk button. "Yes?"

"I'm all set. Can you see me over in the woods?"

Tanya looked in his direction and panned left and right. "No. Just trees and snow."

"They'll be here soon. Sure you don't just want to run away with me?"

"I'd like to, but you know I can't."

After a long pause, Tanya said, "I can see a car and a pickup coming slowly on the main road. It must be them. I'm putting the radio in my pocket now. Don't forget me."

Matt couldn't see up the plowed lane and watched Tanya rather than the road. He could just see the top of the pickup as it slowed. He couldn't quite see the shorter car.

Tanya hopped off the sleigh and down to the plowed road. The truck pulled up to her. The car used the turnaround to point itself out before pulling up next to her.

A tall bald man got out of the car's right front door and scanned the
area. From Tanya's description, it was Volcheff. He motioned to the men
in the truck to get the bags from the sleigh. Tanya went to the car. The
back door opened, and Webb stepped out. He took her hand and hugged
her. Matt was about to ring the radiophone when he saw something move
on the road across from the lake—tops of several cars and large SUVs, as
well as State Police Jeeps. Matt could just see their large bubble flashers
through several breaks in the trees and shrubs.

Matt felt cold. He hit the call button. Everyone jumped when the phone
in Tanya's pocket trilled. She hit the talk button, "Hello."

"You've got company. Don't panic." Matt said. "There is no dope
in the bags."

Tanya turned and looked at the cars approaching and then back at
Matt's general position. She threw the phone toward him. It disappeared
into the snow.

Watching her through the scope, Matt thought the gesture was more
frustration than panic. He didn't move. He was breathing fast, but was
sure his foggy breath would not show from the turnaround. He didn't know
what to do, but running was out of the question.

13

Busted Bust

NOW, CARS OVERFLOWED THE PLOWED AREA. Matt identified Drug Enforcement Agency people with big DEA padded vests over suits and coats and Michigan State Police with their Mountie hats and generally neat, blue uniforms or blue-gray winter coats. At least twelve officers total. Matt could hear them yelling from his position.

Do law enforcement people think everyone's deaf?

The officials had seven people—two from the truck, four from the Lincoln Town Car, and Tanya—lying on the snow, hands secured behind them. They grabbed handguns from some of the prone men and removed a shotgun from the truck. The law enforcers worked fast and rough. Matt cranked the scope to ten power.

Some DEA people closed in on the sleigh in a feeding frenzy—cutting the ropes with jackknives and opening the contents, while others set up video and still cameras. When they found the first life preserver, they became quieter. The people on the snow now stood in a line on the far side of their truck, which blocked his view. Through the truck's windows, he could see Tanya's blaze-orange vest moving. The mass of law enforcement swarmed over the sleigh, going through each bag and the briefcase. They drifted into three groups—the prisoners with a guard of two State Police officers, the other State Police officers, and the DEA agents.

Lots of angry looks and gestures flared among the law groups. They came for drugs but found goose decoys and arrested people for possession of old life preservers. The State Police stomped around, pointing at the DEA agents and shouting. A DEA agent jabbed a finger into a state cop's chest, others kicked at the snow banks. One agent slumped against the Lincoln's fender and pulled out a cellphone. In the chaos, the bad guys moved into the open, exchanging puzzled glances, offering each other questioning shrugs, and finally breaking into smiles. Matt watched Tanya. She seemed either sad or in shock or both.

The DEA and State Police appeared to make a deal, and tempers cooled. The agents did not want to let go of this bone without chewing it thoroughly. They hustled Tanya and Webb and his crew into the police cars and put all the bags into their SUVs. The convoy of DEA SUVs and State Police patrol cars and Jeeps all left the way they came. Two troopers remained behind, apparently waiting for tow trucks to pick up Webb's vehicles and the sleigh. Matt checked his watch. Three p.m., he missed Tanya already.

Matt waited another thirty minutes. The tow trucks arrived and wrestled the truck and car onto flat beds. Local people had arrived, rubbernecking from the road. Matt recognized some of them. Three snowmobiles roared in to check the situation out. The police waved them away, but they came right up to the turnaround's plowed edge, obliterating the single set of tracks Matt had left. Matt chuckled as the two troopers tried to communicate with the snowmobile drivers through their mandated plastic helmets. On departure, the threesome raced right over Matt's tracks to the main road.

The Trout Lake and Naubinway Bars would buzz with rumors for days.

A little after 4:00 p.m., Matt moved from his hiding place. He unloaded his rifle and secured it against the side of the seat. He shook out and folded the tarp and put it on the seat and over his rifle. He dug some moss and dirt from around the tree's base and rubbed it over the fresh wounds from the branches he had broken off. White fresh breaks on a tree are easy to pick out in evergreen woods. The body imprint in the snow made a good hiding place for the branches, and he disguised most human traces by kicking some snow. A scan of the area with the telescopic sight showed no cars and no traffic. Matt started the Indy and headed into the field, pushing "call" on his Cobra radio several times to locate the other radio Tanya had thrown into the snow. Retracing his tracks in the fading light, Matt worked his way back toward the cabin. Each mile made him lonelier.

He reached his road and found it plowed.

Thank you, Leon Johnson.

He drove down the road at a good speed and found the plowing had been done perfectly: right into the big quarry building. There was a sign on the door: "Took 2 beers—Come see us—LJ."

Matt parked the Polaris and stashed his rifle safely in the Yukon. Inside, he poured three fingers of brandy and went upstairs. Tanya had neatly made the bed. Her pillow still carried a little of her scent. For a moment, it all seemed dreamlike, until he remembered the pistol in his pocket, the $250,000 in the forge, and the millions of dollars of cocaine in the cave— but the woman he wanted so badly was in custody with killers and smugglers. He expected visitors soon. The police could probably trace him, eventually, what with all the material they had just confiscated. He had the feeling the bad guys would find him too. Scattered thoughts tumbled through his brain. He needed to get to a town and do some shopping. He wanted to hide the cocaine better. He wanted to know what Tanya was doing. He wanted to know who called the law. He wanted to keep out of jail. He didn't want to be attacked by bad guys.

The town trip seemed like the best idea for right now. The nearest State Police post was at St. Ignace where the grocery stores and sporting goods stores stayed open late during deer hunting season. He would go there looking for Webb's vehicles and crew.

While sitting in the Yukon waiting for it to warm up, it occurred to him his money stash might be discovered by a good police dog. He took several plastic gasoline cans and put them on the forge. They held mixtures of gasoline and oil for various chainsaws and outboard motors. It was a logical place for them, off the ground; in fact, he wondered why he had not stored them there before. He spilled some chainsaw fuel mix down the side of the hole that held the money, hoping to confuse a dog. The forge itself looked so solid no one would think about an air hole unless they were 1910 forge experts.

He put Tanya's .22 in a little drawer on the back of the console between the front seats. He kept the SIG in his hunting jacket pocket and tossed the big satellite phone on the passenger's seat.

Then he put the Yukon in four-wheel drive and headed for town.

14

Trout Lake & St. Ignace

MATT DROVE TO TROUT LAKE. He topped off his tank with expensive gasoline. Famished, he went into his favorite of the town's two bars, where he knew most of the regulars, and ordered a large burger with cheese, fried onions, and a bottle of Bud Light. He ate at the bar. The bartender, a second cousin by some complex sets of intermarriages, was either a Lamoreaux or a Rivard.

"How's it going? Get your deer?" asked Matt between wonderfully greasy and juicy bites.

"Got two hanging and I'll go out for black powder too," said the bartender. "You hear about the big bust at Garnet Lake?"

"No," said Matt. "I've been at camp until I ran out of eggs and bread."

"Well, it was a real big deal. Leon's oldest daughter, Barb, was in here. They saw the whole thing. Two truckloads of people were taken away. They were meeting on a road that Leon just opened up for snowmobiles to park at."

Lou. That was the man's name.

"Yah," Lou continued, "we saw them troop right through here, like a friggin' parade. We had government people in here, too. They wanted to know if we saw any strangers around. I says no, just the regular hunters that come every year. Old Walt that lives by the tracks near Garnet was here with two untagged deer inside his pickup camper. He about shit a brick when government cars drove up and a State Police Jeep parked right behind his truck. He had to have three Hartley shots before he could calm down. How you been, got your buck?"

"I'm fine," Matt replied. "I got a buck opening day, and it's all in a freezer at home. I've still got a doe permit to fill."

He finished his beer and wiped his fingers on a bar napkin. "I was enjoying just wandering around in the woods until the storm hit."

"See you later, Lou." Matt paid and gave a dollar tip. "Good luck with black powder. The deer should be moving by then."

Matt took Highway 123 to I-75 and drove into St. Ignace. He saw the blue State Police sign at the interstate exit. It was the finest State Police post Matt could imagine. Most were old red brick buildings with a garage attached, not big enough for a family of four. The old St. Ignace post was now used by the Mackinac County Road Commission. The new post was on prized land on the west side of the north end of the Mackinac Bridge. Matt took the last off-ramp before the tollbooths. The road offered a great view of the State Police post and the bridge. He drove slowly by the post. Then he pulled over and got out his hunting binoculars and scoped the area. As far as any observer could tell, he would be looking at the bridge, which loomed over the post and across the Mackinac Straits.

A dozen cars filled the normally empty parking area in front of the post's main entrance. Matt could also see the garage area with the regular line of blue vehicles and State Police special machines—snowmobiles, a winterized and shrink-wrapped boat, and other vehicles under winter canvas. No sign of Webb's pickup truck or Lincoln. Matt drove slowly forward on the one-way road and saw the pickup by the garage area. It was dark, and he could see lights in the garage. He felt sure Webb's car was inside the garage, having a very thorough inspection. He couldn't see into the office area, but lights glowed everywhere. He decided to check out the hunting and sports store before it closed.

Ace Hardware had sporting goods as well as any tool anyone would ever need and was busy for a Monday evening. Matt went in looking for large duffel bags or sport bags. He found what he wanted in the hockey section. They had large equipment bags on sale, larger even than the duffel bags that had held the cocaine. Matt checked the stitching and the handles. They were well made. They needed to hold 100 pounds without ripping out a handle or seam. He bought four bags in various colors, making a remark about the expense for parents of hockey players. The girl checking him out showed no interest whatsoever. Despite the ring in her eyebrow and every fingernail a different color, she was smart enough to put three bags into the last one. She handed him his copy of the credit card sales slip without checking his signature.

Matt drove back the way he had come but stopped at a brightly lit supermarket—Glen's Supermarket, the largest in the area. He cruised up and down the aisles buying groceries on autopilot, thinking about Tanya in the police post. He thought of her dark hair against his cheek as he selected some expensive frozen shrimp and some mediocre fresh produce but couldn't find pure maple syrup. He remembered the feel of her body pressing against his while paying the $65 bill and gathering up his five bags. He drove the short distance to the police post and noticed that the pickup and about half the cars were gone. Matt continued past the post and onto Highway 2, pulling over in a widely plowed area near the I-75 entrance ramp.

Frantically searching for ideas, he jumped when Ivan's cell phone warbled. Matt smacked his leg on the steering wheel.

"Ouch!"

He picked up the satellite phone, fumbled with its opening mechanism, turned on the overhead map light, answered with a higher than normal, "Yes?"

"It's me." The tension in Tanya's voice was accentuated by the tinny speaker and the cold void inside the vehicle and inside Matt's heart. "Where are you?"

Matt took a breath. "I'm in St. Ignace."

"So are we."

"You all right?"

"Yeah, I suppose so." Tanya paused. "Look, just please—please—listen to Mr. Webb."

Matt asked, "Where are you?'

No reply.

"Tanya?"

"Shut up and listen," Webb stage-whispered. "We just ordered some food in this shitty restaurant in this shitty little town."

The just-noticeable lag reminded Matt that, though only a mile separated them, their voices had to travel from ground to satellite to ground and back again to make the communication.

"So, splurge and get yourself a pasty with gravy on it," said Matt, trying to sound brave and casual to mask his real feelings. The suggestion made him suddenly hungry, heightened by the aroma of fresh bread from the back of the Yukon.

After the thousand-plus miles of light-speed delay, Webb replied, "Listen, you shithead. I don't know what kinda crap you're trying to pull, but we will find you and your family and we will get our stuff and you will be sorry for messing with me."

"The fact is, I didn't call the police," Matt protested. "I wanted to hold on to the drugs as leverage until I was sure you'd be there. And I didn't want Tanya around the drugs. We can still do business, and you can be in some big city tomorrow."

"I'm listening."

"How about if I take you to pick up the stuff and then I bring you back to your boys? Then I'm out of it."

After several long seconds, "Right." Webb's calloused voice echoed in the car, haunting the familiar surroundings. "I'll send a couple of men—"

"No deal," Matt cut him off by talking over him. "You need to take as big a risk as me."

More seconds ticked off in the cold vehicle, Matt watching the phone like it was a vicious animal.

Webb finally broke the silence, "Tanya says she will go with me, this in chess is double jeopardy. She feels she can make everything go smoothly, no one getting hurt. I just want to get this fiasco over with. I get the stuff and I want that phone too. When can you pick us up, and where?"

"There's a supermarket by the interstate ramp just before you go over the bridge. It's on the east side of the interstate and south of Highway 2. It's called Glen's. It lights up the whole area. Be there in thirty minutes. Park in front, go in, buy some beer and snacks, and wait by the main doors. Have your friends park in the middle of the lot under a light, and have them stand by their vehicles so I can count them. I want you in the seat beside me and Tanya in the back seat. I have the pilot's gun."

More seconds crept by, and then Webb said, "Okay, we can find the supermarket. We'll be there in about forty minutes, our food just got served."

Webb broke the connection.

Matt looked at the phone; it still had a good charge. He wondered why it was so valuable to Webb. The cocaine wasn't valuable enough to Webb to risk his involvement. There was something else being planned. Matt had forty minutes to try to think what sneaky deal they would try to pull. Whose side was Tanya on? He really wanted to believe she was on his side...and really wanted to hold her slender, firm body close.

He drove to the sporting goods store to get some watch-cap-like hats to pull down over his soon-to-be passengers' eyes, but the store was closed.

Damn! Now what? Plan B?

He thought about the grocery bags and emptied two of them. He rolled them until they were about the right size for hoods and carefully tore a few small holes to provide air but not sight. He put them in the back seat, planning to use them just before reaching Trout Lake.

In the supermarket lot, Matt put duct tape over part of his license plate and smeared mud and slush over the rest. A dark Yukon in the U.P. was nothing special. In a moment of inspiration, he also taped part of his taillights and one license plate light. Even if Webb's men covered all the roads out of town, they wouldn't have a plate number and the Yukon would look different to someone following him when he took the tape off the lights. He'd have to stop and search Webb and Tanya when they got away from town.

If only I could take my time "searching" her.

From the far end of the parking lot, Matt again used the small Steiner 8x22 binoculars he kept in the door pocket of his vehicle to scan the lot. Only a few cars there. He thought about the best route. The road would be so lonely on a Monday night he might not even see another car from Trout Lake on. Webb's two vehicles arrived ten minutes early. They circled the lot and pulled up under a light in the middle of the brightly lit lot. Matt watched through the binoculars as Webb emerged from the back seat of his car and spoke to the driver of the pickup for a few minutes. Two men climbed out of the pickup and stood beside it. Webb returned to the car. Volcheff stepped out of the front passenger's seat, followed by another large gangster from the back seat. For several more minutes, Webb and the two men huddled at the right front fender, talking animatedly. Then Webb opened a back door and Tanya slipped out, looking a bit drawn but gorgeous.

Matt's heart thumped in his chest. He wanted to run to her. *Easy, boy. One step at a time.*

Tanya and Webb walked, without talking, into the market. Matt scanned back just as the driver of the car got out and stood by his door.

That makes Volcheff plus four others, Matt thought. *They look like the same guys from Garnet Lake.*

Matt waited and watched through his binoculars. After a few minutes, Webb and Tanya came out with bags. The exit was a good distance from the car and truck parked in the middle of the lot. Tanya and Webb stood at the curb in the pick-up area and waited. Tanya stared at the ground, shoulders slumped.. Webb stood erect, shoulders squared, glaring across the parking lot, scanning the shadows beyond.

Matt checked the SIG and chambered a shell. He held the pistol in his left hand with the hammer down. He pulled out the left armrest of the passenger's side seat—another barrier between Webb and himself. He quickly drove to the pick-up lane and stopped by Webb and Tanya. With the butt of the gun, he pressed the button to lower the passenger's side window.

"Webb in front, Tanya in back. Keep the bags on your lap and keep your hands on top, where I can see them," said Matt.

Webb and Tanya did as they were told. Bigger than Matt had thought, Webb filled the right seat. His thick, heavy body mashed down the seat. Matt lifted the SIG slightly to make sure Webb saw it, then glanced at Tanya. She smiled briefly, then averted her eyes.

"So, you're the hunter that got more than his deer this season?" Webb asked.

"Yes, and I hope you can believe I can shoot you without any of the respect I feel for a deer."

Webb chuckled and shrugged.

They drove, without talking, north on the almost deserted I-75. Matt exited in about eight miles at the Highway 123 exit to Allenville and Moran. After the exit, he crossed over the Interstate, pulled over, and watched the highway. The next exit, seven miles north, didn't go west. The Rudyard exit was another fourteen after that, twenty plus miles to Trout Lake. No cars turned off or slowed, several went on northward. Matt opened his door and pointed the SIG at Webb.

"Slowly pass the bag back to Tanya and get out of the car. Step away from the door. Do everything slowly. Tanya, when Webb is out and away from the car, you do the same, get away from the car."

Webb did as directed, then Tanya. Webb's eyes followed Matt's every move. A hint of a smile creased his mouth.

Matt went around the Yukon. Webb seemed too relaxed. Matt moved behind Webb, ten feet away, and kept Tanya in sight.

"Put your hands on the car," Matt said. "Spread your legs and move them back until I tell you to stop. Remember, I'm not going to mess with you. You do anything fast and I'll shoot you several times."

Matt cocked the hammer, again: theatrical but always impressive. Webb leaned over and spread his legs. Matt had never searched anyone, let alone a gangster boss. He checked outside, then inside his legs, socks, and ankles. Webb wore briefs. Matt patted Webb for weapons in his coat or shirt, or under them. Matt very carefully checked around his back and belt. Finally, Matt checked his collars. The man's shoulders and arms felt hard as oak. He had a wallet and some cash in his pockets, the bills in a money clip. Matt pulled up the wallet to the top of the pocket and let it fall back. Everything seemed normal. He had Webb move into the car's headlights as he searched Tanya.

She smiled slightly as he felt inside her down vest. She wore briefs, too. But Matt knew they were black lace and had a little red rose on the front elastic. He finished the search and put her back into the rear seat. He motioned Webb back in and made sure he put his seat belt on. He had Webb put his hands on the dash and came around the back, pulling off tape as he did so and got in. He decocked the gun in his left hand. He made one last look down the interstate and saw only two cars as far as he could see. None were exiting.

"There are two brown paper bags in the back seat," Matt said. "Put them on, please."

Without complaint or comment, they both put on the bags.

Silence reigned on the drive back to the cabin, except for Webb asking how much longer they had to drive. Matt told him they'd get there when they arrived. He had to use both hands to drive, but Webb kept one hand on the dash and the other on the overhead handhold. The bags proved a good idea. Tanya remained silent and kept her balance with the handholds and her foot on the console between the front seats. Matt pulled into the quarry shop building and up to the cabin before saying, "You can take off the bags now."

Webb removed the bag, looked around, and said, "What kind of place is this? And I really enjoyed your damn dirt roads. Damn near made me sick."

Matt opened the Yukon's back door "Grab some bags, okay?"

Tanya and Webb both picked up bags but didn't seem to notice the rifle in its dark padded case.

"Consider this the seventh-inning stretch and bathroom break." Matt pointed to the cabin's door. "Then we'll get the cocaine and get your asses out of here." Tanya put her bags on the kitchen table then went to the bathroom. Webb put his bags down and looked around, checking out some of the pictures and deer antlers on the wall.

He smirked and shook his head. "I can see why you need the money."

Matt put away the items that needed to stay frozen or cool, without ever turning his back on Webb. Tanya returned and put away the rest of the packages. Her familiarity with the kitchen wasn't lost on Webb, who sat in the chair that last held Ivan.

"You know," Webb said, spreading his arms and glancing around. "I came from a small town in Russia, 200 kilometers west of Moscow. We would have called this place a palace. My village no longer exists. It was a battlefield three times." Webb lifted himself from the comfortable chair and moved to the wall festooned with pictures, antlers, and various racks for coats and hats. Matt watched him carefully and kept several pieces of furniture between them.

Webb talked as he looked at pictures, "I was lucky to make it out of Russia and into the shipping business. Now I can move anything to anywhere on the globe. I tell you this because you are in the middle of many plans. You would be wise to get out of our business."

Webb touched the topmost points of a twelve-point antler mount, allowing time to appreciate and absorb the last point. "We don't take prisoners. We see governments and borders as inconveniences and impediments to commerce."

He turned to face Matt, eyes narrowing. "You would be wise not to become an inconvenience or impediment. We can reward you for helping us or remove you for getting in our way."

Webb shrugged. "But I talk too much. What are your plans?"

Matt checked out Webb's Italian shoes and guessed they were 10½, his size, so he went to a metal coat closet, rummaged around, and found an old pair of Red Wings with some wool socks stuffed in them. "Put these on or you'll freeze your toes off," he said. "We're going to be walking through some snow."

Webb frowned at the boots.

Matt threw some wool knit army glove liners to Webb. "You'll need these too."

Tanya came out of the bathroom. She looked beautiful. Matt wanted to nuzzle her neck, nibble her earlobes, kiss her…He shook himself from his reverie and asked, "Are you all right?"

"Sure," she replied. "Not that the police thing was any fun. I thought we had had it. What made you take out the cocaine?"

Matt answered, "I didn't want you traveling with the stuff. I thought I could get it to you later, more safely. I also wanted to have something they wanted in case Webb didn't show up and my rifle wasn't enough to protect you."

"Those cops were pissed," broke in Webb. "Said they were acting on solid informant information. The DEA's still trying to get indictments and have a grand jury warrant issued for some other things they think I'm into."

"And I suppose you're innocent?" Matt asked.

"Doesn't matter," Webb replied. "When they struck a dry hole, they were royally screwed. I can get them for false arrest, harassment, and whatever my lawyers want to throw at them. Good thing I brought my Michigan boys. They had concealed weapon permits. One of them is former police himself. So, how the DEA knew about the meeting if you didn't do it?"

Matt shook his head. "Damned if I know."

"Maybe they were using a spy plane or some other Star Wars shit," Webb said, pulling on the old, well-broken-in boots. They fit fine. "Just like our phones, there's a lot of space-age technology in the business these days. These satellite phones cost us almost $5,500 each, not to mention the money that goes to the computer nerds that set them up for us."

Webb looked natural in work boots. He could have been a longshoreman or a lumberjack. He had a good Columbia snow jacket on, but would have looked great in a Woolrich checkered wool coat. Snugging up the laces, he said, "Nice boots. Good boots are important in the snow."

"Glad you like them," Matt said, annoyed at the man's relaxed attitude. "We've got a little walk in the snow and will have to drag the bags back. Tanya and I will each carry one bag and, Webb, you look strong enough to carry two, and we can put more in your bags."

Matt grabbed a pint of Hartley's and ushered them outside the cabin. He put the bottle in the Yukon and took out the five-cell he kept under the seat. He felt he would need a drink when this was over. He gave the hockey bag stuffed with hockey bags to Webb and pointed the light toward the door in the far wall. The snow had blown in and formed a fine, white delta that went from no depth to nearly two feet at the door.

"The brandy's for later," he said. "When we get this stuff out of here. I'll shine the light, and you walk where I point it. It's only about seventy yards. Coming back we will have a trail broken."

They walked out the doorless opening into the calm world of brilliant white snow under the flashlight and the total black of the empty quarry space. Drifts piled up around the boulders. The snow crunched underfoot, meaning dropping temperatures. Matt had not looked at the thermometer outside the cabin door, a habit broken only by his total distrust of Webb. Soon, Matt could make out the snowmobile tracks, whose packing action made the walking easier for the three trekkers. They came to the cave door and Matt opened it. He handed Webb and Tanya each a Coleman lantern. Tanya's was battery powered, and he turned it on. He would wait to light Webb's white gas Coleman until they reached the bottom of the stairs.

"This is some place," said Webb. "Who made it?"

"Nature," Matt replied. "Probably ten thousand years ago. There were a lot of caves here, but the quarry…anyway, we use it to hang deer."

Idiot, he thought. *Your teacher's big mouth's gonna get you in trouble. Always gotta explain everything to everybody. Why not just give him the GPS coordinates for the damn quarry while you're at it.*

Downstairs, Matt hung Tanya's lamp on a ceiling hook so they could see most of the room. Matt moved around the table and motioned Webb to put his lamp on it. Matt pumped it up, got out his lighter, turned the valve control to start, opened the gas knob, and lit the gasbag when he heard the hiss of vaporized white gas. The flame blossomed, then settled down. The painfully-white light filled the cavern.

As the hanging deer popped out of the dissipating shadows, Webb and Tanya jumped back. Webb seemed embarrassed.

"The bags are behind the steps on shelves." Matt took the bright, gas Coleman to show the shelves of white bags. "There are three more bags in the one you're carrying, get them out and fill 'em up. Tanya and I will watch."

"Why don't you two help?" asked Webb.

"I want to keep your hands busy," answered Matt.

Webb made short work of the job. His strength and coordination confirmed everything Tanya had said about him and validated the long-shoreman image Matt had of him. In only a few minutes, Webb had four bags packed, zipped, and piled at the foot of the stairs. He checked his watch and nodded, apparently satisfied at his elapsed time. Two bags filled completely, two about half filled. Webb's agreeableness worried Matt more than if he'd argued about everything.

"I'll go up the stairs first," Matt said. "Then you, Webb, can bring up the bags to the landing and then Tanya can bring up the last lantern." He felt in good control. His plan was working well.

With Webb's first step the whole structure swayed and groaned in pro-test. He wisely made two trips with the heavy bags. He gave a smirk as he easily tossed the first heavy bag at Matt's feet. Matt knew the bag could have been thrown with deadly effect.

With no more incidents, his charges and bags outside, Matt secured the cave while watching Webb standing in the snow. With a "go" from Matt, Webb lifted his two heavy bags without complaint or excess effort. Tanya used two hands and struggled with the weight. Matt brought his bag over his back with no problem.

Webb must be carrying nearly three hundred pounds. Jeez, you'd think it was his laundry.

Webb's feat impressed Matt, as did his knowledge of the cocaine's weight. He'd carefully loaded Tanya's and Matt's bags with just what they could carry. Webb had moved drugs before.

They labored back to the cabin, Matt staying focused on Webb and their path. Webb passed through the shop door opening, then Tanya. As Matt stepped through, a shotgun barrel punched into his neck. Matt looked left directly into the cold eyes of Volcheff, all in black with a watch cap pulled over his ears.

"Drop gun or die," he hissed.

Tanya and Webb had not seen him as they entered the quarry shop building from the north door. He had concealed his tracks so they could not be seen in the snow blown through the open windows and door. He knew about tracks and concealment.

Matt's guts twisted. His breath caught in his throat. He'd never had a gun pointed at his head before.

Volcheff stepped back a safe five feet away.

Matt thought about trying something but just dropped the SIG into the snow when he looked into the black eye of the 12-gauge barrel.

15

Prisoners

V OLCHEFF WHISTLED, and four men emerged from the cabin. They took the bags from Webb and Tanya. Webb grabbed Tanya and shoved her toward the cabin.

"Tie this asshole up," Webb ordered. "And her too."

One of the men led Matt into the cabin, tied his hands behind him with short lengths of quarter-inch nylon rope. They knew their business and worked quickly. Matt could feel one set of knots—a simple half hitch with an overhand knot finisher. A snug knot that would tighten with any pulling. Matt didn't pull against them. They pushed him onto a kitchen chair and secured him with a double pass of rope around the uprights, tying the bowline knot in front. Again, efficient and not something he could get out of with six men in the room.

Tanya pleaded with Webb as they tied her hands behind her and her ankles together. One of them kicked her feet from under her, letting her drop onto the couch. She repeated several times that she had done nothing wrong. No one said anything to her.

Webb sat in a chair facing Matt. "Where is the money bag?"

The slap came so fast and untelegraphed, Matt wasn't sure Webb had done it. Matt and his chair toppled over. He hit the floor hard. His ear rang, and the left side of his face burned. His eyes teared. His nose ran. His stomach heaved.

Two men brought Matt and his chair back to the upright position. Matt's hands numbed as the ropes tightened from the fall.

"You will tell us everything we want to hear, sooner or later," said Webb. He then went over to Tanya and undid the button and zipper on her wool skirt. Webb pulled off her skirt. Tanya glared at him, glanced at Matt, but said nothing. Webb then snapped his fingers and held out his hand. Volcheff handed him a single-blade, folding knife. Webb slowly clicked the blade open. The room fell quiet as he sliced her sweater from the waist to the neck, opening it to expose Tanya's silk camisole. He then slit the silk in the same fashion.

"Stop," Tanya pleaded. "I can't help you. I...I've done nothing to harm you. You've got to believe me."

"I believe what I see, first, and what I hear, second. I know this man will tell the truth rather than see you hurt," said Webb. "I can have Volcheff do things to you that even I couldn't think of."

He turned to Matt. "Tell me where the money bag is, and we may leave you alone."

Matt knew Webb was not bluffing. He knew he would have to tell them at some point. He needed to change the numbers against him and fight in a different place, if he was to have any chance. Gauging his words carefully, he said, "I can't tell you, but I can take you to it. It's in the woods in an old deer blind."

"Just tell us, and we will find it," ordered Webb.

Matt's stomach continued its somersaults. He inhaled deeply, eased it out, and fought to stop shaking and to slow his heart. "Look, it's about a mile through the woods. The trail only goes part of the way, then it's unmarked. The blind is good because it's hard to see even in the daylight."

He hated the high pitch of his voice and the tremor in it. "You'll need me to guide you, and you'll need lights and a shovel if you want to get to it tonight."

Webb considered his suggestion but said nothing.

"How did they find this place?" Matt asked Webb.

"I told you we were space-age, asshole. We planted a homing beacon on both Tanya and me. One works on radio waves and the other works with a satellite signal. You didn't search us very well. You spent too much time giving Tanya a cheap feel."

"We almost can't find this place when we know direction," said Volcheff, his voice higher than Matt expected. "You really live in the boondoggles. Not from my childhood time do I see so much snow. This is funny house in a barn."

Webb took Volcheff to a corner and said something in a foreign language, probably Russian.

Hoping he would not make matters worse, Matt broke into their little meeting. "You know the police will find this place from the stuff that I put in the dope bags. I did that in a hurry and at the last minute. There are names on some of the stuff, many people know my sleigh. I've got relatives all around here that might drop in. It's hunting season and many people hunt from this cabin and on this land. You'd be smart to get out of here while the getting's good."

Volcheff and Webb continued their whispered conversation. The other men stood around. Matt took a good look at them. They seemed trained for quiet and menace. They didn't volunteer any opinions. The three of them looked fit—two tall, one short but built like a boxer. The fourth, and smallest, man looked sneaky. Matt figured he was the limo driver, as he still wore fingerless driving gloves. With the exception of the driver, they dressed in mid-calf boots and new outdoor clothes. Everything they wore rustled when they moved. The boots, though warm enough, would fill with snow if they stepped off a path. Matt noted they had dress socks instead of outdoor wool or insulated types. Their leather gloves would suffice for church, but not the woods. Their orange hunting caps might work for bird hunting temperatures but not the U.P. in November.

Webb stepped over to Matt and cut rather than untied the rope around his waist. He snapped, "Stand up."

Matt got up, and Volcheff, who had moved behind him, patted him down, removing his knife and wallet. Volcheff opened and passed the wallet to Webb.

"You are Matthew M. Hunter, you live in Gladstone, Michigan. Where's that?" asked Webb, standing to one side of Matt.

"It's about a hundred miles west," answered Matt.

Webb went through the wallet. He put the cards and various pictures on the table. Matt was surprised at the amount of information about his life he carried in a wallet.

"Who's this?" Webb pointed at a picture of Matt's son at about sixteen.

"My son," said Matt.

"He is a good-looking boy. Does he play sports?"

"He ran cross-country and played soccer and hockey in high school. He still keeps in shape." Matt fought back worry over Webb's interest in his family.

"Here are my daughter and wife," said Webb, displaying some wallet pictures of a beautiful, dark-haired girl and an older copy in blonde, obviously the mother. "My wife was in Moscow Ballet, my daughter is also a dancer and a gymnast in her school in Chicago. We love Chicago. It is like Moscow would be if it could, and the weather is better. We love the restaurants, museums, art centers, and performing arts. I like it better than New York; the people are friendlier and the lake is wonderful. We have a boat in walking distance from our apartment."

Webb kept looking through Matt's papers, pictures, and cards. He held up the Michigan Education Association card. "You are a teacher?"

" I was, just retired," said Matt. Then he silently cursed himself for giving more information than he needed to. It also told Webb that a workplace wouldn't be missing him. *Dumb blabbermouth mistake*, thought Matt. *Got to think faster and talk slower. This guy's friendly chatter is truly disarming.*

Tanya moved on the couch, now wearing only her black leotard panty hose and her black bra, her slashed sweater and camisole spread open. She turned on her side toward the back of the couch and looked over her shoulder.

"Matt," she said. "Just get them the money, and maybe they will get out of here."

She looked at Webb. "Untie me. I'm no threat to you and these big, strong men."

"Lay there, I like to watch your nice bottom," growled Webb. "Look, Mr. Hunter, you go get the money bag and then we talk about what we do with you and Tanya."

"It's over a mile and in heavy snow. We can take the snowmobiles most of the way and it would be faster. I can't drive a machine with my hands tied."

"Can any of you city boys run a snow machine?" asked Webb.

"I've got two and we go north several weekends a winter," said the largest of the three men.

"I've been on a machine a couple of times," said the smaller, boxer-built man.

"Okay, leave him tied, put him behind you." Webb pointed at the smaller man. "You follow them and if anything funny happens, beat the shit out of him."

"I need my outdoor clothes," said Matt.

Webb nodded, one of the men untied the ropes.

Another mark of a good rope person, Matt thought, *to be able to untie knots they have tied.*

Matt put on his hunting coat, feeling the lighter and compass in the pockets as he took it off its peg. His Swiss army knife and wallet still lay on the table. He donned his army wool gloves and black Kromer. They retied his hands, with a little more space between them to allow for the coat. The two men detailed to guard him put on their coats, leather gloves, and hunting caps and pushed him out of the cabin.

Matt had them turn on the cabin's outside lights, lighting most of the area around the two snowmobiles. Matt knew one machine had little gas, but they were not going very far. The bigger man started the first machine and showed the other man how to start the second machine. After a brief warm-up, the smaller man mounted one machine and Matt straddled behind him.

Matt lifted the Velcro-secured storage lid to use as a handhold. The men headed toward the large main door.

"Where to?" Matt's driver asked.

16

Escape

MATT DIRECTED HIS DRIVER to follow the road south for a few yards, then up a path that left the quarry. They went north on an old logging road for more than a half-mile—deep snow with no packed trail. They wound through the arboreal tunnel enveloping the snowmobile's headlight. The second machine stayed behind at an intelligent distance. Matt had no chance of sliding off his sled and running into the woods before the second mob muscleman could run him down.

It was cold, in the high teens, but with almost no wind. The clear sky allowed Matt to catch a few of the Big Dipper stars. There was no moon, but the two snowmobile headlights would make him easy to see. Matt needed them to get away from the machines and their lights. He knew the woods by feel, smell, and slant of the ground. An escape plan slowly coalesced in Matt's brain. Risky, but possible.

They drove slowly for another several hundred yards. Matt called a stop. The second machine glided up behind. Both machines sat idling, casting their lights a hundred yards down the wooded trail. The land rose to their right, the beginning of the ridge with the old deer blind. Matt stepped off the back of the machine. The two men got off their machines. They expertly stayed within one quick step of him, one on each side.

Matt pointed up the hill. "The deer blind is up this hill about a quarter of a mile. Kill the engines and bring the flashlights and shovel."

"We'll keep the first one running, pointing up our path," the big man said. "It's idling well and there's lots of gas in the tank."

"If you say so." Matt arched his back to stretch out the kinks. It had been a long day. "You guys got names?"

"I'm Ray," the smaller man said. "That's Al."

Al took a small Coleman pop-up lantern from the back of his machine, and Ray had a two-cell flashlight. Al also carried Matt's army surplus entrenching tool—a pick and a shovel blade that folded onto a very solid wooden handle, covered by a leather sheath.

"Lead the way." Ray pushed Matt into the untracked snow. "Don't do anything stupid and we won't have to put a bullet in your leg.."

Matt led them up the slope and along the ridge. Ray and Al panted and gasped, unaccustomed to trudging through snow that varied from knee to thigh deep. They grumbled about cold feet and hands—plus getting wet from sweating under their nice ski jackets, which they kept zipped up tightly rather than opening for ventilation, as any cold-weather hunter would know enough to do. Matt thought of leading them around some, but changed his mind when he realized how out of shape they were and how much they stumbled along the basically decent path. The snowmobile's engine sounded more and more ragged. Matt knew the engine would stop soon, with its old spark plugs and need for its first real tune-up in several years. The Indy worked very well at high RPM but not for long-duration idling. Matt hoped to make a break when the engine died and the light went out. The little flashlight and the lantern didn't really put out much light. If he could get down the slope and into the cedars, he would be hard to find. He could circle them to get back on their tracks and then later slip back off their tracks. Many deer had fooled Matt by doing just that.

`Unfortunately, the machine kept running and soon they reached the blind.

"You need to clear the snow out of the entrance," said Matt. "Or I'd be glad to do it for you, if you untie me."

"Sure," Al said. "And when we take the shovel out of our heads, we'll all become friends."

Al pulled the leather cover off the shovel, pushed a button on the hinge, and opened the blade fully. He started digging at the drift that had formed over the entrance.

Seeing how much the drift sagged into the blind, Matt wondered how much two and a half feet of standing, wet snow added to the weight of the dirt held up by the rotten cedar logs and rusted, corrugated steel.

Al put the lantern on the highest part of the drift facing the blind. He worked his way through the snow. Ray moved behind Matt and kept his flashlight on Al's progress.

The digging took some time with the small shovel. Matt watched Al throw snow to both sides as he worked, half of the cleared snow was added to the weight on the blind's roof.

Ray shivered as his lack of activity allowed his sweat to turn to cold water. Whatever he wore under his jacket was soaked and getting colder by the second. He stomped his feet, also wet and cold. Matt stood still, thanking the good folks at Danner who made his boots. His thick poly-propylene-and-wool socks and excellent boots would stand another twenty degrees of cold before he would wish he had on his Sorels.

There is no such thing as bad weather, just bad clothes, and these guys are wearing bad clothes.

He knew these big, bad city gangsters would be in serious trouble if left in the forest overnight. Matt wondered if they had a lighter or matches on them.

"Where are you from?" Matt asked Ray.

"B-Birmingham." Ray's teeth chattered. "Al's from Bloomfield Hills, outside Detroit. Used to be a city cop."

Al, a hard worker, had almost dug into the blind, but the shovel's small blade suited dirt, not snow. Al resorted to slicing blocks and lifting them out. He was on his knees when he finally cleared an opening—a black hole in the sparkling snow bank. He grabbed the lantern and put it into the sinister-looking black mouth. Snow also choked the far opening, turning the blind into a cave.

"It's dry," said Al, wriggling into the deer blind. "The ground's not frozen."

"Where is the money?" asked Ray as he moved around Matt to see into the blind.

Matt peered over Ray's shoulder. "You need to move the boxes out and dig into the floor on the far right side."

He moved against Ray and tried to point with his right foot because his bound hands were useless.

Al passed out a plastic milk crate they used as a seat. Ray took it, becoming progressively more interested in the treasure hunt. An old wooden apple box came out next. Ray bent to a knee to take it and toss it away from the entrance, using one hand while his other held the flash-light. Matt moved behind Ray, still very close so Ray wouldn't feel him trying to get away.

Matt sat on the plastic crate behind Ray and brought both feet up and behind Ray's back. As Ray reached for another box, he kicked Ray into the blind. Darkness enveloped them as Ray fell on his flashlight and his body blocked the light from the lantern.

Matt jumped up and onto the roof of the blind. It gave under his weight and collapsed several feet. He scrambled for solid footing and, once he had some leverage, rolled forward over the far side of the blind. Ray and Al yelled and cursed as he rolled down the steep northern slope. Several small bushes snatched at his clothes, some small pines nudged him away, and finally an immovable stump stopped him short. Although padded by snow, the stump still knocked the wind out of him. As he got to his feet, he looked up the slope, saw no light, but heard muffled, panicky voices. He didn't know how much of the roof had caved in. Still only halfway down the slope, he needed to get away from them and get his hands free.

The rope had tightened on his wrists during his tumble down the hill. He had lost his black Kromer and knew, on a black night, he'd never find it. His hunting coat had a hood, but he needed his hands free to use it. In the meantime, snow packed in his hair and ears and jammed down his neck, making his ears ache from the cold. He shook himself like a Lab coming out of a lake. The dry snow didn't stick to his clothing but turned to ice water on his face.

Matt started to walk around the hill, toward the snowmobiles. If he could get there before Al and Ray got out of the blind, he might be able to get his hands free. With his hands bound, he struggled on the slope and kept losing his balance and doing a header into the snow. He had to circle the hill more than he wanted to avoid the steeper slope. Just before the cedar swamp, he could see the snowmobile's headlight over the crest of the hill. As he watched, the light turned yellow, then brightened, then yellow, then dark.

Matt realized that there is dark, and then there is really dark. A cedar swamp, with no moonlight and no stars, is really dark. With the headlights on just before darkness had descended, the contrast proved even more dramatic. Matt stood still, listening and letting his eyes adjust as much as they could.

The human eye is a miracle from God. The ability to appreciate a sunset in color has a trade-off—limited night vision. Matt used his knowledge of the human eye to get the most of his low-light ability. He scanned the forest, letting his peripheral vision pick up shapes that were not detected by looking straight ahead. The lighter snow all around him blanketed the black trees. Luckily, he was looking at the light when it went out. He stamped a large path directly ahead toward the machines. If he kept the steeper slope on his left and the swamp on his right, he should stay on track. He would walk slowly and try to check his back trail. He knew he had to concentrate to walk a straight line for several hundred yards.

Walking through a forest at night with your hands tied behind you is an exercise in self-control. A fall is not only undignified and dangerous, it is disorienting. Matt had several hundred yards to travel. Matt knew these woods as well as a human could know the woods. However, it was hard to remain calm and objective when his life depended on getting to an exact spot in a totally darkened woods. He knew right-handed people tended to circle left. Slowly and carefully, he fought this trend and hoped to avert overreaction. He had no way to retrieve, or use, the compass and lighter in his jacket pockets. In the occasional open areas, he could just make out his back trail. He felt the ground rise slightly and the trees opening to the sky. Through the limbs of leafless hardwoods, a welcome sight after the smothering darkness of the cedars and pines, Matt could see stars again. Relieved, he spotted the handle of the Big Dipper right where he expected it. He continued south, certain he was on or near the old logging road. Another thirty yards and he could see a pale white finger of snow—the old trail he had walked hundreds of times. He could make out broad, solid maples and tall, pale birch trees that had formed sentinels for the hundred years man had dragged wood and game along the trail. Soon, he could discern the dark shapes of the snowmobiles.

Matt stood by the machines for a full minute, catching his breath and listening for anyone moving in the woods. He heard a coyote call far to the north, answered by calls even farther north. Some creature would be a late dinner—road kill or a wounded animal. Nature despises waste and made the coyote an excellent hunter.

Back to reality. Matt stood in the inky woods with his hands tied. He needed something to cut the ropes. Matt slouched onto the seat of the first machine, not breathing hard but thinking hard.

Matt crouched beside the tool kit on the right side, just above the foot opening. With some difficulty, he snapped it open and removed the spark plug puller. Too smooth to do any cutting. He scrambled to his feet and over to the other machine. Backing up to it, he slipped his feet into the loop on each ski tip. With good footing, he held the plug puller against the small of his back and against the headlight lens.

It should work.

With the plug puller against his belt, he rammed it back into the lens. It didn't break. But the theory was solid and, on the fourth try, the lens broke. As the plug puller smashed through, he levered pieces of glass into his hands. His wool glove liners had excellent feel. He selected a three-inch piece of the thick glass. Nice sharp edges. He tried both sides on the rope. After a few seconds of sawing, he felt the rope part, then give way completely.

Having two hands in front of him was a wonderful thing. He yanked the ropes off his hands, then pulled up his hood. The absence of cold and the build-up of heat was also a wonderful sensation.

Matt listened again for nearly a minute. He heard neither human sounds nor crunching of snow in any direction. He could start the machine...and go where?

North to his cousins' camp just south of Highway 28? They might be there. They would help him, but Matt couldn't get Tanya, tied on the couch, out of his thoughts. Emotions flooded his mind—from lust to pity, from anger to love. Ignoring his own cautions about the fate of lifesavers who jump into the water, he chose to help Tanya. Saving himself became secondary.

What about Al and Ray? They wouldn't last long left in the woods. Frostbite and hypothermia would overcome them by morning. They needed a good light to backtrack well. The flashlight and lantern weren't very good. Were they still buried in the deer blind? Recognizing his own softheartedness, he knew he couldn't let them die in that deer blind.

Matt started the Polaris. Its light made the forest seem safer and normal in a microsecond. He followed the tracks up the slope, easy work with two hands on the handlebars. He watched for lights or movement. In either case, he would turn left and work back to the trail, then north to help. They could never follow or catch him. He stopped one hundred feet from the blind. The headlight illuminated the top of the blind area. He didn't see anyone or any new tracks. He made sure the Polaris was idling well, needing its light, and dismounted. He worked left around the lit area, using trees and bushes for concealment. He came up on the blind by cutting across the steep northern side. He heard whimpering and coughing—and voices of desperate men. Matt approached the shooting slit without presenting a target. Light glowed softly through the snow.

"Ray and Al!" yelled Matt.

Al yelled back, "Get us out of here, we're freezing. Ray's hurt and can't breathe good."

"Okay, I'll get you out, but I want your guns first. Any funny stuff and I leave you here."

"How do we give you guns we can't get at?" asked Al in desperation.

"That's your problem. I'm going to open up a hole and I want two guns to come out or I'm gone and your asses will thaw out sometime in late March." Seeing light coming through the snow between the old cedar logs, Matt scooped snow away. The light brightened as he dug. He punched and clawed at the rotten logs, making an opening the size of his hand. He could hear labored breathing and squirming.

"I don't have much time. Either push out your guns or you're on your own. Do it now," said Matt.

More squirming and muttered curses, then a gloved hand pushed a semiautomatic through the opening. After a few more seconds of movement and grunting, a second pistol came out. Matt put them in separate jacket pockets.

"Can you get the shovel out?" asked Matt.

"It's coming," Al replied. "Every time we use it, more stuff comes down."

"Help us." Ray hacked and gasped. "I'm stuck...from my waist down."

The entrenching tool eased through the opening. Matt took it and widened the opening. Ray and Al stared at him, with fear replacing toughness in their eyes. The shooting slit, eight inches tall and three feet wide, was two feet from the top of the blind. Matt could feel that snow and dirt had fallen past the opening. Moss-covered cedar logs formed the rest of the blind's north wall, now under a foot of snow. The steep slope didn't support a drift. Matt chopped at the rotting logs with the shovel. The old cedar, like wet paper, broke up easily. Using the tool's pick, Matt easily ripped out large pieces of log. He widened the opening to three, then four logs. He backed away and asked if Al could get out. Al wormed his way through the opening, falling into the snow of the steep north side. He then turned and tried to pull Ray. Ray was stuck.

"Stay here and help Ray," Matt warned. "I'll try to get some of the snow off and pry up on the metal. Don't do anything cute or you'll be wearing this shovel. And remember, I'm the only one that can get you out of these woods. You could end up a white, frozen coyote turd if you don't do what I tell you."

Matt worked to the top of the blind. From the original entrance he began to move snow, working for almost fifteen minutes. He took off his coat while he worked, but put the smallest pistol in his pants pocket—a lightweight Smith and Wesson short-barreled revolver—after confirming it was loaded. The light repeatedly cycled bright-dim-bright as the snowmobile's RPM varied. He needed to hurry. He hooked the pick under the edge of the corrugated steel roof and lifted. The metal hardly moved. He jammed the shovel under and pried up.

"He's coming out," Al shouted. "He's out!"

Matt grabbed his coat, ran back to the Polaris, and revved it up to steady the light. The two cold, wet, and nonbelligerent gangsters staggered down the broken trail toward him. Matt took out the semiautomatic Beretta, checked its breech for a shell, and flicked the safety off. He used the gun to motion toward the snowmobile and make sure they knew he had it. "Walk on the other side of the machine and go down the path. Stop when I tell you." With Al helping Ray, they slogged fifty feet down the trail.

"Stop there. Don't move while I turn the machine around."

Matt brought the machine down, around the slope, and back on his incoming track. The two gangsters stood on the track looking like deer in a car's headlights.

"Move on down the hill to the other machine," Matt ordered. "And start gathering dead limbs off the trees as you go."

Matt followed them. Twice, he stepped off the machine to strip loose bark from birch trees and fallen birch logs that stuck out of the snow.

Shivering, Ray and Al waited beside the other machine as he pulled up. He stopped twenty feet away and threw the shovel to them. "Dig a hole in the snow down to earth. Make it about four feet across. Stack the wood near the pit."

They did as they were told.

"Now, go sit on the snowmobile and don't move."

Matt moved into the pit they had dug. He laid several sticks down, put the birch bark on top of them and built a log cabin of sticks around it. After several layers he put the driest and smallest sticks across the top of the cabin structure. He lit the birch bark and watched as it flamed and caught the sticks on fire. Soon the whole structure was burning, producing the comforting crackle, light, and smell of a pinewood campfire.

"Gather more wood," Matt said. "Some larger limbs. They break off easily."

Ray and Al worked fast and soon had a large pile of wood near the fire.

"Good, start your machine and get it closer, over here by the fire. You'll need a dry place to sit," said Matt as he pointed the gun to where he wanted the machine.

They moved the machine and sat back on its seat, shivering with cold.

"I'm going to save your lives. But don't try anything while I'm helping you," said Matt. "I want you to get longer branches, put them across the edge of the pit in front of you. You'll need to put your feet on the logs while you dry your socks and shoes. Be careful you don't burn up your stuff.

Open your coats and start getting dry inside. You've got to dry out before you can bundle yourself up."

"Why don't we just get back to the cabin?" asked Ray.

Matt shook his head. "I've got to leave you here for the night. Give me your flashlight and lantern. The light's broken on your sled, and I wouldn't recommend trying to drive back without it. I'm going to make some false trails, so don't be stupid and get yourselves lost. Just stay put by the fire until dawn. Then you should be able to find the quarry by keeping the sun on the left side of your face."

Al said, "Webb will kill you if you don't give him the money."

"He may not be as tough as he thinks he is. And he's on my land." Matt held out a hand. "Now, give me the lights."

Matt took the lights, removed the batteries, and tossed them in different directions deep into darkness. He hopped on the Polaris and looked at the two men. "By the way, you don't have much gas. Another reason to stay put. Keep the fire going, stay awake, get dry, and this will be a great story at the bars."

With those words, he thumbed the throttle and drove south toward the cabin, then east on another logging road. Working back to the main trail, he circled the quarry to approach his cabin from the south.

17

Volcheff

MATT STOPPED HIS MACHINE behind the large cement structure that once housed the equipment for crushing limestone and loading it into freight cars. Only two large cement arches remained, fifty yards from the shop building. Matt checked his weapons. He carried the Beretta with a shell chambered and kept the Smith and Wesson in his right pocket. He kept the hammer down, instead of cocked, as his only concession to safety. The double-action Beretta would fire with a pull of the trigger.

Matt slowly came up the plowed road to the shop building. He moved right around the large building to the empty windows on the side nearest the cabin. The snow was deep but easy to move through. At the cabin, he climbed through the shop's old, open window. The cabin's light was still on. He didn't want another Volcheff surprise. He peered through the hole he had shot through the wall with the SIG. He couldn't see much, but did see Tanya doing dishes at the sink and talking to someone on her left. Matt couldn't hear what they said. He had four more people to locate. Matt moved slowly along three feet of space between the back wall of the shop building and the cabin. He circled around to the other side of the cabin, waiting several minutes in the dark, listening for sounds of movement or cars running or someone stomping his feet against the cold. The temperature hovered in the teens, making the snow squeaky. The Yukon, still parked across from the cabin door as he had left it, could easily and quickly head back through the main door. He slipped out another empty shop-building window and sidled around to the wall and window opposite the Yukon. He could see the gangsters' truck parked just outside the entrance, apparently unoccupied. The Yukon's windows, however, had fogged. Occupied recently or maybe still. He looked for tracks going to the vehicle, but he saw none on his side. He slithered along the outside of the huge building, watching for more tracks. Fresh tracks headed away from, but not toward, the vehicle.

Matt almost laughed. *Clever boy, Volcheff. Walking backward to the driver's door in my own footprints. Probably waiting for me right now in the back seat behind those tinted windows.*

Matt respected Volcheff. He came from some eastern European country where stalking and killing were more popular than American country-club golf scrambles, but without the handicap system. Anyone below par stopped aging.

Matt assumed Volcheff waited for the snowmobiles to return. A safety valve in case Matt had gotten the better of them and brought them back under the gun. Good thinking by a cunning opponent.

Had Volcheff found the Remington? Matt was sure Volcheff would appreciate a truly fine hunting weapon. He probably had also found the little .22.

Matt doubted Volcheff could have seen the snowmobile's lights as he came up the road. Not with the high banks and the cabin lights masking the glow off the snow that would have been visible in a darker situation. Matt had several options. He could just wait, always a fine option for the hunter. The impatient are often lunch in the animal world. He could sneak up on the Yukon, open a door...and most likely get shot in the face.

Bad idea. He would wait.

Webb had to be worried about his money-retrieval team, now more than an hour overdue. Webb would have his people on alert. Hurting Tanya without Matt's presence would not accomplish any of their objectives. She was no longer tied. Webb probably had only used her to get Matt's cooperation.

Matt studied the Yukon and its big mirrors. Volcheff no doubt had them adjusted so he could see behind him. Matt doubted anyone could see him moving around the outside of the shop building, but his tracks would give him away if they had a roving patrol. He would just wait until his prey moved. He eased to the window of the shop building closest to his Yukon and shuffled the snow around to give him some room to change position with minimal sound. He pulled his hood tighter, but kept it loose enough so he could hear. He was the hunter. They were his prey.

Matt felt the cold seeping into him when the Yukon's rear door opened. Volcheff got out. He stretched, waved his arms about, and stomped his feet. Obviously cold, too. Or he realized frosted windows gave him away or were too hard to see through. He looked around and headed for the dark corner and the door where he had ambushed Matt several hours ago. Matt knew Volcheff would see his tracks outside the huge building even in low light. Volcheff's steps crunched on the snow, louder as he approached the doorway. Matt moved quickly along the building, losing sight of Volcheff for only a few seconds. He stopped three feet from the doorway. He heard Volcheff approaching. Matt held the pistol in both hands as he knelt in the snow. Volcheff would have to be very, very quick to get off a first shot.

Volcheff's shadow fell across and through the doorway, lengthening as he came closer. Matt had forgotten to breathe. He forced a slow, controlled breath, hoping to slow his racing pulse. In through the mouth and out through the nose, slowly to stop any telltale cloud of moisture in his breath from alerting Volcheff.

Volcheff stepped through the door and turned away from Matt. He unzipped his fly, began to pee, and signed with relief.

Matt almost laughed. What a stupid way to give away your position. Most really serious hunters have a jar or bucket for this need. You don't move in and out of a blind during prime hunting hours.

Matt let this prey finish his business. When Volcheff crouched to zip his pants, Matt worried he might identify tracks as his eyes adjusted to the darkness outside the building.

"Don't move or you die," mimicked Matt, in a harsh whisper. He cocked the pistol too. In a whisper, he continued, "Let's go for a little walk. Stay in the path. If you stop, jump to one side, or reach into your coat, I'll shoot you full of holes."

Volcheff turned slightly to see Matt with the pistol pointed at him.

Enough light was coming from the cabin through the open doorways and window opening to give marginal light across the open area that led toward the cave. Volcheff voluntarily raised his hands.

Matt directed him to the cave door. The well-trampled snow made the going easy. Matt stayed carefully behind him. At the cave entrance, he commanded, "Open the door and step away from it."

Volcheff fumbled with the unfamiliar bolts but finally got the door open. Not wanting him to enter the dark cave, Matt said, "Step back more."

Volcheff took two steps back.

"Get on your stomach and spread your arms and legs."

Volcheff stiffened, as though ready to attack. Matt held the man's gaze and kept the pistol pointed solidly at his chest. Volcheff could never cover ten feet between them without taking several bullets.

Volcheff lay in the packed snow and held his arms and legs outward.

Trying to keep an eye on Volcheff, Matt entered the anteroom and turned on a Coleman lantern. He squinted at the sudden bright light. He carried the lantern outside and stood behind Volcheff. "Turn over and cross your ankles."

Volcheff turned over.

"Open your coat with your left hand, very slowly."

Volcheff obeyed, glaring at Matt. The gun in his belt was positioned for a right-hander, and he wore his watch on his left wrist. Right-handed.

Matt ordered, "Take out the gun with your left hand, use two fingers and just drop it in the snow." Holding the gun butt between his thumb and forefinger, Volcheff paused for a moment as though considering his options. Finally, he let it drop into the snow.

Matt then made him turn over again and stretch out. Matt retrieved the gun, another Beretta. Very cautiously, he patted Volcheff down at his ankles, back, neck, and sides. Although there were still places left to hide weapons, Matt didn't want to give Volcheff any chance to grab the gun or wrestle with him.

"We're going inside. Just believe that I'll shoot you for any quick moves."

With the lantern in one hand and gun in the other, Matt directed Volcheff down the stairs. Matt kept the light low to heighten the effect of darkness and strange surroundings. At the bottom, Matt first set the lamp on the table, then moved it to the floor, on the far side of the table from Volcheff. If the lamp was turned off or broken, the darkness would take some of the advantage away from the person with the gun. Matt found the masking tape they used to wrap the venison packages. He tossed it to Volcheff.

He said, "Put your feet together and wrap the tape around your ankles several times. Then hop over to the table and lie on it face down and put your hands behind you."

When Matt had taped Volcheff's wrists together, he said, "This is just masking tape, you can get out of it. But you can't do it quickly enough to keep from being shot. "Do you know how to light a Coleman lantern?"

"I grow up on them," Volcheff replied. "Many parts of my country without electric."

"Okay, here's what is going to happen. I'm going to leave you here for a time. I'll put another lantern at the top of the stairs. I'll leave some matches too. You can get out of the tape easily. Also, I know there are knives in the drawers. When I come back I'll want you down at the bottom of the stairs before I'll come in. Any tricks, and you'll have no future," said Matt.

"I freeze here or will air go?" asked Volcheff.

"It's forty degrees in here. You can stand it for a long time. Stay near the Coleman. There's water in the orange container. In any case, I'm being better to you than I believe you would be to me. The Coleman will make it smell some, but the air will stay good."

Matt started up the stairs, and then went back and checked Volcheff's pockets. He found the keys to their truck, a small but very impressive single-blade knife, a money clip thick with one hundred dollar bills, and a wallet with Illinois cards and licenses, including a concealed-carry permit. Matt took the keys, then opened the jackknife and jabbed it into the table near Volcheff's ear.

Volcheff jumped.

Halfway up the stairs, Matt said, "If you wreck anything in here, I'll take it out of your money clip."

The battery lantern showed a rather gruesome tableau in the cave room. From its position on the floor, it made a silhouette of Volcheff on the table and a pool of lighted limestone under him with the hanging hindquarters of the deer casting ghostly shadows on the rock wall.

Back in the anteroom, Matt picked up a white gas Coleman lantern with sufficient fuel and an intact mantle. He set it and a box of matches inside the metal door and swung the door closed, pushing the large welded bolt onto its welded fitting. He snapped a large master lock into the lock fitting and spun the dial. The combination was on the door in black permanent marker. All the lock had to do was stop a bear or badger, and they couldn't do numbers or combination locks.

In the dark anteroom, Matt felt for the wooden outer door and slowly opened it. He paused to let his eyes adjust to the dark.. He could faintly hear Volcheff banging around inside the cave. He studied the tracks outside the entrance, checking for any new tracks around the cave or between the cave and cabin.

He closed the wooden door and secured it with its outside wooden latch. He had taken two steps when a flashlight beam lanced out of the dark, probing the trail. He backed up the trail and hopped off it, crouching behind a five-foot-high boulder. He threw some snow on his last track and watched the light coming closer. The person was too big to be the driver and too small in the shoulders to be Webb. It was Webb's third gangster from Chicago. He intently followed the fresh tracks. Matt's Danner boots had "Bob" soles, 47 little rubber nubbins surrounded by an outer ring of rubber cleats. They gripped well, didn't hold too much dirt, and were fairly quiet and very comfortable. But, they left easy-to-follow prints.

The man tracked like a real rookie. He looked just at the tracks in front of him, concentrating so much on the immediate trail he never looked ahead. Matt remembered doing the same thing on Isle Royale—after hiking many miles he came upon a fresh set of large moose tracks that filled with water as he watched. His vision was as limited as his tired brain. After several yards of watching water filling the tracks, it finally dawned on him that a moose had to have been in those tracks not too long before. Finally he glanced up the trail and found himself eight feet away from the south side of a north-moving moose. Moose goosing can be bad for the health, but he'd learned an important tracking lesson about looking up any trail you are on.

Matt watched the spot of light edge closer. The man had a rifle, probably Matt's Remington. A bolt-action rifle against a semiautomatic pistol at close range is a mismatch. The pistol wielder could shoot five or six shots while the rifleman worked another shell into the chamber. However, even one hit from the Remington would be a very serious proposition.

Matt did what all good hunters do. He kept very still, very quiet, and waited behind his rock. He monitored his breathing, even breathed into a gloved left hand to reduce noise and breath condensation.

The man and the flashlight beam slowly moved closer, flashlight in his left hand and rifle in his right. He held the rifle at its point of balance, under the bolt and telescopic sight. A good way to carry it, but requiring extra time to get your finger on the trigger. The rifle had no iron sights so the shooter would need to find his prey in the scope, difficult at night at close range. Matt had to assume the man would shoot from the hip, gambling on a literal "luck of the draw." Some people can shoot a rifle very well instinctively, particularly if they had service or police training. Most hunters have never even tried a hip shot because it wastes expensive ammunition and marks them as idiots in the eyes of other hunters.

Now, the man played the beam farther ahead on the tracks. Matt ducked down to hide his white face. The bright beam on the snow beside Matt made his night vision dull for several seconds. He closed his eyes and waited for the man to go by him and let the light and the sparkling snow work to his advantage. He just hoped the man wouldn't pick up the slightly disturbed snow by the rock, or detect Matt's jumping off the path. With so many tracks at the cave entrance, it would take the man some time to sort them out.

The man passed Matt's rock and stopped at the cave door to examine the tracks, then smoothly brought his hand to the grip and his finger to the trigger.

Matt had waited too long, wanting to catch him with his finger off the trigger. Matt waited some more. The man looked at the tracks at the door but didn't try to follow any of them. The "Bob" sole tracks, appearing like a rash of dots in the snow, are hard to read. Volcheff's snow angel could be seen. The man set the flashlight on the snow bank, pointed at the door. He studied the tracks and the snow angel, apparently in no hurry. Minutes passed.

Bong. Bong. Bong. Volcheff testing the ship's door.

The man jumped back and snapped the rifle into hip-shot position as though he'd done it many times before. He was quick. The man didn't earn his job by being awkward. Matt watched the man slowly open the wooden latch on the outer door.

Thud. Thud. Thud. Volcheff ramming something into the door.

The man pushed the wooden door all the way in and stepped back, trying to understand what he was seeing. The old ship's door in a limestone wall must have seemed both incongruous and intriguing. The man kept his eyes on the metal door as he moved back to get the flashlight.

"Don't move a muscle or you'll be shot by your own Beretta," whispered Matt.

The man froze in the light of the flashlight.

"Slowly put the butt of the rifle in the snow bank. If you drop it or hurt it, I'll shoot you out of spite. Move!" ordered Matt.

The man put the rifle into the snow, butt down. The deep snow held the rifle upright.

"Step into the room and put your hands on the metal door," said Matt.

Reluctantly, the man stepped in and leaned against the door.

Matt retrieved his rifle and, using the leather sling, put it over his shoulder. Then he picked up the flashlight.

"Open and lift up your coat, I want to be sure you aren't carrying another weapon."

Slowly, the man complied. Matt kept his distance inside the anteroom. The banging had stopped.

"Move to the right and you'll see a combination lock. The numbers to use are on the door. Open the lock. And you might want to let Volcheff know you are doing it so he doesn't kill you."

The man worked the combination several times because of the dim light and his nervousness. When he had it open, and before he removed it from the hasp, he yelled, "Volcheff, it's me, I'm opening the door. Can you hear me?"

"Ya, I hear you." Volcheff yelled. "Did you get the asshole hunter?"

"No, he got me."

Matt said, "Tell Volcheff to go downstairs. We'll wait for him to get away from the door. Then open the door and go down the steps. The man yelled the instructions to Volcheff, waited a minute, then took off the lock and pulled the door open. Bright Coleman light shone on the landing. No sign of Volcheff. Matt moved to see past the gangster as the heavy door swung open.

18

Death on Burning Snow

A FLICKER OF LIGHT, NOT FROM THE COLEMAN, caught Matt's attention. Before he recognized it, a Molotov cocktail sailed up from the dark stairwell and smacked him in the chest. Unbroken, it fell to the hard packed snow. Had it broken, Matt would have become a human torch. The fuel drained onto the snow, a blazing pool at Matt's feet.

Thanks to his complete surprise, Matt had not fended off the projectile with the flashlight or the pistol in his hands. Either action could have broken the bottle in flight. Matt staggered backward as the flames spread at his feet.

Volcheff sprang from the door, teeth bared and eyes wild, clutching a filleting knife over his head, swinging the weapon down. Matt had no time to block or avoid the attack. Volcheff's white skull and face seemed suspended in the surrounding blackness of the cave entrance. The flames outside and bright Coleman light inside freeze-framed Volcheff as he passed through the doorway. The knife lanced into Matt's left shoulder. Flinching from the pain, Matt reflexively fired two shots. Volcheff and Matt, locked together by the implanted knife, tumbled into the snow and slammed against a boulder. Volcheff yanked the knife out and swung it toward Matt's neck as Matt fired three more times while warding off the thrust with his left arm. The knife raked Matt's arm as the force of the shots pushed Volcheff back.

Volcheff rolled away from the light, nearly invisible against a boulder. Silent. Unmoving.

Matt struggled to his feet, trying to ignore the pain in his shoulder, attention focused on Volcheff. The other man grabbed Matt's gun hand from behind and twisted it very professionally behind Matt's back. Matt turned away from the hammerlock and, fighting back the pain, swung his left elbow into the man's face with a solid impact. Matt's thick coat lessened the power of the blow, and the man kept control of his wrist and gun. Matt tossed his head back into the man's face, hard, sending the shock all the way to his own jaw.

Matt bridged against the attacker, trying to free his gun hand. The man grabbed Matt's coat and held on. Matt felt his left arm weakening from the knife wound, but shock and adrenaline dulled the pain. The man, no rookie street fighter, vised Matt's neck in a choke hold while maintaining the arm control. In this match, no out-of-bounds line or clock would stop the contest. Their heavy coats dampened the choke. Matt twisted into the hammerlock and straightened his arm slightly, then totally. The man put more faith in the choke hold, gave up on the arm bar, but kept Matt's right wrist in a solid grip. Matt thought of dropping the gun so he could use that hand, but couldn't risk his wrestling partner getting it.

Matt's twenty-five years as a wrestling competitor and coach kicked in. Other than his left arm, his muscles were still good and thousands of hours on the mat had honed his muscles and balance. His opponent had made two mistakes: giving up one good hold for a lesser hold, and moving into a "high" position that gave Matt better leverage. With the man still clamping the wrist of his gun hand, they pirouetted in the flaming snow. Matt worked further under the man, lifting him higher and higher as the man put more strength into the neck hold. Halfway through their second little dance spin, Matt seized the man's choking arm above the elbow, using what strength his left arm could muster, and leaned forward. The man's feet came off the ground, and he gave up the gun wrist for Matt's right shoulder to avoid being thrown forward, exactly what Matt hoped. Matt took two short steps to gain momentum and did a twisting lunge into the rock he had earlier hid behind.

Their combined weight crashed into the frozen limestone with the man's head and back hitting first. Matt heard a solid thud as when tapping a ripe melon, a sound that fills a coach with dread and makes mothers scream. Matt twisted and pushed the man off him. He backed away from the man, now a dark blob at the base of the rock, and held the gun on him. The fire had died to a few flames on the rag at the bottle's neck. The dropped flashlight amid the dwindling fire, still on. The Coleman shone brightly from the cave.

Matt picked up the five-cell. His wet wool glove steamed from the heat. He swung the beam at the man he had put into the rock. The man lay still. Matt swung the light to Volcheff. He had opened his eyes and moved up against the snow bank. He looked at Matt for several seconds then fell forward onto the path. Matt wasn't going near him, treating him like a shot deer that you wouldn't go up and kick. Hunters have acquired scars or ended up on the wrong side of a wake that way.

Matt watched both men. Neither moved. Matt elected to wait.

He picked up the Molotov bottle. An old Coke bottle with a green cast to it, made back when they made bottles to last. Who knew where it came from? Something warm ran down his chest and ribs, soaking his shirt.

Blood.

His stiffening left shoulder ached.

Matt's leg muscles started to shake. He had fought and killed two men. Unlike a movie or a play, they wouldn't get up for another take or come out for a curtain call. A matter of life and death and only he remained standing. He needed to stay focused on what he had to do—take care of Tanya and face Webb. He looked down, his gun hand shook, his mouth tasted like metal, and he felt sick to his stomach.

He looked at the Beretta. It still had shells in it. He couldn't remember how many it held or how many he had shot, but it was still locked, cocked, and loaded. The Beretta's stopping power hadn't impressed him. He had put two shots into Volcheff without even slowing him down. He had shot him at least several more times and rolled around with him before the shots seemed to have any effect.

Several more minutes passed and neither man moved or made a sound. Matt couldn't hear any breathing, but his ears still rang from the gunshots and the battering his head had taken on the other guy's face.

He squatted behind Volcheff and put an ungloved left finger on his neck. No pulse and no breathing. Matt waited another full minute to make sure. The knife partially showed under Volcheff, and he still had a firm grip on it. The man was a wolf alright.

The other man's head had smashed on the rock. Matt checked his pulse and breathing. He too was done dancing.

Matt realized that his nice, quiet land now had four dead people on it. Two by his hand. He would have to do some serious explaining when the cars with the lights on top arrived. Moral judgment about his actions could wait, but he knew they would come.

Sharp pain brought Matt back to the moment.

19

Playing With Pain

MATT PICKED UP THE RIFLE that had fallen off during the fight. Although he couldn't tell if the scope had been damaged, the rest of it seemed unhurt. His numbed brain suggested he should check for snow and ice in the barrel. He stepped into the anteroom and pushed the wooden door closed. A small hasp held the door closed from the inside. Downstairs, Volcheff had been busy in such a short time—using the big meat saw to saw off a large part of the stair railing for a lever or ram. He had used white gas from the Coleman for his firebomb. Matt resolved to keep his money as he had warned him.

Matt felt a little floaty as he descended the stairs, the missing railing making the stairs seem steeper. The Coleman, pistol, and rifle felt heavier with every step. He hung the Coleman on its regular ceiling hook, providing plenty of light. He took off his coat, checking the two rips made by the knife. The tough material had saved his arm from most of the slice, but the initial stab had done real damage to his shoulder and left his wool sweater blood soaked. It hurt like hell when he pulled it off over his head. He had to peel the black polypropylene undershirt away from the wounds before he could work it over his head, too.

Blood had started to coagulate around the deep cut, but removing the shirts had started it flowing again. The thin, razor-sharp blade had hit the collarbone and gone into the muscle. If it had gone below the bone, it would have gotten the heart or lungs or major arteries in the chest. Matt had missed dying by an inch and some instinctive reflexes.

Matt always carried a small pack of Kleenex in his back pocket, handy for many uses in the woods. In this case, it would help stop up a wound. He got some water and soap and used a wet paper towel to clean the blood off the wound, wincing with every wipe. The thin blade had gone straight in, leaving a small, almost surgical incision, but the slice on his arm bled steadily, not in spurts. The long, superficial slice ran from mid-biceps to mid-forearm. The blade must have entered his sleeve and raked down the arm as it was pulled and pushed away. He washed his arm too. He needed stitches, but masking tape would have to do for now. He held wet towels on both wounds as best he could while he looked for tape. The one he used on Volcheff was on the floor. He found a new roll in a drawer along with three Band-Aids. People frequently nicked their fingers when butchering meat.

He dried the area, stretched his arm on the table, put the Band-Aids on one side of the slice, and pushed the sides together, pushing the tape down on the other side. It made a difference, but blood still welled up along the cut. He used a folded paper towel as a bandage and wrapped masking tape to hold it on. He did five double wraps and then a running tape on down the entire wound. The shoulder wound hurt. Several muscles must have been cut. He could move his arm and shoulder, but they felt like very sore muscles. He hoped no nerves or ligaments had been cut. He put a third of the Kleenex pack on the shoulder and taped it into place. He wasn't sure the masking tape would hold. He turned his long-sleeved undershirt inside out and carefully put it back on, leaving the cuts and slices on the right side with the left side covering and protecting the bandaging. He did the same with his sweater. He couldn't do this trick with his coat, so he taped up the sleeve to stop the cold seeping in through the cut. He also placed a little tape over the comparatively small shoulder hole.

He drank several cups of water. He had not slept or eaten normally for twenty-four hours and didn't know if his light-headedness stemmed from shock, low blood sugar, adrenaline, wounds, loss of blood, or fear. Probably all of the above.

He checked the time—2:30 a.m., Tuesday morning. Could only thirteen hours have passed since he and Tanya had left for the meeting on Monday? Matt still shook from his adrenaline high. He knew this chemical rush would run out at some time, but for now it reduced his bleeding, made his muscles stronger, but used huge amounts of his body's energy. Eventually, he would face some payback for this survival gift from his distant animal past. He needed food, more water, and, most of all, rest—in a safe place. He would give a lot for a quart of the milk in the cabin's refrigerator. Tanya was in the cabin, but so were Webb and the little driver.

He had to deal with Tanya and Webb. They had probably heard the shots—two shots muffled by the coat but others in the open, echoing off the rock walls.

Thanks to Webb, Matt had lots of guns. He wondered if Webb also had a gun. He put Volcheff's Beretta into the drawer after taking out the chambered round and putting it in the magazine. Then he exchanged the full magazine with the partially used one from the other Beretta and dropped the partially loaded magazine in his pocket. He also had Ray's two-inch-barrel Smith and Wesson—so light it felt like a toy. Matt opened the cylinder—five .357 Magnum shells. Lots of power, but it would kick like somebody hit your hand with a ball bat. Matt pushed the ejector bar, and the shells fell onto the tabletop. He closed the cylinder and put the gun into his left jacket pocket. He wanted to see if the gun would cock and fire in his pocket.

His whole arm ached and had become very stiff. It felt better with support from the pocket when he put his hand in it.

Matt put his hand around the little gun and squeezed the trigger. He heard a solid click. He squeezed three more times and nothing caught on the pocket fabric. He brought the gun back out and reloaded it. His coat might go out in a blaze of glory if he had to shoot that gun in the pocket. He would send it to L.L. Bean and give them a good story.

He chambered a round in the Beretta and slipped it into his belt, ready for a right-handed draw. He would leave his nine-pound rifle tucked back under the staircase. He already had enough firepower.

Carrying the Coleman, he slowly climbed the steps. He closed the metal door, secured it with the bolt but didn't lock it. He turned off all the lights. He carried the five-cell in his right hand and the Beretta in his belt with his jacket unzipped, giving him easy access to the Berretta and more range of motion for the little revolver. He wouldn't freeze between the cave and the cabin. He didn't know what to expect, but he would stay patient. Matt waited in the dark room for a full minute while his eyes adjusted to the darkness. He saw spots for some time thanks to the painfully bright Coleman. His shoulder tightened with every heartbeat. His neck muscles stiffened, and his right eye twitched from the tic he usually got when very nervous or tired. He inhaled deeply three times, letting each breath out slowly and steeling himself for the challenges ahead.

Matt stood silently in the outside doorway to the anteroom for some time. The clean air smelled good after the sickening stench from the Coleman's fuel. Matt pulled in several good lungfuls of the cold morning air. The cabin lights brightened the dark night. Matt had to cross more than sixty yards to reach the cabin. He wondered if Tanya was asleep. Upstairs or down? Or would they be sitting in the living room waiting? Had the second guy come out on his own? He might have been the one awake, on watch for the snowmobiles to return.

The latter scenario could work to his advantage. He would give them a snowmobile returning. He would give them a story that Al dropped him off and wanted to go back to help Ray, who was stuck and hurt. Any story that would get Matt into the cabin and let him gain control would work. He would sneak back to the snowmobile and drive in noisily, right up to the cabin door, stop for a moment, and pull it away from the view of the door.

It was a plan.

Of course, Webb checking tracks or watching him move across the snow-covered quarry floor could mess it up. It could turn into a disaster if Al and Ray had made torches and worked their way back to the cabin. Or if Matt just passed out.

He stepped into the night without turning on the five-cell. Matt poked Volcheff again with the flashlight from behind. He stuck the five-cell into the snow and reached into Volcheff's pocket and took his money. He left one bill in the clip and pushed it back into his pocket. He jammed the wad of loose bills into his own pocket with the extra Beretta magazine. Unexpectedly, Matt felt no regret or pity for the dead man, remembering instead the evil he'd sensed while fighting with Volcheff. His dead, cooling body still seemed to emit malevolence.

Good riddance.

Matt picked up the flashlight, turned, and walked slowly away from the dead men.

The trip to his Polaris took nearly a half hour. Matt kept stopping and becoming part of any boulder or little shrub that had the ability to find enough dirt and was tough enough to grow up from a quarry floor. He made his tracks zigzag and got behind drifts and rocks that would break up any human symmetry Webb might be able to see from the cabin. He felt more tired than the trip warranted. He started the machine, glad the starter handle was on the right, although the effort still hurt his left shoulder. The contrast as the noise and light exploded into the previously quiet darkness shocked him. He was glad he had thought his plans out ahead of time, his thinking had already slowed, forcing him to concentrate to remember it.

Matt roared into the huge building and made a sweeping right turn by the cabin. The right turn used his left arm less. He let the sled idle for a few seconds before roaring twenty feet away, where he hit the kill button. He got off the sled and stood in front of the door with his hands behind his back, a movement that pulled on his painful shoulder. He looked into the cabin.

Webb walked up to the door, dressed but looking like he had been sleeping. He opened the door and asked, "What took you so long?"

"We got stuck going in and coming back."

"Where's Al and Ray?"

"Ray hit a tree and bent the sled up some. Al dropped me off. They should be right back."

"You got the money bag?"

"Ray's got it back there with the bad sled."

Matt stepped up to the door. No sign of Tanya inside. The driver slept on the couch with a blanket over him.

As Matt stepped into the room, Webb jumped at him, going for the gun that Matt stupidly exposed as he moved through the door with his hands behind his back. Matt moved back around the table and threw a chair into Webb's rushing path. Webb grabbed the heavy wooden kitchen chair by one leg and picked it up like it was a tennis racket. He held it like he was going to hit an overhead return, using Matt as a ball, then he stopped, looking at the Beretta pointed at his nose.

"I've already killed two of your men, including Volcheff," Matt whispered. "I have no problem killing you. I remember your slap. Back up and drop the chair."

Webb dropped the chair and backed away, pleading, "While you were gone, I promised Tanya I wouldn't kill you."

Matt smirked. *Big deal, who's got the guns here?*

"Matt!" Tanya stepped off the stairs into the room, wearing Matt's old T-shirt again. She came to Matt and kissed his cheek.

She smelled so good, and the kiss hit a wind-down switch for Matt. He suddenly felt very tired. Trying to sound authoritative, but feeling his energy getting lower every second, he told her, "Tie up Webb and the driver."

"No need for that," Webb said. "We can get along."

"Shut up! I'm very tired of people trying to hurt me. I need some food and some rest." He turned to Tanya. "Tie 'em up or I take 'em out and shoot them."

Tanya looked at Webb and then at Matt.

Webb moved to the easy chair and held up his hands. "Okay, but not too tight."

The driver wasn't all the way awake, but moved to a sitting position on the couch.

Tanya picked the same rope that had earlier restrained Matt and tied Webb's wrists.

Matt found some braided electrical wire and white athletic tape in a drawer and tossed them to Tanya.

"Do his ankles too. First the wire twisted together then the tape over it. It doesn't need to be tight, just so he can't walk. Just tie the driver where he is and cover him with a blanket."

When she had finished, she returned to Matt and leaned against him. He stuffed the Beretta back in his belt and looped his good right arm around her, pulling her close. She looked tired, but still lovely. Her warmth seemed to take away the guilt of killing and, more importantly, the killing hate Matt felt toward Webb.

Reluctantly letting her go, he walked over and checked Webb's bonds, then the driver's. He also searched them for any weapons. He wrapped the tape, meant for ankle wrap, around their ankles and wrists a few extra times.

Matt winced as he tried to shake off his coat. In an exhausted voice, he said, "Help me with my coat, please."

Tanya helped from behind Matt and, as Matt's left arm came out of the coat, she said, "You're hurt."

Matt took the coat with his right hand, not wanting her to comment on its extra weight due to the Smith and Wesson in its pocket. He hung the coat on its regular wall peg and locked the cabin door.

"Why did you do that?" asked Tanya

"Al and Ray are still out there. I left them by a campfire with no flashlights and a snow machine with no headlight. They should come in at first light unless they went to sleep and let the fire go out and froze to death. Or refused my advice and drove off in the dark and got lost." He turned to Webb. "Do you have any more guns? What about the shotgun that Volcheff had?"

Webb shrugged. "Beats me. Volcheff had it."

Matt walked to the door, unlocked it, and paused. "Tanya, would you make me some eggs and toast, and I could drink a whole jug of milk, I've got to check the Yukon."

"Sure. No problem."

Nodding, he unlocked the door and walked outside.

The Yukon had its keys in it, where Matt usually left them. The passenger seat was way forward. Matt could almost see Volcheff crouching in the back. The far rear door was open a crack, the dome lights set to stay off. Matt found the 12-gauge pump propped against the back of the forward-pushed seat. He closed the far door and checked for the little .22 in the back of the console drawer. Still there. A good spot for it. He then went to the pickup and quickly checked it for weapons, leaving it locked. He went to the truck bed and opened the tailgate. He couldn't see anything big or obvious in there in the dark. He closed the tailgate and headed back toward the cabin, stopping at the Yukon to put the shotgun under a blanket in the back after unloading the four 00 buckshot shells. The 12-gauge was a very powerful weapon. No class, no range, no accuracy, but very deadly at close range—like being shot by nine .30-caliber bullets all at once. Matt never knew anyone who hunted with buckshot. He had to get some sleep before his mind wandered too far. Matt locked the Yukon and went back to the cabin.

Tanya led him to the kitchen table. "I've got a lot of questions for you. But first, how bad are you hurt?"

"I'll live."

The smell of cooking made his mouth water. His stomach growled its approval. He enjoyed the T-shirt movement as Tanya wriggled the spatula into the right angle to lift out an egg. The bacon and toast smells completed a wonderful sight-and-sniff ensemble.

Matt grabbed the milk from the refrigerator and started to drink it from the half-gallon plastic jug but, wanting to show Tanya he was really quite civilized, poured a large glassful instead. He chugged the cool liquid in just a few seconds and refilled the glass. He set the jug on the table and collapsed into a chair.

"How did you get hurt?" asked Tanya as she filled a plate with eggs, bacon, and toast and placed it before Matt.

Between bites, Matt explained what had happened. "I saw Volcheff waiting in the Yukon. I got the drop on him when he went out to pee and locked him up in the cave. Then the other guy came out looking for Volcheff. and I grabbed him too. As I was putting him into the cave, Volcheff tossed me a firebomb and stabbed me. I shot him. Then I wrestled with the other guy while he tried to get my gun and strangle me. His head got smashed into a rock. Both of them are by the cave, dead."

Matt wolfed down the food and guzzled the remaining milk quickly.

Webb watched silently from the chair across the room.

Matt winced and tried to find a position that eased the pain in his shoulder. "I don't know what to do with your boys on the snowmobile. I don't feel strong enough to go get them. I think I'll leave them outside like bad dogs and let them cool off."

He turned to Tanya. "Any good with bandaging and dressing wounds?"

"I've had some training for my captain's license and diving certification. I'm good with coral scrapes and sea egg spines. I use lemon on everything."

"Maybe you can check me out," said Matt as he put the pistol on the table and started to remove his sweater. The stiffness and pain in his shoulder and his overall exhaustion threatened his mental and physical dexterity.

Tanya helped him out of the sweater and his undershirt. She shook her head, her lips pursed. "This isn't good, you need a doctor, stitches, and antibiotics."

"We have antibiotic salve in the bathroom medicine chest as well as sterile gauze packages and several kinds of tape. Take a look, and then we need to do some doctoring. If I need stitches, it'll have to wait."

Tanya sucked in her breath as she removed the bandage on the shoulder wound. Then she held his arm as she looked closely at the arm cut. "The arm's easy and should be okay with some salve and good bandaging. That puncture wound can become a problem. It can get infected, and who knows what's cut inside."

"Just raid the medicine chest and do the best you can."

Tanya went into the bathroom.

"What are you going to do with us?" asked Webb.

"I really don't know. Maybe you should think of some options that I can believe. I really didn't want to hurt, let alone kill, anyone. They didn't give me a chance to talk it over. You might as well sleep. We will wait for Ray and Al."

Tanya came back with her hands full of medical materials. She put it all on the table on the other side of Matt from the gun. She studied his injuries. He wanted to close his eyes and sleep. "The shoulder wound has stopped bleeding, I'm going to squeeze it a little to see what comes out."

She moved the shoulder and gently squeezed the wound. The shot of pain drove away Matt's building drowsiness.

Matt smelled her hair and the soap she had washed her hands with.

"It's oozing a little blood," Tanya reported. "But there can't be any big vessels involved. I'll use a little hydrogen peroxide to help clean it, apply some antibiotic salve, then bandage it. It's all we can do right now." When she had secured the bandage on his shoulder, she started on his arm. She soaked a cotton ball with hydrogen peroxide and wiped it along the slice. It fizzed up, in its normal painless and spectacular way. She used the salve and cleaned the sides of the wound with alcohol. Matt grunted as a bit of it ran into the wound. Tanya used the alcohol not only to clean but, more importantly, to dry the skin. She then bridged the cut with several pieces of the micro-pore tape. Matt was impressed with how she brought the wound together and held it with the tape. She worked quickly. Soon, she had the bandage on and a gauze wrap over the entire wound. The shoulder had an X of half-inch tape over a small, neat bandage.

"We'll have to watch for infection or nerve damage," Tanya said, picking up the debris. "Do you want something for pain?"

He shook his head, knowing he couldn't keep his eyes open much longer. "I think I can get to sleep if I can count on you to watch Webb and wake me when the campers come in."

"Sure. Now, go on up and get some sleep."

Matt eased out of the chair, feeling woozy and unsteady. "I'll set the clock for 7:00 a.m. I don't think Al or Ray would make a move before then. That'll give me a few hours sleep." He put the Beretta in his belt, locked the door, and—for good measure—wedged a chair under the doorknob. He put some forks and knives on a plate and balanced it on the chair. He then picked up his coat and headed for the stairs.

"I'll help tuck you in," said Tanya with a little smile.

Matt shuffled up the steps into the bunk area. He stopped at the bed he and Tanya had shared for four wonderful days and nights.

"Do you want help with your boots?" she asked.

"No," he replied, pointing at the dresser. "Just get me a new long-sleeved undershirt from that drawer."

He threw his coat on the top of the closest bunk bed and an old army blanket on his bunk where his boots would rest. He set his alarm for 7:00 a.m., an hour and a half later than his normal hunting setting.

Tanya found a clean white undershirt and helped Matt into it. Matt got on the bed and rolled onto his back. He would have preferred to remove the boots but didn't want to slow down his response if he had to act fast.

Tanya helped arrange his pillows and leaned over him. She kissed him softly and cupped her hands around his face. Matt touched her side with his right arm. He started to bring his left arm around, but a twinge of pain warned him to leave it at his side. He smelled her scent and wanted her beside him.

She stood up. "Get some sleep. I'll make coffee and keep the watch."

Matt started to say something manly, but his eyelids drooped as he fell into a deep sleep.

20

Betrayed

MATT HAD A WONDERFUL SLEEP, dreaming of Tanya. He hadn't had dreams about a woman for a long time. He wanted to keep sleeping, but his aching shoulder made him aware of his bed and how quiet everything was.

He had a feeling that it was later than his dawn alarm setting. No expected glow from the Seth Thomas clock's face. Despite the light coming up the stairs, he couldn't read the time. He reached for the clock and felt the stem of the alarm still out. He picked up the clock. The plug dangled from the end of the cord. He looked closely at the clock face. Its hands showed 5:15.

A small window at the far end of the bunk room showed strong light coming through the edges around the closed blinds. He had seriously overslept.

His coat was not on the bunk where he distinctly remembered leaving it. He felt under the pillows for the SIG. Gone. He looked over the edge of the bed in case he had pushed it out of the bed. Nothing but a few mating dust bunnies.

Apprehension swept over him like a cold shower. He got out of bed. His weight made the plywood floor creak. He grabbed his sweater and slipped into it. As his face came through the neck of the sweater, a change in the light from the stairs caught his eye just as Webb's short-cropped hair appeared at the top of the stairwell.

"Good morning, Mr. Hunter, you're just in time for a little brunch." Webb smirked and motioned Matt to precede him down to the main room. The SIG's butt poked out of Webb's belt. Webb's face creased in a wide, friendly grin that confused Matt more that anything.

"What's going on? Where's Tanya?" asked Matt.

"She's playing short-order cook right now."

Matt slowly moved down the steps. He used the left-side railing, and his left arm and shoulder confirmed the reality of the last few days.

The scene in the kitchen looked like any deer camp. Al, Ray, and the driver, hunched over their food, looked up but said nothing. Al and Ray didn't look too bad for spending a winter night in the north woods.

Webb pulled out a chair for Matt. Matt sat and looked at Tanya's back as she worked at cooking breakfast.

When she placed his breakfast in front of him, she couldn't look him in the eyes but turned to get a cup of coffee.

"How is your shoulder?" she asked, setting the cup beside him.

"It's sore and stiff, but I can move it," said Matt. "What in hell have you done?"

"I made a deal with Webb." Her eyes pleaded with him. "He'll explain it. Just eat your breakfast and listen."

She nodded at Webb to give his explanation.

"Tanya is a reasonable person. She knew that making me a prisoner or killing me would not be good business. I've already made phone calls that got her parents off the hook. We'll leave them alone, and they will have most of their notes marked paid by the end of the day. They will own a good business free and clear with no strings attached. We even worked out the tax implications of them paying off the boats. We have an explainable paper trail for their profits and reinvestment. We will have nothing to do with them in the future. I gave my word and my instructions on the agreement."

"I'm happy for them," Matt mumbled. "What are you going to do now?"

"Now, we get out of here. We found the gym bag hanging on a rack so we know you have all the money hidden—fine, keep it, payment for not involving us in anything—how does that sound?"

"It sounds fine, but what about Volcheff and the other guy?"

"We wrap them up in something and take them with us." Webb placed his palms on the table and leaned close to Matt's face. "We have places we can put them. I'd like to give Ivan a good burial, but for now, the plane needs a pilot and a passenger. Maybe later we can do something with him."

"What about Tanya?" asked Matt.

"She goes with me. We need her…for some business in Chicago and Detroit. Then she can go back to Florida." Webb paused. "That's the deal: helping her parents, your good health, a clean-up job, and you get money. What do you say?"

"Let me think just a little," said Matt. He looked at Al and Ray, who avoided eye contact. Not a good sign. "How'd you like your night in the woods?"

Al glanced up, then turned his attention back to his plate. "It was okay. We got dried out like you told us. We stayed warm; heard wolves howling and saw deer walking right down the trail."

"We saw a hawk get a rabbit too," said Ray, with more boy-like enthusiasm than a good gangster should show.

"Anyway, it wasn't so bad and we got back with no trouble," mumbled Al between bites.

Ray held out his right hand. "Thanks for pulling us out of the dirt. That was a bad situation."

Matt shook his head, trying to decipher the undercurrents.

Webb sipped the hot coffee thoughtfully, then said, "Okay let's clean up and get out of here." He put the coffee cup on the counter and turned to Al and Ray. "Get something to wrap up two bodies and put them in the truck along with the coke. Then get the truck out of here as soon as possible. Mouse will drive Tanya and me in the limo. Ditch the bodies and drop the bags at the garage on McNichol's Road. Call me on a pay phone at my Chicago number when you're done. Say you'll be late for our afternoon meeting. You got that? The Chicago number, you'll be late for the afternoon meeting."

Al and Ray nodded.

Webb turned to the driver. "Mouse, go down the road and get the Lincoln, back it up by the truck and let it warm up."

Matt watched as Al and Ray pushed back from the table, then said, "I can help. I've got plastic tarps and ropes outside."

Webb held Matt's gaze for several seconds without blinking. He shrugged. "No tricks or you'll get hurt."

He looked at Al and Ray. "Let him help, but remember how he took you guys before."

Matt got his coat, lighter without the pistol. He snatched another hat from the rack, a blaze-orange number someone had left. Too tacky to take home, it featured a drawing of two deer screwing and said, "The Buck Stops Here." Better than no hat.

Outside, Matt noted the weather was warmer but still overcast. They hadn't seen the sun for several days. The snow was packing down—four-foot drifts now two feet, more of a problem for driving. It felt like snow again soon.

Matt gave Al and Ray the tarps and ropes and led the way to the cave.

"How did you take Volcheff?" asked Al as they walked.

"I surprised him outside the building and put him in this cave we use for a cold locker. Then I got the drop on the other guy—what was his name?" asked Matt.

"He was Mel something; I only met him when we got up here. He was Webb's muscleman from Chicago. He and Volcheff were real close. They were bad news. I never would have thought you could have taken one of them, let alone both. You were either real lucky or you're real tough," said Al.

"Go on with the story," said Ray, getting closer behind Matt and Al.

"Well, I locked up Volcheff in the cave. I got the drop on Mel and took my—his rifle away, then as I had Mel opening the cave door, Volcheff threw a burning bottle of white gas at me and jumped me right after he threw it. He had a knife and got me in the shoulder. I shot him a lot of times before he died. Then Mel jumped me from behind and tried to break my arm and choke me out."

"Mel had been a Chicago city cop, they like choke holds," added Ray.

"We wrestled around for a time and I threw him into a rock. I didn't want to kill anyone. It just happened fast," finished Matt, thinking he sounded like any hunter telling an adventure. He wondered if he was still in shock.

At the cave entrance, frost covered the flesh on both bodies. Volcheff looked liked a rolled up road kill, and Mel looked asleep up against the rock. Canine tracks, probably from coyotes, circled the bodies. They had sniffed but had not started chewing on anything.

"Shit," said Al.

Al and Ray went to work. They were a good team and seemed to have done such work before. Mel was hard to wrap up because he was all spread out. But the plastic tarps were big and the ropes soon made a misshapen bundle out of Mel. Volcheff rolled into a bundle easily, once the knife was pried out of his frozen fist. "We can go through their pockets and remove information later. Hell, they'll probably wind up in a foundation or cremated." said Ray.

Al gave him a warning look like he was talking too much. "Let's just get this job done."

Deciding that it would take too long to get a snowmobile, they chose to manually skid the two plastic bundles across the snow-covered flat area. They had just closed the truck's tailgate on the bodies when a pickup truck bounced up the road and honked.

21

Tanya Leaves

THE VISITORS WERE THE LAMOREAUX BROTHERS in their red Dodge diesel pickup sounding like someone stirring stones in a steel drum as they pulled up. Matt appreciated the silence when Dick turned off the engine.

"Eh Matt, how's it goin'?" Dick Lamoreaux asked, leaning out the open window, "I see you're wearin' the hat my wife won't let me have at home."

Matt briefly doffed the hat and nodded.

Billy Lamoreaux leaned across from the passenger side. "We came to chop up the little doe we had hangin'."

"Hi, boys," Matt said, pointing at the two gangsters. "Meet Ray and Al. They're from Detroit and both got deer this weekend, nice-sized does. We just packed them up in their truck. They were about to leave."

Dick swung open the door and hopped out, handing Matt a can of Budweiser.

Billy slid out the other side and held out a can of beer in each hand to Al and Ray. "You better have some beers for the road then. Draggin' deer is hot work."

Billy pointed at the drag tracks from Mel's body in the snow. "That one looks good size."

"You got lights?" Dick asked. "We passed a couple of U.P. Power trucks. They were working on the lines."

"We're fine," Matt replied. "Just some flickers during the storm, but it never went out."

"I'm sorry for not putting the sleigh back," Billy said. "I got it unhooked to turn around. There wasn't much snow when I brought in the deer. It got dark by the time I got the deer downstairs and hung up. When I got back on the sled, I forgot about rehookin' the sleigh. You get it back okay?"

"Sure, no problem. Listen, I got to tell you I used up most of the deer you had hanging. We've been eating on it for five days. There isn't enough left to make a good stew. I owe you a deer. I hope you weren't counting too much on the meat."

"Hell no," Dick said. "We didn't even want to work on it today, but we figured we had to get it cut up. I got called back to work at Munising so I'm done hunting. Billy just came along to help me wrap deer and drink beer."

Tanya, looking gorgeous, came around the truck. She smiled and said, "Hello."

Dick and Billy scanned her, glanced at each other, then grinned at Matt.

Matt ignored their looks and said, "Tanya, I want you to meet two of my wildest cousins, Dick and Billy Lamoreaux. They provided the deer meat we've been eating. Boys, this is Tanya. She came up for Thanksgiving with Al and Ray."

Dick eyed her from head to toe and back again. "For sure, it's good to meet you. Want a beer?"

"Thanks, but I better not," Tanya replied, appearing amused at Dick's attitude. "We have to be on the road for a long drive and I don't want to call a stop before we get over the bridge."

Al and Ray relaxed and drank their beers. They looked relieved that the Lamoreaux boys seemed to accept the story so easily and were happy to look at Tanya and not the "deer" in the truck.

Matt said, "I'd invite you in, but they're just packing up and cleaning the cabin. I may be going for a few days too."

"No sweat, we can catch you later. Nice meeting you guys, glad you had a good hunt. Don't let the meat get warm." Dick again turned his full attention to Tanya, reached out, and shook her hand. "Nice meeting you too."

Dick climbed back into the truck, started the rocks in a barrel sounds again. Billy slipped back into the passenger's seat and slammed the door, rocking the big truck. He toasted the group with his beer as Dick turned around in the plowed area and drove away.

Matt took a long drink of his beer. It tasted wonderful. Beer at noon is almost as good as beer at breakfast. He looked at Al and Ray. "That was close. Two minutes sooner and we'd have had real questions to answer.

Good thing Tanya came out and took their minds off the deer. They know what a deer drag looks like and those aren't right. They're way too deep. We were lucky."

With a smile that indicated she had known exactly what she was doing when making her appearance, Tanya said, "We should get out of here before more people come by. Let's load the cocaine and get on the road."

Inside the cabin, Webb had the satellite phone to his ear, finishing up as they entered. He closed it and looked up. "What was going on out there?"

Al replied, "Two of his relatives came by. He got rid of them real smooth. I don't think they suspected anything."

Webb nodded. "They're expecting you at the garage and will take the bundles in the truck."

"We should get out of here before any more people come by," said Tanya.

"Yeah, load up the truck. Then I want to talk to you guys alone." Webb put the phone into Ivan's briefcase. He considered Matt and Tanya for a moment. "You two can say goodbye outside."

He pointed at the two heavy bags. Al and Ray carried them out. He pointed at the two small bags, and Mouse struggled out the door with them. Matt took one of the bags to help the little man. Tanya followed them outside.

Matt and Mouse dropped the bags by the pile of bags at the truck's open tailgate. Mouse went to the Lincoln and started it, then popped the trunk lid. He then went back to the cabin with Al and Ray to get the rest of their things.

Tanya came to Matt and hugged him, whispering in his ear, "Trust me and love me."

They kissed, and Tanya held herself tightly against him.

Matt tasted her, felt her, and smelled her. He wanted to totally focus on her, to give himself up to her, to think about nothing else. He wanted to talk to her, make plans with her, to be in love with her. But he couldn't let himself go. He felt a sad control coming back into his mind and body as she pulled away

"Why are you going?" asked Matt.

"I think I know what I'm doing. Trust me."

"What are you going to do?"

"Don't worry. Why not come to Florida for Christmas?" She gave him another kiss and hug and turned away.

Al and Ray came out.

Ray looked at Matt and jerked a thumb toward the cabin. "Webb wants to talk to you."

Matt returned to the cabin with Al and Ray following. Tanya remained standing by the truck.

Webb stared unblinking at Matt for a few seconds. "If you can keep your mouth shut, you can come out of this with some money and a longer life."

He turned away, transferring some socks, underwear, and his leather toilette kit from his large carryall to the old gym bag, and left. Mouse trailed behind him carrying the last of the luggage.

"Webb really wanted to ice you," said Al, pulling out his Berretta. "Ray and I said it was a bad idea. Your cousins have seen us. You are involved and should keep your mouth shut. And you could have done us in but you didn't. So, consider we're grateful. Tanya did a good job convincing Webb you'd keep quiet."

"So then what's with the pistol?" Matt asked.

"Don't sweat it," Al replied. "We need to tie you up or something so you can't contact anyone for a few hours."

He turned to Ray. "Find some rope."

Matt turned his head to watch Al move around the room. He felt a movement behind him and got hit on the side of his head. Stars flashed just before the floor rose up.

Then everything went black.

22

Alone

MATT WOKE ON THE COUCH, tied hand and foot. His chin, nose, and the right side of his head hurt. For some time, he lay still trying to recall why he was at the cabin. His own drool had soaked the pillow under his head. He couldn't tell what time it was.

Then he remembered Al and Ray. Ray must have whacked him from behind. So much for thinking Al was the mean one. Ray took him out with one hit, probably from the butt of the Smith and Wesson. They had put him on the couch. Nice touch. He would like to return the favor. He had never been knocked out before. His head throbbed, and his guts threatened to heave. His slobber stank of stale beer. He hoped to avoid throwing up on the couch—he liked it, and it would be hard to clean.

Slowly, painfully, Matt turned onto his right side then worked himself to a sitting position. His hands were well tied, but his feet were tied with slack between them—allowing him just enough movement to baby-step to the kitchen in search of something sharp to cut the ropes. Matt struggled to stand, but his shoulder hurt like hell if he tried to use his left arm even a little. Finally, he got to his feet.

The room swam, his muscles trembled, he fell backwards onto the couch. Better than fighting the vertigo and possibly falling forward onto the coffee table or the floor. He scrunched his eyes shut, fighting back the nausea and dizziness. After a bit, he tried again to stand but changed his mind. Instead, he rolled off the couch onto his knees. He felt safer being low, another wrestling thing. He knee-walked his way to the kitchen area. He pulled out a drawer with his teeth, dumping the contents so he could isolate a carving knife. He rolled onto the pile of utensils and grasped the knife. He first cut the rope between his legs, allowing him to spread his legs for better balance. He worked slowly on the wrist ropes. The good news was that the dull knife didn't slice his wrists. The bad news was it took time to saw through the relatively soft clothesline rope.

Matt made up an ice pack from a ziplock bag, cubes from the freezer, and a dish towel. He mentally thanked Tanya for filling the trays. He applied the ice to his face and temple. The many random thoughts tumbling through his hurting mind included replays of the three-time heavyweight Olympic boxing champion from Cuba, Teofilo Stevenson, who would hit his opponent in the temple, not on the jaw. He had lots of knockouts and, now, Matt understood why. Matt still felt sick and pain radiated from five or six places. Next, he thought of a friend, a Marine Scout in Vietnam, who claimed "pain is just weakness trying to get out."

Matt felt he was losing a lot of weakness right now.

Late afternoon—by the wall clock, the gangsters had their several hours. He was alive and Tanya was gone—and he couldn't remember if deer gun season was over today or tomorrow.

23

The Law

MATT GUZZLED THE SECOND HALF-GALLON of milk he had bought in St. Ignace, washing down two aspirin and one Vicoden. He didn't care about thinning his blood, just wanting the pounding in his head and the pain in his shoulder to go away.

Standing in the open cabin door, he observed small flakes drift through the late afternoon air. His Yukon looked okay. He walked to it and found the keys in the ignition. He started it, satisfied that he could drive away. The little Beretta remained hidden in the back of the pullout drawer behind the console. But they had taken their shotgun and the rifle case was empty. He felt sick.

Those bastards took my rifle...

Matt shut the car off and checked the engine area just for fun. No cut hoses. No bombs either, good thing, he had started it without checking. He felt dumb. Blankly staring at the engine, he heard the powerful motors of several vehicles coming down the quarry drive and up to the shop building.

Just what he didn't want in his weakened condition: The Law.

Seeing three vehicles, he wondered, *Do these people always travel in packs? Are they going to yell at me?*

At least they parked outside the building. A pack of five formed and came toward him. He put the Yukon's heavy hood down—a fine, solid shutting sound. Matt liked the sound. He turned and took some deep breaths.

"Mr. Matthew Hunter?" asked a man in a dark topcoat. He was flanked by two clones and two state police in Smoky Bear hats and gray-blue winter jackets. The State Policemen looked like they could be his students. The two clones, wearing topcoats, looked like undercover agents working in a bank or J. C. Penney's men's department.

"Yes, I'm Hunter," said Matt.

"Are you hurt?" asked clone number one.

"Yes, I'm hurt," answered Matt.

"Do you need medical attention?" asked the original.

"Why are you here?" asked Matt.

"We have been advised you were in trouble," said clone one.

"Who told you that?" asked Matt.

"That's not important, do you need help?" answered the original.

"It is important to me to know how you knew to come here," said Matt.

"We can't tell you that," snarled clone two authoritatively.

Matt snorted. "I've been beaten, firebombed, stabbed, sliced, knocked unconscious, tied up, threatened with various forms of death…and I didn't fill my doe permit."

"You've got until tomorrow for rifle season," offered a blond trooper. "But black powder goes for ten more days."

Matt liked him and forced a shaky smile. He looked liked a kid who used to wrestle for Ishpeming.

"Can we take you to a doctor?" said original for the clones.

"If you can drive me in my vehicle. I'd appreciate it," said Matt.

"Can we look around?" asked clone two.

Matt stared into the man's flinty eyes. "No, I don't want people wandering around my place without me here."

"We can get a warrant," said clone two.

"Well then, get a warrant."

The clones exchanged glances with the original, who shrugged.

Matt continued, "I'll just hang around until I can get a friend here to keep an eye on you. I don't like people going through my stuff."

"Hiding something?" the original asked.

Matt ignored him and asked the blond trooper, "Do you have a cell phone that works from here?"

"Our radio can get to a phone, sir," said the blond trooper.

The "sir" made Matt feel old. "Call Leon Johnson in Garnet and let me talk to him."

Matt walked towards the cars. The radio in the State Police Jeep quickly transferred to a landline, and Matt gave them Leon's number. Leon answered.

"Leon, this is Matt. Do you have some time to babysit my camp for several hours, maybe even overnight? I've got some law people here who may want to look around. I need to go to a hospital for a few stitches, and I don't want strangers rummaging."

"Give me fifteen minutes," Leon replied. "But what the hell's—"

"Just get here," Matt cut off the torrent of questions he knew would follow. "Thanks, Leon."

This was big gossip stuff, and Leon loved to be the first at the bar with the facts, or, if not facts, at least the first "he said, she said..."

Matt handed the mike back to the trooper. "Let's go inside until Leon gets here. Inside...means you are guests, not a search party. I want every right the Fourth Amendment gives me."

They all moved into the cabin and took off their coats. The clones all had dark gray wool, three-button suits, even the same ankle-height shoes. The troopers checked out the antlers and old pictures.

"Will you tell us what's been going on?" said the original of the clones.

"Maybe. After I see your IDs."

The clones all produced DEA identification cards—Edward, Stanley, and Frank.

"I've been held prisoner by drug dealers. I fought with them and was almost killed by a firebomb, a knife attack, and a stranglehold. I was just knocked out and left tied up for several hours while they got away."

"Can you describe these people?" asked Edward.

"If I help you, I'll be killed and so will other people."

"We can assure you you'll be safe," said Frank.

Matt looked at each of them in turn. Their faces said they all knew that Frank was full of shit. "Let's talk after I get fixed up and can think better. I'm really tired and hurting."

Edward said, "Yeah, you don't look too good, Mr. Hunter."

"I'll live," Matt replied. "If you want something to drink there is juice and beer in the refrigerator. I can make coffee."

Trooper number two—older, maybe twenty-five—motioned him to sit down. He looked fit, moving like an athlete. "I can make coffee, you sit down. Do you want some juice?"

"Sure." Matt eased into a chair at the table. He felt very tired, and his head pounded painfully with every heartbeat.

The trooper got Matt a glass of orange juice from the refrigerator and found the coffee and filters without being told where they were. He started to use tap water to fill the coffee maker.

Matt started to say something, then thought, *Good enough for you.*

Then the trooper switched to the gallon of bottled water on the counter. No dummies, these troopers. He asked Matt, "Do you want some coffee too?"

"No, thank you, but help yourselves," Matt replied. "There are some cookies and donuts in the cupboard."

The trooper set the box of cookies and the unopened donut package on the table and asked, "You own this place?"

"Yes, originally it was bought by my grandfather in the '30s. It was a quarry," Matt babbled. He wanted to talk but knew he shouldn't. You can't keep a tight story if you ramble on. Yet on he went. "I own most of the forties that aren't national forest for a mile or so around here."

Shut up, dummy, he reminded himself.

Edward picked up a cookie but didn't eat it. "Could I see your driver's license?"

Matt said nothing but took out his wallet and handed him the license. A lot of Volcheff's money was in the wallet, but no one seemed to pay any attention to the wallet.

"You live in Gladstone?" asked Stanley, looking over Edward's shoulder.

"Yes, and at the address shown on the license."

"So," Frank frowned for a moment. "How did you get involved with drug dealers?"

"They followed me here from St. Ignace. And that's the last question I'm going to answer until I get some medical help and some rest."

The blond trooper said, "You said you had been stabbed. Where?"

"In the left shoulder," Matt replied. "It needs cleaning out and stitches, and I probably need antibiotics too."

"If you can describe them, we could get them before they get out of the U.P.," said the kitchen trooper.

"They're long gone. I was out several hours. They're already across the bridge or maybe even across the Sault into Canada. If I thought you could catch them, I would tell you." *So much for my vow of stony silence.*

The orange juice seemed to revive him some. Even his headache was going away. However, his shoulder hurt more and throbbed incessantly. *Infected?* he wondered.

While Matt watched the DEA people look around and the troopers set themselves up with coffee and donuts, he heard the door of Leon's truck slam.

Leon rushed through the door and stopped, scanning the assembled officers. After cursory introductions, Leon asked Matt, "What's going on here? And who beat the shit out of you?"

"It's a long story," Matt replied. "Bad people, drug dealers, beat me up. I need to get to a doctor. One of these men is going to drive me to St. Ignace to the clinic."

"You okay?" Leon asked, looking concerned.

"I'll be fine. But I need you to watch the place. I've not given my permission for them to search the place. There's nothing illegal here and I have nothing to hide, but I don't like people searching through my stuff. If they get a warrant, we can't stop them. But I want you to list anything they take or touch. If they bring a lot more people, call for help—cousins or my aunts."

"Easy, sir," Edward interrupted. "We aren't here to hassle you. Believe us when I say we're here to help you out of a bad situation."

"That may be so, but right now I need to get medical help and some rest."

"We can drive him in our car," said Stanley. "Let the State Police get back to their work."

Edward nodded. "That would be best. And we can talk to you on the way back. You shouldn't be driving back anyway. If they keep you overnight, we'll just stay in town and wait for you. We have a lot of stuff to talk over."

He sounded very official, but certainly not hostile.

"I guess that's the best thing," Matt agreed. "I'm hurting too much to argue. Let's go."

"We'll follow you back to St. Ignace," the blond trooper said. "The roads aren't really great yet, and there're some good-sized drifts and holes on the road getting to the highway."

"Watch the place for me, please," said Matt to Leon. "I'll get back as soon as I can. And thanks."

"No sweat, Matt."

"We can all fit in the Suburban," said Frank. "And you won't have to worry we will go through your place."

"Are we treating this as a crime scene?" asked the older trooper.

"Not yet," Edward replied. "But we are interested in what went on, more than isolating prints. I don't think we'll need warrants, if we can get a little conversation with Mr. Hunter."

Leon took this all in, looking visibly relieved. He asked, "You still need me?"

"I guess not. I was worried about people tearing the place up," said Matt. He turned to Edward. "I have your word that no one will be searching through my place until I get back?"

Edward nodded. "You have our word. But could you lock it up until we get back. We'll explain what we are looking for when we drive in, if you're up to it."

The troopers each took a donut and headed for their vehicle. Matt caught their looks at the DEA men and between themselves. They knew the DEA hadn't told them everything, and Matt knew there was a lot they hadn't told him.

The blond trooper opened the door, careful to keep the white powder from the donut on his finger off the floor and off his dark uniform. "Take care of yourself, sir, and good luck."

24

Medical Help

LEON, WITH HIS COAT STILL ON, followed the State Troopers out of the cabin. He didn't understand all that was going on but knew the answers would come in their own time, and he already had enough news to accompany two or three beers at any local bar. His started his powerful Ford diesel truck and sprinted away. The State Police Jeep had already gone. Soon, silence again enveloped the quarry.

The three DEA officers helped Matt into their vehicle's front passenger seat. Frank drove and did an expert job of negotiating the snowy and narrow road. When they hit bumps he slowed and even said "sorry" as Matt painfully bounced against the passenger's door.

They didn't say anything for some time. Matt's pain increased as they drove.

Finally, Edward broke the silence. "Where is the plane?"

Matt was nearly nodding off with only pain that throbbed in unison with his heartbeats keeping him awake. But, when he heard the word "plane," he snapped awake on full adrenaline alert. In a voice he hoped sounded calm, he asked, "What are you talking about?"

Frank shot a sideways glance at him. "We're talking about a plane that crashed and has several bodies in it."

"We can help you and you can help us, if you can trust us just a little," said Edward. "We didn't want your neighbor involved. We want the plane and everything about it to be our secret. We'd like to have it off your place with no one around here but you knowing about it. It's important that you trust us. We looked stupid in front of the State Police, but we don't want them involved. We're playing for some big stakes on this deal. The information we can get from you will help us. In exchange, we will clean up all the mess that happened here. All you need to do is be honest with us and keep your mouth shut afterwards."

"I don't know…"

"Ease up on the guy, Ed," Frank offered. "The man's hurting."

"You're right." Edward turned to Matt and said, "We can wait until you're fixed up. I just wanted you to know we aren't the bad guys, and you don't need to be afraid of us."

Stanley broke in, "You're lucky as hell to be alive, Hunter. You were messing with some big-league bad guys. We've been working for many years to get something on them. They control and have knowledge of most of the drugs and smuggling activities in this hemisphere."

They drove in silence the rest of the way into St. Ignace.

They entered the clinic's emergency entrance, no other patients visible. Six caregivers in various rooms and behind various counters looked up as Matt entered with his escort of three men in official-looking dark overcoats. The momentum of all this officialdom broke like an ocean wave on the rocks of medical paperwork. A young, plump medical aid girl ushered Matt into a small office and, very patiently and thoroughly, explained all the information they needed before anyone would even think of helping a person who had survived a knife attack and had been knocked unconscious by underworld gangster types from Detroit. Matt had gotten home loans with less forms and exchange of personal information. The girl didn't even bat an eye or seem really interested that the subject of her paperwork had been stabbed and hit on his head with a pistol butt. She insisted on completing every blank on her screen and every form within her domain. Matt presented his MEA insurance card, the magic key to the kingdom of health care.

The forms took nearly thirteen minutes to complete. Matt thought he could have been spurting blood and, as long as it didn't splash on her computer keyboard, the completion of the forms would have taken the same time. The Hippocratic Oath seems of no concern to any health organization until they file the paperwork.

Matt signed the paper that said he would pay any unspecified bills—issued by the medical group, doctors, ambulance, radiology, lab, pharmacy, cable TV, and cafeteria—that his insurance would not pay. A wonderful document; it gave all power to the medical folk and total servitude to the patient. Patients certainly had to be patient.

Finally, they went to another area that was the emergency room triage area. There, a very nice-looking, middle-aged woman in a nurse's uniform with a badge announcing her as a licensed practical nurse took his blood pressure, weight, and temperature. When he mentioned the knife wound, she actually looked up at Matt and his escorts. She informed them that she had to report all knife wounds to the police.

Three leather cases slapped open, exposing three shiny badges. She actually jumped at the coordinated efforts of the DEA men. However, she informed them they were not the police to whom she had to report knife wounds. She needed to call the city police or sheriff's office. She picked up the phone.

Edward finally spoke up. "We have been here for more than thirty minutes. This is a badly wounded man who needs to have medical attention. Is there a doctor on call at this facility?"

"We have our procedures that need to be followed," said the practical nurse practically.

"When can we expect to see a doctor?"

"You will be taken to a room shortly, and the doctor will see you there," said the nurse. She left the room with her clipboard complete with the vital information.

A nurse's aid appeared from a nearby office and escorted the party to a small medical room. "Please stay in here until the doctor can see you."

The room had an examination table, two chairs, a sink, and a counter over multiple drawers with labels for their contents. There were closed shelves of more materials, all labeled.

Matt sat on the examination table. Frank and Edward stayed behind while Stanley left for parts unknown.

Another twenty minutes passed. They studied the certificates on the wall—degrees from Ain Shams University School of Medicine in Cairo, the American University of Beirut, and several from the Universities of Michigan and Wisconsin Medical Schools.

Five minutes short of an hour from entering the medical facility, a doctor entered the room. An East Indian woman who seemed intelligent and in control. She repeated the same questions. Matt provided the same answers. She repeated the blood pressure check on his right arm. She pointed at his left arm and asked, in a stereotypical Hollywood Indian accent, "Is this the arm that is injured?"

"Yes, this is the arm that is injured. I put bandages all over it so I didn't get it mixed up with my other arm that didn't have a ten-inch slash or a puncture wound in the shoulder."

"I see…" said the doctor, not saying "smart ass," but leaving room for it. She carefully helped Matt get the undershirt off. The bleeding had stopped, but started again as the bandages came off.

The doctor put on rubber gloves. "Are you allergic to rubber gloves?"

"I don't think so," said Matt, wondering what a yes answer would have changed.

She looked closely at the wound, lips pursed. "This is a long cut, but it is superficial and not into the muscle. It needs to be cleaned and stitched and bandaged. Are you in pain?"

"I'm kind of tired and numb right now. My shoulder's what really hurts."

"Oh, your shoulder is hurt too?"

Didn't I just say that? "Yes, that hole is under that bandage and it has been written down twice in your paperwork."

"Let us look at the shoulder wound," directed the doctor. She looked and pushed on the wound. "Does this cause you pain?"

"Yes." Matt clenched his teeth. "It was made by a fillet knife and went in several inches."

"Did the bleeding go on for a while?"

"Not very much."

"There seems to be some inflammation. We need to have blood work done. We need to start you on antibiotics. When was your last tetanus shot?"

"Two years ago."

"Can we verify this?" she asked.

"Why? Would I lie and risk lockjaw?"

"True, if you are sure, we will not give you another tetanus shot."

She worked on the wounds for several minutes. She left the room and returned with an aid, a cart full of medical supplies, and several syringes of various liquids. She efficiently jabbed him with several shots, and applied some numbing ointments, a general antibiotic, some stitches, and neat, professional bandaging.

Satisfied with her work, she told him, "If the shoulder wound gets inflamed or if your blood work indicates infection, we may need to open the wound and put in a drain and go to other, more specific antibiotics. I will give you a scrip for oral antibiotics and a painkiller. Drink lots of water and rest the arm for at least a week. We will put it in a sling. Leave the sling on unless you are in bed. It is normal for it to be stiff and for it to itch. Come back in a week."

She headed to the door, but paused to say, "I'll have your prescriptions and instructions at the front desk for you to pick up before you leave."

She had worked on Matt for nearly a half hour. Before Matt and the agents returned to the vehicle, they stopped at the pharmacy in the clinic and picked up his prescriptions. Matt took the Vicoden and antibiotic pills. Very tired, he dozed on the return trip.

The DEA men helped Matt into the cabin and up the stairs.

Edward said, "I need to know specifically where the plane is located and I need your permission to bring people on your land to get the plane and haul it out of here. We already have engineers coming with a crew. They'll be here at first light."

What the hell. Matt told him how to find the lake and the plane. He was too tired to get into how they thought they could get it out of the cedar swamp and off the lake.

Matt crawled into bed, carefully propping up his arm and shoulder on a pillow Tanya had used. He had barely pulled the covers up before falling asleep with the scent of Tanya's perfume—actually his old aftershave—filling his head. He wanted to worry about her but couldn't keep the thought or make sense of the day's actions. Like Scarlett O'Hara, he would worry about that tomorrow.

25

Plane Magic

MATT WOKE TO HEATED TALK from the table below his sleeping area. He thought for a moment he was home in Gladstone and needed to prepare for a day teaching eager minds. Then, as he tried to prop himself on his left elbow, the various pains and weaknesses quickly told him he had only been dreaming about teaching. In the past week, although retired, he had lived a book's worth of adventures. The men downstairs in his hunting cabin were talking loudly about something. He wanted to get out of bed and needed to use the john. He rolled over and pivoted on his right shoulder, getting out on the wrong side from his usual exit.

Wrong side of the bed? Hope that's not an omen.

He sat on the wrong edge of the bed for a few minutes, head in his hands. Recent memories flooded his brain. The clinic and its hassles. The solicitous DEA agents, almost too nice. They'd asked about the plane.

Who told them? Had Webb or some of his men been captured? Did he have an informant in his Chicago or Detroit operations? What about Tanya...and her fate? Had they caught her with hundreds of pounds of cocaine and a major gangland boss?

The image of her behind bars sickened Matt. He couldn't help her much by mentioning her unwillingness to help Webb, but he could hurt her by implicating her if they had made it safely to Detroit or Chicago. Tough choices coming up.

Time for the bathroom and some coffee before finding out about the commotion downstairs. Matt slipped on warm clothes and fur-lined moccasins. His shoulder, more stiff than painful, and his arm didn't want to flex, but his muscles and nerves seemed fine.

Downstairs, five other men had joined the three DEA agents, who still looked neat and professional in fresh shaves, white shirts, and ties pulled up to the button-down collars. Impressive dedication to the official image. The other men wore warm, solid clothes designed for outdoor work—Carhartt vests, heavy shirts with long underwear showing at the neck and sleeves and good, well-cared-for boots.

They all looked up as Matt entered the room.

"Good morning, Mr. Hunter," said Frank.

"Coffee?" asked Edward, taking a clean mug from the cupboard.

"Yes, thank you. Give me just a minute," said Matt as he went into the bathroom. Three shaving kits, for three DEA agents, sat in a neat line on the far shelf. Somebody had cleaned the mirror after steamy showers. Three towels draped neatly over the shower curtain rod.

These guys are neat people.

After satisfying natural needs, he shaved and sponged off with a cloth to avoid wetting his new bandages. As he crossed to the kitchen, he scanned the new personnel before picking up the steaming mug of coffee waiting for him. He asked, "So, what's going on?"

"These men are plane salvage experts," Edward replied, waving a hand at guys in work clothes. "They're here to move the plane. They already had a bulldozer out to the plane and back."

No one introduced them to Matt. They huddled over some hand-drawn sketches and several pages of calculations, all laid out on the table.

Matt sipped the not-very-hot coffee and took the last donut in the box. He glanced at the papers on the table. Nicely done, and accurate. The coffee salved his parched throat. He must have snored like a chainsaw last night. In a voice weaker than he expected, he asked, "How do you get a plane that size up a road?"

"We unbolt or cut off the wings and engines and put everything on flatbed trucks," said one of the workers. "We'd rather take the engines off before we lift the wings, but these guys want speed and want us to take the wing and engine in one piece."

Another worker poked a finger at a sheet of calculations. "We think the weight is too much. The ice isn't real thick at the end of the lake or on the edges either. If the dozer goes down, nothing around here will pull it out."

Matt thought for a moment before deciding he might as well continue to help. "How about skidding the wings out on to the lake before you load them? Also, the water at this end of the lake—" He pointed at the diagram. "—where you come off is very shallow and all rock under a little sand and mud. Your bulldozer wouldn't have any trouble pulling something off the lake."

The first worker nodded. "We thought of the skidding maneuver, but the lake edge is still a problem. We're getting planking now to help, but everything takes time. The ice is only about six to eight inches around the plane. The middle of the lake had over a foot of good solid ice. We can get a flatbed, dozer, tow truck, and backhoe involved with reasonable safety. We're going back now. With luck, we'll be done by noon or shortly after."

The first worker looked at each of the others in turn. Sensing no disagreement, he gathered up the papers and stuffed them inside a metal clipboard and snapped the cover shut. Almost in unison, the workers left the cabin. In a few seconds, Matt heard a heavy diesel engine start and huff away toward the lake.

He turned to Edward. "You don't waste time."

"We need the plane out of here before it's known in every bar in the U.P.," Edward said. "So far, none of your friends have been around. We have people to stop them from coming down into the area, but we would like to do our business and be gone before we draw a crowd."

"Why are you doing this?" asked Matt.

"We want as little known about the plane and its passengers as possible. It is very important that you never mention it. We need your oath to be silent or we'll be forced to detain you. We'd like to avoid that, because of the questions it'll raise. The longer we can keep the plane from being a story in Detroit or Chicago, the more useful the information and technical hardware we now have will be to us."

Edward held up a hand. "Look, that's about all we can tell you at this point, and it's more than you need to know. We'll take the plane, talk to you some more, and be out of here before evening…if you're truthful with us."

"Can we go down and watch them work?" asked Matt.

Edward shrugged. "I don't see why not, as long as we don't get in their way."

"How's the shoulder and arm today?" Frank asked.

"Sore and stiff to both, but everything works. I guess I was pretty lucky overall."

Matt smeared butter and peanut butter on two pieces of toast and filled a thermos with coffee. He washed down two 500 mg aspirins with a large class of orange juice and put a Vicoden in his pocket just in case,

He accepted Edward's help with his boots and jacket and, carrying the toast and coffee, got into the DEA Suburban. Edward slowly drove down to the lake.

The lake shore looked like a military beach operation, with piles of snow pushed eight feet high on the sides of the road that led onto the lake and wood planks at the lake's edge. Three flatbed trailers sat out on the lake. About a dozen men swarmed under, over, and around the plane, clearly visible now that they had removed the snow from it. A cleared and packed path led directly to it, with drifts made by a large snowblower.

Smart, thought Matt. *Spread the weight of the snow across the marginally thick ice.*

Good working weather too—mid-twenties, no wind, overcast—but with the smell of incoming snow in the air. Power tools and winches whined. A boom-equipped, small front-end loader with tracks lifted a wing, swung it around, and placed it onto a flatbed in one easy motion. Workers swarmed to the other side of the plane and out of sight. The bulldozer hitched to the trailer and came toward Matt and the DEA men, who had parked and exited their vehicle.

Somebody started one of the trucks and began to position it to take the trailer. Men with large black tarps and ratcheting tie-downs prepared to cover and secure the wing and motor. Their organization and speed impressed Matt.

As the dozer approached the lake edge, the ice cracked and popped, breaking under the weight. The ice rippled as weight passed over it. If the driver went too fast, the ripple might break like a wave at the shore. It was dry under the ice where the water had expanded onto the land as it froze. The sound made the dozer driver's eyes widen, but he grimly kept his pull on the trailer. The dozer made land, its engine snorting with the power of accomplishment or relief, and pulled the trailer into the clearing. Men quickly unhooked the dozer, which returned for the next wing and engine.

Matt and the DEA men watched workmen secure the wing with large Styrofoam blocks and the tie-downs, then cover it with the tarps. They finally secured everything with ropes and more tie-downs. The truck snorted, the driver found a suitable low gear, and the wing and engine were on their way.

Matt checked his watch. A little after 11:00 a.m. They had the other wing and fuselage to go.

They couldn't drag the wing and engine out onto the lake without taking the fuselage. It turned and skidded across the ice easily, pulled by a winch and cable on the bulldozer. They quickly loaded it on a flatbed and brought it to shore.

Matt noticed no bodies in the cockpit, as the men clambered over it to secure it to the flatbed. They supported the tail with 2x8's supported, in turn, by other braces hammered into the trailer's wooden bed and finished with the ropes, tie-downs, and tarps. They worked like they did this kind of work everyday. They hooked up the next truck, and it growled up the plowed road.

Matt checked the time—12:15.

The last wing and engine posed a problem—partially frozen into the lake. Trying to pull it out, the men ripped out tow points and broke heavy nylon straps. The wing tore, exposing a gas tank that didn't rupture but made working with torches more interesting. They decided on haste rather than careful work. Men sliced the ice with chainsaws, and the dozer yanked the wing and engine onto the ice. The last flatbed trailer accepted the mangled cargo, and the workmen rode their equipment back from the far side of the lake. They maintained a reasonable, safe distance between the equipment and came off the lake looking relieved that nothing major had gone wrong, and no equipment or worker had gotten wet. All the work crew and equipment had left the lake by a little after 1:00 p.m. They spent another hour back-blading and trying to cover the tracks of all the trucks and marks of heavy machinery. Impressed, Matt decided he would change his mind slightly about the usual jokes concerning government workers. The remaining tracks and the mess on the snow could be explained by a pickup going through the ice and using a dozer to clear the snow for the wrecker. They even removed the planks.

Matt felt cold from too many hours with too little activity. He and Edward got back in the DEA vehicle. Thankfully, it warmed up quickly. Frank and Stanley said goodbye and rode away with the last trucks, after announcing they would stay with the plane and dismiss the road patrol up by the highway.

26

Beer Buddies

A T THE CABIN, EDWARD AND MATT AGREED they were hungry and proceeded to search the refrigerator and pantry. Matt took his second Vicoden of the day for his now throbbing shoulder.

After fifteen minutes of preparation, they had lunch meat and cheese sandwiches, hot tomato soup, and buttered crackers on the table. They ate and talked about the efficiency of the work they had watched at the lake. They talked about Matt's teaching and coaching. Matt found out that Edward had two sons who wrestled and played football. He also had a daughter who was a star in cross-country at her high school. The wallets came out, pictures and stories were shared. Matt produced two cold beers to make the meal fit the deer camp criterion for completeness and decorum. They finished up with some Monterey jack cheese in a block, more crackers, and more beers. They talked about Edward's career. How many times he had moved. How hard it was on teenagers to change schools. They talked about sports and agreed that competition shapes kids: competition in sports is very close to the competition experienced on the job, kids need to learn to know the importance of preparation for a big game or meet and deal with their internal demons, win or lose. Their discussion reached total agreement when they listed similarities between teamwork in sports and teamwork on the job.

By the third round of chitchat and cold beer, both Matt and Edward were sure that each was a useful and dedicated person. They decided they could talk to each other and trust each other.

Edward cleared the table except for the nearly empty third beers. As he sat back down to finish his beer, he said, "We need to do some business before my lips go numb. How about starting with your version of what happened when the plane went down, how you became involved with Webb? And I'd like to know, on a personal basis, about you and Volcheff."

"How do you know about all this?" asked Matt.

"I can't tell you a whole lot. We have people in the field who give us information. They are at great risk. We can't talk about them. Without these people we don't stand much of a chance against the bad guys. We know Volcheff's probably killed a dozen people in the last five years. You were very, very lucky. He used a knife on a lot of people. He used a piece of wire on an agent of ours in Chicago. We found the guy wired to a light pole across from his house. His kids found him as they went to school. We had a good description for him, but the witness ended up going to the Bahamas and living in a condo that someone gave her. She retracted her statements. Volcheff was the kind of person who makes a good cop carry a throwaway piece just so he can do Volcheff in an alley and claim self-defense."

His blue-eyed gaze met Matt's as he continued. "Talk to me, I'm not writing anything down and I'm not recording anything. We may need to talk to you officially sometime, but that time will have nothing to do with what you say now. We just want to know as much as we can. Our information is generally brief from an inside person. You could help us put some meat on the bones."

Matt took the last swig of his beer. He got up to get another one. He looked at Edward, got a what-the-hell look, and brought two cans to the table.

Matt started with the plane coming down. He told everything completely and in time sequence—except he left out Tanya. He kept Ivan alive in his version a little longer to make the time line seem better. He mentioned the cave and hiding the cocaine. He talked about the fancy phones and the contents of the briefcase. He talked about Ivan dying and returning the body to the plane. He told of the meeting and how he had set it up to see what they did and about watching the bust that was a dry hole for the DEA.

They both had to stop for bathroom breaks and another round of beer.

Before Matt could continue, Edward said, "You're leaving out Tanya."

"Well, I guess I did skip over her," answered Matt. "Leaving the best for last."

Matt backed up and explained Tanya and her injury. He made it worse than it was and left out the fun of all kinds they had. He mentioned that she had been forced to work for Webb through leverage applied on her and her parents. He told about her involvement in saving his life when Webb wanted him dead. His story went back and forth. The time line got messed up a little. Edward helped him get it straight, less the interrogator than a buddy helping him keep events in good order. They both laughed at the deer blind story and Al and Ray's night in the woods. Webb's use of electronic tracking interested Edward, and he said he would like to talk about it more later and asked if Matt minded if he made a note about it. Matt nodded and smiled at a law officer asking him for permission to write down something. He felt Edward was a real solid guy.

Edward made his note and put the pen and pad away, needing two tries to get the pad in his shirt pocket. "You know, these SOBs sure have the money for fancy electric stuff."

Matt knew that five beers made people start sentences with "You know," and he was glad to see that he wasn't the only one at the table who was feeling his beers. Matt thought, *I'm taller and heavier than Edward, should be able to stay with him in the brewski department.*

"Tell me about Volcheff," Edward asked.

Matt described his first meeting with the man, looking down the wrong end of a 12-gauge pump. He told about sneaking back and getting the drop on Volcheff who had been waiting in the Yukon.

"You really are a hunter, Hunter!" said Edward, louder than necessary.

After recounting the incarceration of Volcheff in the cave, Matt mentioned the other guy coming up the path with Matt's Remington. He smacked himself on the forehead and said, "Oh, shit! That's where my rifle is—still in the cave. That's why my case is empty. Worst place in the world for a rifle. How about we go get it while it's still light out? You can see the cave, and the fresh air will help burn up some of the beer." suggested Matt.

As they walked to the cave, Matt demonstrated how he captured Volcheff, starting with the yellow circle in the snow by the door and reenacting the drama of the event. He made Edward be Volcheff.

They got to the cave entrance. Matt pointed out the spot that Volcheff came at him, reenacted the shooting, wrestling, and ended up breathless before the big rock. He looked at the rock, blood and tissue still plastered the limestone. This wasn't like a good hunting story anymore.

Matt dropped to his knees in the packed snow, touching the stained rock. "His name was Mel something," Matt mumbled. "Dumb son of a bitch couldn't wrestle for shit. You can't get high on a person; gets you thrown every time. Poor guy. A couple of feet either way and he'd have been in a snow bank. It happened fast, you know," said Matt. He also knew when you say "you know" at the end of a sentence, you've been drinking too much. He had just told a lawman everything about the two deaths, including the place where they occurred. The mood was more sober than Matt's brain.

Edward helped Matt up. "Clearly self defense."

Shaking off his sense of having screwed up, Matt fetched a pair of lanterns and said, "Come on in, it's warmer in here, and I need to get my rifle." He led Edward into the cave but almost fell down the steps because he forgot the railing he always used was gone. He took two giant steps, shot to the floor of the cave, and ran across the room, stopped hard by the far wall; on his feet, but aggravating his aching shoulder. When he looked up, Edward stood at the top of the stairs grinning.

"Can I just walk down, or is that how real Yoopers go down steps?" asked Edward.

"Railing gone," said Matt, feeling that articles and verbs were no longer needed in polite conversation.

Matt lifted the lantern he still had in his hand and went around the steps, found his rifle and, using the sling, brought it over his right shoulder as he put the lantern in his left hand. The left hand and arm protested the weight, so Matt put the lantern back in his right hand.

Edward surveyed the room. "This is some place. You use this as a cold locker for your deer?"

"Yeah. It stays about forty degrees all year. Sometimes the weather is warm during hunting season, and this cave is a real meat saver. We have a lot of meat hanging then. This year it's been real cold and most hunters take their deer with them and finish their work at home. This room has been here from the early 1930s. Actually it's about 10,000 years old. When the quarry had hundreds of people here, they used it like a community refrigerator. We keep it clean and have very little in it; stuff gets damp and moldy if you don't watch it." Then he said, "I think I'm sober enough to try to make it up the stairs with only one railing."

As Matt put the lanterns back on the anteroom shelf, Edward stepped outside and stood before the indentation that was Volcheff's last fall.

Matt followed Edward's gaze, "He was fast, but I was a few steps further away than he thought. The bottle didn't break or I would have never seen him coming. I can guarantee he won't be a problem to the DEA anymore."

"We haven't found his body or the other person's. I'd like to see him very, very dead, just like the Wicked Witch of the West," said Edward as they walked.

The giant steps down the stairs and the cold air were clearing his beer-affected brain. Matt thought that Edward was telling him something. *They have not found the bodies; therefore, they didn't have the whole Webb crew, including Tanya? They couldn't have found Al and Ray who were to take care of the bodies or maybe Edward was just being closemouthed.*

"Do you have Tanya in custody?" asked Matt, trying to sound sober.

"Can't answer that." Edward sounded very sober. "Sorry, buddy."

"What do we do next?"

"Look." Edward stopped and turned to face Matt. "I'm going back to Marquette to meet with the rest of the team and the state drug group. We have a lot going on, more than just these guys. Webb's activities are the responsibility of a national enforcement group, and I'm on the task force."

"Am I free to go and move around?"

"Sure. I'll give you my card. But do keep me posted on your whereabouts in case we need you. And give me your phone numbers, email, and however else we can get in touch with you."

"No problem,"

Edward resumed walking. "It might be a good idea for you to get out of here for a while. Keep a low profile. Also, don't be afraid to call me if Webb or any of his associates show up or contact you. I really mean it."

Back to the cabin, Edward gathered his briefcase and papers, while Matt gave him the best route to Marquette and a note with the numbers Edward wanted. Matt walked him to his vehicle. They shook hands congenially just before Edward slid behind the steering wheel. Matt felt like he had made a friend—or was it just the beer?

Matt watched the car drive away. He stood still, listening to its sound fade into the gray afternoon quickly turning to evening. It started to snow little dry flakes that would make everything white and sparkly in a few hours. If it kept up all night, it would cover a lot of the day's busy activity of machines and men.

Inside, Matt unloaded and cleaned his rifle. He would fire it tomorrow to make sure the fight hadn't damaged the scope. He would then reclean it and put it away for the year.

He felt alone. He wanted to go into Rex and have a greasy hamburger and a few more beers, but he didn't want questions. He also didn't think more beers were a good idea.

He ate a dry sandwich and some stale potato chips that someone had opened and not closed well. After finishing the orange juice in the refrigerator, he went to bed. He couldn't find the Griffin paperback but found an old Dick Francis mystery he had read years ago. He couldn't remember the ending.

While reading, he dropped off to sleep.

27

Clean Up

M ATT WOKE UP EARLY; it was still dark outside. He put on some old camp boots and walked outside to see how much snow had come down overnight. Four inches of new fluff. The low-teens cold penetrated his sweater. This hunting season produced more snow and cold than they had had in over ten years—more like the 1960s and '70s that averaged over 200 inches a year with snowmobile tracks made in November reappearing in March. Two years ago, they had hunted in shirtsleeves and vests and, in January, had to trailer their machines to Marquette or Grand Marais to find snow for trail riding. Matt couldn't keep his mind from wandering. Random thoughts drifted through while he tried to work out a plan. Coffee, he hoped, would help him with the logistics.

Back inside, he started the coffee, used his last egg to make French toast, and fried up the last of the bacon. Matt had to think hard about what day it was. He needed to read a newspaper, listen to TV news, anything to pull him back into the real world and provide some meter for his days to come.

All the activity in seven long days had left him totally exhausted in body and mind. He needed to find a place to lick his wounds and rest. He thought of Tanya's invitation to come to Florida for Christmas. The thought of the beautiful green-blue water, warm breezes, and rustle of palm branches rushed into Matt's brain. He would like the feel of flip-flops, baggy shorts, and a cotton T-shirt. However, most importantly, he had a burning desire to find Tanya. He had no way of contacting her. She had no way to reach him here at the cabin, and he didn't want to go back to Gladstone to sit by a phone. Waiting.

He would take Edward's advice, he would get out of Dodge, get out of the chill and white of the magnificent north. Use some of his ill-gotten fortune to head south and find some warm sun.

Matt spent the next two days doing jobs around the cabin. He shot the rifle and proved to himself it was as true as ever. He recleaned it and put it in its case in the Yukon. He packed ammunition into a folding case and zipped it in with the rifle. He made sure the sling was dry and everything was perfectly oiled, ready for long-term storage. At the cave, he straightened things up, sliced off what he could from the deer, and put the rest in the woods for the coyotes and other critters to finish. He cleaned off the rock and jury-rigged a new railing out of several 2x4s stored by the cabin. He didn't work fast, but just kept getting job after job done throughout the two days. Each evening, he showered and checked his shoulder and arm for infection then ate what was easy to fix and went to bed.

The bad dreams got worse, he now remembered them when awake. They slipped in between pain pills and antibiotic-aided sleep. Flashes of Volcheff looking like a monster from a silent movie. Tabloids of dead people. Being arrested by groups of men in long coats. Storm troopers taking everything from his home in Gladstone while the neighbors looked on and gossiped. The most frequent and compelling vision was of Tanya saying goodbye, then slipping into black water where he couldn't reach her.

On Sunday, while fitfully trying to sleep late, voices in the cabin stirred him awake. Leon and several friends had come over to find out what was going on.

"Hunter, get your sorry ass out of the sack and get down here," Leon yelled up the stairs.

Matt threw on clothes, stiff-legged it down the steps and concentrated on supplying the coffee maker with water and drip grind. Behind his back he heard the pop of beer cans. The troops came armed with their own plastic-bound six-packs. Five guests were with Leon, they chattered and clattered like boilers—questions building like steam needing relief. Their questions came in bunches.

"What happened to you? Who was the girl? Why did they come here? Why didn't you get some help? Why all the truck tracks? How long were they here?"

After everyone got their questions out and had either a beer or fresh coffee laced with brandy, Matt started his story.

Matt conceded that he'd had a problem with gangsters who had tried to hide out at the cabin after being caught and released by the police on Monday. They had just looked for a lonely plowed road and some camp to hole up in for a time. He said they had left after pounding on him some. The police finally tracked them to Matt's cabin, but only after the bad guys were long gone. The police had compounded their lateness by driving down the wrong road in a hurry and had gotten stuck going toward the lake. A wrecker had to haul them out.

Everyone agreed that patrol cars had a tough time on the snow and ice. Going down the lake road was what you would expect of city cops.

Matt tied in what people knew about the Garnet Lake incident with what the Lamoreaux brothers had seen and talked about and Leon's DEA experience.

Questions kept coming back to the girl—because Billy had told everyone, "I'd drag my ass over a mountain of glass to spend some time with her." Luckily, the Lamoreauxs weren't in attendance or there would be real issues with time lines, cars and people. Matt knew everything would be analyzed and chewed fine once the gossip mills got into full gear. Matt just said she might be coming back alone sometime—drawing knowing smiles and general agreement that you can't do much with two other guys in a small cabin. Soon, beer and brandy flowed freely, and everyone pledged that they would have shot the SOBs had they known Matt was in trouble. They swapped some good deer stories about this year and a few hits from the past. An impromptu morning party was a special treat for everyone.

Matt showed them the bruise on his temple from a gun butt. Everyone was impressed, until a cousin topped it with two AK-47 wounds on his butt from his Vietnam days. Matt almost showed the knife wounds out of pure one-upmanship. Leon asked about the Garnet Lake plowing job and Matt got around it by saying his friends had called off the snowmobile trip because their kids had gotten the flu that'd been going around.

Matt said he was thinking about a trip south for some sun and rest.

To solidify his decision, he cleaned out the refrigerator and freezer of all perishables that would spoil with time or a power failure. The group would leave with paper bags of food and heads filled with wild tales to share with their families. They all knew Matt hadn't told them everything, but they respected a man's right to keep some secrets to himself. They also knew that Matt was going through a time of adjustment after his retirement.

When asked where he was going, Matt told them he was heading south for a driving vacation. No set destination, just driving until he saw palm trees and sandy beaches. They all agreed retirement was wonderful with no family or jobs to tie you down.

Besides, gun season had ended. The Packers and the Lions would provide the only real excitement for the rest of the season, and they only played one game each per week. The guys had hunted enough, and black powder was good for some guys, but the caps got too cold and didn't always work well, and they weren't going to buy the newer in-line black powder guns because they didn't look traditional and all their wives thought they had enough guns anyway. The brandy and beer ran out. It was time to go, everyone agreed. They took their packages of booty, put the empty brandy jug in the garbage, bagged up the redeemable empties of the beers they had brought and headed outside: talking about the football game that started after supper, and agreeing that West Coast games let a person get more done on a Sunday.

A first cousin asked if he could black-powder hunt at the cabin, and Matt said fine as long as he cleaned up afterwards and held no big parties with naked women all over the place. Everyone laughed and scattered to the pickup trucks that would get them home.

28

To the Keys

MATT PACKED SOME SWEATSHIRTS, socks, and underwear in a gym carryall. Two pair of pants went on good hangers, covered with two light shirts he had at camp. The New Balance jogging shoes would be fine for travel. Heavy clothes went back into the upstairs drawers and closets. Without any light jackets, his camo hunting jacket would have to do. Toilet articles fit into a couple of ziplock bags and a paper bag. Matt filled a medium-size cooler with ice and assorted pop, then loaded everything into the Yukon.

Matt stood at the large door of the old machine shop building and listened and watched for several minutes. Satisfied with his privacy, he dug his cached money out of the old shop forge. He put the money in various places: some in his coat pocket, some with Tanya's little .22 in the drawer of the console, but most in a black plastic garbage bag stuffed in the side panel behind the jack. He would buy whatever else he might need along the way. It wasn't worth the 200-mile round-trip to Gladstone to pick up summer clothes. He would check with the cell phone people about his roaming capabilities and costs, and he would call his Gladstone friends while he was on the road to check on his home and let people know his travel plans. He would call his son from the road and the Vegas' as soon as he had good cell phone reception.

He drove past the road to the lake by mid-afternoon. Fresh snow had covered most of the activity of the previous days. If anyone went down to the lake, they would have a lot of questions. But at least they wouldn't find a crashed plane with two dead bodies inside.

Matt drove to St. Ignace, heading south to cross the bridge, passing the state police post on his right as he slowed down to pay his toll. He shook his head over the memories of the night he drove around the post like some adolescent high school boy driving by his girlfriend's house. It was windy and clear as he drove over the magnificent, five-mile-long Mackinac Bridge. He could just make out the white porch of the Grand Hotel on Mackinac Island to his far left. Passing old Fort Michilimackinac on his right as he exited onto the solid ground of lower Michigan, he smiled at the thought of warmer climes ahead.

He planned to take Interstate 75 all the way south, with a shortcut on US 23 between Flint and Toledo to bypass Detroit.

Driving south felt good, he enjoyed the freedom and thoughts of somehow getting closer to Tanya. The think time was a problem. He worried about Tanya, his felonious cooperation with gangsters, all the things he had told Edward and all the things Edward had not told him.

Matt slept poorly at an overheated motel and hit the road again at dawn, hyped on coffee and donuts.

Though he felt good about heading toward Tanya's home, honoring her last words to him, he feared calling Mr. Vega and the possibility of bad news or no news. He didn't want to hear something that would make him turn around. As the white lines flashed past, he imagined hundreds of scenarios—ranging from Tanya answering the phone to her father sobbing with news of her going to jail...or worse. He lingered on the best fantasies and procrastinated as the miles rolled beneath his wheels. He called Islamorada information for the Vegas' number. Twice, he coded the number into his phone and, twice, turned it off, using excuses like traffic, gas, food, or potty breaks to keep from hitting the send button.

At last, he called the Vega home. A recording told him to call the dive shop and gave a number. Matt wrote it down.

Taking several deep breaths, he dialed the dive shop. The phone was answered on the second ring. A young woman. For a second, Matt imagined it was Tanya and stopped breathing. He felt stupid having high-school anxiety over a phone call.

"Tanya?" asked Matt.

"No, Tanya hasn't worked here for a long time. May I help you?" asked the woman.

"Is Mr. Vega in?"

"Yes he is, but he is with customers. Is there something I can do for you?"

"I'll wait for Mr. Vega. I'm on long distance."

She set the phone on a counter, and Matt could hear voices and movement in the shop. He waited less than a minute. He watched the seconds on his cell phone tick by. At 52 seconds, Mr. Vega answered. "Yes, this is George Vega."

"Hello, this is the person who last talked with you from the Upper Peninsula of Michigan. Do you remember me?" asked Matt.

"I sure do. When are you coming down here and getting some sun?"

"Do you know where Tanya is?" asked Matt.

"I haven't heard much, nothing I can repeat on the phone. Maybe if you come down here, we will know more. Where are you?"

"I'm in Michigan, nearly to Ohio, and driving south."

"What's your cell phone number? I'll call you after work and give you directions to us. Know anything about diving or boats? Maybe we could put you to work."

Matt gave Vega his cell number, and they broke the connection with a hardy wish from Vega to have Matt drive safely to the Sunshine State.

Matt drove into Ohio while thinking of the phone call. Vega actually told him a lot by saying very little. He couldn't talk about Tanya. He didn't seem too worried about her; in fact, he hadn't asked Matt about her. He had more to say, but not on the shop phone, and he sincerely seemed to welcome and invite Matt to come there. On a scale of one to ten for good, the call was at least a seven.

Matt drove around Toledo and into heavy traffic. Everyone was cruising at eighty and seemed frantic to get by and around any other car on the wide highway. The flow of vehicles pushed around corners three and four lanes wide, concrete barriers on both sides, with no reduction in speed. Truly white-knuckle driving for a Yooper unaccustomed to more than one pickup truck per three-mile stretch of road. At this time of day, Matt was more used to stopping for deer than having a truck's Jake brake growling behind him and seeing only the grill of a Peterbuilt four feet from his bumper while roaring into a three-lane corner at eighty.

Matt was glad he had leather seats; the high pucker factor from driving around Toledo at rush-home hour would have sucked up large quantities of cloth seat covers. He passed Ohio Highway Patrol units who also looked scared and frantic. Matt prayed that Vega wouldn't try to call him. If he could just survive a few more miles. But, after a while, he knew he was doomed and gave himself up to taking as few people as possible with him.

He only hoped he wouldn't be pinned and burning while people went by him and the emergency vehicles were hopelessly trapped in other crashes or were blocked by the thick smoke of the burning tires of the truck that had crushed his Yukon.

Somehow, the traffic finally thinned and he saw signs for Bowling Green, Ohio. It brought back memories of college trips from Western to Bowling Green and great football and basketball contests. *Lucky to be alive,* he thought, *damn Toledo traffic's more deadly than Chicago, where traffic doesn't move much.*

Around Chicago, you worried more about your car overheating than being crushed at 80 mph by a Mack truck with the words "No Prisoners" written mirror-backwards on the plastic bug screen.

Gratefully, peacefully now, Matt enjoyed the drive through the Ohio farm country. It was totally dark when he passed Lima. He wasn't tired, but his neck and back hurt from the tension of the Toledo I-475 loop. Matt vowed to think ahead and get a good set of maps so he could plan to avoid further big-city traffic.

The cell phone's tune caught Matt off guard. He jumped. He didn't remember the tune and had forgotten how loud it was. He opened the phone and tried to put it to his ear. The charger cord stretched across his wrist and caught on his elbow. He yanked it out and let it drop.

"Hello, this is Matt."

"Hello to you. This is George Vega. Sorry I couldn't talk much at the shop. I think our phone is tapped. I don't want to say anything about Tanya that could be of interest to the government or...other people. I'm at a safe pay phone up at Key Largo."

"Do you know anything about Tanya?" said Matt

"We haven't heard from her since you and she called us while you were snowmobiling."

"Damn, I was hoping for some good news. The last time I saw her she was driving away with some seriously bad people. She didn't seem afraid and she said to come down there for Christmas. So, you seem to be the link she wanted me to establish."

"She's very strong and has a good head on her shoulders. I'd say no news is good news. Just get down here and we can worry together. We have a lot we can talk about. And we're shorthanded. Interested in working on a boat or helping with diving groups?"

"I would be glad to help any way I can. I've spent a lot of time on twenty- and thirty-foot boats and know most of the newest electronic fishing gear. I've got my NAUI diving card. I don't have any gear with me, though."

"Well, don't worry about it. We've got plenty of gear here. Listen, just get here. We'll set you up. Tanya said you saved her life and she said she liked you. She hasn't liked a boy or a man in a long time, after…anyway, we'd like to meet you. Got to go, I used coins and it's beeping at me. Call me at home early, before 6:30 Eastern time, if you get up early, or after 8:00 p.m. Keep the conversation light, don't mention Tanya. Talk about boats, and I'll get you any information I might have. Got to…"

Dial tone.

Matt drove on.

Childhood memories swept over Matt as he saw signs for Chattanooga. He had visited Lookout Mountain with his grandparents twice when he was a grade-schooler. Matt remembered the many observation areas and being bored at first by sightseeing with his grandfather, but eventually learning to appreciate the old man's intellectual and military insights. Those exchanges reminded him of tracking lessons in the woods and instructions on stalking and rifle shooting. Finally, Matt was honored to listen to a man who knew what he was talking about and could make a science out of details that most people couldn't even see.

Thinking about all these flashbacks reminded him how much he truly missed his grandfather. He would have liked to have advice about his decisions and maybe some forgiveness for his actions. With a sigh for what couldn't be, Matt finally drove off the interstate and took Highway 24 to the base of the mountain at the big bend in the Tennessee River. He slowly went up the winding road that led to the top of the mountain. He always wondered what happens if they were to get snow or ice. He could see scratches on railings and rock sides that explained that the trip down could be a real thrill under slippery conditions. At the visitor's center, he put his money into an automatic machine that allowed him entrance to the park that overlooked Chattanooga. He walked along the lookout points, past cannons and monuments, past placards of Confederate and Union casualties. He leaned on a metal railing and watched the river bend aptly called Moccasin Bend. From this very spot, he remembered his grandfather talking about how decisiveness and good organization had made Ulysses S. Grant the top general here.

Old Manfred wouldn't talk about his WWI service, but he would talk about how individual soldiers might feel and act in battle. Matt knew in this way he was telling Matt what would keep a person alive in a life-and-death situation. Manfred's brothers and two sons, including Matt's father, were killed in WWII and Korea. Matt knew Manfred felt he had not talked enough to them, and felt he might have saved them with some advice never given.

Matt wanted to feel Manfred's strong hand on his arm and see the thick, callused finger pointing at a trench line or a cannon position, and the deep voice explaining how troops were used or misused: how small groups with inspiration and determination can decide a major battle. Matt wondered what Manfred would say about the battle at their quarry. Manfred had talked about reactions versus thinking in a battle. Usually the thinker got killed by the person that just reacted. Matt knew that his grandfather was telling him to act quickly and instinctively, but old Manfred would never get specific. The WWI talk often ended with general anecdotes, such as "the gas killed the lice and rats in the trenches."

Matt enjoyed the view and memories and let his mind relax from its near-constant worry...and thoughts of Tanya, Webb, and the two dead men he still fought. Realizing he was at a tipping point in his life, he walked down the cobblestone pathway and stopped at a low stone wall topped by a tubular steel guardrail. Spectacular view. He grasped the rail with both hands. The action made him think of the bar on a merry-go-round or on a Ferris wheel. These thoughts made a playground come to mind. He saw himself on a teeter-totter. This thought led to an awareness of the risk on a teeter-totter: if the other person rolled off while you were in the air, you came down hard. Matt wondered how Tanya used to play as a little girl. He remembered how she had played as a big girl.

Lookout Mountain seemed an appropriate place to decide his actions and his future, located halfway between the snows of the north country and the sunny south—high on a column of rock, Matt teetered between returning to the familiar north and his friends or tipping to the south with its new people and real dangers...and Tanya. Flashes and feelings of bad dreams, dead frozen faces, badges in leather folders, the feeling of a strong arm tightened to strangle him and finally Tanya's face and lovely eyes and mouth that were so inviting he couldn't resist their call. His forearms ached, and he stopped squeezing the cold metal railing. As he released his vise-like grip, he felt Manfred's loving spirit enter his brain. He could also hear the words from the old man: "You survived your first battles, you don't come from timid stock, be careful but be bold, realizing a dream is worth effort and risk."

Matt looked at the river below, then turned toward the leafless trees, smelled the damp leaves littering the park floor, and slowly walked back to the Yukon for the careful drive down the mountain and the hunt for a good motel. Maybe he would get one with a good pool and start swimming to build up his wind and muscles for his coming experiences in the Keys.

Matt found a larger motel. He swam for nearly an hour. He ordered a pizza delivered, an experience he never had in the U.P. He ate two slices, washing them down with two beers. He was too tired to do more that day, too tired to call George Vega even though he had told himself he would.

He woke at dawn, with cold pizza on the other bed and the television still playing quietly. The early morning news. Early enough to call the Keys, a few minutes after 6:00 a.m.

George Vega answered on the second ring, sounding glad to hear Matt's voice. "I've been waiting for your call. I've got a boat ready for you, moored just outside the marina. You can live on it and work here for as long as you want. She's not listed for charter until mid March and will be free lodging for you just for keeping it shiny and free of salt spray. We may need her for a couple of day cruises or some short fishing trips, that's all."

"Doesn't your daughter take out charters?"

"Yes, but she's on an extended trip right now so we are getting by without her. We could use your help around here. When can we expect you?"

"I'm almost into Georgia now and should be there in another day and a half. I'm not pushing too hard. I'm going shopping for some warm weather clothes this morning."

"We'll look for you day after tomorrow. Drive carefully," said Vega and broke the connection.

Matt did some shopping in a large Chattanooga shopping mall, buying a full wardrobe of summer attire and supplies. He stopped at an upscale outfitting and sports store and got an overpriced rain jacket, windbreaker, and several sweatshirts and cotton V-neck light sweaters. He wanted to look acceptable to the boating crowd. He had bought some soft-sided luggage on a sale that made it only a little overpriced. His last purchase was a hundred-dollar pair of Polaroid sunglasses.

Kinda fun, having some extra cash to blow on nice things. Too bad Tanya's not here to help me spend it.

He headed south on I-75 and made a good run through Georgia, including a smooth passage around Atlanta and then a good part of Florida. He stopped in an almost new Best Western just south of Ft. Myers. The 500 miles of travel seemed to pass quickly in the sun and the green of the south. He ran with the air conditioning on from Atlanta southward. The west side of Florida had turned into one large construction zone since his last visit several years ago, with building going on everywhere. The west side would soon be as tightly packed with shopping centers, condos, and motels as the east side. Florida looked very prosperous. Matt felt good. He would be at Tanya's home the next day.

Matt swam for over an hour in a beautiful pool, ate in the motel's restaurant, and was asleep before the evening news.

The next morning, he saw the first sign for the Keys. He took the less traveled US Highway 41 over to US 1, the only main road in the Keys. He drove on 41 as a reminder of home, as it stretched continuously from the U.P. to Miami. It ended or started, depending on your point of view, in Copper Harbor, Michigan. Matt got off the southernmost part of US 41 east of Miami, and then he drove the Florida Toll Road that took him to the Keys at seventy-five mph. The day was perfect, white clouds skittered across an eye-hurting blue sky and the temperature hovered in the mid-seventies with a lively west wind off the Atlantic. He exited the toll road at Homestead and got on US 1. He lowered his speed to see more of the surroundings. The beautiful blue-green water glistened under the causeway to Key Largo. Boats and marinas seemed to occupy each bridge and safe harbor he passed. The bird nests on pilings and power poles were distinctive to the climate and the Keys. Pelicans and cormorants everywhere. He stopped for lunch at a tavern that overlooked a large channel. As he watched people launch their boats, he ate the first of two hamburgers just as greasy and good as any he could find in Trout Lake. He noticed several Michigan cars. His Yukon was noticed, too, as people looked around to find the kindred spirit from the same state, but Matt didn't feel like exchanging pleasantries with others. Matt wondered what Vega looked like and what life around a Keys marina would mean to him. He reconsidered each of Vega's words on the phone—about the boat and Tanya—and wondered what it all meant. He also appreciated that Vega had more to say than he would trust to the phone lines or microwave towers.

Matt knew that locations in the Keys were noted by their mile markers and he had just passed the 100 marker a few miles before the restaurant. He knew Islamorada stretched between markers eighty and ninety, with Key West at zero. He finished his hamburgers and iced tea, nervous and excited about what would happen in the next hour.

Matt asked some locals for a car wash recommendation and was directed to a good one. Before reaching the car wash, he stopped and organized the back of the vehicle. He piled gear over the rifle and put luggage and the cooler against the sides of the panels that held his money. He wished he still had the plastic cover that pulled over the rear storage area, but he had removed it as soon as he got the Yukon to have more room and to make it easier to raise and lower the rear seats. At the car wash, he got out of the car while six or seven people swarmed over it, inside and outside, to turn the mud-, dust-, salt-, and even bug-spattered Yukon into the shiny, solid piece of GMC machinery he had bought used several years ago. He watched their every move, and they were all work. The Yukon came out of their doors looking like new. He wanted to present himself well to the Vegas. He couldn't believe how youthful he was acting. He was like a high-school boy going to his first prom and wanting the car perfect to pick up his date.

He stopped at a liquor store and bought several bottles of good wine plus beer, bourbon, gin, and vodka to stock the liquor cabinet of the boat on which he would be living. He picked a fine bottle of red wine for the Vegas and had the clerk put it into a separate bag. The store didn't have flowers. Just as well, as it kept him from making a total ass of himself.

Rolling down US 1, he smiled as the mile markers counted down ten every ten miles. At least some government system still worked perfectly. He cruised through Plantation Key and saw the signs for the Holiday Isle. He drove onto Islamorada when he crossed the bridge at Tavernier Creek. Not really a creek, just a passage between the Atlantic and Florida Bay. The compass on his rearview mirror indicated due west. It fools a lot of people when they discover the keys run generally east to west, not north to south. On his first trip to the Keys, thirty years ago, they had looked more like truck stops connected by bridges. At that time, the Holiday Isle was run by two German ladies and cost less than $40 a night for an ocean-view room. Now, businesses were much more commercial, neater, cleaner and everywhere constructed to please and claim the interest and money of the tourist. Matt turned into the Holiday Isle by the gas station that had been there forever, went a little further, and parked in front of the Dive and Fishing Charter Shop.

29

Islamorada

MATT HAD LET THE YUKON COOL DOWN with the AC off for the last three or four miles. He still liked to think of the vehicle as a living entity and liked to let it cool down after a long run. He knew the treatment was not really necessary, but he did it anyway. He was getting a little warm when he got out of the vehicle and locked it. He could smell the sea, the hot asphalt, fish, and just a hint of diesel. The shop was dark and cold compared to the brightness and heat of the parking lot. Seeing no one, he rang the bell on the counter. The sound summoned a good-looking man in his sixties wearing a Dive Shop T-shirt, less than Matt's six feet but standing straight and carrying himself as though used to a pressed uniform. He had dark, sparkling eyes and laugh lines around his eyes and mouth.

He asked, "Matt?"

Matt nodded.

The man stuck out a strong, tanned hand. "Welcome to the Keys, Matt."

"It's good to be here," Matt said, noting the man's firm grip. He looked around the shop. "This is a fine shop."

Vega looked hard into Matt's eyes. "Would you like something to drink and see your boat?"

"Sounds great," answered Matt, knowing Vega wouldn't do much talking inside the store.

Vega disappeared behind a curtain and returned with a can of Diet Coke, which he handed to Matt. As Matt popped the top, Vega came around the counter and led him through a side door to the marina side of the shop.

"We have two charter boats inside the marina. They're rigged for diving or fishing groups. We have a fifty-four-foot Hatteras moored outside the main marina. Picked it up at a very good price last year. The previous owner, a very rich guy, lived on it from time to time and had it reconditioned. We use it for longer diving or fishing charters and for occasional cruising customers."

As they walked around the outside of the marina, Matt felt sweat beading down his back, making his shirt stick, and wondered why they hadn't taken his car.

Vega stopped when they were nearly around the marina, pointed at another one-room boat and diving shop a short distance ahead and said, "We own that shop too. More of an office for the dive and boat activities, while the other's more of a store. Keep looking around as I point. I've got things to tell you."

Matt stood beside Vega and sipped his Coke.

Vega kept his voice low, even though they were thirty yards from the nearest building. "You can't repeat what I'm going to tell you. Don't even try. Tanya is fine. She contacted me several days ago. The DEA has Webb in custody, and she will be a part of the case against him. What he does and how much he helps the DEA will determine when we see Tanya again. But the bottom line is she's fine and knows you're here. She told me she loves you." He glanced at Matt, and a smile flitted across his face. "You're older than I expected, but I'm happy if my daughter's in love, safe, and happy. My wife and I know Tanya's a good judge of character. We also know you saved her life and even stood up to Webb and his gangsters. That's better than I did."

"I'm sure you did what you could."

Vega put his hand on Matt's sore shoulder and gave it a manly squeeze. "I'm grateful to you in many ways."

Matt winced a bit and hoped the wound wouldn't break open. "Why the secrecy and what can we say about Tanya?"

"Webb's people have ears as big as the Federal people. I've walked a thin line between both worlds. Tanya has too. We don't talk about her because we don't know what information might hurt her with either the mob or the government. We live in a continual state of worry. It's less than it was, but it still hangs over us. Tanya said she'd explain everything when she is able to see us. In the meantime, we're to take care of you, keep you happy, and not let you get sunburned or run over by a boat. She's the one who suggested you use the Hatteras. But it is most important we mention nothing about Webb being in custody. Tanya broke major secrecy to tell us."

"What's my reason for being here?" asked Matt.

"Let's say you met Tanya after you retired from teaching, and she mentioned I was looking for some help. You came down to help out until she gets back."

"That's close enough to the truth. I can use my true identity. After all, I have always loved fishing, diving, and boating. So I shouldn't have too much trouble keeping that story straight. I'll keep my feelings for her to myself."

They walked over to the larger boats moored outside the marina, but still protected by the natural harbor formed by the Holiday Isle and the highway. Eight large, moored yachts faced out between large pilings. In the third slot rested a beautiful, white Hatteras.

30

The *Reefer*

MATT SMILED AS HE STEPPED ABOARD the Hatteras, feeling the big boat rock gently on the water.

Vega gestured around the deck. "This was Webb's boat, but we never mention his name. I hold the papers on it, but I had to let him use it anytime and keep it ready for sea. Several years ago he paid about $800,000 at a government auction—they had impounded it—and then put more money into it. The hull's special as are the engines. He sold it to me for a quarter-million dollars last year on a sort of land contract—I can't even put it up for sale. Tanya had something to do with the transaction."

Vega paused to point at the other boats moored around them. "The boats are expensive, but we need them to stay in business. Since Tanya was our primary captain, things are a bit tight right now. By the time we cover the loans, interest, upkeep, fishing or diving equipment, and then pay a captain, we don't make much."

"I understand this is an expensive business," Matt said.

"I didn't even mention insurance, a crippling expense these days. We maintain large deductibles and pray for safe journeys." He shook his head. "You should see our release form for the tourists."

"Damn lawyers make everything expensive," Matt muttered.

Vega laughed. "Tanya mentioned you wanted to get captain's papers. Maybe I can help you out there. The classes are demanding, but an ex-teacher should be able to handle it. The biggest limitation is the hours you need at the helm of various-size boats." Vega led him to the cabin. Matt admired the palatial salon as they entered from the aft deck. It looked like a movie set. Large leather couches lined both sides. A large bar and a small galley. Two staterooms, a master and a forward, with separate heads, showers, and televisions. The guest head could also be entered from the main passageway. The bow had a large storage area, like a walk-in closet. A stacked washer and dryer sat just forward of the galley. The craft had more room than many apartments Matt had stayed in. The air conditioning kept everything dry and cool. The engine room, big enough to stand up in, contained two large diesels and multiple other motors and machines that Matt couldn't identify. Everything shipshape and spotless.

On the large flybridge, Matt discovered he was familiar with most of the controls. Parts of the console looked like something you would expect in a Boeing 747 cockpit.

He leaned over to look at the electronic fishing and navigation equipment. "This is expensive stuff."

"Webb likes nothing but the best," Vega said.

Forward of the controls was a comfortable seating area, above the flybridge a marlin tower with more controls and instruments. The fishing equipment and rigging were all top of the line and looked new. A marlin-fighting chair sat on the aft deck, and compartments opened to expose a bait preparation center, a tackle center, a live bait well, and a small sink.

"I hope you can be comfortable here," said Vega, giving Matt a wink.

"I'm overwhelmed. I just came from several weeks at my hunting cabin where we're glad to have inside plumbing and working electricity."

"Think you can adjust?"

"Look, are you sure you want me here?" Matt asked. "I could find a motel."

"No, Tanya wants you here. Besides, you can help me by keeping this thing shined up and I'll go with you to check it out on a few charters. You can run it, get some helm time, and get up to speed on the navigation gear. Webb had the usual three-bedroom configuration modified to just two very nice cabins. The salon can sleep another four. It can cruise 600 miles depending upon your speed, and it makes over 600 gallons of fresh water a day if you're out of port. The ice maker can keep your drinks iced or keep your fish cold in big freezers."

"All the...well," Matt chuckled. "I almost said all the comforts of home, but my home can't compare to all this."

Vega shrugged. "Money can change your perspective on necessities. In fact, this hull design is found only on a few Hatteras boats, with a special reduced-draft bottom with prop pockets. Webb invested more than seventy grand in rebuilding the two 1200-horsepower MAN diesels, which still have low hours. This boat'll haul ass."

"I'll just bet it will," Matt said.

Vega showed Matt around for another hour, explaining how to work the basic equipment: the heads, the twenty-kilowatt auxiliary generator, the six parallel-switched batteries, and the complex inverter-controlled electrical system with its soundproof generator. Vega showed him the plastic barrel that held the Avon eight-person life raft, and how to use the davit to load and unload the Boston Whaler secured to the main deck. He showed Matt the checklist for shore hookups and remote anchoring.

When Vega fired up the radar and navigation equipment, Matt held up a hand. "Whoa. I've been on the road for three days. I'm starting to feel like a man trying to drink from a fire hose."

"Sorry." Vega patted him on the back. "This boat always gets me excited. But let's stop for now. Just one more thing."

Matt followed Vega into the salon where Vega opened a beautiful wooden cabinet with a desk that contained the navigation and electrical control station. He pulled out several books and manuals. "You need to go over these so you know where the information is in case you need it. You have two GPS systems on board, a Furuno and a Northstar. You have a color video depth sounder and a 96-mile radar both by Furuno."

"Can that wait until tomorrow?" Matt really wanted a shower and some time to relax.

"Sure. But, right now, let's look at the important stuff." He showed Matt how to run the TV satellite dish and the Sony entertainment center. "You also have a satellite phone, but it's not activated."

"Guess I won't lose touch with the world."

Vega laughed. "Not unless you want to. I'll show you the rest when we're ready to use it. Let's walk back and get your car. I'll give you a sticker so you can park right by the dive office."

As Vega ushered Matt out and closed and locked the salon door, Matt said, "I doubt there are any hotel rooms around here that can compare to this."

Vega handed Matt the key on a floating ring. "Don't worry about living here, we'll get some payback work out of you."

The two men continued talking on the way back to the main shop. Vega asked questions about Matt's background and interests. Matt gave him a quick outline of his life, ending with his time on fishing boats and ocean charters, his diving skills, and his land in the U.P.

Back at the shop, Vega asked, "My wife and I would love it if you would come to dinner tonight. Around seven?"

"Sure," Matt agreed. "My pleasure."

"Good. I'll tell you about my Air Force career over cocktails before dinner. We eat late and get up early so if you see us nodding off at 11:00, you'll hopefully understand."

Vega gave Matt a map and got a ten-minute tour of the shop. They stocked only first-rate equipment and clothes, meaning expensive. Matt met the girl he had spoken to on the phone. Young and energetic, she probably wore her clothes out from the inside. She seemed to never stop moving.

Matt moved his gear and booze aboard the boat. The *Reefer*. Whether christened by Webb or the original owner, Matt hoped the best connotation of the name would fit. He planned to anchor it over lots of reefs. He couldn't believe the luxury that surrounded him. He changed into shorts, T-shirt, and flip-flops. He turned on the stereo, picked up a heavy crystal-rock glass, put in nearly round ice cubes from the built-in ice maker, poured in some bourbon, and swirled it around. It made an expensive sound. Up onto the aft deck, in perfect temperature out of the afternoon sun, he sat in the marlin chair that had a chrome label reading "Murray Brothers." He put his feet in the footrests and leaned into the comfort of the padded chair. Out in the marina, boats were returning from a day catching, or trying to catch, fish. Their captains efficiently, skillfully eased them into the moorings. The customers—in their bright clothes and sunburned cheeks and noses—stood quietly as the captains and crews worked over the boats, securing all the lines, icing the catch, in some cases cutting up the fish, washing down the decks and working areas and, finally, shaking hands, loading fish and tackle into pickups, and securing their boats for the evening. Matt watched this process repeated a dozen times over three bourbons. He felt wonderful and a little bit at sea—literally. The slight rocking comforted him. After the third bourbon, he laid out his new slacks and best-looking shirt on the master stateroom's queen-sized bed.

While showering, he thought about his two logistical problems: the money and his rifle. He would move both aboard after dark.

He needed groceries too. Although semi-stocked with canned and dry goods, the galley contained no fresh food and its freezers were empty. He remembered passing a large grocery store as he drove through Plantation Key. Ending the shower, Matt dried himself and contemplated the complexities of this floating palace, unlike anything he'd ever experienced.

He needed to find some hiding places and resolved to start with the bow and slowly work aft until he knew every part of the boat. Then he could decide where to stash his contraband.

31

Meeting the Parents

MATT SPENT OVER $100 on five bags of groceries, finding most items more expensive than in the U.P. The fresh produce and the in-house baked breads were a plus in his book for the Winn Dixie or Piggly Wiggly or whatever they called the store. They had the air conditioner in high gear, Matt shivered while checking out. The warm air outside felt good.

At the marina, Matt parked in his approved spot. Two young athletes from the dive shop came out and helped him carry the bags to the boat. Vega must have talked to them, as they were very polite and good-old-boy sincere as they answered boat questions. Obviously familiar with the boat, they showed him how to turn on the anchor lights and work the various lines that secured the *Reefer* to the dock and mooring posts. They said they would be around if he needed any help and suggested Matt should get a dash cover for the Yukon if he was going to park in the sun all day. Though they didn't ask him any questions, Matt could sense they were full of them.

Matt changed from a T-shirt to a dark polo shirt. He put on his new Dockers, Top Siders, and sunglasses, then checked himself out in the aft salon mirrors. He didn't think he looked his age. He carried a light sweater in case the Vegas chose to sit outside. He knew evenings in the Keys could get cool. Although used to the cold and snow of the U.P., there he wore wool and long underwear. Cotton wouldn't keep him warm if, like many southerners, the Vegas set their air conditioners at temperatures designed to keep meat fresh.

Matt locked the boat up as instructed, checked the lines as instructed, and drove north, which was really east, to the Vega home as instructed. He arrived ten minutes early and slowly drove by the house to the end of the road, which meant to the Bay. He turned around and checked out the neighborhood. The Vegas lived on a road of older bungalow homes. Their backyards either ended in mangroves or a canal depending on how much someone had spent on excavating before laws were passed to regulate how much of the Keys one could dig up to get bay or ocean to their property. The Vega's home sat on about an acre and had a well-tended lawn of the domesticated quack grass popular with those who wanted a green lawn. Several young palm trees grew on one side of the house and a hedge of oleander on the other. The circular drive ended in a garage and portico that shaded and protected the entering guest. Matt noted they had a roof and eave system that caught rainwater, indicating that the house was fairly old, constructed when builders and owners worked at getting all the free water they could. There had to be a cistern somewhere in the side yard. Matt drove slowly back up the road and turned onto the well-groomed and sealed asphalt driveway.

George Vega stood at the entrance when Matt stopped the Yukon. Vega greeted Matt as he got out of the vehicle. "This is some vehicle. Just what you need for snow and hauling deer. How's the gas mileage?"

"Depending on the wind and load, I get around seventeen or eighteen miles per gallon. It rides well and you can see over most cars," answered Matt, completing the compulsory initial meaningless chitchat.

"I worked with almost every type of piston motor the Air Force had for over twenty years. I still like to take things apart and see how they work." Vega held the door for Matt to enter the house. "I restore old cars for a hobby. But I haven't had the time for the last several years. I just sold a 1929 Star that I worked on for five years. I haven't started another project."

"Great hobby," Matt said, stepping into the house.

"It is, but our business takes most of my time now, and I don't get into the machinery very much anymore. Most of the boats we have now are so new I either don't need to do much or I don't have the computers and such that they need. The day of the real mechanic is about over. Everything is solid state: sealed-component-and-replace versus the old fix-it technology."

The house, 1960s layout, could have served as a set for the old TV show "Father Knows Best." A large main room stretched across the front with a lannon stone fireplace that looked like it never had a fire in it. One archway led to the dining room and kitchen, on the garage side, and Matt assumed the other archway led to the bedrooms and bathroom. The walls, pale yellow stucco, seemed freshly painted and nicely complemented the light-colorful furnishings. Vega led Matt into the large kitchen that opened onto a screened porch overlooking a small back lawn that ended at a dock with a moored, center-console fishing boat, an eighteen- or twenty-footer.

Mrs. Vega looked to be making fruit salad and stopped to dry her hands. Thin, small, probably middle-European ancestry, with high cheekbones and light hair mostly gray, she seemed nervous. Matt remembered Tanya talking about her mother's problems with ulcers. She held out a delicate hand. "How do you do, Mr. Hunter. Welcome to our home. We've heard how wonderful you were to our Tanya."

As he shook her hand, Matt wondered just how much Tanya had said about how wonderful things between he and Tanya had been. "It's a pleasure to meet you, Mrs. Vega. Thank you for inviting me to your home."

"Call me Anita. Mrs. Vega was George's mother." Mrs. Vega gave him an easy, gentle smile. "I hope you like grilled fish and vegetables. Dinner is ready whenever George gets the fish done."

"I love fish. I've got a bottle of wine in the car. I'll go get it. It's red but the appreciation is sincere even if the wine is the wrong color."

"What do you drink?" George Vega asked with one hand on the refrigerator door handle.

"A beer would be fine," said Matt, remembering the three bourbons he had had in the afternoon.

Vega opened two Coronas and handed Matt one bottle. "Let's get that wine and I'll show you the garage and house, then I can put the fish on the grill. If we time it right, that will be just about time for another beer."

Vega and Matt went into the garage, a mechanic's dream. Tools lined all the walls above well-placed and well-lighted workbenches and power tools stored in shelves made for them. Matt identified grinders, drill presses, and a radial arm saw. Everything neat and shiny clean. The paint had a military look.

"You keep a neat shop."

"Military habit, and as I get older I need to put my stuff back in a particular spot or I can't find anything," said Vega as he turned on a half-inch drill press and moved close to Matt. "We need to talk seriously about some things. Did Tanya tell you about what has been happening here over the last few years?"

"She mentioned how you and she had gotten involved with Webb. She talked about her problems at work and with Webb using you both when it suited him," said Matt.

"We're talking here because I don't want to make my wife more nervous, and I am fairly sure this area isn't bugged. I know we're being watched. I don't know if it is government or mob people—or maybe both. The girl at the marina, Webb asked to hire her as a favor. He acted like it was just a favor for her family, and she works hard, but I don't trust her. I've got Air Force buddies living all over the country, and they have caller ID; but when I call them they don't see our name and number, just locations in Colorado or Atlanta. I think our phone is tapped."

Vega pulled out a shop stool for Matt, motioning for him to take the seat. After a long drink from the clear bottle, he continued, "We get expensive charters for the Hatteras, people who put down deposits that are not refundable and then they don't show up. We keep the *Reefer* shipshape and we get regular amounts of money for having it that way. We almost expect the monthly money now. Our bank debts were built up because Webb made me buy some bigger boats we didn't really need. Now, the notes have been paid up. The bank won't give any information other than the debts have been paid and the titles are clear and in my name. This makes a paper trail that I can't explain. It all looks great on a balance sheet, and we pay all our taxes. It's just I know I'm being manipulated, and I can't do anything about it. I can't even figure what Webb or whoever is trying to do. We haven't taken any shady charters for several years. We haven't sent out any suspicious, no-questions-asked, bare-bones rentals for some time. My retirement and social security and the shop were enough to keep us comfortable, but now we are worth several millions. I'm telling you this because Tanya trusts you and wants you here. I want you to know what is going on in case you decide to stay. Just be careful what you say and where you say it. Don't talk about Tanya or Webb. She contacts me only though a pay phone system."

"Is there any way I can talk to her?" Matt asked.

"Not really at this time. I'll try to set something up but it will take a while," said Vega as he turned off the drill press and ushered Matt through the side door of the garage toward the patio.

On the patio, a fire burned in the grill and a plastic container with the fish sat nearby. A variety of spices and spatulas stood ready for the chef.

"Anita does all the work, I put the fish on for a few minutes a side and get all the credit for being a master chef," said Vega as he expertly prepared the grill surface, seasoned the thick fish fillets, and put them on the grill.

He pointed at the thick fish steaks with a spatula. "Sailfish. They dry out easily so I need to stay right with them. The whole trend to blackened fish cooking is just because people are too lazy to watch what they are doing. We soaked these in a soy sauce marinade and I keep brushing them with a mixture of butter, oil, and a little garlic. I think you'll like it."

Matt inhaled the aroma of grilling fish. "It smells great. The last real cooked dinner I had was with your daughter."

A hint of pain flashed in Vega's eyes as he gestured a toast with his beer bottle. "Let's hope we can all be together again soon and share some great food on the grill." Over a fine meal, they talked about Matt's hunting experiences, his son, his work in the classroom and in athletics. They answered questions about Tanya but didn't talk at length. Matt soon understood it was painful for them to relive stories of her growing up. Great sports fans, they knew all the top football and basketball teams, collegiate and pro. They talked about fishing trips and how the area off Islamorada has a seamount that brings deep currents to the surface and provides some of the best fishing in the Keys. They talked about diving on various reefs. Matt went over his history in the area. They shared the pleasant serendipity of living in a place where Matt had vacationed several times. They talked about retirement. The Vegas had considered selling everything to avoid the long hours needed to run their business profitably. Although nobody mentioned Webb and they only briefly talked about Tanya, both seemed to cast a silent presence at the table.

They had coffee and Key lime pie out on the screen porch. The conversation turned to Matt's plans. They agreed he should stay as long as he wanted, working on the boats as a crew member, building up his time at the helm, and working toward his captain's papers. When Matt saw them tiring, he thanked them for their warm hospitality and the fine meal. George Vega shook Matt's hand firmly. Anita hugged him warmly.

"Thank you for taking care of my daughter," she whispered in his ear before letting him go. Matt backed the Yukon into his parking spot in the well-lit marina with the rear bumper very close to the heavy chain link fence so no one could open the back doors. He left the money and rifle inside. Matt decided the Yukon was as safe as the boat for now. He decided to bank most of the money in the next few days.

Matt had half a Key lime pie to put into his refrigerator, a gift from Mrs. Vega with the admonition that it "will get soggy if you don't eat it right away."

Tanya's parents had impressed Matt favorably. He could not help but like them both. As Matt entered his new floating home, curiosity overwhelmed his desire to kick back and relax for the rest of the evening.

The instruction manuals and logs still lay on the navigation table. Matt turned on the light over the table and planned to just scan the pages to acquaint himself with the scope of the material. He found the log the most interesting, with each voyage since the boat's renovation recorded. Just short notes about number of passengers, crew, weather, where they had gone, and what they had done. Most records detailed deep-sea fishing charters and several captained cruises into the Bahamas or the Dry Tortugas. Most entries were in the neat printing of George Vega and two were in Tanya's script. Matt looked for an earlier log and found one. The boat was older than it looked—early 1993 vintage. The older log entries, incomplete and not well organized, were probably written by the original owner, arrested when the Feds had impounded the boat. Matt wondered why Webb would buy an older boat and fix it up. Webb had a lot more money than time.

Matt finally found some of the renovation bills in a business-size envelope inside a manual for the washer and dryer. They covered work on the master and guest staterooms and heads, the windows, carpet, and couches in the salon, and upholstered headboards in the master and forward staterooms. He found a separate bill for installation of the new washer and dryer with line items for custom paneling and woodwork. Matt added the bills in his head. Over $100,000. The bills were from a person in Miami—simple, hand-printed on the yellow part of a three-part business form. Matt believed extensive work had been completed on the instruments and mechanical equipment, but found no bills. The manuals for the radar and depth sounder were only a few years old. The plastic canvas over the flybridge looked very new. Matt wondered again why Webb would fix up an older boat and then support it at the marina with regular no-show charters.

Too tired for more detective work that night, Matt went into the master stateroom, washed up, and went to bed. The bed was truly wonderful, the rocking and jerking against the ropes was cradle-like. Matt tried to think about all that was happening—giving thanks that Tanya was safe—but fell asleep within minutes.

32

Marina Life

MATT WOKE TO A KNOCKING on the door frame, surprised that he had not felt the boat move when the person had stepped aboard the aft deck. Then he realized the slight change that a 200-pound person would bring to a 70,000-pound boat. Hard to detect in the harbor waves.

"I'm with the pumping service," a man's voice called out. "You living aboard now? You want to be pumped out one time a week?"

Matt slid the salon screen open, not yet totally awake. At least now the question of sewage was answered. Stifling a yawn, he said, "Sure. Who do I pay?"

"I give the bill to the shop, and they settle with you." The man handed Matt a business card. "If you need more pumping, call me or tell the shop. Number's on the card."

"Thanks." Matt looked at the card and nodded. "What day do you come?"

"Monday later or Tuesday early."

"Okay. Appreciate your stopping by."

The man paused to admire the salon. "Nice boat you got here."

"If only it were all mine," Matt muttered, as much to himself as his visitor.

"I hear you. Banks own most everything," the man said with a smile and left.

Matt put the card in the navigation table drawer and decided he was up for the day. He made breakfast, then took his coffee cup and treated himself to another tour of his temporary home. Truly a beautiful craft. He had always heard of the Hatteras as one of the world's best-built boats. Burtrum or Grand Banks owners might argue the point, but everything Matt saw on his tour impressed him. The *Reefer* was made for cruising, fishing, and living aboard. He found the dive platform stored in the engine room. It would take two men to carry and rig it on the stern. The German V-12 diesel engines were also marvels of mechanical beauty. Matt resisted the urge to fire them up. He needed to check with Vega first.

Succumbing to the natural camaraderie among boat owners, Matt introduced himself to his neighbors.

To port, an expatriate Cuban-American doctor and his family from Miami occupied a 51-foot motor sailor. A beautiful wife and three teenage children. They talked freely to Matt. They planned to head out for a sail to Key West then on to the Dry Tortugas. They invited Matt to dinner the next time they came down for a weekend. Matt admired their organization as each family member jumped to their tasks with little prodding—storing provisions, untying lines, disconnecting shore hook-ups, warming up their small diesel, and checking their gauges and tanks. In less than thirty minutes they were heading out the channel toward the Atlantic, with the oldest girl at the wheel. The father pointed out landmarks as his family moved over the deck, pulled the protective canvas off the sail booms, freed jib lines, brought out the chrome crank handles, and stowed their docking lines and cables.

Wistfully, Matt watched, fighting the siren song of the open sea that urged him to follow them.

To starboard, a dark gray 40-foot trawler, more work boat than pleasure craft, seemed a little out of place among all the fiberglass and chrome. Upon closer inspection, Matt recognized its functional beauty. All locked up, its dark portholes and cabin windows made it look almost sinister. Its perfectly conditioned teak deck and very nautical cord whippings on the handrails and line ends looked professional. Its antennae and radar rigging announced up-to-date electronics and navigational equipment.

The marina had come alive with boats starting and idling, loading up and filing out the marina entrance, and turning left to parade out the channel to the deeper water. Matt watched them, reveling in the way the greens and blues of the sea varied as the sun and clouds played over the surface, like a perfect, ever-changing painting.

Reluctantly, Matt returned to the *Reefer*, cleaned up, made the bed, and walked to the main shop. He found George Vega talking to a customer about wet suits. The protracted discussion ranged over two-piece vs. one-piece suits, about two mil or thicker suits, about long or short legs. The customer ended up with a short legged, short-sleeved, one-piece suit. George ran the credit card, and the man left.

George turned to Matt and said, "Too many choices these days. And the Internet hurts us. People come in and use our time and knowledge, take notes, and buy their suits below our costs."

"Then they'll wonder where the little shops went," Matt said.

"I suppose so. But that's not your problem. How about we get you fixed up for a short dive late this afternoon?" After reviewing the many options, Matt selected a one-piece with short legs, long sleeves, and a front zipper stretching all the way down the left leg. Made by Bare, it's neoprene was only 3mm thick. He also bought a U.S. Divers mask, full-foot flippers, and a snorkel. Vega sold him a new top-of-the-line Sherwood buoyancy compensator several generations more advanced than Matt's old equipment. He bought an eighty-cubic-foot aluminum tank and a new top-rated Sherwood regulator and two breathing mouthpieces , his most expensive single purchase. The regulator's assortment of gauges displayed volume, depth, and maybe the direction to the nearest bar. Vega threw in a used-but-serviceable diving bag to hold the gear. The total came to a Vega-adjusted $1,200 with tax. Vega raised an eyebrow but said nothing when Matt put a neat pile of hundred-dollar bills on the counter.

"I'll get a bank account and some local checks soon," said Matt.

"I like my bank in Key Largo, but you might want to shop around," said Vega. "I'll have your tank filled and one of my boys bring everything to the boat, along with my own stuff. We can check you out on the *Reefer*, too. How about four-ish?"

"Sounds good."

"That gives us calm waters and decent light for several hours. Have some beers and sandwich-makings on board, and we can stay out until dark. You need to know how to find this place at night. Anyone can come in during the day."

"Why don't you bring your wife if she'd like to come along?" Matt asked.

"That's a good idea. She wouldn't dive but she loves to be on the water at sunset. We'll see you later." Vega turned to another customer that the shop girl was showing spear guns.

Back at the *Reefer*, the cool salon provided welcome relief from the unaccustomed heat outside. Deciding he shouldn't delay any longer, he decided to clean out the hot-as-an-oven Yukon, removing the wrappers and bottles and cups that had built up during the drive down. He aired it out and carried the Remington into the boat, wrapped in all his jackets and his sleeping bag. No one paid him any attention. He took three shells from the twelve in his shell holder and, contrary to his usual safety measures, he loaded them into the magazine. He stored the rifle in a pull-out drawer under the bed, wrapping the rifle in the extra blankets it contained and putting the two extra pillows on top. Not bad for a storage place: easy to get at and not too noticeable. He could grab the rifle and quickly chamber a shell, if he needed to. Vega's need for secrecy and his wife's nervousness seemed like a warning, and being able to blow away anything that walked produced a certain sense of security for Matt.

Matt decided to check all the new construction, starting with the master stateroom. Using the twenty-five-foot Lufkin metal tape measure from the Yukon's toolbox, he measured the under-bed drawers and the distance across the bed. Twenty-six inches unaccounted for. Matt pulled out the drawers, finding solid wood behind them. Matt removed the bed covers and lifted out the foam and innerspring mattress. The bed's woodwork had not been designed for easy disassembly. Marine spar varnish and stain coated everything. Excellent work, the kind one would expect on a million-dollar yacht.

That left the end panel. Matt slowly covered each inch, looking for joins or panels or levers. Just as solid and with the same careful work. After an hour of thumping, examining, and measuring, Matt could find no way to access that twenty-six-inch by six-foot-three-inch space under the mattress. The drawers didn't go all the way through because they could only come out so far within the confines of the room. Nothing moved or sounded loose about the end of the bed. Matt put everything back and made up the bed.

Matt next inspected the forward stateroom. All measurements fit and all woodwork looked perfect. The bathrooms went quickly. Most of the fixtures were brass and chrome of the highest quality. There were showers in both with the master having a small tub. Matt's inspection revealed nothing that moved when it shouldn't or showed any scrapes from swinging or moving. Again, impressive workmanship and material quality. And very clean.

It occurred to Matt that somebody might access the master stateroom bed space from the engine compartment. He found a hatch that opened to a space below the bed area, only large enough to allow inspection of the top of fuel tanks and to snake wires and tubes though the boat. He could crawl forward for only five or six feet before the space became too narrow and low for further movement. Matt checked the space with a flashlight but, again, no evidence of a hiding place or hidden panels. It was all very clean, and Matt could just detect a faint smell of diesel fuel, not surprising because the tanks held over 1200 gallons of the stuff.

Matt's inspection of the *Reefer* merely showed everything in perfect order and extremely clean. Someone had followed a regular schedule to keep the bright work, deck, and windows so clean.

Matt slipped into slacks, collared sports shirt, and leather shoes and drove the Yukon east until he found a large bank just north of Key Largo. They had full service and safety deposit boxes. Matt opened an account with $1,000 and rented a large safety deposit box. He told the truth about staying on a boat in a marina and wanting to secure valuables that might be easy prey on a boat. He declined the checking service but applied for the ATM card they offered. After putting most of his money in the deposit box, he felt better about leaving the Yukon out of his sight.

Matt felt he had paid some dues for the money and hoped it would give him some power over events. He planned to add money over time to the account and use the ATMs located throughout the area. He would have his Visa card statements forwarded to the Islamorada address. He saved a $10.000 bundle and hid it behind the jack in the Yukon. It wouldn't fool any real good search, but it might foil casual searchers. He had another pile of bills aboard the *Reefer* in a lock box used for customers' watches and rings when aboard the boat.

He returned to the boat in the early afternoon and found the diving gear inside the salon. Vega had another key. He stowed the equipment outside on the deck, in the shade. He ate lunch, donned a swimsuit and T-shirt, and continued exploring the *Reefer*. He sat at the controls on the flybridge, the instruments alone worth several times what he had paid for a complete Lake Michigan fishing boat. He climbed to the top of the marlin tower, more than eighteen feet above the water with a fine view of the marina, the channel, and Highway 1 that passed to the north.

The Vegas drove up as he sat in the elevated position trying to identify each radio antenna, GPS dome, the radar apparatus, and the TV satellite dish. They carried paper bags.

Supper and snacks, Matt hoped.

They didn't look up as they came aboard and he surprised them when he called down, "Welcome aboard."

"Oh my." Anita Vega put a hand to her chest and smiled up at him. "I didn't see you up there."

"Sorry," Matt said, "didn't mean to startle you."

"That's all right, I'll recover." She held up a paper bag. "I brought some snacks, cocktail fixings, and ham-and-potato salad for a supper."

Vega waved at him. "Come on down to the engine room, and I'll show you where the fuel line's emergency shut-off valves are located. You should never start a diesel without knowing how to shut it off."

They went below, and Vega demonstrated how to ready the engines, check for oil leaks, and manually inspect the bilge and safety equipment. They went over the fire control system again, the personal flotation devices, the first aid kits, then went to the flying bridge, where they checked the various radios and the compass. Then they turned on the blowers, checked all their gauges, and started the diesels. Matt closed his eyes for a moment, absorbing their powerful bubbling sound. They turned on and checked all their navigation instrumentation and also made sure they had the appropriate charts on board.

Vega told him, "What we just did is what I would expect of a captain before taking out any boat. You are never in too much of a hurry to make these inspections. Now let's see if we can get out of here without dragging the dock away with us."

They carefully unplugged their shore connections and stored them either in their place on the dock or their place on the boat.

"Tie the leeward bow and stern spring lines together, keep them dry and reachable for our return. Then take off the lines as I tell you. I'll let you do it so you learn," said Vega.

Matt got all the lines untied, either returned to the boat or secured on the dock. He was tying the windward, port, and spring lines together when he felt the props engage and the *Reefer* get underway.

"Come on up and take us out. It's about two hours past low tide so we need to stay strictly in the channel," Vega said.

Matt took the wheel with his left hand and held the two throttles with his right. The boat turned easily under the engines' effortless hum. Matt stayed in the middle of the channel, which thankfully no other vessels were using. He could see the shallow water on both sides. It looked a foot deep, but Matt knew it was really five or six feet and quickly going to ten and twelve. The incoming tide was not a factor.

"We draw about five feet," Vega said. "But you should panic at six feet. These props cost five figures." Even at their very slow speed, the two GPS units refreshed every few feet. Matt increased speed as they left the channel, heading for the half-mile-long Alligator Reef, the largest and easiest-to-find reef in the Keys. Its 136-foot tower can be seen for thirty miles. Once in deep water, Matt turned east while Vega showed Matt how to use the GPS, the radar, and the depth sounder.

"We've marked all the diving places on our charts and loaded them into the GPS." Vega pulled a pair of binoculars from a drawer. "She can drive you there on her own while avoiding the major reefs. You do need to watch out for the minor reefs, other boats, and junk in the water,"

"Will she make me coffee too?"

"Almost," Vega replied. "Let's go up to the marlin bridge. It's really some feeling moving over the water from up there, and you can see better. But only in calm water and at slow speeds."

The view from the marlin bridge almost took Matt's breath away—360 degrees of blue-green water. The *Reefer* hummed along at fifteen knots. The relatively flat ocean with its one- to two-foot swells had settled into its afternoon calm.

"Open her up for a few minutes," said Vega.

Matt pushed the throttles forward. Fifty-four feet of Hatteras lifted its bow out of the water and doubled its speed with an effortless exercise of power and fine boat design. Thirty-two knots and still accelerating. At thirty-seven, Vega made a hand signal to ease her down. Matt brought her to a nice cruising speed of twenty-five knots. Vega went down to the flying bridge and took the helm while Matt came down. The instrument panel's dials and meters all indicated a happy boat doing what it was designed to do.

They came to the reef and its tower in just a few minutes. Matt would have liked a longer run, but Vega had other ideas. Vega slowed the *Reefer*, while pointing out how the GPS, radar, and sounder all confirmed their position. The reef depth ranged from about eight to forty feet. They steered wide into deeper water near the buoy-marked wreck of the USS *Alligator*. Then they brought the boat around and, going slowly, approached a row of buoys with eight dive boats moored.

Vega waved an arm at the scene. "This is the dive area where we take ninety percent of our first dive customers. The tower gives people in the water a reference and we can dive on the reef and the USS *Alligator* on the same trip." Vega brought the boat to dead slow about a quarter-mile from the tower and had Matt attach a bow line and secure it aft to the closest buoy. Vega idled the engines for a minute before shutting them down.

Quiet. Calm. Beauty fit for a postcard.

"If it wasn't for the buoys, the anchors of the dive boats would have completely destroyed every good reef in Florida," said Vega.

The two men wrestled the diving platform into place and locked it down.

"How about a little snorkeling first?" Vega asked.

He and Matt put on their wet suits and sat on the diving platform, only a few inches above the water, to put on their flippers and masks.

"Follow me," said Vega as he held his mask and rolled forward into the clear water.

Matt followed him into the calm water with visibility as much as eighty feet. Matt inspected the bottom of the Hatteras with its twin propellers tucked into formed pockets, making them less efficient at low speeds but better at higher speeds, and impressive twin rudders. Finishing his brief inspection, Matt noticed that Vega had continued toward the reef, forcing Matt to work to catch up. Vega made a surface dive to some coral heads in about twenty feet of water. He turned and motioned Matt down.

Matt got the drill. Vega wanted to know if he could dive.

Matt followed Vega wherever he went. Then he went ahead and made several long underwater runs along the reef in ten to fifteen feet of water. Matt enjoyed diving the reef, which was not as alive as twenty years ago, but again who was?

There were still live coral groups, schools of colorful fish, and the constant clicking sound of life underwater. Matt watched Vega take something from his wet suit. Soon, hundreds of fish swarmed around him—parrotfish, grunts, and a few larger striped groupers. Moving closer, he saw that Vega was distributing bits of soft tortillas—a coaching point not wasted on Matt.

They moved along the reef for several hundred yards before turning back. They took turns pointing out various corals, sponges, schools of fish, a stingray and, in the deeper water near the boat, a school of two- to three-foot barracuda.

They reached the boat and heaved themselves onto the diving platform.

"Be careful of this platform if you take people out in any real waves. Lots of times they hang on when it is going up and get pulled under it, then it comes down and they get a good bump. It's the most dangerous thing they do all day, just when they're the most tired and relaxed, thinking they are safely back to the boat," said Vega.

"Good point," Matt agreed.

"How about an easy tank dive to the USS *Alligator*?"

"Sounds like fun."

"You feel up to driving?" asked Vega.

"You bet," Matt said, glad Vega had asked.

Getting to the next dive area proved easy. Once again tied to a buoy, they only had about an hour of light left, maybe less. They donned their vests and tanks, checked each other, and slipped quickly into the water.

They went to the bottom at about forty feet and worked their way to the mound of ballast stones that is the wreck of the USS *Alligator*, a ship of the pirating days that hit the reef in 1825. Matt followed Vega around coral heads and valleys. The water surface above reddened from the setting sun, producing a beauty Matt had never seen before. He had made night dives but never saw a sunset from underwater.

Vega kept the dive short, obviously satisfied with Matt's skills. Vega pointed at a scorpion fish with its deadly spines. Matt signed that it was a no-no. They slowly circled the wreck and worked their way back and up. At the buoy chain, they paused at ten feet for ten minutes just to make sure they had completely decompressed—more drill than necessity for their short, shallow dive. Surfacing at the stern of the *Reefer*, Matt admired the beauty of the lighted boat, its tower still highlighted by the setting sun.

Aboard, they rinsed off with fresh water, put on dry shorts and sweat-shirts, and rinsed and stowed the dive platform. As the sun hit the horizon, they settled into folding chairs on the aft deck with filled wine glasses. Anita had crackers, salsa, and chips on a folding table.

Matt raised his glass in a toast. "Here's to the good life and new friends."

They all clinked glasses. Matt felt that, somehow, Tanya's fourth glass clinked with theirs, at least in spirit.

Sunset failed to produce the green flash in the Key West advertising brochures but dazzled Matt anyway. They described their dive to Anita, and she told them about the huge manta ray and turtle she'd seen from the boat. Over their second glass of wine, they ate the ham-and-potato salad and marveled at the beauty around them and their good fortune. Matt relished going barefoot in December with seventy-five-degree breezes wafting across eighty-degree water. After dessert—yesterday's Key lime pie that tasted even better than the day before—they climbed up to the flying bridge. Vega added the running lights to the already-on anchor lights. The console glowed like that of an X-wing fighter in *Star Wars*.

"Do you want to take it in?" Vega asked.

"For sure!" Matt replied.

"Good answer. You know I've been testing you, but it's the only way I know to be sure a person can handle a boat or a dive. Let's see if we can get this big hunk of plastic into a slip sometime this evening." Vega's grin showed he knew conditions were perfect: slack tide, no current in the channel.

With the helm station lights glowing and the nearly full moon overhead, Matt could see the cars on the highway. Using binoculars, he identified the marina lights. He kept his cruising speed low, looking for the buoys, not content to just follow the GPS. Matt brought the 70,000-pound boat to a stop several times and made 360-degree turns to port and starboard. George and Anita laughed at the resulting confusion on the GPS caused by the captain feeling out a new craft. Finally, they reached the red and green channel markers.

In the channel, the *Reefer* handled easier than Matt's own twenty-four-foot aluminum boat. The big Hatteras didn't blow around and could almost turn on its length. Matt wished Vega would back the boat in, but George sat comfortably in the far seats of the flybridge as Matt backed between the mooring pilings, an easier task than expected thanks to better visibility. Vega already had the stern line secured and the spring lines adjusted by the time Matt had cooled the engines, shut down, and secured the console. Anita had already done the dishes and gathered her jars and containers.

As they said good night with handshakes and hugs, Matt thought of Tanya and silently wished she had been part of their otherwise perfect evening.

33

Strange Neighbor

MATT CHECKED ALL THE LINES and rechecked the newly attached shore power and water. Just as he shut off the exterior lights he thought he saw a light go on and off on the sinister-looking boat next to him. Possibly a reflection from a passing car or someone turning around in the parking lot, but he had a bad feeling. The light seemed secretive, so he decided to watch the darkened trawler.

He quickly changed into Levis, a dark sweatshirt, and a dark, billed cap. He took the excellent Steiner 8x50 binoculars from the main cockpit drawer and headed for the Yukon. He made lots of noise and drove away toward the highway but quickly circled back into the driveway of the gas station that fronted the whole complex. He slowly drove along the quarter-mile asphalt strip along the Holiday Isle and pulled off the road just prior to the bridge leading to the lower keys. He turned off his running lights. The main beams would not go out until he turned off the engine, but the traffic on the bridge would mask them. He turned off his engine and fought the inoperative power steering to crank the vehicle around to face the marina. The *Reefer* and the metal trawler next to it floated about sixty yards away.

Matt naturally dropped back into hunting mode, using concealment, patience, an alert mind, and an awareness of the slightest detail. He also trusted his feelings. Something about the dark boat threatened...but what? The binoculars' fifty-millimeter lenses brought in a lot of light. Matt could see the water line and the spring lines clearly. He could only see part of the

Reefer; the metal boat blocked the aft third. He studied the water lines of both boats and their respective movements for nearly an hour. Just when he was feeling dumb for his caution, a light flashed from the metal boat—a flashlight or someone opening and closing a door that let light escape. The marina was well lit, with tall floodlights on all four corners and smaller lights along the marina docks and at the entrance to the outer mooring dock, as well as lights at the water entrance to the marina. Each boat moored outside the marina had an anchor light. Matt had shot many deer in much lower light conditions and from much longer distances.

The water lines changed slightly from their patterns. Matt wouldn't have noticed it if he hadn't studied their rhythms. The lines moved again. Someone was moving around on the darkened boat. Through the binoculars, he watched someone come out onto the aft deck and move quickly toward the *Reefer*. Matt started the Yukon and drove to the dock, directing his brights down the dock. He grabbed the Beretta .22 from the drawer behind him and confirmed a shell in the short, two-inch barrel.

Matt jumped from the vehicle and sprinted toward the *Reefer*. A man—average height, slim build, sandy brown hair, round face—came out of the *Reefer*, stopped, and looked at Matt. Breaking his deer-in-the-headlights pose, he turned and ran away. Matt broke into a full run. The man raced down the dock, jumped into the water at the marina entrance, and swam toward the dock on the other side. Matt didn't follow him but watched for him to come up on the dock. He didn't. He could have worked along the dock and boats and merged into the groups at the Tiki Bar and its crowds. Matt went back to the *Reefer*. The unlocked sliding door had not been forced. Matt turned on the lights, finding nothing out of the ordinary. He would check more carefully later. Right now, he wanted to play a little cat and mouse with this wet mouse.

Matt ran back to the Yukon, hopped in, and raced out of the lot. But, just around the corner from the outer mooring area, he stopped, jumped out, and sprinted back to the dive and charter shop. Peeking around the building's edge allowed a view of the dock and parking lot that the mouse would have to use if he was as smart as Matt thought he might be.

After ten minutes, wet sandy brown hair slowly appeared over the dock from a ladder on this side of the marina. The man had doubled back to escape, hoping to avoid the row of shops, many still open, or groups of always observant yuppie partiers. The man slowly walked down the dock, past his boat, and headed across the parking lot, coming directly toward Matt.

Matt scanned the area—three cars parked behind a bar closed for renovation. Matt moved behind the farthest car, gaining cover just as the man ran around the corner toward the first car. The man struggled to get his keys out of his wet pants pocket. Matt waited until the man's keys jingled as he prodded for the keyhole in the dark, then slipped up behind him, the black .22 invisible in his hand.

Quietly, hoping he sounded at least a little threatening, Matt asked, "How was your swim?"

The man whirled and aimed a backhand at Matt's head. Matt ducked and backed away. The man tried a front kick. It fell short too.

"You have to be from the government," Matt observed.

The man assumed some kind of karate stance and made a sucking sound.

"Calm down, all I want are some answers," said Matt. "Why are you spying on me and sneaking into the boat I'm on?"

The man tried to bolt past Matt. Matt slammed the gun down across the man's nose. The man sank to his knees, leaning forward and clutching his face. Matt grabbed the man's neck with his left hand, pushed him to the asphalt, then leaned his knee into the man's back. The man had no real muscles. Matt thought he could pull the jerk's head off if he tried real hard. Matt seized a fistful of hair and banged the head down lightly a few times until resistance stopped. Putting the not-needed pistol in his pocket, he used both hands and hauled the wet mouse toward the Yukon.

We are going for a ride, thought Matt.

Blood oozed from the man's nose, forehead, and the bridge of his nose. Matt slumped the man against his Yukon and bound him with duct tape. He blotted the blood with paper towels and pushed him into the rear storage area. The man, clearly scared, tried to look nasty. Matt emptied the guy's pockets, finding a wet wallet, a mass of keys, and a small Leatherman, like a whole tool kit the size of a pack of gum. The plastic pocket liner of an advanced nerd poked out of his shirt pocket. He watched Matt with equal portions of fear and hostility.

Matt drove to Vega's house and into the driveway. When Vega came to the door, Matt asked if he could come to the boat and show him how to turn on the water heater. Vega said he thought the heater was automatic, but he told his wife where he was going and got into the Yukon. As they drove away, the man moaned and demanded to be released. Matt pulled into a parking lot and told Vega what had happened.

Vega said nothing but sat thinking, staring into the darkness, lips pursed. "Have you considered your options?"

Matt handed him the man's wallet. "Take him to the police. Take him out to sea five or six miles and feed the sharks. Or just talk to him and let him go. What's your opinion?"

Under the Yukon's map light, Vega perused the wallet's contents. "Most of these cards look like government. His name is Ron Miles. Maybe on the team that's watching Webb and his group. That boat's been there six months. No one knows what they do or who they are. Miles and a few male friends were all we've ever seen. We figured it was a bunch of guys from Miami who only used it once a month or so. They never talked to anyone and always stayed in the boat."

"What do you have to say for yourself, Miles?" Matt asked, twisting around to see the trussed-up mouse in the back.

"I've got nothing to say, except you're in big trouble, fella. You can't hit me and get away with it," Miles warned, in an adolescent voice.

"How about illegal entry, and assault?" Matt asked. "Not to mention being terminally bad at karate. How about various violations of the Fourth Amendment? Maybe I should take your boat apart and call the news people and let them know that the government's spying on retired school teachers and retired Air Force people with no criminal records. How much taxpayer money are you wasting spying on solid citizens?"

"I've got nothing to say."

Vega said, "I say we take him to Sheriff Root. I've known him for fifteen years, and he was an Air Force officer for ten years. I'm tired of being cute with these guys. Let's get stuff out in the open."

Matt drove back to the marina. Matt left Miles in the Yukon after packing his nose with cotton from his first aid kit. Scared and hurting, Miles looked like a drowned rat with a hurt nose. Vega phoned Sheriff Root, and he showed up in fifteen minutes.

Root was no movie-stereotype southern sheriff: he was not fat, he didn't sweat, he was neat and businesslike. He reminded Matt of the best of the Michigan State Police officers—squared away, the kind of person you could trust. Root listened to Matt's story. He never interrupted. He looked at Miles's identification. He looked at Miles's keys.

"May I see your boat key please, Mr. Hunter?" Sheriff Root asked.

Matt had the key in his pocket on its little floating ring.

Root slowly looked at it and in the light of the Yukon's back area slowly went through Miles bunch of keys. Holding up two matching keys, he asked, "Mr. Miles, why do you have a key to Mr. Hunter's boat?"

"I'm not going to answer anything, you don't have any jurisdiction in this situation," blurted Miles.

Matt thought, *Never tell cops they don't have jurisdiction.*

In an emotionless, profession tone, Root said, "I'm going to arrest you for unlawful entry based on this witness and the fact you ran or, more in evidence, swam to escape, plus you are accused of attacking Mr. Hunter. We may have more charges. I'm holding you while I try to get a warrant to search your boat. You need judges and just cause to spy on American citizens. The government's duty is to protect the public and make people more secure. I hate the thought that people are being spied upon by people we expect to protect us. Also, you are being totally uncooperative."

Root put Miles into the back of his patrol car. He carefully recorded Matt's statement. He tried the keys on the *Reefer*.

"Don't touch the door handle, the glass, or the frame. We might get a print. I'll send forensics out tomorrow morning. I can't legally enter Miles's boat but need to verify that it's secure because I'm locking him up. I want you two to witness that I don't take anything."

Root boarded the metal boat and, using a handkerchief, tried the latch. The door opened. Not finding a convenient light switch, Root used his Maglite. Heavy, dark cloth covered the windows. Recorders and other electrical equipment, red LEDs glowing, packed the lower salon, looking like a mass of mad rats. Still cameras and video recorders on tripods pointed at the *Reefer* and the dock.

Root flashed his light into the nooks and crannies, then said as he locked the boat's door, "I'll bet he had a microphone or a recorder on your boat. He might be able to beat all of this if someone from high up pulls enough strings. I'm still going to do my job and make them explain themselves. I'll keep you informed and I'll be back tomorrow morning. I doubt the marina surveillance cameras can pick up activity out here, but I'll check." On the trip home, Vega kept taking deep breaths and didn't say much. He seemed to have aged in the past hour. In his driveway, he stepped out but, before closing the door, said, "I hope we did the right thing."

"I think we did," Matt said. "Don't worry about it."

"I suppose. We've got an afternoon charter you might want to help with. I'll call you about noon. Good night. Again." Vega closed the door and walked back into his home.

Back on board the *Reefer*, Matt used the edge of his T-shirt to carefully slide open, close, and lock the salon door and avoid unnecessary fingerprints. He searched for a half hour and found nothing amiss. The busy day, diving and fighting, had numbed his body and brain, so he showered and went to bed.

34

Crime Scene

M ATT WOKE TO VOICES AND LIGHT coming through the overhead air vent. He rolled over to check the brass clock on the wall—a few minutes after 8:00. As he slowly got out of bed, his muscles told him he had used some that had been comfortably working their way to atrophy. He stretched, got into shorts and a T-shirt, and went aft to the salon. Several uniformed and presumably plainclothes lawmen worked on and around the trawler. Matt carefully opened his salon door and stepped onto the open deck.

"Good morning, Mr. Hunter," Sheriff Root said. "Okay if we finger-print your door area and look around inside your boat?"

"I'm just living on it, it belongs to George Vega," Matt replied. "But you're welcome aboard. I'll make coffee if your people say it's okay. I've been careful about touching anything in the main room."

Two of the plainclothes people on the dock by the trawler followed Root onto the *Reefer.*

"These are our crime scene people, they'll check for prints and microphones. I'd like to look around too," explained Root.

The two crime scene people started on the door and door frame—a middle-aged woman and a young male trainee. They each carried a metal box with tools of their trade. They set up on the deck and went to work. Within a few minutes, they found and captured prints.

Root asked, "Okay if we go inside?"

"Sure, boss," the woman replied.

He and Matt went into the large salon.

"This is a beautiful boat," said Root as he began to search, with a small flashlight, under tables and behind any space that could hide a microphone. He found the bug on top of the navigation desk bookcase but didn't touch it. He called out to his crime scene people, "Just found a bug in here!"

They stepped into the salon, and the woman photographed the salon and the bug in its hiding place. The trainee, under the woman's watchful eye, carefully lifted the bug. Stuck down, it came away with a little effort, and he dropped it into a plastic bag.

Matt made coffee, and he and Root, from facing couches, watched the two people work for fifteen minutes until they cleaned up and closed their boxes. The investigators quietly left and went to the trawler.

Root sipped his coffee and said, "We ran Miles through the system. He was a government worker. He is no longer on any payroll that anyone will admit to. He hasn't admitted to anything. I have a warrant to search the trawler on various charges, including that it might have been a crime scene. Miles is not even admitting the trawler is his. We're running its ownership down. There's a lot of funny stuff here. I wouldn't be surprised if we get a hands-off from Tallahassee or Washington. That's why we're working fast while we can. Based on your description of the time Miles had on your boat, I doubt he got past this salon, but we have a bug-finding device that we'll use later this week. It's in use right now. If that's all right with you?"

"I'd appreciate that. Has Miles called anyone yet?"

Root glanced at his watch. "He oughta be making his call this morning, right about now."

Root finished the coffee and went over to the trawler. Matt made some breakfast and, while cleaning up, heard an "Ahoy" and "Permission to come aboard." Vega stepped onto the deck, looking much better than last night.

"Morning, George," Matt called out.

"That was a nice dive yesterday," Vega said, entering the salon. "We need to do more. Just remember that it's a lot different when you have five or six customers in the water. You don't see anything but people."

"I can imagine."

"You'll get the hang of it fast enough." Vega gave a dismissive wave. "I just talked to Root. He's a fine man, and I feel we did the right thing last night. He said he found a bug here and lots of surveillance gear next door."

"Yeah. What do you think is going on?" asked Matt.

"Well, it could be a lot of things. DEA, ATF, IRS, FBI, or some other government alphabet group interested in Webb's boat. It could even be Webb just keeping track of things. He's like that. He always seems to have multiple checks going on, spying on everyone. It could also be some of Webb's competition. Root'll tell us what he finds. My position is to be an honest public citizen and to let the investigation do its thing."

Root came back aboard the *Reefer* and announced, "A call just came in from Tallahassee. It was the state Attorney General himself. He asked that we release Mr. Miles. Because he asked and didn't demand suggests that calls have come from above him. He explained the official position as no harm, no foul, and hopes you will not press charges. Mr. Miles and his boat will be gone by the end of the day Saturday. I called the FBI in Miami. They haven't called me back. I wouldn't expect any interest from them or they would have been back to me almost immediately. They're probably still checking their brother agencies. And that's about all I can do as a lowly Florida county sheriff."

"I really appreciate your help," said Vega. "I don't like snoopers around the marina. It's a good place. I know all of the divers and fishermen who come through here. We fuel up some muscle boats from time to time and get big boats with twenty-year-old owners who got their money who knows where. Of course, we do have several corporate lawyers and four or five investment bankers million-dollar boats they may not have worked very hard to buy. But I don't know how any government group could justify a long surveillance operation at this marina."

"I'm with you, George," Root said. "Government workers shuffle among projects and agencies, but many projects seem to have no off switches. Our government always seems to start new agencies or committees rather than fine-tune or direct the ones we have. And have you ever heard of an agency being eliminated?"

"I always wanted to work for the Department of Redundancy Department," added Matt with a grin.

They all laughed, and each added several examples of government disorganization and overlapping responsibilities. They solved most of the major governmental flaws in another half hour of pleasant discussion. Finally, Root's cell phone played a Bach tune. He stood up to answer it. Matt could see the Air Force officer in him.

Root listened intently, while Matt and Vega sat quietly. After two minutes, he ended with a clear, "Yes, sir."

Matt and Vega waited for an explanation as Root put his phone away. He looked up and said, "That's it, Miles is free and it's not even 10:00 in the morning. We are to put everything back that we took from the trawler. I have been criticized for holding him without a phone call until this morning. He will be moving the boat by this weekend. No one is saying anything, but I'd bet the farm this is federal stuff."

"Well, you did all you could, and I really appreciate it," said Vega.

"Hey, it's not all over," Root said. "Between you and me, and I mean you and me, we aren't all done. We have the bug that wasn't a part of the verbal orders I have been given. We also had people look at some of the videotapes. I'll find out what was on them just for my own curiosity."

Root shook hands with Vega and Matt and, before leaving, told them to stay vigilant and to feel free to call him anytime.

35

Waiting for Tanya

O VER THE NEXT SEVERAL DAYS, Matt assisted with diving and fishing charters on Vega's 26-footer, earning the respect of the man Matt had quickly come to consider a friend and who had taken him in as though he were already a prospective son-in-law. On the charters, he discovered Tanya's neat printing on clipboard-mounted checklists, equipment lists in the storage areas, and even on the yellow foam float on the boat's ignition key. The boat carried her mark, literally. Matt missed her but satisfied himself, for now, with just immersing himself in her world.

Vega found him a slot at Key Largo's Sea School in the last class of the season and insisted he take the *Reefer* with him. Vega also coached him through several practice runs with the big Hatteras, making sure he understood its complexities and how to operate all its equipment. Matt knew he had a lot of catching up to do to meet the minimum requirements for a captain's license, but vowed to take the class, work the boats, and get his papers as soon as he could satisfy the required ninety days of experience on near-coastal or open ocean waters.

The night before leaving for Sea School, Matt sat in one of the seats forward of the helm on the flybridge watching the sun go down. He had the *Reefer* all ready for the trip and the two-week stay. From his vantage, he could keep tabs on the surrounding marina while staying inconspicuous. As he opened his second beer and considered turning on some of the *Reefer*'s many lights, two men, bigger and meaner-looking than Miles, boarded the trawler. In a few minutes, its engines started. One man efficiently freed the lines and shore attachments and held a bowline until the businesslike boat edged out of the mooring. As they moved into the channel, the line-tender walked back to the aft deck to scan the marina behind them.

It was Al, Webb's henchman he'd met in the U.P.

Shocked, Matt dropped low on the flybridge, hoping Al couldn't see him. The man on the trawler wore slacks and a short-sleeve shirt instead of winter clothes, but Matt recognized him. Definitely Al. The other man was smaller and quick, probably Ray.

Matt's gut twisted with remembered tension from those distant, but not so long ago, days at the deer cabin. All his insecurities and hunter-prey instincts swept over him. He stayed low and got the binoculars from the helm. The trawler gleamed in the reflected reds and yellows of the sun setting over the Florida Keys. The glasses brought the trawler's bridge and aft deck clearly into Matt's view.

Two men. Definitely Al and Ray.

They handled the trawler far better than the landlubbers Matt had thought them. Once through the channel, they increased speed and headed west, down the Keys, and quickly pulled out of Matt's sight. Matt switched on the *Reefer*'s radar and watched their track creep toward Key West. Ground clutter on the radar soon masked the trawler. Matt would have liked to follow them, preferring to keep his enemies under surveillance. But he had to leave for Sea School the next day.

He spent the rest of the evening pondering the unexpected sighting of Al and Ray. Although not government, they motored off in a government boat, or at least one with high government connections. Matt remembered the admonitions from Ivan, Tanya, and Webb about falling into something way over his head. He had last seen Al and Ray in a pickup with cocaine and two dead bodies. So, how did they get to Florida? And this particular marina?

Matt massaged the tender spot where Ray had hit him. He would like a chance to return the favor. Somehow, the two men had evaded capture. Did they know Webb had been arrested? Were they still working for Webb or somebody else? Either scenario spelled bad news for Matt, George Vega, Tanya, or all three of them.

The comfort of the Reefer and the gentle rocking of the waves lulled Matt to sleep with multiple questions, but few answers, tumbling through his mind.

On the day he left for Sea School, he thought about the complex world into which his life had crashed. He resolved to take it as a challenge with Tanya as the wonderful prize for success. He had been alone for many years. His son, his students, athletics, hunting, fishing, and the town he loved had filled his life for years. The seasons, with their requisite preparations and activities, had always filled his life and given it a steady meter. He had chosen to leave teaching to change that rhythm. Though this latest adventure had changed things, he sensed no new rhythm yet nor even understood the new rules in his new world. He resolved to play the game out and emerge victorious, counting on his native instincts, smarts, and luck to keep him ahead of the powerful factions challenging him.

Vega joined him on the cruise down to Key Largo. After Matt told him about the events of the previous night, Vega said, "I don't know who's watching who anymore. Webb always had a lot of people getting him information. Al and Ray may know he was arrested or maybe not. Webb has enemies inside and outside his organization. They'll attack any weakness, eliminate any informers. Webb's friends and enemies are involved at the highest levels in politics and law enforcement. Al and Ray may be following instructions Webb gave them and not know about anything else. Al and Ray weren't hiding themselves—that must mean something. I'll try to contact Tanya to see if she has any ideas."

Matt agreed they needed advice and, thinking about Edward, told Vega, "I'll call a DEA friend of mine to see if he knows anything about this, or is willing to admit it. I'll use a public phone at Key Largo."

Anita had driven to Key Largo and met them at the marina. She and George returned home after introducing Matt to the Sea School's director, a retired Coast Guard Master Chief. Watching the Vegas drive away, Matt's mind again raced through his many questions. He longed to hold Tanya, tightly, again. He wanted to know what was going on. His speculations on the many variables merely twisted any possible answers into an exhausting maze of possibilities. One thing he knew—Webb and Tanya held the keys to the puzzle.

Again sitting on the *Reefer's* flying bridge with a beer, watching the setting sun, he decided to concentrate on the school, keep his eyes open, find a way to contact Tanya, and call his new DEA buddy Edward.

Or maybe not.

Matt considered that the balance of payments in information rarely had worked out in Matt's favor when they traded information.

After watching three quarters of the second NFL game of the evening on the boat's satellite TV system, Matt put on dark clothing and went ashore. He left the TV on so the flickering light might create the illusion that he remained aboard. He strolled around the marina, checking out the other boats, noting that the *Reefer* was the only lighted boat in the small marina. Rows of docks lined the waterfront as far as he could see. Key Largo, the city, glowed to the northwest. The main road offered the only walkway due to all the fenced yards and the marinas fenced off with security guards or gates. Matt walked for a half hour. Several dogs barked at him, and investigative lights came on a few times. So, having learned only that peace and quiet reigned on Sunday evenings along Marina Road, Matt returned to the boat.

Matt enjoyed Sea School. The fifteen-member class looked like an ad for diversity with both sexes, most age ranges, and many ethnic backgrounds represented—two old fishermen with decades of experience on the local waters; four women wanting captain's licenses to help with the family businesses; three obviously rich, retired people mostly wanting the license and education for planned months-long voyages; and a half-dozen young men hoping eventually to gain their Master's License. The excellent instructors showed good classroom skills. Training proved stimulating, educational, well structured, and fast-paced. Matt and two other students had boats in the marina. The class frequently gathered on one of the boats or at local bars for cocktails, often moving on to restaurants to savor the local seafood.

The days passed quickly. Matt learned many new things and refreshed his knowledge about others. Navigation training proved the most difficult, but also the most useful. He knew the rules of the road but now had to memorize them.

Vega showed up late during his first week of training accompanied by a technician to set up the satellite phone. While the technician worked below, Matt and Vega talked on the aft deck.

Vega said, "I talked to Tanya last night. She figures Al and Ray somehow got away from the people who picked up Webb's car. No clue how. She thinks they may not know about Webb. She also said that if they come across you, you must stick to the waiting-for-her story and admit no knowledge about Webb or his activities. She said Webb is being very cool, but cooperative. It makes her nervous. She's only seen him one time since the arrest—in a room she knew must be bugged and filmed. Webb doesn't know who set him up, but thinks it could be Al, Ray, his driver, or even her. Being caught with many kilos of cocaine gives the government all they need to issue indictments and initiate asset-seizure procedures."

"You'd think the feds could just about wipe him out financially," Matt said.

"Exactly what Tanya told me. She thought that threat would force him to cooperate. She said she's heard he's planning to work some kind of deal with them."

"I'll bet." Matt took a long swallow of beer. "He's a smart guy."

"True," Vega said, then added with visible relief, "She's hoping to come home soon. I'll give her your new sat phone number."

Vega's news cheered Matt. The thought of seeing, and holding, Tanya again excited him.

One problem solved, or so he hoped.

36

Tanya

S MATT CHECKED THE DOOR LOCK, he gave a final look at the deserted marina. A shadow crossed the dock under the marina's parking lot lights, moving toward him. It didn't look like anyone from Sea School. Matt opened the small white box in the bottom drawer of the navigation and communication table and took out the Beretta .22. He turned off the one remaining light in the salon. He moved through the door and around to the far side of the salon rail and crouched. The person jogged directly toward the *Reefer*, moving like an athlete. A weak dock light spotlighted Tanya just as she jumped onto the deck.

Matt wanted to shout a greeting, but her secretive approach to the door made him stop. Tanya tried and then opened the heavy sliding door, stepping into the darkened salon. "Matt?"

He moved from his crouch and came up behind her, whispering, "You looking for maple syrup, lady?"

Tanya jumped and spun around. "Oh, you shit! If I'm wet it won't be from love as much as being scared to death."

With a pleased sigh, she slid into his arms. Clutching each other as though afraid the moment would vaporize at any moment, they kissed. After they were both sure the moment was real, Matt locked the salon door and pulled the shades. He turned on a light over the dinette, leaving the main area in shadows.

Tanya stepped through the master bedroom into the bathroom, throwing clothes on the floor. She said, "I need a shower and you, in that order."

Matt turned down the bed, dimmed the lights over the headboard, and put on a CD of baroque music. From the galley, he brought two glasses of red wine, set them on the counter in the steamy bathroom, pulled off his sweater and shorts, and joined Tanya in the shower stall. They kissed and touched each other until both were too excited to stop. They made love in the shower, then filled the tub and made love again. No conversation. No hurry. Tanya's series of expressive moans provided sufficient verbal communication. Matt quickly and happily learned the new language.

Matt had never felt so wonderful. Reality with Tanya beat any fantasy he had ever had. She fit in all the right places, and she had wonderful pressures and contacts. And best of all, Matt didn't feel selfish; she enjoyed him as much as he enjoyed her.

They finally let the water drain from the tub, restarted the shower, soaped and rubbed each other all over. They would have made love again except Tanya said they should try the bed next time. They dried off with one set of towels, wrapped themselves in fresh dry towels, and picked up their wine glasses. Matt followed Tanya as she roamed the boat.

"Isn't this a beautiful boat?" she said in a soft voice. "I've been dreaming of being with you here since we first made love. You are much better than my dreams."

Tanya stood in the middle of the salon and turned toward Matt. The most beautiful woman he had ever seen. Even with wet hair, no makeup, in a large white bath towel, she glowed with love and health.

"I've got so much to tell you. It'll be difficult to get it all straight. Is this room free of listening devices?" she asked. Before Matt could answer, she turned up the stereo system.

"Yes," he replied. "It was searched and electrically swept the day before I left your marina and I've been on it or around it all the time after that. I could see it from our class room. I expect your dad told you about the person filming and bugging the boat."

Tanya nodded agreement, took a sip of the wine, then a deep breath. She stood directly in front of Matt, holding eye contact for several seconds. Matt knew she had something important to say.

Finally, she said, "I have been working for the DEA for several years undercover. It kept my father out of trouble. He doesn't know. He thinks I got involved just like he did, because of entrapment and coercion. In a way it was true, except the government made a better case of coercion than the gangsters. Before I give you the whole story, let's have more wine and something to eat. Besides, I need to dry my hair."

"Are you going to leave the towel on?"

"For now," answered Tanya, as she moved past him to the master stateroom.

While the hair dryer nearly drowned out the boat's stereo, Matt made a wee-hour snack of leftovers from the refrigerator—cold pizza, boiled shrimp, pasta salad, cold salmon. He sliced some leftover sirloin into bit-size pieces. With a glass of wine and a plate of food, Tanya curled up in the corner of the biggest salon couch, tucked her legs under her, and fixed her towel so as not to distract Matt. She ate a large, cold shrimp with her fingers, took a sip of wine, and started her story.

"My job was to get Webb caught dirty—and get information on their communications. When you switched the drugs on the sleigh, it really messed me up. It also made Webb know someone was informing. If you hadn't gone along with the second deal, I don't know where his anger would have led. He might have had Volcheff kill us all, just to make sure he got the informant. That's how they do things in Russia. He didn't know how to read you. When you took out Volcheff and the other guy, you really confused, and impressed, him."

"Yeah, well," Matt said, "impressing gangsters has always been a life-long career goal."

"You succeeded." Tanya laughed briefly. "Anyway, Webb knew that the Feds were targeting him and that his days were numbered. The various indictments he had narrowly avoided were getting stronger and stronger. He was setting up to make a run anyway. The federal indictments were circling him like vultures. He has cashed out and turned over ownership of most of his business. Several people in his organization and rival groups were working against him. He had power over many, many high government people and cops in this country and others. He thought out loud when we drove with Volcheff. When they got to the good stuff, they went to Russian. I knew they tied you up, they wouldn't let me see you in the cabin."

When she paused to take a few bites and drink some wine, Matt said, "You don't have to go through this whole thing tonight. There's always tomorrow."

"No, I do. I mean, I want to." She downed the last of the wine in her glass. "We left in the Lincoln about ten minutes after the pickup. We were arrested just as we got to the main paved road. The line repair people were all DEA. We had over thirty kilos of cocaine in the trunk. Someone must've gotten confused when they were loading it."

Seeing her wide, beautiful grin, Matt asked, "You?"

"Yeah," she replied, leaning closer. "It was a solid bust. We all acted surprised. Webb wanted to kill someone. I think he thought it was the driver because he carried out the small bag. The driver had left the trunk open. I covered the stuff with coats. DEA was to get the truck before it got to the bridge with the bodies and cocaine, but they got away somehow. We didn't work with the State Police because we wanted to keep it all DEA. Major mistake. They kept Webb, his driver, and me isolated at a huge, old Air Force facility south of Marquette. They interrogated us for several days, then flew us on a private jet to Denver. I just flew to Miami from there and rented a car. The most important confiscations were the satellite phones and the computer. They are enabling the electronic surveillance people to listen to important traffic on phones and the Internet."

"So, Webb's cooperating?"

"Sort of. He's talked a lot, but hasn't really said anything we didn't know. They're offering him the witness protection program. Personally, I can't see him running a dry cleaners in Cleveland. I only saw him once in Colorado. He was sorry I got caught with him. He told them I was just window dressing and knew nothing about the business. He told me to make any deal I could to stay out of prison; I really think he meant it. He said he was worried about his wife and daughter, figuring if the word got out about his arrest, the organization would target them to keep him quiet. After all, he's done the same thing to others. He's also worried about what he called a feeding frenzy from high-placed politicos who'd like to see him taken out completely."

"How did you get away?"

"In a moment. I'm starving." She paused to eat, smiling at him between bites. Holding her glass to indicate she wanted a refill, she continued, "The driver, Mouse, rolled over big time. I couldn't believe it. He was a two time loser, something he hadn't told Webb, and he didn't want to be behind bars and on Webb's short list of informers. He gave up all sorts of trafficking and smuggling information and named lots of names in Chicago. A real vein of gold for warrants and indictments. With him, they no longer needed me for anything official."

Matt poured wine in her glass. "How did you call the DEA from the cabin?"

"The sat phone. Ivan might not have known how to change it to unscrambled calls, but I did. It's just an encryption on or off choice on the menu. I talked to Edward, whom you met; we set up the bust at Garnet Lake. Then, when we were in the St. Ignace State Police post, we used the plat books to find your name and your land. I told them you saved my life, and you'd help trap Webb. My time was limited with Edward. The DEA has some numbers that can't be traced on a printout. I couldn't call Florida. My dad's number would have been a red light to the people who pay for the phone."

Tanya finished her food and sipped the wine.

Matt poured some more wine in his own glass. "How did you get the DEA to cover where our road comes out on Highway 123?"

"We were being trailed when we left the State Police Post in St. Ignace. When we headed back toward your cabin in your vehicle, they figured we were going back for the cocaine and money. They were supposed to be following Volcheff, too. I don't know all the particulars, but I think they used planes at night with night-vision and heat-sensing equipment. Volcheff was too smart for bugs or regular tails. I guess your changing the taillights was considered smart, but they were watching the car when you got out to take off the tape. They didn't know about the electronic devices Webb and I were carrying. I couldn't do anything about that. I was just hoping either Volcheff or we were being followed. I didn't want them coming right in and busting us—it would have meant you or I were the informer and Volcheff would still be on the loose. I couldn't get to a phone, at first, and then when you had Webb at gunpoint, I saw a chance to get him and the coke and the bodies away from you. Before you took out Volcheff, I had Webb convinced I could get you to do whatever we wanted, and killing you would be a problem he didn't need."

"If you'd batted your gorgeous eyes at me, I probably would have," Matt said, leering a bit. "Maybe." Tanya restocked her plate and rearranged herself comfortably on the couch. After several bites and sips of wine she continued, "Webb knew you were really fond of me, but he went with us easier than I expected. He used me on the couch like he did because he knew you would do anything to protect me. Later, after you tied him up, he promised to let my family off the hook and not to kill you if I let him free. He knew all my need buttons too. However, I believed him. His word is very good when he gives it in a clear and straightforward way. I wouldn't have let him go if I hadn't believed him. He said he was just going to scare the hell out of you, not kill you. I know him real well; I also knew you wouldn't kill him."

"I don't know," Matt mumbled. "I just might have...under the right circumstances."

"If he'd gotten away, he would have done something like use your son as leverage to control you. He would have sent him some present and explained to you that it could have been C4 explosive. It's how he works.

He set the standard for terrorizing families. My mother has aged ten years in the last three because of Webb and his minions. He gets what he wants, but he doesn't kill if he can get around it. He can be totally heartless if he has to be, but he has a sense of honor. He has power and a fascinating charm, maybe like a tiger."

Tanya finished her wine, then stretched and yawned. Her towel slipped open. She let it fall down. She stood and headed for the master stateroom. "Isn't this better than long underwear and hypothermia? I don't have any extra clothes or even a toothbrush. I guess I'll just have to be naked for a while."

Matt thought about cleaning up the dishes—for about a nanosecond—but followed her instead.

The next day, Matt was late for class. He missed the introductory lecture to a plotting exercise about chart symbols. But, he thought, life was very, very good.

Matt checked on Tanya at noon. She was not dressed yet. She had commandeered a T-shirt and boxer shorts and was making a list of items she needed. She planned to make a trip to some Key Largo stores, then return the rental car and have them drop her back at the boat. After she demonstrated how his boxer shorts kept slipping down, Matt almost forgot about the upcoming lecture on radiotelephone procedures.

That Friday, Matt turned down invitations to bars, dinner, and hints he should take the class out on his boat. He jogged back to the boat, worrying he had dreamed the whole thing and Tanya wouldn't be there.

Tanya's kiss quelled his fears. She nibbled his ear and whispered, "Welcome home."

She had prepared frosty Margaritas, chips, and salsa. She had called her folks, and they would be there with supper in about an hour. She reminded him not to bring up Webb or anything related to him within earshot of Tanya's mother. Despite facing a whole day of school on Saturday, Matt could not disguise his disappointment when she announced plans to go home with her parents after dinner. She assured him she would return with her car by the time Matt finished class. He knew he was being selfish about sharing Tanya. He considered pouting but, after the first Margarita and Tanya's promise to spend all day Sunday with him alone, decided he should be a real man and not threaten to eat worms and die to get his way.

The Vegas came early, carrying in several boxes of various dishes. Everything smelled wonderful. Luckily, he liked garlic. They had Cuban *Picadillo*, a hamburger, onion, and tomato casserole, black beans, and rice they cooked on board. They talked constantly over the wonderful meal and continued throughout the evening. George and Anita's relief at Tanya's return was obvious. Matt appreciated their love and happiness. After dinner, the women cleaned up, while the men watched boats coming and going on a busy Friday evening.

George told Matt that Root had come by to say Miles had never returned to the motel he'd paid up for several weeks. They found his rental car at a local steak house. The names Al and Ray hadn't meant anything to Root. They were now looking for the trawler with no results.

Matt resolved to call Edward in the morning.

Tanya came up and gave Matt a deep kiss in front of her father, who only smiled. Then the three Vegas left for home, leaving Matt alone watching the taillights disappear.

He showered, laid out his sea clothes for the morning, set his clock, and slept without dreams.

The Saturday class used a boat moored only three slips away from the *Reefer*. They spent all day in a cool, rainy mist—no problem for a Yooper. The day passed quickly. By 6:00 p.m., as they made their last set of docking procedures and tied up, Matt felt tired, a little cold, and longing for Tanya.

She waited for him on the *Reefer*, dressed in her new jeans, a large black sweater, and sandals. She had already turned on the heat, giving the boat a different smell. He inhaled the satisfying aroma of food cooking.

Tending a pot of something on the stove, Tanya said, "My mother likes you very much. My father doesn't say much, but if he didn't like you, he would say something. They suggested I should cook for you so you know I can."

He gave her a love pat on her nicely-rounded rump. "Like I care if you can cook. I'd be happy to do all the cooking."

"But I'm multi-talented."

"So I've noticed. What are we having?"

"*Arroz con pollo* and a fruit salad, topped off with Cuban-style coffee and *flan*. Mother also sent some of her special bread."

"Sounds great. I'm famished!"

"The Chablis is chilling in the refrigerator," she said, looking truly beautiful and very domestic.

They ate and talked about Matt's class and Tanya's parents, who had told her how happy they were she had found a good man to love. They made plans for a Sunday cruise and swim. They would anchor in a special cove Tanya knew, catch some fish for dinner, and ignore any bad weather.

While Matt enjoyed the superb *flan* and bitterly strong coffee, the phone rang.

Tanya answered it—her mother offering last-minute *flan* instructions and suggesting a light syrup for topping. Tanya suggested maple syrup, a joke her mother didn't understand but which made Matt and Tanya laugh. Matt took the phone at last and thanked her for the fine bread. He also thanked her for producing such a beautiful, charming daughter and fine cook. Mrs. Vega laughed with happiness as she said goodbye.

They arose late on Sunday morning. They fired up the *Reefer* and passed the channel buoys just before noon. The rainy weather had passed but an overcast hung on. The sun was bright enough to make the deck warm and the air conditioner kick on. Matt turned the helm over to Tanya, who immediately began hot-rodding, keeping the throttles to the stops for several miles. She slowed slightly to weave through a series of channels between the ocean and some mangrove islands. She finally slowed the large boat and pulled into a cove, surrounded on three sides by mangroves and trees with a snow-white beach. She eased the *Reefer* within a hundred feet of the beach before they set the anchor. They started to fish, but spent more time just holding each other and watching the birds and shallow-water schools of small fish. They oiled each other and stretched out on sunning mats on the fore deck. Their world, safe and beautiful, seemed completely within their sight. They spent most of the day in the cove, stopping on the return trip to snorkel dive on one of her favorite reefs. The coral was alive, and the fish made the living rocks seem to be trees with colored leaves that fell and swirled and took their places again on the tree.

Tanya, confident in the water, did nothing awkwardly. All her moves were efficient, graceful, and sleek. Matt followed her and marveled at her beauty. She seemed pleased that Matt could easily keep up with her on even the deeper dives.

Returning to the *Reefer*, they used the outside freshwater hose to wash off. After rinsing their swimsuits, and hanging them over the marlin chair, they raced for towels in the master stateroom, where they found little use for towels.

With the sun just setting, they worked the *Reefer* slowly into its slip at the Sea School Marina. The day, although very different, had proved as wonderful as their previous time together in the Upper Peninsula snow and forest trails. Their love and enthusiasm for life and each other created a common ingredient.

The rest of the Sea School time established itself into a rhythm. They shared breakfast early. Matt went to class. Tanya drove to see her parents and spend time at the shop, or on a dive boat. She was always back in time for dinner and an evening with Matt.

Graduation Friday brought hard rain and violent seas and winds just short of official tropical storm status. The Master Chief gave a talk, and two Coast Guard officers attended and handed out the graduation papers and licenses. Many family members attended. The Vegas attended and photographed Matt and Tanya with the Master Chief. With his new operator's license, Matt could now take out six or less passengers for diving, sightseeing, or fishing in coastal waters in the smaller boats that Vega owned, needing more hours for his master's papers.

Matt, Tanya, the Vegas, the Master Chief, and his wife had a small celebration party on the *Reefer*—the rain precluded inviting the whole class for a real outside party.

When the graduation party broke up, the rough weather and late hour prevented Matt from running the *Reefer* back to Islamorada. Matt and Tanya decided to boat back in the morning. Mrs. Vega drove Tanya's car, following Mr. Vega home.

Tanya and Matt locked up the boat and went to bed, but not to sleep.

Saturday morning arrived still rainy and cool. Matt and Tanya decided to walk a few blocks to a local restaurant for breakfast and let the cold front pass through the Keys. The forecast called for clear skies by noon. They found rain gear and left the *Reefer*.

37

Webb

TANYA AND MATT RETURNED to a very quiet marina a little after 11:00 a.m. The wind had eased up and the temperature had gone up fifteen degrees. They walked with their rain gear over their arms. Too much breakfast and too much coffee had been consumed while they speculated on their futures and the wonderful opportunities before them. Step one was getting the *Reefer* back to its home marina.

Matt sensed something wrong when they stepped into the salon. The shades, closed more than when they had left, made the room darker. Matt took Tanya's hand and started to pull her toward the door to leave the boat. Matt opened the door while still looking into the boat. When he turned to step onto the aft deck, he ran into Al.

"No noise, move to the couch and sit," ordered Al, holding his semi-automatic at his side.

Tanya turned to run into the lower area of the boat. Webb's appearance on the steps stopped her after one step. He had no visible weapon, but his sinister look and presence intimidated more than Al with his gun.

"Welcome aboard." Webb showed no emotion. "Sit down. We have a lot to do, and you need to listen carefully."

Tanya took a step backward, brow furrowed. "Why are you here? Didn't you have a deal going with the government?"

"Ya, they had a great deal for me. Tell all I know, roll over on the biggest drug traffickers in the world, get on about four hit lists, worry about your wife and daughter disappearing at any time or have them hanging in a closet when you get home some time, and for a reward we get to live in Cincinnati, Ohio, working at a hospital supply company. Without even a view of the river."

"You'd have had protection."

Webb laughed humorlessly. "Right. Then some people wanted me transferred to Washington, D.C. So, I called in several favors, gave up some good information, and persuaded some people high in the Justice Department that they didn't have that good a case. I was in transit in the custody of U.S. Marshals when they cut me loose at the Detroit Airport. I wouldn't have lived twenty-four hours in Washington."

"What do you want from us?" Matt asked.

"I need your help. I'll pay big for it. I don't want your support because of threats, but I'll play some tough cards if I have to. Tanya, I've got a solid paper trail that implicates your father in drug smuggling, tax evasion, money laundering, and various levels of fraud and conspiracy to defraud. It would put him in a cell and your mother in a hospital."

"What do you want from us?" asked Matt again, watching Tanya turning pallid and thinking, *So much for Webb's cabin promise to help Tanya's father.*

"I need to get my wife and daughter out of Miami. I need to get across to Bimini. Once we are there, I will be out of your life. I'll release this boat to George Vega. It's a good deal for about a hundred-mile sea trip. What do you say?" asked Webb.

"What choice do we have?" said Tanya.

"I hope none. But understand, I've not been convicted of anything. They could get new indictments, but there would be no one to serve them on. Where I eventually go, they're not likely to entertain any extradition claims from the United States. Or if they do, it will take a hundred years to get them acted on.

"I can live very well, and my family will be respected and protected. Once I get my contacts all set up with my protected status, no one will be interested in my wife or daughter, unless they want to risk their family and everyone they ever knew. I have no choice but to get out of the country immediately."

"And spend the rest of your life looking over your shoulder?" Matt asked.

"Like I wouldn't be doing that if I stayed here and cooperated?"

Matt shrugged, unable to come up with a reasonable argument.

"I want you to get this boat fueled up and out of here within the next half hour," ordered Webb.

Matt and Tanya looked at each other. Al leaned against the door frame behind them. Webb stood on the stairs below them. They didn't say anything for nearly thirty seconds.

Finally, Tanya asked, "Will we live through this if we help?"

"Yes. You can believe me. I need the cover of a charter and your papers to get to where I need to go. It will only be a day or so. You have my word. I'll let you know where the file is on your father when we arrive at our destination. I'll do the boat deal via the phone as soon as we are underway. The papers are already signed at the bank. Also, I figured out either you or my driver turned me in. Since I know he rolled over on me in Colorado, he's probably dead by now. It would go a long way with me if you'd help me through this without needing Al's gun in your ribs all the time. What do you say?"

Matt and Tanya looked at each other again. They both nodded.

Suppressing an uneasy feeling in his gut, Matt said, "Okay, we can leave as soon as we cast off the lines. She's full of fuel." He rose and walked to the door.

Al put his gun into a shoulder holster under his jacket and followed.

They started the diesels, cast off the lines, and reached the channel within fifteen minutes. The weather was clearing. Al handled his duties well and seemed to know what to do even before Matt could say anything.

They went to the flying bridge, where Matt started setting up all the electronic gear. He coordinated the GPS and radar, checked the depth sounder system, and began to plot the run toward Miami. While working, he asked Al, "Where's Ray?"

"Ray drove up to Miami to set up the deal to get Webb's wife and daughter away from the guys watching them. Look, I can keep us on plane and on course for a time. Why don't you go talk to Webb and get the whole skinny on what we're going to do."

"Well, I don't—"

"I can call you if I need you." He pointed to one of the several microphones in the overhead communication complex.

Downstairs, Matt found Tanya crying.

Webb looked up as Matt entered. "I wasn't trying to make her cry. She's upset about calling her folks. She's worried about her mother and about lying to her." Matt put a hand on her shoulder and said, trying to sound calm, "Let's just ask if we can use the boat for a long weekend and come back Monday or Tuesday. You can say we want to go up to Miami and on the way back we might even try some marlin fishing. Tell your mother we'll call her every day. That will also give us a little insurance too. If they don't hear from us, they'd probably put out an alert on the boat."

"Ya, that's all good thinking," agreed Webb. "Go wash your face and make the call. "

Tanya went to the master stateroom. She returned in a few minutes looking composed. Matt and Webb just watched each other silently during her absence.

Webb handed her the sat phone. "You can tell your parents mostly the truth. We're going to a marina in South Miami Beach. Ray will have the marina expecting us this evening. We need to be there by 8:00 p.m. Tell your mother you're going to Joe's Stone Crab for dinner."

Tanya made the call and pulled off her ruse very well. Her father thought some deep-sea fishing would be a good idea. He advised them on bait and warned them not to put too many fish remnants down the sink. Her mother urged them to be careful in Miami and asked her to call daily.

While she talked, Webb found a bottle of good wine in the built-in rack. When she hung up, he tipped the bottle toward her, "Let's have some wine and relax. Then I'll tell you about my clever plan to get my wife Karen and my daughter Carla."

Matt opened the wine and poured three glasses. Despite the boat's rolling through the larger ocean waves of the Straits of Florida, the large-based glasses remained steady on the counter as Matt poured.

Webb sipped his wine and began, "Here's the plan. They will have dinner this evening at Joe's Stone Crab, they'll go to the washroom together after they order, they'll switch clothes and wigs with look-alikes in the women's washroom. The look-alikes will continue the dinner. Ray, outside on Washington Avenue, will pick up my ladies and drive them to the marina. They'll board, and we will have a lovely night cruise to Bimini. We're really going to the Cat Cays Club south of Bimini. I'm a member there and will buy you a great breakfast. We need you to cover us as a charter. I'll have the customs clearance people there Sunday morning. Once we have our names all registered with our false passports, I'll pay all the cruising permit fees and will take care of your refueling. We'll catch a plane, and you'll be back in the Gulf Stream by noon tomorrow."

While they finished their wine, Webb reminisced about his daughter. Then Matt and Tanya went to the flybridge to take over from Al.

They slowed the boat and checked their course for Miami—an easy run putting them there well before dark. They would have time to top off the tanks and check the weather and Gulf Stream conditions for the

Bimini run. They would also have time to get some provisions—expensive in Miami Beach but even more so in the Bahamas.

The weather improved as time passed. They steered well clear of the regular cruise ships as they approached Miami Beach. They motored slowly past the exclusive luxury enclaves of Fisher Island. They entered the marina after calling on the ship-to-shore to the port authority and marina people, then stopped at the fueling area to top their tank. Webb paid the bill in cash and gave the dock boy a tip. They were directed to a slip near the marina entrance easily accessible from the road. Webb's attention to detail impressed Matt.

Tanya and Al went for provisions for their several-day cruise.

Webb grew nervous as the sun set. He made several phone calls out of Matt's and Tanya's earshot. He double-checked the lines and inspected the *Reefer*, and checked the security of the whaler on the fore deck. He checked the davit and windlass, looked over the navigational gear, and started the generator while pacing in and out of the engine room. His uncharacteristic nervousness made Matt nervous too.

While Webb prowled the boat, Matt located Cat Cays on a Bimini chart, making himself look nautical while opening various drawers around the navigation table. As though searching for something, he muttered about needing the smaller parallel rule. Checking the bottom drawer, he was relieved to feel the weight of the Beretta still in its white box where he had hidden it. He put the box on the desktop and went to work on the charts. Making sure nobody watched him, he slipped the .22 into his waistband. He then put the box back into the drawer and continued making calculations and using the dividers and rulers on the charts.

Mostly to himself, he commented, "Cat Cays and Cat Cay are actually two different islands. Interesting."

Everyone ignored him. He worked out the angle needed to compensate for the northern flow of the Gulf Stream to reach their destination. He turned on the radio. The National Weather Service reported the light northerly winds would shift to east or southeast winds for the next twenty-four hours. Calm seas and a light wind offered ideal conditions for a Stream crossing. No one else paid any attention. He put everything away and went to the master stateroom head.

With the door closed, he checked the gun for shells. Seven hollow point, long rifle shells in the magazine, none in the breech. He popped a shell out of the magazine and pushed the lever on the left of the gun. The barrel opened like a shotgun. He slid the shell into it and snapped the two-and-a-half-inch barrel and breech closed. The gun's design made it easy for people without the strength to work the slide action. With the shell in the breech, it was a double-action gun, semiautomatic after firing the first shell. Matt put the gun in his pocket, feeling less helpless. He wouldn't do anything unless Webb or Al started to change the situation. The .22 was a very small caliber, but easy to hide. Matt had read that the Israeli Mossad used the Beretta .22 as their weapon of choice. The little 41-grain bullet wouldn't appeal to Dirty Harry, but what it lacked in power it made up for in concealment and, if you aimed it right, it would definitely ruin a person's day.

Tanya and Al returned with several boxes of food. Smiling as they put the items away, she said, "You wouldn't believe the prices for eggs, cheese, bread, and milk. Captive clientele, I suppose. A really rude checkout guy. Anyway, Al paid for it. I thought for a minute he was going to pull his gun and shoot the grocer. Then I laughed and he laughed too."

Matt shook his head, puzzled.

"Well, you had to be there." Tanya chuckled.

Webb walked in and checked his watch against the ship's clock. Not even 7:00 p.m. yet.

Webb pointed at the supplies still on the counter. "Let's get this stuff stowed. We need to get out of here the second we have them aboard. I haven't seen my wife or Carla for over a month. You and Matt can sleep where you are. We'll take the guest cabin. I don't think I'll be sleeping much anyway. There's a lot that can still go wrong."

Matt thought Webb looked older and more wound up by the minute. Webb made three short phone calls. They couldn't hear much from the galley area, but he was short and direct with whomever he was talking to. Finishing the calls, he stalked into the galley area to make sure the area was shipshape and somebody had dumped the empty boxes in the dumpsters at the end of the dock. He sent Al for reading material while he checked the lines and went over lists he had already checked earlier.

Matt and Tanya went to the flybridge and put up the rear storm enclosure. It would be nice to be dry and warm if the Gulf Stream turned rainy. Matt liked the covers—all custom work with everything snapping and zipping into place with perfection. As they finished, Webb popped up the ladder and agreed with what they were doing. He also made sure they were not on the radios.

They all returned to the salon and waited. Al came back with several papers and magazines. Webb sat at the salon coffee table and absentmindedly scanned through the pile without pausing to read anything. After a few minutes, he glanced at his watch and ordered, "Al, go wait in the parking lot. I don't want them wandering around looking for the boat."

Al put on his jacket and left.

"You got any sweaters or jackets they can wear?" asked Webb. "They'll only have whatever they're wearing."

"I've got a couple of sweatshirts and one jacket," replied Tanya. "I came away from Colorado without a lot of clothes. I bought some at Key Largo, and brought a few things from home, Matt has jackets and sweaters. I think we can manage, for a day or so."

Webb stared out at the parking lot without really listening.

38

Killers

WEBB LOOKED OUT THE DOOR at the now-lighted parking lot.
"Here they come. Let's get the engines going and start
casting off the lines."

He jumped to the flybridge and started the engines. Matt spotted a group coming from the parking lot. It looked like more than the expected four. But he went forward and began to cast off the various lines. He got back to the aft deck just as the women reached the boat. Matt thought he had remembered the daughter of the wallet picture as dark-haired like Webb, but this girl was blonde and the woman with her had long, light brown hair. He saw in their faces that something was wrong.

Two men loomed out of the shadows from behind the women and Webb's men and motioned everyone into the salon. As Webb stepped off the ladder from the flybridge, one of them shoved a gun roughly into his side. The other man grabbed Matt and pushed him into the salon.

"Get into the boat. One fast move and you're dead," said the second man, a swarthy, mean-looking Latino in a dark sport coat. He carried a silenced pistol. Despite the gun in Webb's ribs, Matt could see his urge to attack, his need to protect his family almost overpowering good sense. With a physical posture that reflected his decision, Webb quelled the urge and obeyed the gun-carrying men.

"Who sent you?" Webb asked as the men pushed the seven of them down onto the various couches in the salon. Having them sitting made it difficult for a fast attack on the gunmen who stood at both ends of the salon. The hum of the engines created an undercurrent for the ensuing silence. Webb's wife clutched his right arm. His beautiful daughter sat on his other side, looking terrified. They wore light sweaters, and in the better light below, Matt could see they also wore wigs. Some dark hair peeked out from beneath the daughter's blonde wig. Al and Ray were also on the larger couch, openly glaring at the gunmen. Matt and Tanya sat together on the couch across the salon. They, at least, didn't have a coffee table in front of them. The two dangerous-looking men spoke Spanish to each other. While the one who had ordered everyone below stayed behind, the taller gunman left the salon. Soon, the *Reefer* was moving slowly out of the marina. They were making a wake as they turned left at the marina opening and were on plane before they were past the south end of the marina's sea wall.

"I asked who sent you?" repeated Webb.

The gunman leaned against the counter that bordered the steps to the lower part of the boat, his eyes and the set of his jaw indicated an innate cruelty. The scars on his chin and across his left cheek and his black, ponytailed hair heightened the impression. He could have been handsome except for his thin lips and weak chin. "I am supposed to say *hola* from some people you know in Maracaibo and your capital city."

He ended his speech with a tight grin that made him look even more sinister. His dark eyes showed no emotion.

"Whatever you are being paid, I'll double it and get you to wherever you want to go in the world," said Webb.

"We have a job and you know what happens if we do not do it well. The people who were watching your women are still watching those other women eating their Key lime pie. Fools. We saw what was going on from the bar area. We knew they would lead us to you sooner or later. Those other guys will not be fooled forever. So, we must be well out to sea before they wise up."

The boat slowed and broke plane. Matt couldn't see anything but knew they had not exited Government Cut yet. Not with such smooth water.

The gunman noticed Matt's curiosity and said, "We got another boat off Fisher Island that will be following. They are my brothers. We need to be sure they know it is us."

"What do you want with us?" asked Tanya.

"I just want you to be quiet and not to move. When we get out on the ocean, we will tell you everything you need to know."

There's death in his eyes, Matt thought.

"Let me talk to Cortada," Webb said. "I can work this out. You don't want to hurt us. It can destroy a lot of people."

"I got orders from my boss, who has an arrangement with some very important people in Washington who say you got to go and your files with you. You can make it easy or hard. It's up to you. I don't care. My brothers don't care. We're poor fisherman, we do this right and we're fixed for all our lives and the lives of our children. Raoul, up on the bridge, is my wife's brother. Once we're out in the Gulf Stream, you'll tell us where the files are and face an easy death. Anything less and you'll watch some bad things happen to these women. And that's all you need to know."

Ray lunged at the man.

Two shots spit out of the gunman's silenced pistol almost in unison, both piercing Ray's heart. He collapsed in mid-leap and sprawled across the coffee table, dead so fast he shed little blood. Both bullets passed through him and lodged in the back of the padded leather couch. Carla screamed and crawled across her father to get away from Ray's body. Al started to stand but slumped back into the couch, his hands open in a gesture of surrender.

The semiautomatic, silenced pistol scanned the group, defying anyone to move.

Matt saw the two shell casings on the champagne colored carpet. He saw the two holes in the brown leather couch identified by small tufts of white padding. They were less than six inches apart and made finger-sized ripped holes. Death had become supercargo on the *Reefer*. The slightest wrong move meant instant retaliation.

Webb, suddenly and unexpectedly calm and relaxed, moved his daughter next to his wife and left some space between himself and them, keeping them away from Ray's body. His expression turned nonbelligerent as he said in a conversational tone, "Ray was probably embarrassed that you got the drop on him. How did you do it?"

"We just drove up and asked for directions. When they came close, we had the guns on them. They were nothing. You should hire more competent people," said the man from Maracaibo.

Webb spoke in a near whisper, "I've got stuff on Cortada and half the top people in Venezuela. The same goes for major players in Washington who control the drug interdiction programs. I even have people that help me in the Coast Guard, Air Force, and ATF. Without me, your boss is in deep trouble. So, why is he doing this?"

"Not my call. You can talk to the man if you want to. I get no pleasure from this. I don't want to hurt beautiful women, but you must believe that I will if you don't tell us what we must know."

"Can I get up and use the phone?" asked Webb.

"Okay, but move slowly and don't even think of coming at me."

"What's your name?" asked Webb as he rose slowly.

"Carlos," said the gunman.

Webb moved toward the satellite phone located on the counter near the couch that Matt and Tanya shared. As he edged between Carlos and Matt, Matt palmed the tiny Beretta in his pocket, then crossed his arms, concealing the gun under his left arm.

Carlos noted Matt's movement and fixed his eyes on him. "Don't move again—even to cross your legs. I will give you no chance to even get your legs under you. Do you understand me?"

"Sure. You're the man with the gun," said Matt.

Carlos stood fifteen feet away. The Beretta with its short barrel was not very accurate even in a shooting vise. Carlos's gun looked like a 10mm or .40 caliber, more than three times the power of Matt's. He had just fired two shots offhand with deadly accuracy at fifteen feet in a half-second. Too fast to appreciate the coordination and physics that went into the almost instant killing of a human being. Matt turned his thoughts from Carlos's ability and advantages to ways to put lots of little holes in him.

Tanya moved closer and buried her head in his neck, helping hide the pistol she'd noticed him slip under his arm. She sobbed but, between sobs, whispered to Matt, "I can help."

Carlos watched the movement and dismissed it, more interested in Webb on one side of the salon and Al on the other. He moved farther back into the boat, decreasing the angle between his potential targets. In doing so, he put part of the counter between himself and Matt's lower body.

Tanya moved away from Matt.

"Can I try to help him?" asked Tanya, indicating Ray. She was trying to establish a dialog with the killer and move in a way that would get Matt closer to him.

"Just sit down and be quiet. That man is dead. You can't help him. If you move again, I will be forced to shoot a very gorgeous woman," said Carlos as his eyes moved up and down Tanya.

Webb had placed a long distance call. He spoke in Spanish. The conversation started with some heated Spanish invectives that questioned the family and profession of the mother of the person on the other end of the satellite connection. Tanya blushed a bit, and Carlos smirked. Even Webb's wife could not completely suppress the smile that creased her lovely face; either she understood Spanish or her husband's ass-chewing ability, or both.

Webb's call did not seem to be going well. He cajoled and then made major threats. Matt couldn't follow all the Spanish, but he understood Webb's stiffening jaw line and his crushing grip on the phone. Webb slowly unscrewed the phone set from the satellite cable connection with his left hand, a careful and dexterous movement. To show animation and strength with one hand and subtlety and dexterity with the other was an effort of impressive coordination. With the cable disconnected, Webb put his hand over the phone set. He was going to throw the set at Carlos.

Matt was in a bad position. Webb stood between him and Carlos. Webb could be shot in front and in back if he attacked Carlos with their present positions. Matt needed to change the alignment but had no idea how.

Al saw most of what Matt had seen. He knew Webb would not go meekly into the Gulf Stream. He shifted his feet closer to the couch, preparing to pounce.

Carlos saw this and brought up his pistol. He yelled, "Sit down and cross your feet out in front of you. Señor Webb, hang up and get back on the couch. *Ahora*, now!"

Webb released the phone and put the hand set back on to its cradle. Carlos motioned him back with the gun and moved further into the salon. Sideways to Tanya and Matt, only ten feet away now, he reached into his sport coat pocket, pulled out several white plastic cable ties, and threw them on the coffee table next to Ray's body. He turned to Tanya.

Matt stopped breathing.

"Put these on their wrists and ankles. Start with him," said Carlos, pointing at Matt.

Tanya picked up the plastic strips and turned to Matt.

"Do you want their hands in front or in back?" she asked Carlos.

"In back, but be careful and do nothing fast," warned Carlos.

Tanya moved between Matt and Carlos and bent over to help as Matt placed his hands behind him. No one in the room except Tanya saw Matt move his gun and right hand behind him. Carlos could not help but watch as Tanya's slacks tightened across her bottom as she appeared to work on Matt's wrists. She kept Matt's feet under him and pushed the plastic end through the slit on the opposite end, surreptitiously twisting the plastic so the smooth side, rather than the serrated side, slid against the locking teeth. She moved deftly and smoothly while ensuring that Carlos was distracted by her other moves.

Tanya then crossed to the other couch to tie up the others. Mrs. Webb and Carla sat quietly, numb with fear and despair. Webb glared and looked ready to launch another futile attack when Tanya winked at him. Webb looked into her eyes and relaxed.

With his captives restrained, Carlos moved closer. Six feet from Matt, he stopped and leaned against the end of Matt's couch. The boat's rolling through larger waves announced their arrival in the Gulf Stream. Carlos seemed to relax a little as his plans were working. Carlos licked his lips and leered at Webb's daughter. "I am very impressed with your ladies, Señor Webb. Beautiful women. Maybe we can make a deal with them and let you watch." Tanya finished securing Webb and Al—as ineffectively as she had Matt—and ended her work standing at the far end of the salon, near the door and as far from Carlos as possible.

"I've done them, now do you want to do me?" A tantalizing pout flitted across Tanya's face. She moved into the doorway and held her wrists together. She raised an eyebrow and smiled before turning around and holding her hands behind her. "Do you want my hands behind my back too?"

She did a half turn and gave Carlos a hip shot.

Carlos, assuming his prisoners were properly bound, moved toward Tanya with another cable tie in his free hand. He was focused like some bucks Matt had stalked.

As he passed, Matt smoothly brought up the gun and shot Carlos twice, the tiny slugs impacting just above the right ear. He fell at Tanya's feet, touching Ray's extended hand. His legs jerked and drummed on the carpet, the silenced weapon pinned under his convulsing body.

The noise, even from the Beretta .22, thundered in the salon's close quarters. Mrs. Webb and Carla, so horrified they couldn't bring in the air it took to scream. Webb moved first and clamped his freed hands on their mouths, shaking his head and quietly urging them to silence. He rolled the still shaking body, snapped up Carlos's gun and went outside. Raoul had heard the shots and started down from the flybridge, but Webb stopped him with three shots while the man had both hands on the ladder's railings. He caught the man as he fell and dumped his body along the starboard side of the deck.

Webb rushed back into the salon. Al, now free, leaned over to check on Ray. Tanya helped Mrs. Webb and her daughter into the master stateroom, trying to block the gruesome figure of Carlos, with one eye a bloody lump on his cheek and the body still shaking.

Webb had the sport coat of the man he had shot. He threw it to Al. "Put this on, turn up the collar, get up top and keep the boat on whatever course we are on. We'll keep the lights low and the flybridge covers will make you hard to see clearly. Check the radar to find the other boat. We need to know where they are and if they can see us."

Al retrieved his pistol back from Carlos and returned it to his shoulder holster. He struggled into the sport coat and went topside.

Matt slouched on the couch in shock, staring at Carlos's last quivers. He had shot Carlos without hesitation, knowing he had no choice if they weren't all to die. He also knew the Venezuelans would have abused the three women before killing them. Matt had reacted like a deadly animal facing another deadly animal—fast, unequivocal, and final. No threats, posturing, or mercy, and there shouldn't have been any sorrow. Matt would have preferred to maintain a civilized posture while trying to negotiate, but he knew Carlos already had his kill switch thrown. The outcome was not in doubt, only the time and place.

Tanya shook him. He still had the little Beretta in his hand, the hammer cocked. Tanya took it from him, broke it open, and removed the live shell from the breech. She dropped the magazine and replaced the unspent shell in it. She lowered the hammer, pushed the magazine into the handle, and put the pistol in her slacks. She stroked Matt's hair and said, "You've saved us all."

He did not look up, his mind still trying to sort out his feelings.

Tanya went to the liquor cabinet and poured some Crown Royal into a small glass. She brought it to Matt. He drank it. It burned all the way to his stomach, breaking his stupor.

In the master stateroom, Webb told his wife and daughter to stay put until things were cleaned up. When he returned to the salon, Matt and Tanya had wrapped Carlos's head with towels to stop the small amount of blood from his eye. There were no exit wounds and his dark hair hid the entry points. After they had the head covered, they dragged the bodies out onto the darkened aft deck and put them against the aft gear locker, covering them with an awning tarp. When they returned, Mrs. Webb had started cleaning. Without the brown wig, her short, blonde hair looked stylish. Matt noticed how easily she moved despite the boat's side-to-side rocking and forward bounding motion. They all worked but said little. The blood disappeared, and a blanket and throw pillows covered the holes in the leather. With the cleaning finished, Webb motioned everyone to the liquor cabinet.

Webb's wife came to Matt and took his hand. "We owe you our lives, so don't be sad. Let's rejoice in being still alive."

"I'll get over it," Matt said with a shrug.

She looked at him with luminous blue-gray eyes above high cheekbones and a model's smile. She kissed his cheek and said, "I'm Karen. Our daughter is Carla."

She went to her husband and kissed him too, before turning to Tanya. "You are a wonderful actress and very brave. Thank you."

Tanya accepted a cheek kiss, also, and smiled.

Karen went to her daughter in the stateroom.

"Let's go to the bridge and figure out what we are going to do with the boat that's following us," said Webb.

They darkened the salon to just the galley lights and, with no aft lights burning except the mandatory stern and running lights, climbed the ladder to the flying bridge.

The sea, fairly calm for the Gulf Stream in December, sported well-spaced, two- to three-foot swells—the light southeast wind did not build significant waves against the north-flowing current. The waves further slackened with the decreasing winds. The moon shone brightly ahead, but high enough to avoid silhouetting them. Through binoculars, they could see clearly the moonlit other boat about a quarter mile behind them, directly in their wake. Miami's sky glow silhouetted the other boat and spotlighted many of the city's taller buildings. But how much could the other boat see of them? The after deck would be out of the moonlight and also shielded by the brightness of the stern light that came from the top of the flying bridge and shined more out than down.

Webb spoke, thinking out loud, "We can probably outrun them, but not their radio or their radar. We can set this radar and pick up Bimini from here, but so can they. At some point, they planned to stop this boat and pick up Carlos and Raoul. I don't think they had planned to take anyone else back. They wanted my files or to know where they are. Maybe the other boat was a ploy to make me think they were totally prepared to kill us all. But I would bet they planned to eventually kill us and scuttle us. They must know I have a lot of good friends and support at Cat Cays— they wouldn't pull in there or even Bimini. They may have planned to anchor off Bimini, but that would be a risk and I bet they plan to be done with their work before dawn."

"So, what's our best course?" Matt asked.

"I'm thinking...maybe too deeply. They were fisherman with guns and orders. Cortada, their boss, knew this type would scare me most because they are too dumb to be disloyal and think about a double cross. I've used the same type for the same reason. I want that son of a bitch Cortada to die a bad death. I think I will drop him alive from a plane into his own courtyard so his family can see some blood too!"

"We got our guns back, and we've got their guns; let's stop, turn on lots of lights and when they come in, we do them." Al smiled at his own dramatic bravado.

Matt nodded. "I've got my deer rifle aboard. Only twelve shells, but a lot more firepower than a Beretta. It's got a scope on it. I think I could make a good shot, even at night from a rolling boat at fifty yards."

Webb held up a hand. "They might have AKs and RPGs for all we know. They had a silencer, that's big-league hardware. We're too close to Miami for them to blow us up or to have a fire. We're only a few miles north of the cruise boat lanes. We have to be on a half dozen radar screens right now, not to mention the DEA and Coast Guard planes that can cover the whole area from 30,000 feet. They're counting on the normalcy of two boats going to Bimini using the buddy system. Even if they raft up for a while, they wouldn't cause any concerns on any radar. I doubt you can distinguish two boats tied together. Then after a while, if only one boat goes on, who's to report it?"

"The way things've been going today? Most likely nobody," Matt agreed.

Webb continued, "I bet they plan to tie up together and scuttle us. After we go down, they go away. They may even have something to help us go down, like a shaped charge or something that would make a hole, but wouldn't cause a flash or fire. They know boats, so they would know how to sink one. They would stay off the radios. I say we run another ten or fifteen miles or, they come up on us, slow down, stop, make it look like we have the information they want. If we can distract them enough to get close, we can just shoot the shit out of them. It's either that or we run for it."

"I vote for taking them on as plan A," Matt suggested. "And running if things don't go our way as plan B. If they have RPGs here, they could have backup people they could call in Bimini. Maybe we can capture one or both of the brothers and get some information."

Webb nodded and looked at Al, who also nodded. "Okay, we try to sucker them in. If they get suspicious, Tanya, we'll need your perfect Spanish. With our hailer, your voice should confuse them a little."

"I can handle that," Tanya said.

Webb continued, "Matt, you cover them from the lounge area in the front of this flybridge. It's dark and you'll get a good view if we stay a little sideways. There's too much chop for the marlin bridge and they might see you. Let's have the whaler ready to go in case they do have a rocket or a fifty-caliber that can put big holes in us. I'd like to take them alive. They may know who Cortada has been working with, though I wouldn't hold my breath. Worst case, they'll tell us how to get to Cortada, and I can get some people working on that when we get to the Cat Cays. When the time comes, I'll take the helm, and Al can be on the aft deck, he's good with a handgun. He can have several all loaded and cocked. That's a lot of fire-power, unless they have automatic weapons. They won't see you, Matt; so you take them out if they make a fight."

Webb turned to leave, "Right now, I need to talk to Karen and Carla. I've got another distraction in mind."

"I'll come along," Tanya said.

Webb and Tanya went down the ladder. Al sat in the helm chair with the boat running as Raoul had set it. The autopilot button glowed. The seas, almost flat, shone silver under a silver moon. The lights of Miami on the western horizon made it hard to see the lights of the boat behind them—though not on the radar.

Matt put his hand on the helm chair and watched the instruments with Al.

"Can I ask you a question?" said Matt.

"Sure," replied Al.

"How did you get away from the people that nabbed Webb?"

"A little luck and a little planning. We rented the truck from a farmer who lived just north of St. Ignace. We left him our rental van and gave him several hundred to use his truck for a few days. He's an uncle of a person Ray knew. No way did we want to have the cargo we had in a vehicle everyone could identify. I figure from what Webb told us, they just let us go because they were looking for a Lincoln and everyone you know seems to drive a four-by-four pickup. Anyway, we didn't know Webb was in trouble until he contacted us in the Keys."

"Why did you come down there?"

"You didn't hear this from me, but seeing how you just saved my ass for a second time, I'll tell you. Webb knew people were watching the boat and the marina. He has someone working around the marina. We were to get rid of whoever was watching and find out who he was working for."

"So you met Ron Miles?"

"Yeah, but we couldn't get much from the asshole. He was a weird buckaroo. He tried to put a karate move on Ray and got taken out by accident. Ray was not a good person to attack. He was small but had boxed professionally in Detroit and liked to hit people. We did our disposal tricks and took his boat too. That boat's now in Cuba running Canadian tourists around. Webb set it up. He wants to get in good with some of the top Cuban resort people. He thinks that Cuba will be the best tourist area in the hemisphere sometime soon. Did you know that craft was a Grand Banks, and somebody painted over the beautiful wood to make it look more like a fishing trawler?"

"Too dumb," Matt said, shaking his head.

Al continued, "It had more electronic stuff than a TV studio. Had to be CIA or some other government bunch. It was way past the DEA budget. Plus, they wouldn't have had a person like that asshole working a stakeout."

Webb and Tanya came up the ladder. They went over the procedure to work the hailer. She could use it from behind the helm console and out of sight of a boat coming from any quarter except directly aft.

"We'll put them off our port rear quarter. We want them to see the aft deck but not real good into the flybridge," said Webb.

"I'll tell them to put their hands up or be shot," Tanya said. "Al will have them covered from the deck. Webb will run the helm. And, Matt, you'll be forward with the rifle."

"Karen's agreed to being on the aft deck, looking like she's been beaten," Webb said. "Actually, she suggested it as a distraction. I think she didn't want to be outdone by Tanya. She likes being the star."

"Could be dangerous," Matt said.

"She knows. It's a good thing she doesn't have her tights and a tutu… okay, when they get close, we'll turn on the deck lights. They should be looking at Karen more than Al, who is about the same size as Raoul. Karen's trying to make her darker wig look like Raoul's hair. If it doesn't work, Al can just wear a hat."

"Al, why don't you go down and see how she's coming with that wig," suggested Tanya.

Al left. Matt followed. Karen and Carla began working on Al. The too-small wig made him look like he was being attacked by a light brown Lhasa apso. They laughed, as much from nerves as the foolishness of the wig, then gave up and gave Al a fishing hat with a long visor. Matt found his Remington, checked it, and gave it a few dry fires to reacquaint his finger with the trigger. He put the ammo pack in a pocket and donned a dark sweatshirt. He grabbed a dark towel from the bathroom shelf and moved to the flybridge with the rifle.

Webb pointed at the rifle. "Mind if I have a look?"

Matt handed it to him.

Webb examined it, worked the bolt, placed it against his shoulder, and scanned the horizon through the telescopic sight. "Fine rifle you've got here. You ever shot from a boat or over water?"

"No, and it worries me. If they get close enough, it won't make any difference. This is very powerful. It puts out a bullet that goes faster than 3,000 feet per second. If they close to less than fifty yards, the bullet'll reach them before the recoil brings the gun up. I can almost watch the bullet hit. Simple point and shoot."

Matt went to the flybridge's lounge, just ahead of the helm, little more than a padded seating area. Matt set up on the port side. The U-shaped Plexiglas windscreen had openings on the bottom and sides. Matt wrapped the barrel with the towel and rested it on the window frame. He peered through the scope, but the boat's motion proved too bumpy. He decided to shoot using only the sling for bracing. He tried several shooting positions. From his knees wasn't bad and gave good concealment. But standing gave the best sight picture and allowed the smoothest compensation for the boat's rolling. He would wait on his knees and, when the boat stopped, stand up if necessary.

"We're better than halfway across," Webb said, apparently enjoying the excitement and challenge. "This is about as smooth as you will find the Stream. I think we're ready. Let's go on with the show. I'll go down and get Al and Karen ready. Carla will work the lights. It's better if she has something to do. We will need the light off fast if they start shooting and we make a run for it."

Webb went below, leaving Tanya and Matt alone on the flybridge. Matt held her tightly to him and kissed her deeply. Moonlight bathed the ocean around them. The boat cut through the small waves with animal-like smoothness. They watched the radar. The other boat's blip jumped closer with each screen refresh.

Tanya picked up the overhead microphone and turned a switch. Her voice came over the boat's speakers when she announced, "They're coming up on us."

In less than a minute, Webb stood at the helm, turned off the auto-pilot, and slowed the boat.

Tanya and Matt watched Al loosely tying Karen to the flybridge ladder. He ripped her blouse off her back. He squirted ketchup from a plastic bottle to fake bloody marks across her back. He didn't overdo it. The effect was very good. Karen said something, and Al pulled down her slacks. Matt tried not to stare at her toned body in her nearly flesh-colored lace panties and bra. She looked up the ladder and winked at Tanya.

The sea battle was to begin.

The big Hatteras broke plane and quickly settled and stopped. The other boat was less than two hundred yards out. Matt cursed himself for mental vapor lock as, at the last minute, he remembered he had unloaded the rifle at the Sea School. He moved to the forward lounge, sat down, put three shells in the Remington's magazine—the most it would hold—then pushed the shells down and slipped a fourth shell into the breech. He brought the bolt forward, putting on the safety out of long habit. He couldn't see well enough to read the exact power setting on the scope. He twisted it to about halfway up, four or five power, as a good magnification for a moving target less than one hundred yards away. He could locate the boat quickly and spot any people on it.

The other boat came up smoothly and turned on a powerful light secured to the top of its solid roof, which covered its center console.

"So much for outrunning it, it's a thirty-some-foot Intrepid, it's got us by fifteen or twenty knots," Tanya whispered to him.

Matt scanned the approaching boat. A center console design. Good news, as it left no place for the operator to hide. He couldn't see the motors well, but knew there would be two or three big outboards. As they slowed, Matt picked out two men standing at the console. Less than fifty yards away and coming in slowly.

Webb took the microphone, switched to boat speakers, and said calmly, "Lights."

The Reefer lit up like a Christmas tree. Al waved and turned his back to the boat. He made a slow effort of untying Karen's wrists. She squirmed and cried. The sight reminded Matt of a movie set from a B-movie horror scene. Webb turned the idling Reefer slightly to port with an expert engagement of the starboard propeller. The subtlety was perfect. Matt had a clear view of the approaching boat, and the Hatteras offered itself to a stern approach.

Matt heard the outboards reversing and then idling. The boat was very maneuverable, and the driver skilled. The engines engaged again, and the boat slid up to the side of the Reefer. One man put over two white bumpers and tossed a rope to Al who now had Karen in front of him, mimicking tying her hands behind her. A masterpiece of choreography—Karen, in her panties and bra, with her slacks at her ankles and the remnants of her blouse around her arms, presented a striking tableau.

Al grabbed the line and bent over the cleat as he secured it. Karen fell forward onto the deck. The men moved to the side of their boat for a better view of the nearly naked woman. When they were a few feet from Al, he brought up his pistol and held it in the feet wide, two hand, straight-armed, classic Weaver stance.

Tanya's voice came over the hailer speaker in Spanish, "Put up your hands now, or you will be shot."

Completely surprised, the men raised their hands. Matt moved from the forward part of the flybridge to the aft, where he unzipped part of the plastic covers and poked the rifle out, covering the two men from above and only fifteen feet away. Webb bounded down the ladder and also held a pistol on the men. When Webb was in position, Al, staying out of all lines of fire, boarded the smaller, lower boat and took the guns shoved into the men's belts. He expertly searched both men, finding another pistol on one man and knives on both. He pushed them to the deck and looped the plastic cable ties around their wrists and ankles, correctly allowing the little plastic teeth to achieve their one way grip. In less than two minutes, he had both men trussed securely on the aft deck of their boat.

Webb told Carla to turn off most of the lights. Darkness again settled over the ocean. The moon and stars reappeared in the dark sky. They were alone on the water. With little wind, the two boats thumped gently against the bumpers between them.

Webb helped Karen up. She pulled up her slacks and wore her ripped blouse like a queen's robe over her arm. Webb kissed her. She gave him a sexy look and went into the salon.

Webb got on the Intrepid. There was enough light to see the men. Webb bent low and spoke to them in Spanish. They tried to look tough, but Matt could see their fear from the *Reefer*. Webb looked around their boat. He gave a satisfied snort when he opened one of the forward lockers and pulled out chains and mushroom anchors.

"Put these on our dead guests from Maracaibo and put them over the side so our new friends can watch. Then I'll help you put weights and chains on them," Webb ordered Al, pointing at the bound brothers

Al made quick work of the two dead Venezuelans. He then carefully slipped them over the stern of the *Reefer*. The two men in the Intrepid saw it all.

"What do we do with Ray?" asked Al.

"I'll get him home to Detroit if you think it is what he would want," said Webb.

"I don't know, he always knew the risks. Having his body won't make his family feel any better, and it'd create a lot of problems and expense. If it was me, I'd say the sea is just fine."

"Then do it. I'll try to make sure his family makes out okay," said Webb.

Al weighted Ray and gently put him over the starboard side, out of sight of the two prisoners.

Matt and Tanya watched all this silently, overcome by a sense of unreality.

Tanya finally refocused her mind on business. She checked the radar and GPS, switching them to various ranges. To their south, cruise ships formed an almost straight line. Matt checked the GPS against their previous course settings. They'd drifted almost two miles north. The Gulf Stream's current was moving them at three or four knots, they couldn't feel the movement.

— 39 —

Cat Cays

EBB CAME UP TO THE FLYBRIDGE, still excited, acting more like a college football player after a big game than a crime lord wielding power on several continents. He asked Tanya, "Can you get this boat to Cat Cays?"

"Yes, I've been there several times," Tanya replied.

"Good, we'll follow you. We will use the radio if we need to talk. Keep it on. Al and I will question those men while we travel. Stay on the standard band. Let's move, we need to take advantage of the smooth water. Matt, hide the .22 and declare the rifle and ammo on the customs forms."

Matt nodded.

Webb placed a hand on his shoulder, smiled, and added, "And I want to say thank you. Those chains and anchors were meant for us."

By the time Matt had unloaded the rifle and put the shells back into the carrying packet, Webb and Al had untied the boats, and Tanya had returned the boat to its proper course, guessing at the amount of south angle to compensate for the Stream's flow. She brought the boat to plane. They cruised at a little over twenty-five knots. The Intrepid slid into the *Reefer*'s wake and took up its previous station, back about a quarter mile.

"Radio check, radio check, radio check…" came over the speaker just above them. Tanya, sitting in the helm seat with Matt standing beside her, jumped. She turned down the volume and responded that they could hear him perfectly. She gave their heading, speed, estimated time of arrival, and a warning about the tricky tides in the shallow channels.

Tanya and Matt had the world to themselves again. The sea glistened in reflected moonlight and hissed as the cruiser cut through it. The engines merely hummed. Glad to be alive and together, Matt hugged Tanya and enjoyed her feel and smell. A perfect night.

Pulling her closer in the romantic setting, Matt's thoughts wandered a bit. "You know, I used to tell my students that the Gulf Stream is the single, simplest source of power in the world. Twenty times more water moves between Miami and Bimini than all the fresh water that flows into the world's oceans from all sources: rain, rivers, and melting ice. The Gulf Stream is always moving at two to five miles per hour. I always thought some real smart person would figure a way to tap this energy; maybe using an underwater turbine turned by flowing water channeled to it by giant sluice walls."

She kissed his cheek. "I didn't know that, professor."

"Never mind. It's just good to be alive and too beautiful for a lecture."

"I'll bet you were good with chalk and a board." Tanya put her head on Matt's shoulder.

"Ahoy, up there. Mother sent up some food and drink." Carla stepped onto the flybridge balancing a corked tray with sandwiches, chips, and cans of pop. Carla seemed well over her previous shock. She pointed at a group of lights just visible on a faint land mass. "This is beautiful. Is that where we're going?"

"Yes, that's the Cat Cays," Tanya replied. "And that's Bimini to the north. You can see them better on the radar. We're about an hour out."

"What are we going to do there?" Carla asked.

"It's a very good harbor. It's a private island with pools, beaches, tennis, and restaurants," said Tanya.

"How about shops? We're going to need a lot of clothes." Carla's eyes lit up. She chattered for several minutes. A month away from being fifteen, she liked school and would miss her friends, but looked forward to new adventures and had her mind set on being positive about her future life.

Matt felt her attitude should be isolated and prescribed to all teenagers. Her positive approach to life and ability to shake off the horrors she had just witnessed impressed Matt.

Carla went back to the salon.

Tanya adjusted the GPS and radar to bring the approaching shore into higher resolution and definition. She adjusted the sounder that had finally found a bottom over two hundred feet below. She called Cat Cays Marina—properly pronouncing it "Keys" not "Ks"—and, after several tries, got a sleepy response. The two boats were directed to two consecutive dock spaces and informed the docking fee was $3.00 per foot for three days maximum. Tanya requested customs clearance—someone would be called but might not show up until morning.

The marina also directed them to take the Gun Cay Cut a mile south and to watch the rising tide onto the Grand Bahama Banks. Tanya steered into the channel and watched for the marina markers. A marvel, the GPS showed all the navigation aids, the channel, and even the marina entrance. It couldn't help with the currents or sailboats anchored off the shore waiting for daylight. She monitored the various anchor and navigation lights and the lighthouse. Their depth sounder beeped to signal sixty feet of water under them. She handled the 70,000-pound boat like a sports car, sensing the pushing current and countering the boat's tendency to crab. Matt was glad he was watching rather than steering.

Matt checked behind them. The Intrepid cruised right on their tail with four people standing on deck. This made Matt feel better. He would not have been surprised if Webb had put the gunmen over the side. He bet the two fishermen had some high-pucker-factor moments before reaching an agreement with Webb. It looked like one of the fishermen helmed the sleek boat. Amazing how cooperative a person can become when faced with a possible one-way trip to the bottom of the Florida Straits chained to an anchor.

They finally came to the lights of the marina—a tropical paradise of palm trees and flower gardens. Multi-million-dollar boats moored at the docks and long piers. The sounder bleeped again as they passed over the sand bar into the deeper marina water. They found their slips, and Matt went down to help with the lines and docking.

Tanya brought the *Reefer* to the dock without the help of any ropes or dock attendants. The speed-efficient pockets that partially covered the props forced Tanya to use higher than normal rpm for docking maneuvers. The growl of the powerful twin diesels made more than a few heads pop out of their plastic palaces before popping back down like tanned prairie dogs. Finally, the *Reefer* gently touched the dock, perfectly positioned as Tanya placed the twin transmissions into neutral.

The Intrepid docked almost as smoothly. The fisherman, who had less space than Tanya had, used the fishing-boat technique of touching the bow to the dock with its bumpers before swinging the stern into the dock by reversing the opposite outboard. Matt noted the three Yamaha motors, planning to check their horsepower later. But the 36-foot boat certainly would have nearly twenty knots advantage over the *Reefer*.

Webb carried a bag, probably with their guns, from the smaller boat to the *Reefer*. As he boarded, he told Tanya, "Good job."

Tanya looked up from securing the *Reefer* and hooking up the electricity and said, "Thanks."

Matt followed him as he crossed the *Reefer's* deck and hugged his wife and daughter. He went into the master stateroom and locked the door.

Matt was glad to be at the dock, ready for more than a couple of drinks. He watched as Tanya finally stopped the engines, sparing the marina further din from 2,400 diesel horsepower and returning it to the flapping of flags and palm fronds in the warm ocean breeze. The lines and cables of the sailboats clanked and, from across the marina, calypso music added a festive touch. The wooden dock was wide and perfectly kept. Matt figured the golf carts parked beside several boats must provide the transportation around on the broad, flat property.

Webb came topside and stepped out on the dock, looking around for the harbor authorities. After ten minutes, a uniformed worker pulled up in a golf cart with the Cat Cays Club colors and symbol. Webb spoke to him and the man stiffened in respect. Webb climbed aboard, and the cart hummed away.

Tanya walked up beside Matt. She took his hand and looked up at him. "Hi, sailor. New in port, looking to have some fun?"

Matt smiled. "I'm always ready for some fun, milady, but how about a good drink of rum and something to eat first?"

They walked hand-in-hand to the Intrepid where they found Al trying to communicate with the two gunmen, who looked happy to be alive. They laughed excitedly at Al's bad Spanish.

Matt helped Tanya step aboard and began translating between Al and the two brothers. The brothers looked sad when Tanya mentioned their brother and brother-in-law. They seemed very relieved when she explained they were alive because they hadn't tried to kill anyone. They said they didn't like Cortada much, anyway. Matt could follow most of the conversation as Tanya translated for Al. They understood the killings were in pure self-defense. Tanya told them to stay on their boat until Webb got back. Al sat on a bench on the dock between the boats and kept an eye on the men who had no way of knowing if he was armed or not.

Webb returned in an unmarked golf cart with a second set of seats where golf bags normally were stored. Waving for them to join him, he said, "I've paid for our dockage. The clearance people will be here in the morning. Meanwhile, let's do some shopping, then have a few drinks and the dinner I promised you."

Within seconds, Karen and Carla had piled onto the seat beside Webb, and Matt and Tanya climbed in the back. Al remained behind to watch the boat and the Venezuelans.

Webb drove them to a cluster of buildings and led everyone downstairs below a restaurant to a small boutique opened especially for him. Webb and the women browsed the swimsuits and warm-weather casual attire. Matt already had his clothes on board. Matt totally enjoyed the fashion show as the women modeled swimsuits. They laughed when Tanya and Carla picked the same style yellow bikini. After considerable good-natured debate, they decided it was the best style available and they would be twins. Karen picked a head-turning one-piece—black with a large red spot, no back, and a low-cut halter front. Webb bought some shirts for Al, who had his own sandals and swimsuit.

Webb paid with cash, to the delight of the lady at the counter.

Once again, they crowded into the two-seat golf cart and returned to the *Reefer*. Tanya and Matt listened from the back seat to the far-ranging conversation.

Webb told Karen their plane couldn't be there until the next day. The island's 1,100-foot runway required a short takeoff and landing aircraft, and Webb had arranged a suitable plane from a charter service for a morning flight, but they had slipped the schedule into the late afternoon. This had upset Webb and forced him to reschedule their itinerary. He didn't like hanging around Cat Cays very long, but he was happy to be with his family. He and Karen had been here several times and looked forward to showing Carla the pool and beaches. Carla asked many questions about their destination. Webb assured her that his estate in the Dominican Republic was beautiful with a pool, a private road to a private beach, and a wonderful view. They talked about Carla's schooling in Europe. Webb spoke to her in Russian, Spanish, and some fractured French. Webb explained the importance of knowing multiple languages in business. Before he could lapse into a boring father lecture, they arrived at the boat.

The ladies took their plastic bags of shopping booty and disappeared into the *Reefer*. Webb and Matt joined Al, who still sat on the plastic power-and-water pedestals that also served as boarding steps by each slip.

"What are we going to do with those boys?" asked Al.

"I think we got all the information they can give us," Webb replied. "I know all their contacts and can get to the next levels within their organization. We killed their brother and brother-in-law. I think we let them go back to their families. They'll tell that we are tough, but not heartless. What do you think, Matt?"

Matt furrowed his brow. "Frankly, I was surprised when I saw four people in that boat when you came in. Can they hurt you if you let them go?"

"Not really. They agreed to have radio problems for twenty-four hours. They have more to fear from Cortada when they go back. His men failed, he showed his position. He might find he has a lot less allies now that he tried and failed to get me. But I need to know who the U.S. government person is working with Cortada. I'll find it out in time, but right now I'm vulnerable. I need a safe place for my family and me. I'm not ready to cut and run. I can ride this out for a few months or a year and have everything I ever wanted."

"So?" asked Al.

"I'm going to talk to them again, gas them up, if they need it, and send them back to Miami, or wherever they want to go." On the Intrepid, Webb helped them keep their radio promise as he yanked out the radio microphone and threw it overboard. He talked intently to them for nearly ten minutes. They shook his hand and looked like they would have kissed it if Webb had let them. He walked back to Matt and Al.

"These aren't really tough guys. Cortada chose his gunmen poorly. Maybe all he thought he needed was Carlos, who had killed several people for him. They said they have money for gas. They don't want to be here when the Bahamian authorities come."

The three men watched the brothers start the three Yamahas and back the thirty-six foot boat away from the dock. The boat headed for the fuel dock, and neither brother looked back as it slipped out of sight.

Matt, Webb, and Al turned around just as the three women stepped onto the dock.

Carla, who led the procession, asked, "How do we look?"

The men agreed that they all looked beautiful in their shorts, sandals, and colored blouses, with light sweaters draped over their shoulders. Matt had to admit that, if he weren't so completely in love with Tanya, he would be hard-pressed to pick a winner in their impromptu beauty contest.

Webb slapped Al on the back. "Al, now that you don't need to babysit, let's have a good dinner."

"I'm ready," Al said, grinning and rubbing his hands together.

"Can you two boys lock up?" Webb asked Al and Matt.

Matt locked up the *Reefer*. All six of them crowded into the golf cart under the marina's bright lights and headed past the security guard's shack toward the club's restaurant.

The Cat Cays Club restaurant was better on presentation and service than cooking. They were eating late and the kitchen was limited, but no one complained. They enjoyed good wine and avoided talking about anything unpleasant. Carla had a couple of moments when the day caught up with her. Matt could see it in her eyes. Webb served her wine and kept the conversation moving and light.

They rode back to the boat under palm fronds that rattled in the breeze. The lights around the marina hid the stars. They got to the *Reefer* and went in feeling the long day, the life and death events, and the wine leading them to their beds. Al made up the largest salon couch for a bed. Carla took the cushions from the smaller salon couch and made a bed in the guest stateroom. Everyone was bedded down in twenty minutes, the *Reefer* secured and its internal lights off or dimmed.

Matt and Tanya had their bed back. They were past being tired. Matt fought to stay awake as Tanya brushed her teeth, hoping to fall asleep in each other's arms.

Al woke everyone at mid-morning by announcing the arrival of the Bahamian customs official accompanied by the only Bahamian policeman on the island. They had patiently waited for several hours, observing the Bahamian tradition, a point of national pride, of never being in a hurry. Although the men had no great demands on their time, it was undignified for them to wait too long. After all, they had come to the boat as a courtesy to a valued guest. They had finally agreed that 10:00 a.m. was late enough to sleep in on a perfect day.

Webb handled the whole procedure. He used their real passports. Matt and Tanya were superficially asked for their passports. The simplified paperwork involved only a few lines on several pages. Matt listed his rifle, but they didn't ask to see it. They checked the boat's registration and associated paperwork—George Vega had left photocopies aboard for any authorities who might need them. Webb paid the cruising fees, again in cash. The officials gave them fishing licenses for several months and a Bahamian courtesy flag to fly to keep them from additional inspections and charges as they cruised the islands. The permit was good for twelve months.

While Webb and Al completed the final pleasantries with the officials, Tanya and Karen prepared a real breakfast for the whole crew. Although Carla wanted to get in the sun by the pool, she controlled her teenage enthusiasm and helped with the breakfast. She ate lightly but slowly. While the adults enjoyed their second cup of coffee, she slipped into her new yellow bikini and a large T-shirt, ready to go. Webb sent Al as chaperon. She bristled at this, and Matt saw her first real flash of Webb's blood. She immediately masked her desire for independence and left for the pool with Al. Al carried a rather heavy, rolled-up boat towel, and Matt figured it wasn't suntan lotion.

"We should be out of here by this afternoon," Webb told Tanya and Matt. "Just enjoy the *Reefer*. I've arranged for some money to be delivered when you get back. No strings attached to it or to me. Tell your parents they can sell the business without any difficulty now. If you get married, send us a wedding invitation, I'll get our address to you. If you encounter any political problems, let me know about it."

"I think we'll be fine," Matt said, squeezing Tanya's hand.

Webb continued, "In return for all the good stuff, just forget about everything that happened from the plane going down to right now."

Matt and Tanya looked at each other. Webb wasn't a person you thanked. Anything you got from him was earned many times over.

"Would it be all right if I called my mother?" Tanya asked. "She worries every time I cross the Stream because it can get so rough."

"Sure, why don't you plan on staying here for a few more days as my guest? When we are gone, maybe your folks could fly over and join you."

Tanya called her mother and explained they were fine and needed the rest and sun. She kept the conversation light but did mention they were at the Cat Cays Club and might stay a few days. Webb heard this and looked concerned. Tanya finally hung up.

When Tanya had hung up, Webb said, "I'm not sure mentioning where we are was a good idea. Bimini would have been close enough. I'm going to be very happy to get in the air and out of here."

They all went to the pool and sunbathed, swimming a few laps when they got hot. Tanya and Carla, in matching suits, drew more than a few looks and sparked plenty of conversation, mostly among the older people sitting in the shade around the pool. Matt heard the various conversations as they speculated on the family relationships of the three women and three men. Seeing Webb's heavily muscled body in just a swimsuit made Matt very glad he'd never had to wrestle him. He looked big, even chubby, in street clothes. In a swimsuit, his huge leg muscles balanced his shoulder and arm muscles, and his thick torso formed a logical connection between the two muscle masses.

Karen apparently had to baby her almost ivory skin, using SPF 45 sunblock and keeping to the shade most of the time. She swam well and walked around the pool as though on stage. Matt noted her feet looked hard and her toes didn't match her well-manicured fingers: ballet. But anyone looking at her feet would have to be more than a little weird, anyway. This made Matt wonder why he was checking them out.

They all made one run to the ocean, only a few yards from the pool area. The scene—greenish-blue water against white sand beach lined with palms—looked right out of a Mexican beer commercial.

They had lunch served at the pool. It was better than the dinner the evening before—fruit, chilled seafood, pasta, and excellent fresh-baked bread.

Webb made and received several phone calls, leaving the pool area after each call.

Nervous again, Matt thought.

Finally, Webb suggested that everyone shower and get back to the *Reefer* to prepare for the plane due to arrive in less than two hours. After showering, they all piled into the cart still dripping, drying themselves as they rode back to the dock. Everyone changed into fresh clothing and assembled in the salon area. Carla switched on the television and began channel jumping to find news from the outside world. Webb motioned for Al and Matt to follow him into the master stateroom. When they entered, he closed and locked the door and said, "What I am going to show you would be worth many lives."

He led them into the master bathroom, too nice to be called a head. He opened a lower storage area and took out a short plunger, a plumber's friend. Matt had wondered why a million-dollar-plus boat would have plumbing problems. Webb wet the plunger, pushed it hard onto the middle floor of the tub, gripped the wooden handle with two hands, and pulled the whole lower part of the plastic tub up. It came up easily except where it attached to the drain, and that lifted up with a little back and forth motion. He sat the tub on the closed toilet. The removed tub exposed a large opening that extended under the master stateroom bed.

I knew there had to be a way into that space.

Webb touched a light switch just inside the opening, and several small lights came on, illuminating a wide, plastic case. Webb picked up a wire hook and pulled the case out, then another, and another. The cases, each about twenty by eight by twelve inches, looked very sturdy.

"These are custom-made cases, waterproof and airtight. They even have a pressure-equalizing valve for air travel and temperature changes." Webb thumped one with his fist. "They're about as indestructible as money can buy, made of a special resin that is, overall, better than Kevlar. They contain prima facie evidence—pictures, recordings, tax records, and even a pair of lace panties that a particular federal judge would like to get back. These represent twenty years of work and have been a major contribution to my success. I need to get these on the plane. There are literally fifty people who would give all they own for these, and maybe twenty of those people would kill for them. I don't want them on a plane, but I have no choice. That's why I've had the *Reefer* watched and cared for this long. It could have been sunk or burned and most of this stuff would have come through."

Webb turned off the light and replaced the tub floor. It was back in place in just seconds, and Matt noted that the molded tub and shower combination looked like one solid piece.

"It's big enough for a person if they don't have claustrophobia. We've moved people in spaces like this, but usually we put them to sleep first," said Webb.

They each picked up a case and returned to the salon. Webb's wife and daughter had their belongings in the plastic bags from the boutique. Webb brought an expensive leather and canvas bag out of the guest stateroom, along with a gym bag containing his toilet articles.

"Let's go to the airstrip and wait. I've set up the charter for four people and luggage. They are very picky about weight when they only have a short runway," said Webb.

Matt and Tanya walked. The flying four, their bags, and the three cases filled the golf cart.

There was no formal place to wait for the plane, just a few benches under a typical Bahamian palm leaf gazebo.

The plane touched down a little early. It was a two-engine, high-winged machine. The aircraft's short landing, with runway to spare, impressed Matt.

Matt and Tanya walked toward the plane as the rest went ahead in the golf cart. When Matt got near the plane, he could hear and see Webb was in a fury.

"What do you mean you can't take off? What's wrong with your electrical system? Can they send another plane?" Webb rattled off the questions without breathing, let alone waiting for responses.

Matt recognized the man's fear and frustration—he lacked control, felt vulnerable, and worried about the exposure of his family and his files.

Matt looked into the relatively small plane. He looked at the pilot. The man avoided eye contact. Not a good sign.

Webb and Matt looked at each other through the open window on the plane's open door. They both had the same recognition: someone wanted them on Cat Cays for another night. As though a switch had been flipped, Webb changed from a frustrated, worried man to a philosophical, retired executive in a few heartbeats. Matt had witnessed this transformation by Webb previously—sudden calm under high stress.

Calmly, Webb suggested, "Well, folks, if you got to wait somewhere on this whole earth, can you beat this place? Let's lug this luggage back to the boat and set up a snorkel swim on the reef for this afternoon."

The pilot promised he would have the plane ready to fly immediately after breakfast the next day.

Everyone retraced their steps and actions and returned to the *Reefer*.

Back in the salon, Webb brought everyone together. "We're in trouble. I think the pilot was lying. I think if we stay here overnight, we'll be sitting ducks for whoever wants to kill me."

He looked at Karen and Carla; they looked scared, but not panicky. He added, "We need to be on the water before it gets dark."

Webb, once again the general, sent Tanya to get charts and directions to the best diving reefs around North Bimini, arrange for someone to fuel them as they went out, and ask about good anchorages where they could stay several days. He sent Karen and Carla to the commissary for a modest amount of canned food, dried milk, and salty snacks. Al left to find dark marine paint and any awning canvas that could help change the appearance of the all-white *Reefer* to help fool aerial searchers. Webb would use the radios to check weather reports.

Webb's take-charge approach impressed Matt. An interesting blend of corporate executive and rum-runner.

Webb ordered everyone to return in an hour.

Matt was asked to help with the cases and appointed to check the engines, galley, and navigation information. Matt and Webb returned the cases and a now-emptied gym bag to the hidden compartment. As Matt worked around the boat, Webb spent the rest of the hour on the phone and radios. He called several people to let them know he was vacationing in the Bahamas. From bits of the conversation Matt figured Webb was listening for surprise or fear or the cockiness that might betray the person who was thinking about him a whole lot right then. Matt was at the navigation table reading Bahama charts as Webb worked his way through various secretaries to an Assistant Director at the Bureau of Alcohol, Tobacco, Firearms, and Explosives. After a few words, Webb's alarm seemed to go off. Following a brief exchange, Webb hung up the phone. "The damned ATF! It fits, part of the Treasury and coupled with the Coast Guard. That bastard knows many South American connections. I found him very useful in the past and rewarded him with money and silence about material in my files. I'm not ruling many people out, but he is on my short list of people most likely to work with Cortada to have me killed. I plan to make the list shorter as soon as I have a safe place for my family and these cases.

Everyone came back in less than an hour. Matt and Tanya had the unnecessary Bimini charts and notes that would help leave a false trail. They also had picked up the latest radio and harbor chart kit for the Bahamas. The shoppers had bags of bread, fruit, canned food, whole and powdered milk, eggs, and a meager amount of very expensive and substandard meats. Al's treasures included two blue plastic Bimini tops—the type used on open fishing boats—a gallon of blue anti-fowling paint, masking tape, and brushes of several sizes. He had one small pint can of paint thinner intended for spray painting; they would have to be neat. He also had purchased a machete in a canvas sheath.

They sat down, with a can of pop or a bottle of water from the machines at the end of the pier, to think through their options before casting off. They collectively came up with items they could use, but either their choices were not in the sparsely stocked stores or would give away their plans for a long run 180 degrees away from North Bimini. They got into their swimming suits and T-shirts and looked like a family going for a snorkeling afternoon.

They topped their diesel tanks while Webb made one short phone call from the Cat Cays Club. Soon, they were on their way to the Gun Cay Cut. Their deck speakers loudly played "Red Red Wine" all the way out of the marina. The music actually raised their spirits.

40

Bahama Run

They left the green, clear, shallow banks and cruised into the deep, dark blue of the Gulf Stream, heading northwest for several miles before turning south. The two- to four-foot waves were building from a gentle north wind. The Hatteras comfortably cruised downwind through the waves and swells at twenty-five knots. Bound for Nassau, to refuel, they planned to run all night down Exuma Sound to George Town near the southern end of the Exuma Cays. That was as far as their current plans went. Webb wanted to be anchored close to George Town by morning.

Webb disconnected the Westinghouse Wavetalk satellite phone, concerned about its security.

Al, Tanya, and Matt took on the ambitious task of securing the blue Bimini tops to the flybridge and whaler, not an easy task on a bounding deck at cruising speed. They used lines and lashings. They used punched holes and duct tape to fasten the plastic over the dingy. The two areas of dark blue did change the looks of the *Reefer*. They put dark towels around the Marlin chair and secured them with bungee cords. Their work looked good, even from up close. They felt confident the evening people at a Nassau fueling dock wouldn't find anything amiss and decided to forgo the paint.

The run to New Providence Island took only a little over five hours with the favorable winds and waves. They cruised fast enough that most of the passengers had to sit and hold on to something if they didn't want to be thrown around. The bounding cruiser put most of the people who stayed below deck to sleep. Matt, Tanya, and Webb stayed at the helm, plotting and planning.

They would violate rules by not informing the harbor control authorities of their coming. They planned to cruise in at dusk—fly their Bahamian courtesy flag, slowly motor past all the anchored cruise ships in Nassau, stop at a fueling dock, pump in a couple hundred gallons of diesel, head under the Paradise Island Bridge, and continue southeast into the Exuma Sound.

They accomplished their plan without any problems. They were just one of many beautiful yachts in the harbor at the start of a beautiful evening. The monster cruise ships they passed would have dwarfed World War II aircraft carriers. The Straw Market was well lit with thousands of tourists spilling out onto Bay Street, walking off their usual overindulgence on the floating hotels. Webb found a fueling dock, and they were on their way in less than an hour.

The run down Exuma Sound proved smoother than the passage to Nassau. They decided it would be wise to have daylight and high tide when they entered George Town Harbor on Exuma. That meant anchoring in one of the friendly, beautiful Cays for several hours. They wanted to look like the quintessential touring yacht. They slowed the *Reefer* to a fuel-saving twenty knots to be less conspicuous on anyone's radar. The speed, at an efficient point on the power curve, kept them on plane. They had more time than they needed, but they didn't want to anchor to wait for dawn with an almost seven-hour cruise ahead. They took turns at the helm where the hardest work was staying awake while the autopilot followed its course and the GPS, radar, and sounder kept them informed of everything around and under them. They were not alone on the run. The seas of the Exuma Sound are normally gentle and, therefore, very popular with Bahama travelers. They saw many fellow boaters. The water was over 5,000 feet deep and free of Atlantic swells.

They took turns sleeping and eating. Matt and Tanya used some blankets and pillows to make a nest on the flying bridge's forward lounge area while Webb manned the helm. Webb's wife and daughter brought food and drinks up, then, for several hours, watched the beautiful sea slide by. They talked in whispers and covered their laughs so they didn't disturb the sleeping pair in front of them.

When Webb couldn't stay awake any longer, he and his family retired to their stateroom, and Matt took over.

Al came up several times and offered to take a watch, but Webb only seemed to trust Tanya at the wheel when he wasn't—or, next best, Matt with Tanya no more than two steps away. Al again slept on the salon couch.

41

Exuma

T ANYA AND MATT GREETED THE SOFT PINKS of the Bahamian dawn at 6:30 a.m., the sun peeking over the horizon about fifteen minutes later. The island of Great Exuma lay off their starboard beam. Having covered about three hundred miles since leaving the Cat Cays, they felt they deserved a stop and some fun in the beautiful, clear water. Webb said they wouldn't be going into George Town until the early afternoon.

Tanya checked their charts and tide tables—high tide at 7:48 a.m. with the next high tide in twelve hours and twenty-five minutes. Carla asked how they knew. Matt and Tanya gave her a quick lesson on Earth-Moon orbital dynamics. She absorbed the tide lesson and quickly moved on to helping pick a great area where they could drop their anchor.

They had literally scores of beautiful beaches and secluded bays to choose from. The island, one of the favorite haunts of the eighteenth-century buccaneers, lay only a few miles north of the Tropic of Cancer. They worked their way west of the barrier island that protects George Town. Tanya picked a palm-lined beach with eye-hurting white sand that let them anchor within fifty yards of shore in twelve feet of air-clear water. She backed off to set the anchor. They could still see the anchor over eighty feet away, partially buried in the sand. The water colors varied from aquamarine to jade. Nearby coral heads supported hundreds of resident fish.

Everyone had a light breakfast and was soon on the deck running the davit and getting the Boston Whaler into the water.

Webb and Al stayed on board. Matt became whaler master and ran the outboard as he and his lovely female crew happily headed to the now pinkish white sands to explore the uninhabited beach. They explored the perfect beach until the sun grew too hot, and little bugs started biting them. They then reassembled and made a snorkel trip to the coral heads. Matt stayed in the whaler as the safety man. They only had two snorkel-and-mask sets, Tanya did without and guided Karen and Carla around the groups of coral and into the tide channels. Whatever they saw was not as pleasant as Matt's view of three perfect bottoms bobbing in the perfect water. Matt was just about to call them in when the *Reefer* gave a short blast on its horn. They had fun getting into the whaler without losing their tops. Matt finally helped them.

Back on the *Reefer*, they raised and secured the whaler then washed themselves off with the freshwater hose. They all understood the need for conservation of the holding tank water, but the six hundred gallons of freshwater per day the water maker could produce made several quick, daily, freshwater rinses on the deck something they appreciated. Swimsuits left to dry from ocean diving created a problem. The salt gets into the fabric, absorbs water from the air, and keeps the material perpetually damp. After freshwater showers, the swimmers attacked their hunger and thirst, and soon the salon table and dinette area was filled with food and hungry people enjoying an early lunch.

Once lunch was over, Webb stood up and said, "We need to be in George Town by early afternoon. Tanya can get on VHF 16 and raise the harbormaster at Elizabeth Harbor. Give our last port as Cat Cays. After we fuel up, we'll have more cruising range than anyone can figure because they won't know about Nassau. You can go in like regular tourists, see the shops, and buy bread, vegetables, and maybe some local beer. Stay around the marina within sight and hearing of the *Reefer*."

"Can we get some masks, fins, and snorkels so we all can dive?" asked Carla.

"Sure, but let Matt or Tanya help you so you get something good. I've got to find the airport. Al, you can stay behind on the boat."

"No problem, boss," Al replied.

"You aren't flying out without us?" asked Karen.

"No, there should be a package for me. If it doesn't come in, we will go out overnight and come back tomorrow. We don't want to be in the harbor at low tide. If you hear three toots and another three toots, get back on board as fast as you can."

They all changed into shore clothes while Webb and Tanya weighed anchor. They slowly brought the *Reefer* toward George Town. Tanya called the harbormaster and reported the ship's name, registration number, country of origin, and last port. They gave her channel coordinates and information about the harbor, city docks, and the Shell refueling dock.

In mid-afternoon, they eased into the wide harbor, where many sailing boats enjoyed the excellent anchorage. Passing several beautiful fifty-footers, Matt clearly saw their anchors resting on the sandy bottom in the crystal-clear water. Marine growth fouled most of the chains, which meant they hadn't moved for some time.

A new retirement village, thought Matt.

Tanya brought the *Reefer* to a well-built dock by the island's major one-way road and within an easy walk of the village and its shops.

Webb and Al hopped onto the dock and quickly secured the boat. Several local guides and island-services vendors approached them. Webb quickly struck a deal to hire a driver to take him to the airport a few miles across the island. As Webb boarded a small van, Matt first heard, then saw, a white jet bank onto final approach—a Cessna Citation II, a beautiful executive jet that can land almost anywhere a prop plane can. It would not have made the Cat Cays strip, however.

Matt assembled his harem, leaving Al on the *Reefer*, and headed toward the town and shops. In the little village, charming and colorful, they found several items to buy including several six packs of Kalik beer. Matt sampled two, not thinking about their cost, while the ladies shopped. He told them he wanted to make sure the beers weren't skunky. They had trouble finding the diving gear. Tanya ended up charming the owner of a charter diving service out of some rental gear, paying new prices for well used, but good, gear.

They were ready to walk back when they smelled hamburgers frying. The aroma drifted in on the southeast trade winds, a clear sign from God to increase their cholesterol. They all had a large, greasy, wonderful late lunch. Matt had another Kalik. Life was good.

Matt heard, but didn't see, because of the palms, the jet taking off and heading south.

They were about halfway through the feast when Webb found them. In a good mood, he hugged his wife. He ordered a hamburger for himself and one to go for Al.

Matt knew Webb had pulled off a deal or accomplished a coup. Matt liked Webb better when he showed vulnerability. He was a lot scarier when he held the winning hand. Matt remembered the slap and knew he needed to get Tanya and himself away from Webb, instead of enthusiastically helping him.

Webb acted like the survivor of an extended cocktail hour. However, Matt had never seen him drink more than one glass of wine or booze on the rocks. Karen showed Webb the shops that she liked best. He bought her more overpriced, low-quality tourist junk. He pushed T-shirts on Carla, who turned moody trying to refuse them. They finally worked their way back to the *Reefer* with their booty and Al's cold hamburger.

Although Al seemed pleased with the warm beer and cold sandwich, Tanya warmed the hamburger in the microwave and poured the beer over ice cubes. Al thanked her heartily. Matt made a mental note to learn more about Al the man, rather than just Al, Webb's human German shepherd.

Webb smiled, stretched, and announced, "I've paid our dockage fee. They should be pumping us out anytime. And we can leave whenever we want after that."

"Why are you so happy?" Karen asked. "Good news at the airport?"

Webb looked at her with the you-should-know-better-than-to-ask-that look. Then he changed his mind. He made himself a beer on ice and sat down just as the microwave binged and the salon filled with the universal smell of fried meat.

He swigged some beer and said, "I'm back in some control again. I picked up a special satellite phone. It came in on the jet you heard. Getting it here was my last call on Cat Cays. We can safely make calls again. I've also sent many planes all around the Bahamas. They're making stops, fueling, and flying on to Santo Domingo. Some people are going to go crazy trying to track them. The more they try to chase these planes, the easier they will be to identify."

He inspected the beer bubbles in his drink. "All we need to do is take a nice, easy cruise for a few more days. We will get to our new home and drive our enemies totally crazy."

Matt felt some worry trickle into his three-beer brain. He asked, "That means we are going to the Dominican Republic?"

"Yes, but it's a fairly easy cruise. I'll make it worth your time. Tanya can call her mother to let her know she is fine—without giving our location, of course." He turned to Tanya. "Let's say you're in Abaco trying to catch a record fish or something. I'm going to listen. One wrong word could undo a lot of work by a lot of people, and you could put us all in danger." Discussion stopped when the people with the holding tank cleaning cart showed up on the dock. Webb and Al went out to supervise them. Matt noticed that Al left half his hamburger. A real German shepherd would have finished it.

Matt and Tanya went up to the bridge to consult their charts and books. They had all the fueling and harbor information for the Bahamas, but the DR was not in the Bahamas.

"It's about four hundred miles depending on whether we go for Monte Cristo or Puerto Plata," Tanya said. "If we go north of the Windward Passage between Cuba and Haiti, it's heavily patrolled. And this was once a drug boat."

"I heard Puerto Plata," Webb said as he stepped off the ladder. "That's our destination. I've got a lot of reasons to put in there. We can make the run with our present fuel, but we should plan two overnight stops, make them out-of-the-way places."

Webb pointed at the south end of Long Island and southeast corner of Great Inagua. "They're easy daytime runs and not major cruise ship stops. I know lots of people in Puerto Plata, I can get you in and out fast with no port hassles, some fuel, and you can get back into Bahamian waters where your yellow flag should still be good, or I'll be happy to give you plenty of cash to buy a new cruising permit."

Tanya nodded. "We'll work on it. We'll be in the Atlantic after the Windward Passage. What if we get stopped? What is your status?"

"I've got another set of passports for me and my family if I need them. But why would we be stopped going to the DR from the Bahamas? They're a lot more interest in northern traffic."

No one answered the generally rhetorical question. Instead they discussed harbors, GPS coordinates, and other navigation issues.

Webb left the bridge.

"Do you think we're in trouble?" asked Matt.

"Not as long as his family is with him," she replied. "Plus, he's making a deal. We need to make it business with money and goods for services. I'm not going to do anything but be a worker bee. I don't want to lose you or the wonderful life we can have."

Tanya looked around and checked the microphone setting on the radio console. She leaned close to Matt. Her warm breath on his neck and ear made listening difficult. She said, "I did my job, someone let him get away. Someone way above anyone I know. They can't be in the DEA, but in some agency that is like it and has national power with direct lines to the Justice Department. His driver was the traitor according to Webb. I've got good people watching my back, but if I get between Webb and some other power broker that wants Webb gone, I'm a crushed ping-pong ball. Either one of them would mark me and you expendable."

They worked on the books and charts. They looked at water depths, reefs and small islands, shipping lanes, and safe anchoring areas. Each took a destination island. Their stops would be off the major lists of places to go and things to do, but interesting and beautiful locations nonetheless.

Matt found a good anchorage at Gordon's Settlement, almost at the southern end of the eighty-mile length of Long Island and nicely in the lee of the prevailing east winds. They could make it by sunset with little effort. It had cliffs to identify it, a rare thing in the Bahamas.

Tanya worked on Great Inagua, the third largest island in the Bahamas and home to a zillion flamingos and a million tons of salt production per year. The best port was Matthew Town and that wasn't saying much. Few good diving beaches too. She showed Matt the cruising guide listing:

> *Matthew Town: Profile*
> *Clearance*
> *Matthew Town, Great Inagua port of entry, no marine facili-*
> *ties except a very small man-made inlet. Anchoring off is fine*
> *in calm weather. Habitation and stores southwest of Matthew*
> *Town. Most of the coastline is hostile with no anchorages and*
> *no roads along much of the coast, help will be difficult to find*
> *if a yacht encounters difficulties.*

Tanya reviewed the information and plotting with Matt. Matthew Town could make a decent anchorage if the winds remained easterly. That's why the town was there. They might be able to get fuel delivered by a tank truck to the town dock. They could call ahead when they got closer.

They decided to get underway and work out the leg from Long Island to George Town after they had time to study the GPS, their cruising books, and the fine set of British Admiralty nautical charts in the salon's navigation table. The GPS system was a wonderful instrument but charts were better for some of the tricky shallow areas in the strings of Cays they would have to transit. The British charts, works of art, offered an amalgam of function and beauty. Although used as decorations in their leather map tubes, they were current and perfectly functional.

Tanya, Al, Matt, and Carla made one more run to town for more expensive beer, bread, and fruit. They would be away from a town for several days, especially if they didn't stay more than a few hours in Puerto Plata. When they got back, Webb and Karen had the boat running and the lines ready to cast off.

They left the peaceful and perfect natural harbor on the ebbing tide before the retirees started their earliest cocktails.

42

Long Island

WEBB BROUGHT THE *REEFER* UP to its cruising speed of thirty knots in the light chop. They would make their anchorage in about two and a half hours. The white beaches, green slopes, and palm trees of Long Island soon appeared on their port horizon. They had set the course to avoid even a hint of shallows and the strings of cays or outcroppings projecting from the midpoint hook of Long Island. They steered west of Sandy Cay in a lazy crescent, ending at the southern end of Long Island, which made their trip longer, but safer, than running along the bonefish-filled shallows on the island's west side. Matt noted the island was about eighty miles long, rugged and rather steep on the east Atlantic side and sandy and low on the leeward west side. The color of the water changed, with the light and depth, from cobalt blue to turquoise. Everyone stayed on the deck or the flybridge just to absorb the beauty.

The water was nearly flat in the calm afternoon due to the leeward shore, light easterly winds, and relatively shallow water. They kept a sharp eye on the surface of the water and, using the sounder, the seafloor. Hitting sand, coral, or a floating object at thirty knots would do serious damage. The shoreline lowered as Sandy Cay's topography approached sea level, and they swung further west. Then they followed the deeper water that approached the southern tip of the island. At the end of the island's only road, a few houses formed Gordon's Settlement. They had no need or desire to put in there.

They found a good anchorage about a mile south of the town in a bay that ran into a deserted, breathtaking, pink-white beach that seemed to extend to the northern horizon. They checked their tide charts—low tide around midnight. They anchored in fifteen feet of gin-clear water. The tides would lower them about four feet by midnight and bring them up a couple feet by breakfast. They were but a short boat ride to several shores. They wouldn't have time to find a "blue hole" for snorkeling before they made their run to Matthew Town the next day. However, they did have coral and tide channels for swimming, perfect beaches for walking, and tidal flats for shelling.

Tanya, the marine biologist, identified multiple species of fish below the *Reefer*. She and Carla tried out her new diving gear as far as the closest cove wall. Back aboard, they announced their intent to catch fish.

While Webb and Karen drank red wine and Matt and Al worked on their second Kaliks, they watched with exaggerated interest as Tanya and Carla thawed some frozen shrimp. They tied the smallest hooks in the tackle drawers to the only fishing poles aboard, major-league marlin poles, and proceeded to catch several yellowtails. Tanya then expertly threaded larger hooks through the backs and out the stomachs of the yellowtails. Dragging weighted lines along the bottom, with the leader keeping the yellowtail two feet off the sand, they caught five large snappers and finally a ten-pound grouper, probably eating another snapper eating the yellowtail. Everyone cheered as they landed each fish on the deck. They needed no net as their line could have hoisted a small anchor. Carla caught the grouper, playing it well.

Matt took the fish to the aft-deck sink with its wooden cleaning board that fit over it and a hole to wash water and guts into plastic pail below. Quickly and expertly, Matt filleted all the fish, filling a pasta strainer with so much fish it took two hands to carry it. Webb got into the spirit and produced a grill, secured it to the stern transom, and swung it out over the water. He started charcoal and, within an hour, had grilled the fish and served them with fresh vegetables on a plate of boiled rice. They topped off their gourmet feast with the fresh Exuma bread and more wine. They finished an hour after turning on the anchor lights. Dinner talk included the day's events and the days to come. Eventually, they settled into a pleasant silence, wrapped up in their own thoughts, lulled by the highly muffled generator and occasional waves slapping against the hull.

Matt consulted the *Islands of the Bahamas* book and read aloud that Sandy's Cay was the third island that Columbus landed on in 1492, with Gun Cay the second. Historians still debated whether Columbus landed first on Cat Island or Watling Island, also called San Salvador. Matt started to read about early island industries when he noted his students eyes at half-mast and brought the lesson to an end. Karen and Tanya cleared the table and would not let anyone help them do the dishes—the galley only held two, anyway. Matt, Al, and Webb took coffee to the flying deck.

Sipping their cooling coffee, they enjoyed a perfect evening at a perfect anchorage in a perfect cove.

Matt inhaled deeply, relishing the warm salt air. As though still in his classroom, he launched into lecture mode. "Inagua is an easy run tomorrow. We might get some weather by noon. And about halfway, we'll be in a major shipping lane between New York, the major east coast ports, and Colon at the Panama Canal. They do a lot of cruise ships, I understand. It's about one hundred fifty miles. Seven hours outside, five hours with good seas. Tides and depths should be no problem once we get away from here. Could have bigger waves if the east wind builds up. It might rain in the afternoon. North of the island there are some mean reefs, one has a freighter on it as a very sincere marker and there's a lighthouse noted on the map. We will be able to see Cuba on the radar."

"What about fuel?" asked Webb.

"The book says we should call for a truck at the city dock at Matthew Town. I'd say we have a good chance of fueling. If we don't—and we might want to think twice about taking fuel from a place like this—we'll need fuel in Puerto Plata, for sure. It's about two hundred twenty miles quartering against wind and waves. We would get into Puerto Plata with about two hundred gallons as reserve, less what the generator uses in the next two nights."

Webb stared across the dark ocean, brow knit in thought. Al rose and, without a word, went below.

"What do we do in Puerto Plata?" asked Matt.

Webb slowly turned to look at him, waving a hand dismissively. "I'll be on the phone tonight and tomorrow to set up everything. We have a special dock. No one will ask any questions and no government people will come down who aren't friendly. We come in. I'll have cars and people waiting. We get off and are gone. I'll fill you with diesel juice and pump you out. You can go or stay overnight if you want. It's simple and straightforward."

"I suppose," Matt said, trying to sound reassured.

"You can tell anyone you want who you dropped off. You are clean as Doris Day's bra straps," said Webb, dating himself. "If you get any federal pressure, just say you were coerced and we had guns. Both are true statements."

Tanya came up to the flybridge with her own cup of coffee. Matt, Tanya, and Webb talked about the beauty of the night. Then they checked the anchor lights and generator diesel that would turn on if the air-conditioning unit kicked in or the batteries got low, neither of which seemed likely. They made sure the boat hadn't dragged the anchor—checking shore locations they had noted before dinner and shining a handheld spotlight on the anchor buried in the sand. Nautical tasks complete, they returned to the salon. Webb's wife and daughter had gone to bed, but Al sat watching TV news with a headset on.

43

The Phone Call

WHILE KAREN AND CARLA were getting settled for an early bedtime, Webb went into the guest stateroom and came back with his telephone in a briefcase. He set it up on the dinette table. It was a complex-looking bit of technology. Matt watched Webb open it up and turn it on; it didn't even plug into an outlet. The set probably would run on batteries, wind, sun, or even gerbil power for all Matt knew.

Webb addressed Matt and Al, while Tanya listened from the open door of her stateroom. "This is quite a phone. Nearly seven pounds, an omnidirectional antenna built into its cover. It has already linked with several LEO Satellites, that's Low Earth Orbiting. We can use this underway, too. It's got encryption and, because the satellites switch the signals between them, it's hard to trace and, even if they could, the encryption would stop eavesdroppers if the receiver had the same technology."

Tanya came out of her stateroom. She wore an orange and yellow T-shirt depicting revelers above the word "Jambaloo."

"Could I call my folks? It's not too late for them, and they are up and gone in the morning." Tanya asked.

"Sure, but keep it short and don't say where we are. Maybe tell them we are near Freeport," said Webb. "Dial like any long distance call."

Webb moved around the table so Tanya could reach the number pad and have easy access to the handset with its short, coiled line. The phone had a large battery pack, three small meters, a plasma screen, a small computer keyboard, a number pad, and the handset, as well as a speaker and microphone for conference calls. Matt figured it hadn't come from a Wal-Mart.

Tanya checked out the system, punched in the number, which appeared on the screen, and pushed a green Send button.

She spoke with her father; her mother had gone to bed early. He didn't wait for her to talk. As soon as she identified herself, George Vega told her a man named Edward had been calling several times a day for several days and said it was urgent she or Matt contact him. He gave the number Edward had given him. Only then did he ask if she was all right. Tanya said they were fine, the boat was fine and they would call Edward right away. They swapped weather reports, expressed mutual love, and she hit the End button.

Webb and Matt both came to attention at the name of Edward. Webb acted as if he knew Edward was DEA, and Matt knew he could get Tanya in big trouble.

"We are to call Edward ASAP," said Tanya, looking at Matt and trying not to look worried.

"Let me do it," Matt said. "We got real close at the cabin. He could know something about what they are going to do with me and my playing around with cocaine."

"I want to hear everything that's being said," added Webb. He snapped his finger and Al was not only off the couch, but also at his side. Matt felt a major pucker coming on. He moved between Webb and Tanya and leaned over the table. Tanya punched in the numbers and pushed Send.

In a few seconds, Edward said, "Hello."

Matt quickly said, "Edward? This is Matt. I'm with Tanya on the boat. What's happening?"

"Can I assume Webb is there, too?"

Matt was about to lie when Webb hit the SPKR button and said, "Yes, I'm here"

"Good. What I have to say, you need to hear and believe. My line is secure, how about yours?" asked Edward.

"We're as good as ten grand can buy these days," said Webb.

"You're in trouble if you're making a run to the DR. Some people have you located down to the bay you are in each evening. You're a subject of interest by people outside of the DEA. I'll talk about that later. Also, your driver has died, ostensibly of a heart attack. That fact makes the drug possession and distribution case weak. He may or may not have planted it, but without credible testimony and, after the dry hole at Garnet Lake, it makes an easy defense case for entrapment and planted evidence. Your driver can be linked to the Justice Department. Now follow this carefully. Can you hear me okay?" said Edward.

"Yes, we all hear you fine," said Matt, completely mystified by the fact and, more importantly, by the reason Edward wanted to tell Webb anything.

"Okay, Webb, you were let go by an order from the number two man in Justice. The reason was the lack of credible testimony and their belief they didn't have a case they could win. The paperwork was issued three hours before your driver died. Your driver was under house arrest and in a safe house. He was moved by federal marshals from DEA supervision just as you were. The timings look very bad. Why would they concede a case before they lost their witness? An officer of the ATF and a federal appellate judge are also involved. They are the ones, together with officials in the Treasury Department with links to the Coast Guard, who have many questions to answer. I don't like letting a person like you, Webb, get away, but I'm telling you this to save Matt and Tanya and your wife and daughter who I know are with you. They're all really civilians in this drug war. Your movements are known; your destination has been deduced. The many planes that were tracked and the satellite information that was requested was way out of line for several people and government departments. Many people have showed their hands by either helping you or trying to find you.

"A lot of people will be under federal indictment to testify as to why they were interested in you; we will try to show their past or present involvement with you. Our guess is some were helping and some saw a way to silence you. They were only two hours behind you at the Cat Cays Club. A Bahamian policeman was hurt. They would have picked you up for questioning but we asked them to let you go. So, worst case, we will have a win of sorts by weeding out the people you controlled, or tried to control."

"I see," Webb said thoughtfully. "So, where do we go from here?"

"People will be waiting for you at sea just inside the DR territorial waters. You can't outrun or outflank them. You're being tracked by radar and satellite. We believe they plan to attack your boat with rockets of some type. They have orders to sink the boat and all on her. I can't tell you how we know this, but I hope you believe me for your passengers' sakes. You'll face several go-boats and a large yacht with a helicopter. The big yacht is a locator and blocker, and then the go-boats will take you out and disappear.

If you turn around and come back, we can work something out with you and your family. If you keep going, we only have limited help we can offer," concluded Edward.

"What help?" asked Webb, visibly tense.

"We have a Coast Guard cutter that we can have in the area to escort you. It can try to protect you, but there are no guarantees. I wouldn't risk it, if it were my call."

"It's not your call. But thank you for the information. I'll send you some information that will help your investigations. You'll get a promotion," said Webb.

"We'll make good use of it. Good luck, and I hope you send it before you leave Bahamian waters," said Edward.

The connection was broken.

Matt looked up. Karen and Carla stood in the hallway. The looks on their faces said they had heard everything.

Webb rubbed one hand across his forehead and exhaled loudly. "I can't put you two ashore or on a plane. If they have you, they control me. This is a major power play in Washington, Columbia, and Venezuela. I never thought the DEA would save my life. What a world."

Matt asked, "Go-boats?"

"Small boats with lots of power, open, also called go-fast boats."

Webb went to the galley and emptied the still-warm coffee from the pot into a large mug without offering any to the others. Carrying it back to the table, he continued, "I really thought I was being clever getting out by boat. I have always envisioned this boat in my escape plans. I always liked the stories of the buccaneers. I've made a major error. Right now, I need to be alone to make some calls."

Solemnly, Karen and Carla returned to their cabin. Without a word, Al got off his couch and became invisible. Matt and Tanya put on sweat-shirts, intending to go to the flying deck.

Matt announced, "I'm going to run the radar for a while. Anyone tracking us would have figured we would be around here overnight before we made the long run down the shipping lanes."

Webb grunted a kind of approval and went over a tablet of names and numbers he produced from somewhere.

Up on the bridge, Tanya and Matt stood by the helm chair in each other's arms. The radar showed nothing in the anchorage or the bay beyond. They watched the bright sweep of the screen for a minute, then shut everything down again.

"I'm getting my rifle and bedding down up here," Matt told her. "I like hunting, but not being the hunted. You should get some sleep, we have a long run tomorrow."

"I've got a better idea," she countered. "Let's build another nest up here. You and I are both light sleepers, and there aren't any bugs because of the breeze."

They went below for pillows and blankets. Webb was talking adamantly in Spanish. Something about patrol boats and Bell helicopters, punctuated with several *buenos*. Webb even winked at her as she and Matt carried the blankets and cased rifle out the door.

Webb called after them, one hand over the phone's mouthpiece, "We have more allies than just the Coast Guard. But thank you both for being lookouts."

No one slept well. Lots of anxious pacing. Webb and Tanya got the most sleep. Matt slept like a baby—up every two hours. From the beginning of their trip, the waning moon shone less each night, but the stars and the natural light reflection off the sea allowed Matt to see clearly around the *Reefer*. With the binoculars, he could make out trees on the beaches and individual rock and sand groups in the cove. Several times, Tanya woke up, cuddled closer to Matt, and fell back asleep. Al came to the bridge twice and patrolled the deck every hour with binoculars. Their vigil resulted only in wasted time and lost sleep.

At breakfast, everyone looked tired but anxious to hear Webb's decision. He came out of the stateroom showered, shaved, and smelling good.

Confident and relaxed, he said, "I made calls last night. Lots of people owe me favors. DR has patrol crafts and even helicopters that the United States gave them in the nineties that still work. I appealed to their national pride and how their wives would like new minivans. They don't want South American gangsters shooting up one of their newest and richest citizens. They also have DR officers, called ship riders, on the Coast Guard ships. They'll be on our side, too. We're going to set a trap. It's better than driving the bad guys away and not knowing who they are."

Webb sat down. "We'll have the Coast Guard ship behind us; they will locate the bad guys and drive them to the DR boats who will catch them. I'll try to make a deal to put the women on the cutter. The big yacht is another thing. I've got some other people that will take care of it. Sauce for the goose, so to speak."

"What kind of weapons are we going to be up against?" asked Matt.

"They have an almost unlimited supply of Soviet RPG-7's, 85 mm rockets that can go five hundred yards and blow a hole through a foot of armor plate. You can buy them for fifty dollars if you know where to go. They also could have a fifty-caliber rifle that can shoot through a motor block while being accurate at a thousand yards."

"Shit," said Matt.

"Be brave. It's hard to hit a boat weaving at almost forty knots. The RPG is 1962 technology, some don't even fire, and on the water they would be lucky to hit anything at hundred yards. The fifty-cal, which is a worst-case weapon, is serious firepower but can't really stop us from another boat unless they get within two hundred yards. They shoot three or four times and their barrels are so hot, they burn your hand. If they have machine guns, they'll soon know we have friends who have them too."

Webb added, "We just need to get though the initial contact. They get to draw first in this gunfight. I'd better call Edward again. He might be able to help with some communication matters or, more specifically, to help stop, or jam, some communication."

Waiting for breakfast, Webb set up his phone on the table again. He called Edward and asked about the Coast Guard cutter. Edward said political considerations would likely prevent a Coast Guard vessel from taking on the family of a major drug dealer and smuggler. They concluded the call with Edward agreeing to work out a rendezvous point with their escort.

"You know," said Webb, hanging up, "I'd have a sea plane pick us up, but they are 1940-something flying boats and even the slower helicopters can catch them. There are less than ten services in the Bahamas and Caribbean, making it too easy to cover them all. Same with airports. We could run to Cuba, but I don't trust the Cubans. Working out deals to run along their coast is one thing, trusting them with my family and my life is another. Anyone got any ideas?"

"If we can trust what Edward is saying," Matt replied, "we only have about six miles to worry about. That's the DR's territorial limit. We can skip putting in fuel. We can really get this boat out of the water when we're a thousand gallons of diesel lighter. We can use our radar and maybe talk with the Coast Guard to know where any bad guys might be."

"What about your DR patrol boats, will they help or hinder the Coast Guard?" asked Tanya.

"They'll be near shore until something happens," Webb replied. "They shouldn't be on anyone's radar. They would come out and get us, but I would rather be shot at on the open seas moving fast rather than in the harbor."

"So," Tanya asked, "are we going to stick to our plan and make the run to Matthew Town?"

"Yes," Webb replied. "Plus, I'm going to bring in some help at their airport. It might confuse the people who are tracking us. I'll bring in a private plane early next morning. They will fly in, have breakfast, and fly back to Puerto Plata. We'll see what happens around them. We'll pull out before dawn. It's an eight- to ten-hour run, and we want the sun and the Coast Guard behind us tomorrow afternoon. Today should be a five- or six-hour cruise. Let's get underway."

Matt took the helm, and Tanya and Al brought in the anchor. Everyone was tense but still enjoying the beauty around them, beauty that contrasted with the uncertain dangers ahead. The *Reefer* rounded the last of Long Island and into heavier seas, but the big boat cut through the following four-foot waves with no difficulty. They followed the wide wake of a cruise ship running at twenty-eight knots. They ran at over thirty knots until the great white ship was close enough for them to see its passengers. They saw no gain in passing it as it was making a fine path for them. They reset their autopilot to match the cruise ship's speed and spent half the voyage in the nearly flat V of its wake. They broke from the tandem arrangement in about three hours and angled more east toward the shelter and anchorages of Great Inagua Island. They passed a wrecked freighter, worrying it was a waiting interceptor, but relaxed when they found it on their charts listed as a rusting reef marker. Also, the old lighthouse made a perfect reference point, a rare thing in the Bahamian waters.

They worried that every ship, boat, and plane they saw was a potential enemy. They passed several sailing yachts going one-third their speed or less. They replied on the VHF when any passing vessel hailed them. They listened to all the radio traffic, mostly news and personal gossip from Bahamians saving money on phone calls.

Tanya and Matt worked charts to locate a safe anchorage near Matthew Town.

Soon, the dark line on the horizon shifted to green as they approached Inagua.

44

Inagua

THE LIGHT-GRAY SKY HELD THE PROSPECT of rain with dark, almost black, masses of clouds on the east horizon. Running north along the island coast from Matthew Town, they saw the boats and small workers' homes of the rather drab, at least by Bahamian standards, village. Going ashore on the desert-like island did not appeal to anyone. The marina failed to confirm a fuel tanker for the next day, as originally promised. The *Reefer* anchored between a beautiful beach with several small houses visible and a shallow, very unspoiled coral reef with sand-covered, tidal channels running out to deep water. A score of boats lay at anchor several miles to their south.

While everyone prepared to swim, Webb contacted Edward, who provided the location where they would come under the attention of the Coast Guard cutter. The Reefer's course crossed the cutter's normal patrol run in the Windward Passage and north shore of Haiti. Edward said he would stand by all the next day and confirmed all the planned frequencies. Everyone except Webb went into the water. Schools of fish swarmed around the coral. A manta passed under the *Reefer*, the harmless creature measuring fifteen feet between wing tips as it flapped along like a large underwater bird through the clear water. It passed within ten feet of Carla and Tanya, providing an unexpected thrill. Matt was floating around the coral with Al, enjoying the colors, fish, and warm water. The shrieks of the women through their snorkels brought Webb up from the helm chair in fright. Matt saw the relief on his face when the alarm was only for the black, mysterious ray passing up the channel.

They climbed back aboard tired and happy with the dive. Webb took requests for drinks and served them himself on the forward deck as they dried off from their showers.

Karen and Carla sat with Tanya. They had formed a bond, and Matt sensed the cloud of their coming farewell on their minds.

They prepared a large supper, using up the fresh vegetables from Exuma, cooking frozen steaks, and toasting the dry bread for garlic bread. As they ate, Matt noted that everyone showed more tan than four days before, even Karen, who now sported some freckles on her nose. They chatted about nothing in particular. Webb said very little, but was unusually attentive to the needs of everyone at the table. He poured wine and offered plates to pass. Matt thought he was apologizing with action, not words, for the dangers that tomorrow might bring.

It started to rain hard just as they poured coffee. The rain came down in sheets, amidst thunder and lightning.

They picked from a dozen movie tapes after supper, settling on the John Wayne western *Stagecoach*. They watched it versus the wet Bahamian evening. They had spent most of the day with wind in their faces, and the unmoving screen relaxed them. They rooted for the stagecoach to outrun the Indians with more than a little personal interest.

Everyone went to bed after the movie, agreeing to rise at 5:00 a.m. and get underway shortly after breakfast. There was a steady rain, a good night for a warm, dry bunk. Matt and Al took turns with anchor watches. At 1:00 a.m. both agreed that nothing was happening. Al agreed to sleep on the flying bridge lounge with Matt's rifle nearby.

45

The Run to Puerto Plata

A 5:00 A.M. ALARM WAS LIKE DEER CAMP to Matt. He pushed off the light blanket and put his feet on the floor. Except not a floor, but a deck; not upstairs at a camp, but sitting in a queen-size bed on a yacht with a drop-dead beautiful woman sleeping in a T-shirt next to him. In a few short weeks, he had gone from a not-so-simple ex-teacher hunting deer to a far more complex hostage, lover, killer, fugitive, yacht captain. And, despite the intensity of his love for the woman next to him, this complex new world still felt surreal, especially living on a million-dollar Hatteras. The realization that he had killed three men in as many seconds troubled him, but his conscience was clear; he had had no other choices, given the circumstances. When he thought about the future, perfection seemed an attainable goal—if he didn't swallow an old Soviet rocket today.

He touched Tanya. Warm and real—all the reality he ever wanted or needed. He would fight for her. He would kill for her. Hell, he had killed for her. He would be the best he could be in every way for her. The thought of taking Webb and Al and cruising back to Miami ran through his head. Thoughts of Karen and Carla blunted the idea. Besides, he had been lucky so far, and Webb was not a man to take lightly. Back to plan one. He kissed Tanya's warm neck. She moaned and pulled up the cover. He wondered of what or of whom she was dreaming.

Tanya came into the bathroom as he finished shaving. He had given himself a sponge bath, since he was still clean from yesterday afternoon's dive and shower. She had her eyes nearly closed against the bathroom's bright lights. She settled onto the toilet around the corner from his sink.

It must be love, thought Matt. He toweled his freshly-shaved face and smoothed on a little after-shave gel. He looked around the corner; Tanya was almost asleep on the toilet. He took her face between his hands and kissed her. He whispered, "I love you. I'll make you a Yooper breakfast."

Matt went to the galley and started the coffee, first-one-up rule. He went to work—pancake mix, bacon, old-but-not-green bread, cheese, milk, and eggs. Soon, the *Reefer* smelled like a hunter's cabin before the morning's hunt.

The cooking aromas soon lured a sleepy quorum to the dinette table. Matt served hot coffee and full plates, warmed in the oven, heaped with pancakes, scrambled eggs with cheese, bacon, and coffee with toast and jam on the side. He also put orange juice and milk on the table. Tanya, last to the table, received special service, including warmed maple syrup that Matt purposely dripped on her hand and slowly kissed off. She laughed a low, morning laugh and dug into her steamy eggs and pancakes.

Everyone enjoyed breakfast. Webb even ate the pancakes that were not going to be eaten by his wife and daughter. Al finished up the cold toast with a lot of jam. They went through three pots of coffee.

Webb pushed back from the table. "This could be...an exciting day. If we can pry ourselves away from this table, we should start the engines and begin our run to the Dominican Republic and our new home. I've got a few calls to make before we hit big water."

They quickly cleared the table and prepared to get underway. Tanya, Matt, and Al went topside.

Al folded his blankets and started down the ladder with them and his pillow. He paused and said, "Matt, I left your rifle on the lounge. It can't fall."

Tanya fired up the twin, 1200-hp MAN diesels. They seemed to know they were in for a big day and made their basso hum. The sea was as dark as it gets. Matt brought in the anchor as Tanya moved gently up on it to avoid hurting any coral or catching their anchor on coral rock. She expertly pivoted the *Reefer* within the tidal channel and moved carefully away from the shore. Matt pointed the spotlight into the water ahead, allowing Tanya to watch the coral heads and bottom sand. Just past high tide, the depth sounder showed nineteen feet. Moving a 70,000-pound boat before dawn along an unmarked and strange coast was not work for a rookie. Matt stayed at the bow after securing the anchor. Through the perfectly clear water, he watched the seafloor. Many large fish rushed through the light, each giving Matt a start because they might be a piece of dangerous driftwood or dock in the channel created by tides running off the shallows. They could see lights at the Matthew Town dock and the alternating white-green beacon light at the airport. Several dozen anchor lights glowed like candles around the port. The lighthouse at the point helped them navigate in the dark. Matt reflected on the scarcity of navigation aids for the near-shore sailor in the Bahamas. The generally low topography of the islands made boating a heads-up proposition. Their GPS and the sophisticated sounder made it possible, but probably not prudent, to move at night.

The water quickly deepened as they passed Matthew Town. They moved slowly southwest. Turning off the spotlight, Matt joined Tanya at the helm. She knelt on the helm chair to see over the bow—like a little girl playing in the family car. Matt gave her a pat…and then more than a pat.

"You are taking advantage of me, sir," said Tanya, never taking her eyes from her work.

Matt took the binoculars, padded strap around his neck, and climbed to the marlin tower. From this height he scanned the harbor for boats moving out after them. No boats had more than their anchor lights on and none seemed to be moving. Of course, he would not have seen a small, unlighted boat.

Sunrise would be in a little over a half hour. The eastern horizon already glowed with the sunlit low clouds, possible harbingers of more rain. The stars shined brightly overhead and to the south. Matt seized the handrail with one hand when the *Reefer* lifted onto plane. He could hardly hear the engines, the sound lost in the wind as they accelerated smoothly past twenty knots on their way to their nearly thirty-knot cruising speed, if the seas would allow it. Finding it impossible to use the binoculars from the swaying perch, Matt carefully used both hands on the ladder to climb back to Tanya.

The radar showed several larger blips to the south and east in the commercial sea lanes to the Windward Passage. Matt looked at the sweep behind them—no blips coming out of Matthew Town.

They were over twenty miles toward Puerto Plata before good light brought the prospects of a beautiful day. The clouds that looked dark turned into high cirrus pinking in the rising sun and the sky blued. The waves posed no challenge to the *Reefer*, which cruised easily at thirty knots, over thirty-four miles per hour.

Anticipating the bumpy day ahead, Matt and Webb carefully checked the boat, storing and securing movable items. They double-checked the whaler and divot tackle. They checked the lifeboat in its plastic box. They checked the anchor and all associated hardware. They took down the flying bridge covers, wanting clear visibility on all sides. Handling the plastic covers proved challenging in the thirty-knot wind as did removing the blue tarps used to disguise the boat. Lastly, they confirmed that everything was secured and shipshape in the galley and below decks.

"Where should we put Karen and Carla if we draw fire?" Matt asked Webb.

"Down in the hallway has the most cover, but if there's an explosion they would have no chance to get out from down there. But there aren't many other options." Webb thought for a moment before adding, "Let's put them there and have them brace across the hall. We may be moving fast and making hard turns."

"I figured that when we tied down everything," said Matt.

Webb marshaled his troops—Al, Tanya, and Matt—at the helm. Solemnly, he said, "I've had a little experience with taking fire from boats. If there are no objections, I'll take the helm when we face problems."

Nobody objected.

Webb nodded. "Matt can do what he can with the rifle. Tanya can stay low in the forward lounge area and take over if I get hurt. Al, I'd like you to stay with my family, get them out if something happens topside. Does that sound acceptable to everyone?"

They all agreed to their roles. During the several hours before they were to intercept the cutter south of the Mouchoir Passage, they took turns at the helm. Everything about the *Reefer* was working perfectly. They drank iced tea and soft drinks.

At mid-afternoon, Webb assembled Matt and Al in the salon while Tanya worked the helm. "Here's a packet of instructions I'll put in the navigation desk. It's a list of names and instructions if something happens to me. We have a beautiful place ready in the DR. We have protection and several deals in place. This packet will keep everything going and protect my family. You both know where the files are kept; they hold a lot of power. I really think I'm being overly dramatic, but I am that way."

Matt thought Al might cry. He had never been trusted at this level before, and he took his charge very seriously. Matt just wanted to get away from these dangerous people.

They found the blip of the cutter exactly where they were told it would be. An hour later, they called the Coast Guard cutter in the Mouchoir Passage with their VHF gain way down. Almost immediately came back the strong response from the USCGC *Escanaba*—Matt couldn't believe the serendipity of a ship named after a Yooper town. The captain and the DR officer briefly explained the plan. The cutter would move south and cover them at a distance, advising them if the cutter's powerful radar or satellite systems picked up any boats vectoring on them. Webb brazenly asked them to take his family, but they said they could not honor his request. The Coast Guard captain reiterated that he would warn them if anyone approached them, adding they could not open fire unless the other ship fired first. The *Escanaba* would have their armed helicopter in the air as the *Reefer* neared DR territorial waters. Anyone dumb enough to fire on them or any US-registered vessel would receive return fire. The captain also said they were already tracking the *Reefer* on their integrated radar and satellite systems. Then they signed off.

Impressive, thought Matt. *From almost forty miles away, they had the Reefer and the coast of the DR on their scopes. They must have some great radar and integrated satellite systems.*

Matt had no idea how the Coast Guard systems worked but hoped their helicopter could reach them before attacking boats could blow them away. Matt felt his tax dollars in action.

Everyone was either on the flybridge or the aft deck during the call to the Coast Guard. They all felt better with the type of help it offered.

"How big is the cutter?" asked Matt anyone who knew the answer.

Webb replied, "The *Escanaba* is almost three hundred feet, capable of more than twenty knots, and has armed helicopters capable of one hundred eighty knots. They're tracking us. They have satellite links that cover this whole area with optical and infrared. They don't have satellites all the time, and even with their best efforts little boats can hide with their engines off and a blue tarp over them. We need to look for these little boats. When they chase us, the Coast Guard will see them. But if we don't see them, they can hurt us. Radar doesn't see them. In a while, we'll call the cutter again and ask if they can locate a large yacht off Puerto Plata, the one that will coordinate the little boats that are probably out there with some people sweating their asses off under the plastic."

"We can all be lookouts!" said Carla enthusiastically.

"Good idea, Carla. We can get ready now, but we have some time yet before we are close enough," said Webb.

Tanya passed out binoculars to Al and Karen, a light but powerful Russian monocular went to Carla. Matt had his telescopic sight, but it meant holding a nine-pound rifle at his shoulder. From previous recent experience, he knew resting it on a rail wouldn't work very well, so the rifle went into its case. Everyone picked a spot around the flybridge so they could cover the entire surrounding area. Carla went to the marlin bridge for about five minutes but came down looking a little green.

They decided that eyes on deck would be the most effective use of everyone, and they agreed that, even if they saw one boat waiting for them, each person would keep his or her section of responsibility under watch. They didn't want to turn from one attacker and into another, a contribution Matt made to their strategy. He described deer hunting using "drive" and "post" techniques—explaining what the drivers did and how the post was the hunter waiting for the deer. He talked about wind and how deer liked to go into the wind to be able to smell where they were going. He went through how the drivers kept in line and sometimes barked like dogs. Everyone was interested, especially Webb.

"Does the deer ever get away?" asked Webb.

"Actually, most of the time, if the does and young deer run toward the post hunters, they get shot at. Some bucks lay down in the thick stuff and let the drivers go by them, but the really wise bucks circle behind the drivers and sneak away, even if it's downwind," said Matt.

Everyone was busy arranging their areas of responsibility. Matt checked on his rifle. While uncomfortable playing the deer in this hunt, Matt had respect for the hunters. Although grateful for Webb's knowledge of tarps and hiding boats from surveillance technology, he had to chuckle at how a ten-dollar plastic tarp and a shut-down engine could defeat multimillion-dollar systems. Probably using thirty-dollar walkie-talkies just like his own. He inspected his rifle's bolt and barrel and unloaded and reloaded the magazine. He put the eight extra shells in his shorts pockets. He wanted the shells on him, not in a case.

Matt asked Tanya, "What about life jackets and places to hold onto if we start evasive action?"

"Another good idea, I'll get everyone a life jacket." she replied, serious, but excitement showing in her sparkling eyes. She gave him a cheek kiss and put his hands on the wheel, signifying he had the helm. Then she went below.

The autopilot turned the wheel, aiming directly at Puerto Plata on an ESE heading.

Webb came up with a beer for Matt. Matt thought that beer, maybe two, was a good idea before a sea battle.

"Better get something to eat, we'll be going as fast as we can in about twenty minutes," said Webb. He pointed at the horizon ahead. "There's the mountain at Puerto Plata."

Matt went below, changed into a clean T-shirt, and found his hat. He ate some of the cold cuts and cheese Karen had prepared. He slipped into a collared Stern life vest Tanya handed him. He finished his beer and took another topside. In his cap, sun glasses, and life vest, he felt like John Kennedy on the PT-109. Not a real good thought, when he analyzed it.

Webb just was signing off with the cutter. He turned to Matt. "They're painting the big yacht on radar, five miles due north off Puerto Plata, in DR waters. They don't see any go-boats or movements toward us."

Matt shared his ice-cold Bahamian beer with Tanya. The PT-109 came to him again. JFK's ship was sitting still when the Japanese destroyer ran over them. The image of a small boat bobbing in the blue-green water lodged in Matt's brain. It seemed to stay there.

The DR coastline slowly came into view and, in the distance, the mountain called Pico Isabel, really just a beautiful, green hill. Matt could see how Christopher Columbus would have picked it out on the horizon in 1493. Their radar showed the big yacht clearly, a large, unmoving blip.

"Ready," shouted Webb as he shoved the throttles to their stops, the *Reefer* accelerated to nearly forty knots. They slammed over the swells now with the bow taking air at times. Thirty-five tons going over the water at forty-six miles per hour is impressive. Everyone held on tightly and scanned intently. Webb had the helm, while Al, Karen, and Carla held their lookout posts. Matt and Tanya watched the instruments and the radar screen. Some gauges approached redline, but the temperature gauges stayed in the green. Everyone actively watched forward. Matt glanced at their wake as a puff of smoke appeared just to its left.

"Rocket!" he screamed, so loud his throat ached, and pointed.

Webb craned his head back, saw the rocket, and immediately cranked the wheel hard to port. The rocket screamed by them twenty yards to starboard. It smacked into the water a hundred yards ahead of them, followed almost instantly by a *kaboom* and a 100-foot plume of water. They couldn't see a boat behind them.

"They're shooting at us from boats that aren't running," Matt yelled, his throat still hurting.

Webb completed a smooth circle. He called the cutter to report that they were under fire from small boats that did not have their engines running. He didn't wait for any acknowledgment. Matt took Carla's binoculars and located the little boat only because they were pulling in a tarp and white water churned under their two large outboards. They were coming after the *Reefer*. Webb turned back to starboard and toward their destination. More smoke puffed from their starboard, a long way away. Webb watched it and didn't change their direction.

"They're shooting before they start their engines. They will shoot more when they come after us," yelled Webb.

Matt got his rifle and worked into the sling. He looked at the little boat approaching from the stern.

"Keep looking ahead," Webb yelled at Carla, Al, and Karen, who were having a hard time holding on as the boat slammed through their own wake.

Matt tried to put the pursuing boat in his sights, now three hundred yards away and slowly gaining. He could not even keep the boat in the cross hairs, let alone anyone on it. Another boat joined the chase on their starboard side; it soon was behind them also. Both of them were in RPG range, but they weren't firing. Then both fired simultaneously. Webb heeled the boat to port again and the rockets went by, the closest missing by only thirty yards. Webb kept the port turn until he straightened the *Reefer* out heading away from Puerto Plata and ninety degrees from the pursuers. He didn't want to be the herded deer.

"We'll run toward our help," Webb shouted.

The *Reefer* leapt across the waves. Once the boat sailed off the crest of a wave and slammed down like a breaching whale. The go-boats were slow to change course and lost relative distance. Matt assumed Webb had decided it was better to run from two boats they could see than run into others that they couldn't. Matt scanned the skies for a white-and-orange helicopter.

Transmitting on the VHF, Tanya announced their name and US registry and added, "Mayday! Mayday! Mayday! We are being fired upon by terrorists with rockets."

Calmly and clearly, she gave their speed and course and the location of the bad guys. She announced they would be overtaken in ten minutes. Then she repeated the whole thing.

Webb looked at Matt, nodding appreciatively.

Yeah, Matt thought, *you're right. I've got a good woman.*

They ran on the new heading for five minutes. The go-boats got to within the two-hundred-yard range again, and then suddenly broke off the chase. They turned and ran in different directions. Webb slowed the *Reefer,* giving everyone's muscles a break.

The big helicopter, spotted by the go-boat crews or by the big yacht's radar, approached and passed over them at great speed, low enough they felt the downwash. *Stagecoach* in the Twenty-first Century. Matt and Tanya cheered as much as everyone else on board.

Matt thought of Winston Churchill's statement that there was nothing more exhilarating than being shot at and missed.

On their radar, they spotted the cutter, the blurred flashes of the helicopter, and the big yacht moving along accompanied by several small boats that hadn't shown up five sweeps before. They'd broken the drive, the deer had doubled back, and the post was going home. Life was very good.

"Matt!" Webb called. "Take the wheel and come around and aim toward the mountain. I need to use the bathroom and find some vodka."

Matt took the wheel.

Webb slapped him on the shoulder. "It's good we heard your deer story."

Matt centered the peak of Isabel on the bow and set a comfortable cruising speed. He watched the radar as the big yacht headed east down the coast. He couldn't pick up the little boats. Still under smoke-puff alert, the *Reefer* crew watched the helicopter come back. Matt talked by VHF with both the helicopter crew and the cutter's bridge. The cutter reported that the boats had scattered, and the DR patrols already had several in custody. The crews insisted they had heard no fights, all weaponry had been deep-sixed, and they assured the officials that they were simple fisherman in simple fifty-thousand-dollar motorboats. Matt offered their thanks and waved at the helicopter as the gallant cavalry galloped away with a *thwup, thwup, thwup* never made by a horse.

Matt made a mental note to send a letter to the men and women on the cutter *Escanaba*. He'd find their address and home port on the Internet.

46

Dominican Republic

MATT BROUGHT THE *REEFER* all the way into the entrance of Puerto Plata's busy harbor, flanked by an impressive red-bricked fort to port and green hills and the Pico Isabel de Torres mountain ahead and to starboard. Webb radioed the port authorities, then took the helm and brought the *Reefer* to an old dock area below the fort. It was a blue-collar harbor with older, rusty interisland cargo ships far outnumbering any chrome-and-plastic playthings of the yachting set. The harbor was too open to the sea to be a top-level port. Matt could envision seventeenth century ships tied up at the same pier, with its old timbers, massive rocks, and working road. There was no shore power.

Webb's phone calls en route produced results—many men at the wharf wore jackets or sports coats despite temperatures approaching eighty degrees Fahrenheit. Webb had people watch the *Reefer* while he invited the *Reefer* crew to walk to a bar that had probably pushed rum to the smugglers who sailed out of this harbor three hundred years ago. They passed on the Brugal and Macorix local rums, but Matt found the Presidente beer went down just fine. Webb looked tired, Carla appeared eager to see their new country and its shops, and Karen just looked drained. Tanya said she was happy to be alive.

Webb took Matt and Tanya aside and told them, "I need to get Carla and Karen to a hotel for the night. I'll get them settled and protected, and I'll come back to talk to you. I'll bring some officials with me. Don't be alarmed, they are, as they say in this country, *muy simpatico*."

Two fuel trucks were needed to fill the *Reefer*, and its holding tanks were pumped—just as Webb promised. Webb even paid the multiple port fees and arranged for security guards on the pier to protect the *Reefer* from stowaways or any other unpleasantness.

As they walked back to the boat, two minivans arrived for Webb's transportation. Tanya and Matt helped Carla and Karen into the second vehicle while Webb and Al brought their luggage—soft-sided bags—and the plastic bags from the Cat Cays store. Matt noticed Webb's special plastic cases were not among them.

"I'll see you in an hour or so," Webb said from the window as they pulled away.

Matt and Tanya walked along the dock area, unimpressed with the ships and smells that greeted them. They returned to the *Reefer* and turned on the evening lights. They took beers to the flybridge to admire the green hills and watch the harbor lights come on.

Webb returned in a little less than two hours. He had several more men with him, two in uniforms. Tanya and Matt met them on the aft deck. Webb came aboard alone, and the group of men waited respectfully on the pier.

"Carla and my wife insist you stay with us a little longer. I would like that also. We have a five-bedroom villa, a perfect beach, 147 hectares with all types of trees and crops. I'll be very busy getting security set up and working out some business deals. It would be a favor to me if you could give us a few more days."

"My parents wouldn't understand our being gone so long," said Tanya.

"Call them, tell them you are needed to get me to the DR and I'm very grateful. I'll send a plane for them in a few days if they can get away. You could all cruise back together. Call them twice a day, if you want. You know I like your father. I'm sorry I frighten your mother, but this is a beautiful country and there's no need for them to worry about me ever again. I promise. What do you say?"

Matt looked at Tanya. She smiled and nodded her head.

"It's Tanya's choice. We'll stay for as long as she wants," answered Matt, trusting Tanya's instincts and noting Webb's six men, all within shouting distance.

"Good," said Webb. "Let me introduce you to the people on the dock."

The two uniformed men represented immigration and the port authority. They provided Matt and Tanya with tourist cards after they showed their passports and boat registration. Webb had already paid the ten-dollar-per-person fee for what was really a ninety-day visa. The officials formally explained, as tourists, they could now go to other DR ports, beaches, coves, and anchorages because of receiving clearance at this major port of entry. Webb also introduced two trim and fit young men, Luciano and Mario—their guards for the duration of their time in the Dominican Republic. They carried leather bags and wore light jackets. The last person introduced looked to be in his sixties, small and slender but with sparkling eyes and a ready grin. He wore washed khaki slacks, a white, short-sleeved shirt, and well-made sandals.

Webb touched the man's elbow. "Matt, I want to introduce you to the man that runs the estate. Rafael Morales. He is like you in many ways—a hunter and fisherman—and his wife was a teacher for many years. He'll help you bring the boat around to our harbor. I'd suggest you go out for a good dinner, get to know each other, and make the trip in the morning. We'll be doing some shopping and will see you in the afternoon. Our land and villa are west about twenty kilometers up the coast. It's not marked and has no harbor facilities, but you can anchor safely."

Webb locked gazes with Matt and said, in an offhand manner, "I'll leave some people on the dock all night. Luciano and Mario can take turns on the salon couch. One will be on the deck all the time. Rafael can use the forward cabin. We can move the rest of our gear off the boat over the next few days."

Matt knew he meant the hidden, special cases.

Rafael waited calmly until Webb finished, then he stepped forward and extended his hand to Matt. "Welcome to our island, Mr. Hunter. I hope you find it as Christopher Columbus did when he called it the most beautiful island in the world. I would be honored to show you a good restaurant for this evening and to help bring your beautiful vessel to our cove in the morning."

"I appreciate your help, Mr. Morales," Matt said, shaking the offered hand.

"*De nada,*" Morales replied. "And, please, call me Rafael."

"And I'm Matt."

The three of them watched Webb and the government officials depart.

Tanya showed the two bodyguards the salon and the guest head. Matt showed Rafael around the *Reefer* and took his small overnight bag into the guest cabin. The boat guards both took up station on the flybridge. They maintained radio contact with other men on the dock. The *Reefer* was securely guarded. Matt could only guess at the contents of their ever-present leather bags or under their jackets, incongruous given the temperature.

They all discussed where to eat in Puerto Plata. The bodyguards enthusiastically joined in, their age and machismo led them to suggest several local restaurants featuring ear-pounding merengue music where tourists were tempted to drink the *mamajuana*, a rum and herb drink designed to make you forget where you parked the car. After Tanya said she would like someplace with a fine view and good seafood, Rafael said he knew a perfect place, but they would need long pants and a shirt with a collar. Matt and Tanya quickly changed.

Tanya, Matt, and Rafael walked to a main street and took a cab to Armando's, a restaurant perched on a hilltop. At first stunned at the prices, they relaxed upon realizing that thirty-five DR dollars equaled one U.S. dollar. Rafael remarked quietly that cab drivers or bartenders would sometimes give over forty DR dollars for one U.S. The restaurant featured northern Italian cooking and Dominican favorites. Matt and Tanya had *langosta*, lobster, and Rafael had the *paella*. The fantastic view of the sea and mountain matched the perfectly cooked and served food. They had white wine by the carafe and ended the meal with strong coffee and excellent Dominican rum in snifters.

After listening to Rafael ramble on about his wife and three children who all lived in the United States and learning that he was actually seventy-one years old, Matt asked Rafael about his link with Webb.

"Señor Webb bought the house and land, including land I once owned, over a year ago. He has been here only one other time. His wife and daughter have never been here before. We have been working very hard to repair damage from the *terremoto*, earthquake, we had last September. We did not have much damage, but the swimming pool is still being repaired. The center of the earthquake was at Puerto Plata and it was a 6.5, very powerful. Streets in the city are still being repaired."

Another cab brought them, full and tired, back to the *Reefer*. After passing pleasantries with the guards, Matt, Tanya, and Rafael went to bed. Matt saw a big difference between the men Webb had around him at the cabin and the friendly, talkative Dominicans. Matt appreciated having people watching over them.

Matt woke before Tanya. He heard Rafael and the bodyguards speaking rapid-fire Spanish just outside the stateroom door. He let Tanya sleep. With barefoot silence, he put on shorts and T-shirt, took his place as captain on the flybridge, started the engines, and supervised the lines being cast off.

Rafael brought him coffee and toast and stood beside him pointing out on the radar scope how to navigate around the headland.

At the wheel, Matt enjoyed the breathtaking view—the red fort and green hills in spectacular contrast to the blue-green ocean with its lazy, two-foot swells. Matt sighed with relief at leaving the bustling, chaotic port—a mirror of the street and harbor traffic—behind, glad to be on the open sea, heading west along the beautiful coast. They passed headlands and beaches dotted with impressive homes and vacation complexes. An hour passed quickly, bringing them close to their destination cove that Rafael pointed out as Tanya came to the helm.

"Look," called Tanya, pointing out to sea.

Matt tensed and moved his hands to the throttle controls as he looked where she pointed. His brain thought *rockets*. Happily, his eyes saw whales, about a half mile away.

"Those are the whales that come to play every winter. You can hear them at night. They are humpbacks, very big," said Rafael, who then pointed inland at a low green projection of land that faced a high bluff. "We go there."

Tanya hugged Matt and smiled while gazing at the picture-perfect coast. She said, while adjusting the GPS and sounder and checking the radar screen, "I plugged the phone together and called my mother. She was very surprised to learn we were so far away. I explained we chartered the boat to get Webb and his family to the DR. I made it seem all business and left out the exciting parts. She and dad will talk about coming down; they're very busy right now. She really does not want to have anything to do with Webb, but she didn't say no."

"Then we'll just have to wait and see," Matt said, continuing his scan of the coastline.

At first, Matt could not see the harbor opening, until they had nearly passed it and could see the signs of a channel—no waves breaking at the opening. There were no markers and the seafloor came up quickly. Matt was glad he had 2400 diesel horsepower and wasn't coming in under sail. The windward shore would allow almost no margin of error for a rope-pulling sailor. Matt slowed the *Reefer* and kept one eye on the sounder as he carefully worked the boat through the reefs. The water was calm and still he could hear the waves crashing against the headland. Matt assumed a steep beach and bet on a dangerous undertow or riptide. However, they soon pulled into a fine anchorage—twenty feet deep that decreased to twelve when they came about and lowered their anchor. Matt backed toward the beach to set the anchor. The beach—snow-white sand, palm trees nearly to the water's edge, turquoise-blue water—provided a classic tropic island panorama.

Without delay, they launched the whaler. The bodyguards were really boat guards—Luciano and Mario remained on board. They already had found the food and beer, and assured Matt they would be happy but vigilant. Matt reviewed the boat's operation in case they had to move it or if the anchor failed to hold.

Although the cove provided good anchorage most of the time, Rafael explained, bad weather or hurricanes could require boats to move to nearby Luperon, west up the coast, with its protected harbor and supposedly hurricane-proof anchorage. He pointed out a large hill rising above and behind the closest headland and said, "There's also a larger harbor and dock area around the next headland west. It's very open to the sea, but it is where large boats take on the cocoa and banana crops."

They beached the whaler and secured it to a driftwood log buried in the sand. Rafael led them up the narrow dirt path that led up to the villa. Halfway up the quarter-mile path, the palms, trees, shrubs, and grasses gave way to an open expanse. Looking up the hill, they saw a white villa with a yellow tile roof. An impressive sight.

A whitewashed wall surrounded the house with its two large, covered second-floor balconies and expansive, covered main-floor patio, all facing the ocean. Two structures jutted above the roof—a water tower and a viewing tower offering a panorama of the ocean and bay to the north and the hills and mountains to the south.

Like a fortress, Matt thought.

The path led to a large, thick, double-door gate, suitable for a medieval cathedral. They passed through the unlocked gate and up steps to a wide, terraced patio. On their left, the L-shaped pool held no water, and masonry tools lay scattered around it. Rafael asked them to wait in the foyer while he left to arrange refreshments. Within moments, a maid brought in a rolling cart that held several types of soft drinks, iced beers, and a pitcher of fruit juice. Rafael returned and, grinning, informed them that Señor Webb and his family were delayed because the women were buying everything in every store in Puerto Plata.

They lounged in the comfortable wicker furniture and sipped the cool drinks while gazing across the bay and ocean. Palm trees blocked their view of the *Reefer*.

After finishing their drinks, Rafael escorted them on an hour-long tour around the well-designed and constructed villa. Almost every room faced either water or mountains. The five-bedroom, four-bath house had electrical power and its own generator.

The Webbs and their entourage arrived in a full-size pickup truck and two minivans. Several men took positions around the villa, and two went on patrol along the forest edge. Matt appreciated the military precision of their operation. Al took charge of their positioning. Carla and Karen, flush with happiness and wonder at the villa, could be heard going from room to room and floor to floor with excited bursts of appreciation and wonder at the thought that went into the floor plan. Webb supervised the unloading of several heavy wooden boxes, which they transported into the garage and house.

While his family explored, Webb joined Tanya and Matt in the front foyer. He filled a large glass with ice and poured in fruit juice.

In a low voice, he told Matt and Tanya, "Cortada is still on the loose. He was on the big yacht but took off by helicopter. We need to be careful for the next several days. Don't say anything to Carla or Karen. I've got people on the road and I'll have a helicopter and electronic surveillance equipment coming right after Christmas. The Dominicans I've hired have no love for Venezuelan gangsters. The local police and military are also alerted. If he's going to try anything, it will be now before I get good security systems in place and before we gain influence with the locals."

When Webb paused, Matt asked, "Why is Cortada after you?"

Webb glanced around the room before answering, "I just acquired financial records that prove Cortada is linked to a presidential cabinet member. Cortada and the Washington politician want the records and, as a bonus, my head. This type of material can only be used once—the threat is its real value. I gave up a fair amount of information to get away, hints of the cabinet link helped also, if for no other reason being free makes me a better target. As it stands, department heads may resign, some illegal activities will be interrupted, but as long as the very top people are protected the machine will refit and keep working."

Karen and Carla gaily entered the room offering Webb smiles and hugs. Webb returned the hugs and adroitly switched gears in his conversation with Matt and Tanya. Rafael slipped into the room quietly behind the two women.

Webb swirled the juice in his glass and said, "I have a lot of plans, the U.S. dollar is very important here. The political system is still very structured in favor of the few richest people. I can make the locals very happy and make an honest profit by building a cocoa fermentation plant, an idea I got from Rafael. Fermented cocoa beans are worth twenty-five percent more than unfermented, and the locals have been selling only unfermented beans so far. I believe we can build a plant to service the locals for many miles and produce fermented and dried beans. I can make twenty percent, give the locals fifty percent more than they're getting now, and provide much-needed jobs. A true win-win and—if I keep it relatively small and localized—I shouldn't have any problems with the big producers."

"Interesting plan," Matt said, still marveling at Webb's chameleon personality. "Good luck."

"With enough money, luck is less of an issue," Webb said with a broad grin.

Carla changed into a new swimsuit and cover-up; their snorkeling equipment was still on the *Reefer*. The two women—with Matt and Rafael carrying various towels, beach chairs, and beach bags—headed down the path toward the beach. Webb sent two men with them.

Tanya and Carla wanted to swim, and Rafael agreed to arrange for beach gear. Karen decided to continue exploring her new kitchen and see that the swimmers had lunch delivered to the beach. Webb said he needed to make some important phone calls. Matt and Rafael carried towels, beach chairs, and beach bags, followed Tanya and Carla back down the trail to the beach.

As they walked, Rafael told Matt that the estate covered about 360 acres, the same size as his U.P. property. It seemed bigger with its steep hills, panoramic views, and expansive ocean. Something smashed through the thick growth around them. Still in a cautious frame of mind, Matt turned and ducked, expecting an attack.

"Just a wild pig," said Rafael, pointing to a blur of brown dashing across an open area between thickets. "We have many wild pigs; they were brought here with the Spanish. My boys used to hunt them in these hills and down by the beach. Very fast and very smart. They know when you are hunting them."

"Do you suppose I could do some hunting while we're here?" asked Matt.

"Our government passed new laws for hunting. It would cost you $300 U.S. for fifteen days, but we have no rules here on private land with no road for over a mile, and that road is dirt and goes to the old cocoa dock."

"I'll get my rifle from the boat, and we can try to find that pig while the ladies swim."

Rafael agreed, then added, "Bring a big knife—or, better, a machete—and some rope, in case we need to haul that pig back on a pole."

The whaler made a quick round trip to the boat. Carla returned with diving gear and Matt brought his rifle, in its case, the machete that Al bought on Cat Cays, and some quarter-inch nylon cord. Rafael thumbed the machete's edge, frowned, but said nothing and hooked it to his belt.

He put the cord in his pocket. Matt left the rifle case with the women, loaded three shells, and carried two more. The Dominican guards came over to admire the rifle and check its telescopic sight. Too heavy for pig hunting, they told him.

Satisfied that Luciano and Mario on the *Reefer*, with binoculars, and the two armed men on the beach could ensure the women's safety, Matt and Rafael excused themselves and headed west up the beach. Matt just hoped the distraction of the female swimmers would not prevent their guards from watching the cove's entry and the surrounding hills.

Fifty yards up the beach, Rafael led Matt up a path that led into the trees. The thick cover only lasted a few yards and turned into fairly open palms mixed with bamboo and pinyon pine and, farther up the hill, acacia and banana trees. Small birds and several parrots flitted through the branches and sang songs unfamiliar to Matt. They continued up the hill, heading toward the headland to their west. Rafael pointed to several signs of wild pig: tracks, scat, and root digging.

"With that rifle it's best to get you to an open area. We will go up to the cliffs that look down on the beach by the ocean," said Rafael as they walked uphill. "The morning or evening is the best, but they can be found at any time."

They could see the white of the *Reefer* through the trees as they climbed. Matt could now pick out a pig trail and saw where several crossed their path toward the beach. Rafael was ahead of him several steps, enough so that branches he moved did not swing back to strike Matt. Suddenly, Rafael stopped and got down on one knee. His expression turned serious, and he put his finger to his lips. He motioned Matt forward and pointed to a fresh boot mark in the light soil of the path. He made a walking motion with his fingers to indicate that the boot's owner had crossed the trail heading toward the cliffs overlooking the beach and the *Reefer*. He moved close to Matt and whispered, "Someone is watching Señor Webb's beach."

"Let's see who it is," Matt whispered back. "But be careful and quiet, just in case." They moved slowly and quietly toward the cliff. Matt found palms and small bushes freshly cut along the person's path, something Matt routinely did when making a hunting blind in the woods. Matt pointed out the cuttings, and Rafael nodded he understood. They moved very slowly, allowing the natural sounds of the palm branches and breezes to cover their approach. Ahead of them twenty feet, a pair of boots topped by camouflaged pants jutted from behind a blind of palms and branches stuck into the ground. Matt held up a hand, and he and Rafael froze and remained motionless for several minutes.

Slowly, Matt continued the stalk—Rafael close behind—inch by inch until he stood over the man watching the boat, beach, and swimmers through a monocular scope. Matt had a random thought about writing a doctoral thesis about how men get in trouble by looking at women, but let the thought fly away. The palm branch and grasses rustled in the light northeast breeze, masking their approach. The man had a scoped rifle beside him. Matt stepped on the rifle's stock and pushed the safety off his own Remington. The click of the safety brought the man's head up, he slowly turned his head. Rafael moved quickly to the other side of the man, brought the machete out, and put it against the man's cheek. In Spanish, he told the man not to move. Matt took the man's rifle away—a sniper version of the AK-47, looking malevolent. Matt backed away a few feet and leaned the sniper's rifle against a bush. The man watched him with brooding eyes but did not move.

"Let's tie him up and see if there are more like him," Matt snarled softly. "Tell him if he makes a noise, I'll shoot him."

Rafael translated quietly while Matt removed the sniper's boots, took out the laces, and bound the man's ankles with them. Matt twisted the man's hands behind his back and used some of the nylon cord to tie them. Rafael yanked off one of the man's socks and jammed it in his mouth, securing it a loop of cord over his mouth and around his head. Then they dragged him back from the cliff edge into the banana and cocoa trees. The man lay quiet and motionless on the ground, although with anger flashing in his eyes.

Matt picked up the long-barreled AK-47 and admired the fancy stock that formed a quasi-pistol grip by providing a hole to slip your thumb through. The strange scope showed a confusing array of etched lines and graphs, for distance judging, Matt assumed. No help to him since he'd never used a scope like it.

Matt searched the sniper, finding another magazine he guessed held eight to ten large shells, several energy bars, a canteen with water, and a two-way radio in his breast pocket. Matt turned it on and heard rapid Spanish. He passed it to Rafael, who listened for some time.

Finally, Rafael said, "Men on shore are talking to men on a boat about maps and how long they should stay on the beach. They must be close. These radios only work for a few miles. We need to check out the next bay." They decided to look for other snipers and question their prisoner before moving on to the next bay. They secured the man to a palm tree by a loop of cord around his neck and retied his arms behind the tree.

Matt handed Rafael the AK-47.

Rafael shook his head. "I do not understand this weapon, but I know how to work yours."

"Look," Matt said, "If I don't use my own rifle, we'll both be using strange equipment."

"But—"

"I can show you what you need to know about the AK."

Rafael nodded. "Okay."

Matt demonstrated how to load the magazine into the rifle, work the action, and turn the lever from safe to fire. Rafael watched patiently, took the weapon, put it on his back by its sling, and drew his machete.

They went up and down the path for a hundred yards either way looking for tracks but found none. Then they worked their way across and up the headland to its west side where they could see across the low hills to the next bay. A white yacht, three times the length of the *Reefer*, lay at anchor. Three decks high with a small helicopter on the top aft deck. Two white powerboats appeared to be transporting men and material to the far south of the bay, out of Matt's sight. The telescopic sight couldn't give him any more information than his unaided eyes. They went back to the man tied to the tree.

"*¿Trabaja para Cortada?*" asked Matt.

Rafael placed the machete's edge across his neck. The man's eyes widened. He nodded yes. Rafael took the gag from his mouth, and then replaced the machete across his neck. They whispered in Spanish. The sock went back in.

Rafael walked a few steps away and motioned Matt over. "He says he was only to report if Señor Webb came to the beach. He said they plan to go to Webb's house and capture him and get papers he has. He doesn't know how many men there are; he thinks maybe three or four. But I think he is also a very big liar."

Matt and Rafael untied the man from the tree, hauled him to his feet, and hustled him down the hill back to the beach. Carla and Tanya were still snorkeling along the near reefs. The two beach guards ran to meet them as Matt and Rafael pushed the prisoner up the beach. The guards suggested twenty actions in as many seconds. The sniper was on the wrong end of several kicks before Matt could stop them.

He stepped between the guards and the sniper. "Stop it! We need to inform the house and Webb, get the women to the safety of the boat, then maybe we can screw up Cortada's plans."

They stopped kicking. One guard started to run toward the house.

Matt grabbed his arm, pointed at his radio, and ordered, "Get me Al on this thing."

Within twenty seconds, Al's voice crackled through the radio. "Yeah?"

Matt took the radio. "Hey, Al ol' buddy, this is Matt, down on the beach. We're having a great time, there are a lot of people here but more are coming. I hope we have enough beer for everyone. We got the music so loud I bet the folks in the big yacht in the next bay west of us can hear us. I don't know when they'll be up there but it won't be too long. Do you think you have enough food and booze for everyone?"

A long pause. Matt imagined Al trying to decipher his unexpected warning.

Finally, Al replied, "Let me check on the food and beer, I'll get back to you."

"Just in case they're listening in," said Matt, winking at Rafael and the guards.

They decided to send the prisoner back to the house with one guard and get the ladies back on the *Reefer*. They would plan their next steps after they heard from Webb.

The guard left with the sniper, leaving Matt his radio. Rafael listened to Cortada's radio traffic, but reception on the sniper's radio proved intermittent with the intervening two hills and nearly another mile of distance. The repeated bursts of static let them know that several radios were broadcasting on the frequency.

They drove the whaler out to pick up the swimmers and take them back aboard the *Reefer*. They couldn't call Webb since nobody knew his phone number. Thankfully, their radiophone gave a beep, and Matt answered.

Webb said, "Matt, it's me. We're getting ready for the party. It would be nice if you could keep our guests from leaving too soon."

"What is your new phone number?" asked Matt.

Webb gave the number and hung up. Matt called him on their satellite phone, allowing them to talk without playing games. Webb told him the sniper had become totally cooperative. He wanted Carla safe and the *Reefer* out to sea. Webb asked if his three men could get close to Cortada's yacht, particularly if they would be able to stop the helicopter from taking off.

Matt answered, "Maybe."

"I want to get that bastard once and for all," Webb said. "We'll all be safer when he's gone. He's working with U.S. government people and doing their dirty work. That means you and Tanya have a stake in this. We can stop his men, but he might just get away and try again. I'll have the yacht stopped in an hour or so. See what you can do to take out the helicopter, that's how he got away before. Do what you can. I've got work to do,"

"We'll do our best," Matt replied.

"Good. And, Matt?"

"Yeah?"

"Leave one guard on your boat no matter what."

"You got it. By the way, what do you know about the AK-47, particularly one with a big scope showing lots of lines, arrows, and a graph on the left?"

"A lot. I bought and shipped them by the trainload. Do you have one?"

"Yes, a semiautomatic." Matt carefully described the rifle and its scope.

"It's a Dragunov, and I'm very familiar with the scope," said Webb impatiently.

"Can you give me the *Reader's Digest* version?" Matt asked.

Webb quickly explained how to use the scope. Following Webb's instructions, Matt figured out which chevron to use for distances from one hundred to four hundred meters. The graph helped measure distance by viewing a person in the scope and seeing where he fit on the graph. It read in hundreds of meters out to a thousand. Matt wasn't worried about that. He now knew how the chevrons worked and could accurately sight to four hundred meters. Good enough.

"Webb," Matt said, "Tanya will take the *Reefer* out to sea with Carla and Mario. We will go after the yacht and helicopter."

"Good luck."

"Just remember, you're going to owe me big time if I don't get killed or end up in a DR jail." Matt hung up.

Aboard the *Reefer*, they talked over their plans as they started the engines and brought up the anchor. They tied the whaler behind the *Reefer* and headed slowly out the narrow channel, agreeing to run west out to sea and come in behind the next headland. The yacht would only have a quick glimpse of them because the palm trees of the west headland and the lower eastern anchorage entrance blocked most of its view of the ocean. Plenty of white yachts cruised these waters along the Amber Coast.

They ran at low speed across the anchorage entrance used by the large yacht, which carried them quickly out of the yacht's vision or radar view. The east side of the headland was low, and the reef was over a half mile out. The *Reefer* stopped, and Matt and two of the three guards got in. Just as they were casting off, Rafael jumped aboard. He said he would help them find the old cocoa dock and the best trail over the headland, but Matt could see he didn't want to be left behind as the others launched into an adventure, no matter how dangerous. The overloaded whaler was dangerously low in the water. Waves sloshed on the tense fingers that gripped the sides when they hit the reef waves, but their good timing and strong motor pushed them past the hazards and brought them safely to the beach. They pulled the whaler up onto the sand and hoped the tide wouldn't reach it.

In the palms, they checked their weapons. The two guards had Berettas and small fully-automatic machine pistols, all 9 mm and all using the same shells. Matt had his Remington with twelve shells and the Dragunov with two magazines, confirmed as holding ten shells each. Rafael led the way using his machete and mumbling about its lack of sharpness. Sweaty and breathing hard, they climbed the steep slope of the headland. Rafael found a trail that made their travel much faster and easier. They went about a half mile across the peninsula when Rafael stopped them and told them to catch their breath. Surprisingly, he looked neither out of breath nor tired.

After a brief rest, Rafael said, "The dock is only thirty meters ahead. You can get behind large pillars, and you'll only be fifty or sixty meters from the big ship. I'll take you in closer, but we must be quiet."

Rafael moved into the brush with the two guards right behind him. Matt brought up the rear. They skirted the edge of the cliff. Looking down, Matt saw the dock area directly below and the yacht floating close and glistening in the early afternoon sun. Matt was on the correct side of the sun for scope work—sunlight would not enter the lens or reflect off it. The guards with their small-caliber guns needed to maneuver as close as possible. They agreed to work themselves out on the dock and stay hidden behind the old, three-foot-high concrete wall that stretched along part of the old dock area. Pillars and partial walls, once part of a warehouse, also provided cover. No one would shoot until Matt fired first or they were discovered. Matt said he would shoot into the helicopter as his objective and didn't want to be responsible for shooting people. They whispered "good luck" in Spanish and English as the men separated.

Rafael helped Matt construct a blind at the edge of the cliff using branches he hacked off with the machete. They pulled out any grass that might block Matt's sighting. Matt put both rifles beside him. With his Leupold scope on ten power, he scanned the yacht, less than two hundred yards away and facing the sea. It swung against its anchor as the currents pushed it to and fro, at times coming thirty yards closer. The helicopter seemed an easy shot—high on the big ship. Matt just had to figure where to shoot it.

The mammoth yacht awed Matt. He couldn't see into the bridge area, but he could see three lines of portholes or windows, two ending in open sundecks. The ship had to be 150 feet long. He couldn't see anyone on or around the ship. The davits on his side were swung out and empty. He spotted two speedboats on the far south beach. The old dock was built at about the only place in the cove deep enough to support a large ship. The yacht's radar showed no movement, but he could hear a generator working.

Matt considered his ammunition—hunting shells with bullets designed to expand on contact, not penetrate metal. He checked the Dragunov's extra magazine. It held full metal jacket shells, military type, much more suited to chop up a plastic and aluminum helicopter. Matt hoped he could remember Webb's instructions about the sights. He considered using—

Boom! Boom!

Well off in the distance. Quickly followed by the staccato cracks of automatic weapons, then more booms and more shooting. This continued for several minutes before it stopped. He couldn't see where the gunfire originated.

Shit, this sounds like a full-fledged war.

Matt took a deep breath to steady his nerves. He popped out the Dragunov's magazine, ejected the cartridge in the chamber, and closed the action on the empty chamber. He tried the trigger. A long pull with a stiff release, not in the same league as his Remington. Matt thought the trigger pull on this famous Russian sniper rifle needed a good rework. But, at least, the semiautomatic rifle could throw a lot of big FMJ bullets quickly. The shiny white-and-blue chopper wouldn't care about the trigger pull. Twenty of these big projectiles would make it very sick.

Matt and Rafael did what all good hunters do: they waited patiently. A few more shots and one more boom rang out from over the low hills. Matt swung his Remington's Leupold scope onto the two shore boats. One, with three men in it, frothed the shallow water while pulling off the sand. The boat swung around and raced for the yacht. Matt had no idea what Cortada looked like, but the man sitting down in the middle of the boat looked like a leader, a frightened leader. He was tall, heavy, and soft looking. Matt didn't like him from four hundred yards. Matt reloaded the round into the Dragunov's magazine and found its spring as uncooperative as the rifle's trigger spring. He slammed the magazine in and worked the action, checking with a partial action pull to make sure a shell had been chambered. The second chevron should be two hundred meters and its elevation felt right for a round ballistically similar to the .30-06 that Matt knew well. The stock felt short, maybe made for the Russian winter when the shooter had on four inches of coat. The scope was comfortable, and Matt hoped the rifle's kick wouldn't split his eyebrow on the eyepiece.

Matt asked Rafael, "Think now's a good time to shoot that damn helicopter?"

"As good as any," Rafael replied.

Matt moved the safety lever down to the fire position. The large metal lever had a long throw and clicked loudly. He took a bead on the housing below the main rotor with the second chevron on the Russian scope and squeezed the trigger. The rifle made a solid bang and kicked less than the Remington. The scope didn't slam into his eyebrow, so he fired again. Four shots later, he figured the engine or transmission or whatever was under the housing would be sick, and he moved his sight to the tail area. He emptied the rest of the magazine into the tail rotor. He couldn't see the bullets going in, but stuff the machine probably needed spewed out the other side.

Several men came out of the yacht's helm area, but Matt stayed on task. He put in the second magazine and fired five shots into the cockpit's plastic bubble. He aimed low, hoping to hit instruments as well as to mess up the leather upholstery. He kept five shots in reserve and switched to the Remington with the larger, more powerful scope. The shore boat had reached the yacht. The man in the middle was gesturing for them to get him aboard. The crew dropped a ladder over the side, but the man struggled to pull himself up the rope-and-wood contraption.

Webb's men on the dock sprang into action. They fired at Cortada and the men on the yacht. They didn't hit anyone that Matt could observe, but Cortada went up the ladder much faster under fire.

Matt was caught up in the shooting frenzy and felt like putting more holes in the helicopter. With the Leupold scope, he could see the leaking fuel tanks and fuel stains on the deck under them. He fired at the tank area but couldn't see where the bullet hit. He fired twice more. Matt jumped as the tank exploded in his scope and flames engulfed the entire deck.

The boom split the air less than a second after he saw the explosion. Surrealistically, the flames slowly dissolved the plastic rich man's toy. Matt watched initially through very little smoke at the heat-distorted image as a second explosion flung the main rotor out of the fire. His job was done.

Rafael hissed some Spanish that had included *bueno* in several phrases. Matt glanced at the older man, surprised by his obvious enthusiasm and pleasure at watching several million dollars of damage done in a few seconds.

The big yacht's engines started, it rode up on the anchor, its winch whined as the large Danforth anchor was plucked from the water. The two men on the dock ran out of shells. They couldn't do much at their distance with their small 9 mm weapons, but had given the ship major acne on its port side.

The yacht pulled away, a melting helicopter smoking on its top deck, its perfectly molded lines marred with scores of pockmarks and spider-veined windows.

Matt checked the boat back on the shore, no one had come to it. The other boat slowly turned in the yacht's prop wash and was left behind.

Matt and Rafael picked up their weapons and threw the cut branches back into the trees. Matt picked up his 7 mm Mag brass and observed that the Dragunov was a world champ in shell casing ejection. Its ejected shell casings had sailed out of sight and could probably have drawn blood if they had hit anyone.

Webb's two men waited on the dock for Matt and Rafael to walk down and join them. Instead of walking back to the whaler, they decided to retrieve the abandoned boat just offshore. Luciano stripped to his white briefs, made an accomplished dive into the water, and swam out to the boat. He brought the boat to the dock, and they rode in style back to the beach and the whaler. They easily worked their way through the surf, with only two men in each boat, and pulled up alongside the *Reefer*. They could see Cortada's yacht to the east with a gray DR gunboat on each side. Matt wondered about the DR laws for armed invasion by a Venezuelan army.

Tanya, first white with worry then pink with relief and joy, helped them hoist the whaler into its mounts and rig the big yacht's shore boat for towing. Carla had been crying. They had heard the gunfire and loud explosions even out at sea.

The phone rang.

Carla answered. After a short, happy conversation, she reported that her father said they could return to their previous anchorage. The *Reefer* ducked into Webb's cove well clear of the DR gunboats. They anchored and used the shore boat to get to the beach. Matt had started his third beer when Webb and Karen, driving a small tractor towing a flatbed wagon, arrived at the beach. Everyone shared kisses and hugs. Matt was nearly crushed by Webb's enthusiastic bear hug and knew he would have bruises. They boarded the wagon, and the little Ford tractor dutifully pulled them up the hill. DR police and military vehicles were at the villa when the little tractor finally stopped by the side gate.

Matt expected to see bodies and shell holes. There were none. The villa didn't seem to have any holes, either. Most of the action must have occurred down the hill on the road leading to the cocoa dock. They once again enjoyed drinks on the lower patio. Out of the hot afternoon sun, the temperature seemed twenty degrees cooler. Matt opened two Presidente beers, one for himself and another for Tanya. She clutched his hand and stroked his hair repeatedly. Carla and Karen descended on Webb in excited, even angry, Russian. Karen did not appreciate warfare in her new home. Webb, in full defensive mode, struggled to explain the upsetting incident. Even in Russian, it was patently clear Webb had fallen under the time-honored marital rule that if you're explaining, you're losing. After half a beer's time, Webb broke away and, shaking his head but smiling, joined Tanya and Matt.

Quietly, he said, "Cortada was an idiot to try this like he did. The Dominicans are a very nationalistic and proud people. He'll disappear into a prison for some time, maybe forever. His men may never see their country again. His yacht will probably become some general's property. This incident will never hit the papers, because the effect on tourism would be very bad. Labor riots in the streets of Santo Domingo are bad enough, but shooting and gang warfare of this scale will be kept from the general public and the news people."

Tanya looked around the grounds. "So, what actually happened here?"

"We ambushed them as they came out of the trees. Most of the firing was over their heads. We had three 60 mm mortars that arrived this morning. They went from being unpacked from their South African boxes to being fired in about an hour. We shot over their heads, and the shells exploded in the woods. They fired some small arms for their honor's sake and gave up. Only a few were wounded, and probably by their own fire. Cortada was so far behind them we almost got him with the mortar shells. The dry pool was our firebase, we didn't do the tiles any good, but they couldn't figure out where the shells were coming from. We tried to hit them but the shots went long. It actually worked out better than having holes in the open ground and bodies to bury. I almost went to the beach with you instead of getting the weapons unboxed and inspected, a lesson in taking care of business first. This whole incident will cost me many dollars to make all the officials happy. We had all our automatic rifles and mortars hidden before the authorities got here. They were too excited about having prisoners they could intimidate to ask the questions they may think about later."

"I'm glad everyone's all right," Matt said. "And, by the way, we want to head back as soon as possible."

"I understand," Webb said. "Tomorrow, I'll get the rest of my personal possessions off your boat. This evening, let's all have a good dinner together. Also, Edward from the DEA will be flying in to take some material I have for him. The evidence will pay back several political types who thought they could work with Cortada and put me away. Edward will also be involved with legal maneuvers the U.S. government may want to use against Cortada if the DR ever lets him go. I'll make sure the DEA knows you were both forced to be with us."

Webb clinked his glass that probably held vodka against the nearly empty bottles in Matt and Tanya's hands, and walked back to his wife and daughter.

The dinner that evening was late, following the DR custom. Matt and Tanya were ravenous and enjoyed too much of the wonderful food dishes that were passed before them. The cooks prepared main dishes of baked red snapper in tomatoes and onions, cayenne shrimp with onions and bell peppers, and pork in an orange, rum, and cointreau sauce. Their vegetable was a ratatouille: eggplant, mushroom, bell peppers, and onions. With the exception of the rice, every dish had some degree of garlic. They finished with coffee served with small slices of fudge pie. They all enjoyed each other's company for what they all knew was probably the last time. Even Carla was less then her bubbly self by the end of the meal. With several vodkas under his belt, Webb waxed philosophical about cocoa farming and the myriad fruit trees all around them. Tired, Matt's mind lagged behind the conversation. When the dinner ended, they all hugged at the patio gate and promised to exchange addresses and phone numbers so they could keep in touch. Rafael and Al walked Matt and Tanya back down the hill, saying they needed the exercise after the big meal. They enjoyed the star-studded night. Matt pointed out the Big Dipper and the North Star directly in line with the path. He noted its position, so low compared to the familiar night sky of the Upper Peninsula. There were no lights to pollute the stargazing. The walk down the hill felt almost surreal in its beauty. Al held a flashlight for them as they boarded the motorboats that had belonged to Cortada. The men strained to push the large inboard off the sand.

At the *Reefer*, Luciano and Mario helped them back onto their boat, but would not take the motorboat back to shore. Webb had insisted they remain on board for as long as they stayed in DR waters. Matt and Tanya didn't press the point, but went to their cabin for a good night's sleep.

The next morning dawned gray and breezy—not DR Chamber of Commerce weather. The Webbs and several men gathered at the beach and motored out in the other boat left by Cortada. With some difficulty in the four-foot waves, they climbed aboard the *Reefer*. Webb took Matt to the master stateroom while the ladies gathered in the salon.

After locking the stateroom door, Webb retrieved his gym bag, the three cases from their hidden compartment under the bed, and then reached in with the hooked rod and pulled out a fourth case, older and made of metal rather than plastic. Webb put the case, black with a built-in combination lock, on the bed and opened it to reveal packets of money in plastic, shrink-wrapped bundles and several aluminum boxes the size of cigarette packs. Webb took one box and tore off the tape that secured its top. He poured out a palmful of large diamonds.

He held the diamonds out to Matt. "Here, these are my way of thanking you. They're not stolen or laser etched for identification, and they are each three or more carats. Under pain of death, don't ever tell my wife I gave away diamonds. Keep your mouth shut and live your life so you don't need bodyguards."

Webb poured them into Matt's hand. Matt stared at the gems, not knowing what to say. Webb didn't give him a chance, returning to the bathroom to replace the bathtub floor that hid the secret compartment.

Webb picked up the black case, the gym bag, and one plastic case and asked, "Would you bring the other cases?"

As Matt picked up the cases, he asked, "What's in the gym bag?"

Webb put his load down and opened the gym bag. Empty. Just a well-used, cheap nylon bag. Webb smirked. "The Cortada information is laminated in the cardboard bottom. The Feds went through it and let me keep it with my underwear and toilet kit. This bag was the main reason I got involved with you."

Webb picked up his burdens again and left the stateroom.

After a few seconds of thought, Matt put the diamonds in the amber, plastic, antibiotic pill container in his shaving kit. He carried the two cases that Webb had not taken and followed him to the salon.

The waves swelled even higher, and rain sheeted across the anchorage. They put the cases and boxes in a dry area on the aft deck and waited in the salon for the rain to stop.

The Dominican guards defended the inconvenience of the weather by explaining most lengthy rains occur at night and hard rains in the morning usually pass in an hour or so. In the crowded salon, they discussed inconsequential things—Carla's European schooling, Karen's redecorating plans, and Webb's plans to farm fruit and cocoa. Matt couldn't keep a straight face as Webb tried to explain with real passion how the coconut palms and the banana trees shaded the cocoa trees and how ground litter was important to the midges that help pollinate the cocoa trees. When Webb said "midges," Matt started to laugh and soon everyone joined in with Webb insisting he was serious. Matt had never imagined Webb as a Russian farmer. The Webb-baiting ended when the sun broke through the clouds and the rain stopped. The front had passed, and the waves gradually settled into their gentle norm. After supervising the loading of the boats, Webb stood on the aft deck with Matt and Tanya. Below, Carla and Karen used beach towels to dry the seats on their boat.

Webb smiled and said, "Tell your mother and father they will have no further business with me in any way. Also, there will be no more charters for this boat that don't show up. If Edward contacts you, answer anything he asks, don't get into more trouble for my sake."

Webb said he had smoothed over everything about the attack by Cortada and the status of Tanya, Matt, and the *Reefer* with the Dominican officials. "At least you can't say our time together has been boring."

Webb shook Matt's hand and hugged Tanya. He hopped gracefully into the inboard boat now bobbing gently in the lee of the *Reefer's* stern. The boats made for shore with the ladies waving and Webb standing wide-legged watching his wife and daughter.

47

Homeward

NEARLY NOON, AND TANYA AND MATT were finally alone on the *Reefer*. They went to the helm, started the diesels, rode up on the anchor, and hoisted it to its secure position. They slowly headed out the channel just as Webb's two boats reached shore on the other end of the cove. Webb had told them they could just set their course and leave without further DR clearances.

"The quieter the better," he had said.

Matt had the helm with no definite course except north to clear Dominican waters and return to the Bahamas. They would finalize their plans after Tanya talked to her parents.

Tanya went to the Westinghouse phone in the salon. She called her mother at home and said she had a lot to tell her, that they were fine and still in the Dominican Republic, and would have no more involvement with Webb.

Her mother's voice shook as she said, "Thank God."

Tanya reiterated that everything was fine in every way. Tanya asked if her parents would be interested in getting on a plane and meeting them in George Town on Exuma. From there, they could slowly explore the wonders of the Bahamian Out Islands, celebrate Christmas and Boxing Day, and just enjoy life together. Tanya and her mother agreed that Mr. Vega needed to be contacted.

Matt joined Tanya in the salon as the autopilot kept their slow northerly course. They both talked to George Vega at work; the conversation lasted nearly twenty minutes and an agreement was reached to rendezvous in the

Turks in two days. The Turks, chosen because they were over three hundred miles closer than Exuma for the *Reefer,* had no equals for clear water and great diving. Tanya consulted the maps on the navigation table, excitedly talking about meeting at the Grand Turk Airport, then she and her father went into details about places they could go and things they could do.

Matt returned to the helm. The autopilot didn't know about tankers and fishing boats. Matt clicked off the autopilot and turned a few degrees into the waves to make it smoother for Tanya in the salon. He reflected on the month since Tanya literally dropped into his life and initiated events that had changed him forever. He still missed the woods, the snow, the smells, and the sounds of wind in the white pines. He even missed the loneliness. Mentally jumping to the here and now, Matt witnessed the beauty of the water around him and the magnificent Hatteras under his control, but couldn't make it all feel real. He wondered if Tanya could learn to appreciate the northland.

He wondered what to do with a handful of big diamonds. Webb's gift presented a complication and a temptation to smuggle and avoid taxes. Matt decided that honesty was the only policy. He would ask Edward some hypothetical questions about the best ways to turn faceted pieces of pure carbon into legal tender.

Edward, Matt thought. *Yet another complexity.*

Matt wondered if he would leave Tanya alone or want to use her for further work. Deep in thought, he startled when Tanya appeared at his side with a loving bump.

Tanya had a page from a yellow pad with numbers on it and a chart of the Turks and Caicos Islands. She pushed herself onto part of the helm chair, "My dad knows the Turks and some retired Air Force buddies who are developing condos there. He'll set up docking for us and phone with the information. He also suggested some cays where we can anchor tonight."

"Sounds good."

She snuggled against his shoulder. "I'm so glad to be away from Webb and alone with you."

Matt gave her a hug and neck kisses while she entered numbers and settings into the autopilot. He whispered in her ear, "Will you do something special for me?"

Tanya finished her navigation work and turned to Matt. Putting her arms around his neck and gazing suggestively into his eyes, she murmured, "Anything."

"How about getting two beers and bringing me the container of antibiotic pills from my shaving kit?"

Acknowledgments

The seed for this book was planted by Grandma McGillviray when she showed me around Fiborn Quarry in Mackinac County over forty years ago. She ran the boarding house and raised her four children there in the late 20's and early 30's. We hunted out of her cabin at Garnet for many years, and heaven couldn't provide food any better than her rolls from the wood stove.

While no name is given to Matt Hunter's quarry property, it is in reality the Fiborn Karst Preserve and belongs to the Michigan Karst Conservancy. The preserve has interpretive trails and history displays and is open, following guidelines, to the public. More information is available online at http://www.caves.org/conservancy/mkc/.

My wife Ann provided the most support for this book, patiently and skillfully responding to hundreds of, "Please read this." She actually knew "silowet" had an 'H' in it when my spell checker didn't know what I wanted.

George Sink, my college roommate, read the first crude manuscript and liked it—all I needed to forge ahead. His subsequent help and advice has been a continuation of our friendship of forty-seven years.

My best friend—Archie Davies, a USCG Master Chief and former Michigan State trooper—provided invaluable facts and background throughout the story.

Editing and writing advice was a team effort. Jana Aho from Gladstone's Library was a constant source of help and encouragement. Laborious efforts were also contributed by Frank Reuter, Ph.D., Sharon Berkner, and, most of all, Walt Shiel—author, jet pilot, general expert on all things literary. The talent of Kerrie Shiel, Walt's wife, produced the cover artwork. And kudos to their daughter, Lisa Shiel, for checking and double-checking everything.

Steve Hamilton, very successful author of the Alex McKnight mysteries, graciously helped this fellow IBM'er many times.

My son, Ben, provided solid information about large boats and all things nautical. Paul Bialik helped crash the Cessna 310—an occurrence he avoids as captain of 747s and 767s. Terry Johnson, twenty-seven years a law officer (and fine JV fullback for me), helped correctly kill off Carlos.

Lastly, I need to acknowledge Miss Willits—Senior English—yes, I wrote fragmentary sentences, but they are in style now.

John (J. C.) Hager

Born and raised in Michigan, John earned a B.A. and M.A. in Biology and Science Education from Western Michigan University, taught high school science and coached football and wrestling. He retired from IBM after twenty-seven years on quota. He and his wife Ann live in Michigan's Upper Peninsula on the shore of Little Bay de Noc. They have two grown sons. John dilutes his writing time with hunting, fishing, boating, traveling, and providing laughs and lost golf balls at the Gladstone Golf Club.

CPSIA information can be obtained at www.ICGtesting.com
Printed in the USA
LVOW06s2124240714

395882LV00001B/297/P